Gone Wild

By Señor Fruity

ISBN: 979-8-9993708-9-1 (Paperback 2026 Revised)

Prologue

Benjamin's mom always told him he needs to do the best he can at school and get good grades because if he does, he will have more success later in life. His mom always pushed him to succeed because that's the caring mother she was.

His mom would also tell him that he needs to make friends too, because it's a cruel world that they live in and friends will help you when you're lonely. Benjamin has always kept those words she said in his mind. Benjamin wouldn't show it, but deep down those words that mom said were effective, deep down to his heart.

Benjamin would blush every time his mom would say to him that he needs to get himself a wife when he's older because he will be lonely again. She would always worry about him being lonely because his shyness would always keep him away from people. Benjamin knows that she just cares about him, but still every time he meets a stranger, a new kid he has never met before, Ben would just avoid him. Hide behind his parents' legs if he had a chance.

Every time he did so, mom would just shake her head and repeat the same words: "Ben, you really need to have friends, otherwise you'll be lonely." or "Ben, when you grow older, you need to get yourself a wife. You'll be lonely, honey."

Every time, Ben would just ignore her, but those words would stick to him. Stick to his heart, stick to his brain. She would usually tell him he should enjoy his youth while it lasts because his younger years will pass by quickly.

Well...

He's just ten years old, but he feels like his younger years have already passed because everything he did with his mom is now just memories...

He's sitting on a chair, crying in a quiet waiting room with nobody around. His small body trembles as he cries. The surrounding silence is heavy, broken only by his own sobs and the sound of his dad yelling at a medical receptionist at a counter.

His words are sharp, angry—shouting words that Ben swears shouldn't exist. His dad slams his hands on the countertop, and the receptionist flinches as if she is worried she is the next one to get slammed.

Ben's vision blurs from the tears, and he can barely hear the words. But the anger on his dad's face, the way his hands tremble, is clear.

Why?

Why is all of this happening?

Why did Mom have to go?

2

Suddenly, his dad's footsteps storm toward him. Ben looks up. His dad says nothing, but his face is pure red. His dark hair is a mess, like a crow's nest made with a bunch of crazy random objects. Ben's thoughts feel just as tangled—memories of his mom that used to bring warmth now stab like thorns.

There's something dangerous in his father's eyes. Something cold...

"Come on, let's go," his dad mumbles under his breath.

He grabs Ben's hand and yanks him out of the chair.

Ben wipes his tears away and tries to keep up with his dad's pace as he storms out of the building and into the parking lot. Only then is he released, and Ben follows his father toward his parked car. Out of habit, Ben gets in the back seat, leaving the front passenger seat empty... His mom's seat.

His dad starts the engine without a word. The engine roars to life like his dad to the receptionist. Without a word, he drives out of the parking lot. Ben stares through the window in silence, his mind numb.

Why did Mom have to leave?

She was always so full of light, always the reason he was happy to come home from school. Her voice was soft and calming, like the black-capped chickadees in the backyard—especially the ones that sang "fee-bee." That sound always made Ben feel at peace.

His dad, on the other hand, sounded like a crow—harsh and loud, always yelling. Ben hates crows. They sound like they're laughing at him, and that's what his dad does when Ben's late getting home.

If it weren't for Mom, Ben would've been scared every day.

She was his safety. She was the reason he smiled.

Now, she was gone.

Through the rearview mirror, Ben catches a glimpse of his dad's scowl, and all he can think about is how to make his dad happy. He wants to make him forget the anger, to get him to smile, to feel something good again.

Losing Mom hurts both of them, Ben knows, so they both need something happy to focus on. Maybe then, his dad wouldn't be so angry.

When they finally arrive at their house, Ben's dad is out of the car before it even stops. Ben follows, trying to keep up with his dad's pace. When they get to the door, his dad fumbles with his keys, growling something under his breath until he finally opens the door.

The inside of the house is cool for the warm weather outside, spotless air feels empty without Mom. Inside, Ben passes by his dad and heads upstairs to his second-floor bedroom. There, he takes out his piggy bank from his drawer and gives it a shake; his full allowance rattles around inside.

He had this great idea of how he could make his dad happy. He came up with it on the spot while they were in the car. He'll spend his allowance on two tickets to the movie theater. Watching a movie ought to help take his dad's mind off what happened. It always does with Ben when he is having a bad day.

Ben bursts out of his room, rushing down the stairs to the kitchen. There, he finds his dad slumped at the small wooden table, his head resting on his arms. Three empty beer bottles litter the surface.

Oh, no! Don't tell me he is drunk!

Ben's dad always yells at him when he drinks. He crept up to his dad, hoping not to make him mad. He holds out the piggy and shakes it. The sound of coins makes his dad turn his head toward him.

"What the hell do you want?" His voice thick and slurred.

Ben swallows hard, then answers. "I—I want to go to the movie theater."

"The movie theater? Why?"

"To get our minds off Mom."

His dad stands up slowly, exhaling a deep, disappointed sigh. "I don't want to go to the movies. I've got a better idea. I'm going out." He shakes an empty beer bottle and places it back on the table.

Ben already knows what he means. He runs up and hugs his dad's legs, hoping to change his mind. A desperate last-ditch effort to stop him from going out.

No, not the bar. Anything but the bar.

The bar is full of weirdoes. He can hardly believe his dad wants to go there. Every time he goes, he comes back drunk and miserable.

Why do adults always go there, anyway?

He holds his dad's legs tight so he can't move, but his dad just growls and pushes his son to the floor. As Ben tries to get back up, a beer bottle crashes to the ground, shattering into hundreds of shards barely missing him. His dad's face starts fuming; it's red like a fire engine.

"Goddamn it! That's it! If you try to stop me, I'll kill you!"

With that, his dad storms out of the house, slamming the door behind him. The sound of the door crashing against the frame leaves Ben frozen, his mind struggling to grasp the weight of what just happened.

Did he really mean those words?

His words echo in Ben's head, like Mom's words echo around him. He wipes his eyes, but the tears keep coming.

Collapsing onto the kitchen floor, he lies there, trying to convince himself that it's okay.

Maybe it is, right?

Maybe he just needs to make his dad happy.

He's angry because Mom is gone, that's all.

Ben just has to find a way to fix it, if that's even possible.

If he could make his dad happy, maybe he wouldn't have to leave...

Maybe then, things could get better.

***

The dawn brings another school day. Not that it feels like anything special. Ben can't understand how some kids actually enjoy school. He doesn't want to get out of bed, but he does anyway—mostly because if he doesn't, his dad might yell.

He gets ready in silence: washes his face, changes out of his pajamas, throws on some clean clothes. When he heads downstairs, he finds his dad fast asleep in the living room recliner. Ben tiptoes to the front door, careful not to wake him.

He's determined to do well today. If he tries his best in school, maybe it'll make his dad happy.

Ben rushes across his neighborhood to the spot where the school bus usually picks him up on the sidewalk next to the mailbox. He notices someone there already, which is unusual. It looks like another kid waiting for the school bus.

As he gets closer to the kid, he realizes it's a girl who looks like she's about his age. Girls from his class usually try to look nice, but this one's hair looks like she just got out of bed and skipped the mirror before heading out. It's hard to read her face through her messy hair, but he can tell she is crying.

Maybe she had an awful morning, and that's why her hair is messy, Ben thought. He can understand that. He felt the same way yesterday after his mom died. The girl suddenly looks in his direction. Embarrassed, he looks away. He tries to find the courage to talk to her, but he's too nervous.

Ben has always been shy, especially around girls. He doesn't know what to say, so he keeps his distance from her. Fortunately, the school bus finally shows up, and the girl stands up. After the bus door opens, Ben goes in and finds an empty seat. He sees the girl is also alone, but he doesn't go to her. He understands what she is feeling. He wonders, *who is she? She must be new.* He tries not to think about her too much, instead focusing on how he might make his dad happy.

***

During school, Ben tries the best he can at each of his classroom assignments. During art class, he draws a picture of himself, his dad, and his mom as wolves because that's his favorite animal. He loves animals; that's why he feels excited that they are supposed to draw their favorite animals in art class.

The girl from the bus stop is in his art class too. The art teacher introduced her: Her name is Honey Barnes. Ben thinks Honey is a peculiar name, but it's cute. Her name is exactly how he would describe her because she has blonde hair that has a yellowish hue to it.

Her yellow eyes have a nice contrast with her black pupils. Her eyes make Ben think of honeybees. She is even wearing a yellow-and-black-striped shirt, like a bee. He guesses that her favorite animal is a hippo based on her appearance.

Honey has a seat next to him. Neither make eye contact through class until Ben leans to peek at what she is drawing. He was surprised to see her drawing of a bee instead of a hippo. Guess his assumption of her favorite animal is wrong.

Honey must notice him looking at her picture, as she smiles at him. Ben quickly looks away in embarrassment. He can't believe how red his face probably looks right now the minute she turned her head. Making eye contact is the worst for Ben. He just gets back to drawing his picture.

After school is over, Ben hangs out with his two best friends, Tom Dunkley and Cedric Coy. The three of them are at the school's playground. He wants to make Tom and Cedric happy too because they are the only two friends he has. Cedric is his cousin; Ben's mother is part of the Coy family.

Stacey Coy was her name before she married his dad, Josh Uno. Ben honestly wanted his last name to be Coy instead of Uno, but Uno is still cool though. Ben doesn't have a lot of friends at school because he's shy. The only friend other than Cedric that he hangs out with is Tom. Tom's dad and Cedric's dad know each other, and that's how they met.

Ben, Tom, and Cedric call themselves "The Wolf Pack" because of their love for wolves. The three of them love wolves so much that they even have wolf necklace chains for each other. Tom's older sister made the necklaces for them. That's how they were able to create their group.

What's their group motto, you may ask? "No wolf works alone."

It's kind of cheesy, but they don't care. Plus, it is true, because wolves in the wild work together in packs to make the job of killing their prey easier. The Wolf Pack does the same. They imitate the wild wolves' strategy, even though there are only three of them. The Wolf Pack work together to make it easier to "kill their prey," or in their case, to defeat their rivals: The Cougars.

The Cougars are led by Jack Sims—*Cougar Jack,* as he calls himself. *Jackass*, as Ben calls him privately. Jack is cocky and annoying and clearly doesn't know much about cougars, since those cats usually hunt solo.

Ben suspects Jack picked the name only because he thinks it sounds cool and tough. But Jack? He's just arrogant.

The Cougar crew includes Jack and his sidekicks, Edwin Sharp and Larry Terry. Together, they always manage to beat The Wolf Pack at... well, everything.

Ben's tired of it.

Today, they're at the playground trying to figure out how to finally beat the Cougars at basketball.

"Hey, Ben, I saw you eyeing that new girl in art class today. You like her, don't you?" Cedric laughs, waving his brown trucker cap around. He is always a jokester, and sometimes he says funny things, but other times he just makes fun of Ben. Ben hates him.

"Quit it, man! I'm trying to make a plan here, and you're just joking around." Ben gives Cedric a dirty look. Tom looks at Ben with concerned eyes. "Hey, Ben, are you alright? I know that your mom just died. If you need any help, just ask for it, and we're here for you."

Ben just waves his hands. "I appreciate it, but I'm alright." Ben continues to give dirty looks to Cedric as he stops laughing and puts his cap back on his head.

It has the number 406 on it. The amount of times Ben sees the same cap worn by other people in Montana is abysmal to him. Kind of how his friends' jokes are abysmal.

Cedric looks at Ben with a more serious expression now. "Hey Ben, you know I'm only joking around. If you need anything, just ask us."

Ben just sighs. "Listen, both of you, I'm okay. What I'm not okay with is the Cougars always beating us. It's been two weeks in a row that they have been beating us at basketball, and I'm not having it."

Tom slaps his forehead. "Oh, give me a break, Ben. Just face the facts. The Cougars are better than us at basketball."

"Nope, I'm not having it." Ben lifts his basketball off the ground. "It's training time, Wolves!"

"Uh, seriously, do we have to do this?" Cedric asks as both he and Tom lift their basketballs off the ground too.

Ben points toward the basketball court. "Oh, yeah, we're doing this. Wolves, let's train!"

***

Meanwhile, with the Cougars

The Cougars walk toward the basketball court for their easy matchup with The Wolf Pack. Cougar Jack can't wait to kick Ben's butt at basketball again for the hundredth time in a row. He loves seeing Ben's face every time he beats him at everything they compete at. It's like ecstasy to him. Cougar Jack walks arrogantly with his two friends, Larry and Edwin, by his side.

Suddenly, in the corner of Cougar Jack's eye, he spots the new girl in class, Honey Barnes, watching The Wolf Pack train for their basketball match. She seems to be enjoying herself from her smile. Cougar Jack can't have that! The eyes of the girls at school should only be on him. He's the hottest boy in fifth grade.

Jack throws his basketball at Honey to get her attention. Honey doesn't seem to notice the basketball and gets hit in the face. She falls on her back on some wood chips, then just lays there, seemingly stunned.

"Hey, new girl, how about you stop looking at trash and watch some skilled athletes do it!" Cougar Jack smirks.

He walks up to Honey and lends her his hand. Suddenly, a random basketball hits Jack's head, and he also falls on the wood chips covering the ground. Edwin and Larry also get hit in the head by two basketballs, and they fall to the ground.

Honey looks around skittishly until The Wolf Pack walks up to her.

***

Benjamin offers his hand. "Hey, are you alright?"

At first, Honey just stares at it, like she doesn't trust him. Ben smiles at her, showing that he's not going to harm her, unlike those pesky Cougars. She still seems reluctant, but she finally grabs his hand. He pulls her up.

As if her hair wasn't messy enough, it's now covered with wood chips. Even her face is dirty, a long streak across her face. She still looks beautiful, though. Ben, like an idiot, stumbles over his words trying to say something else to her.

Suddenly, the Cougars get back up, recovering from the basketball raid. They dust themselves off. As if Cougar Jack couldn't get uglier, his face and hair are now covered with pieces of wood chips. Ben didn't think Cougar Jack could get uglier with bangs, but somehow, he manages to do so. His hair is filled with wood, looking like those elk bucks with their antlers, with the leaves and twigs.

"Do you realize you need to put the ball in the hoop, right? Jesus, no wonder you guys' suck." Jack sneers.

Even after getting nailed in the face, Jack's still smirking. God, Ben wants to slap that look right off him.

"Same goes to you, Jackass. When you said you love hitting on girls, I never thought you meant that literally."

Despite Ben's payback jab, Cougar Jack is still smirking. "You can talk all the trash you want, Benjamin, but you will always lose to us. Unfortunately, always beating you in basketball is getting too old for me now. Playing with you guys is a waste of time, and I need some actual quality practice." Cougar Jack starts shaking the dirt off of his hair and flips his head like he's in some shampoo commercial. Ben just has to stand there in astonishment as Jack and his two sidekicks start walking away.

"See ya later, Wolves. You can keep your girlfriend, Benjamin." Cougar Jack points to Honey. "She's a worthless freak. She can't even catch a ball properly; you can have her. She has about the same intelligence as you do." Cougar Jack starts laughing.

Ben is about to run up to Cougar Jack and punch him for making fun of Honey, but Tom grabs him by the arms.

"Hey, Tom, let me go!"

Tom doesn't release him until the Cougars are gone. Ben shrugs him off and turns to check on Honey.

She looks bewildered, like she's still piecing together what just happened.

Ben softens. "Don't listen to Jack. He doesn't even know half the words he's saying." He offers her his hand again. "Stick with us. Those jerks won't touch you."

She stares at his hand again, just like before—but this time, she smiles. She takes it.

"Thank you; I loved seeing you guys play. I think you looked great. I don't know what that kid was talking about."

Wow, Ben has never heard her say a full sentence before, but her voice is as smooth as butter. Exactly the opposite of what a bee would sound like. When Ben hears a bee, he wants to stay as far away from it as possible, trying to swat it away.

Like those crows that sit on the power lines, mocking Ben when he walks back home. Or like his dad when he gets drunk, a fistful of anger.

But Honey's voice is a shy, calm voice that makes him want to hear it every day. It's like a chickadee's call. Like his mom's voice when she tells him that everything will be okay. He doesn't know why Honey doesn't talk more often. He wants to hear it more.

At that, Ben caught himself just staring at Honey for the longest time. Ben laughs awkwardly, stumbling over his words. *Great, what do I say next?*

"Thanks, I don't think we're that great, but you're welcome to play with us, Honey, if you like?"

Luckily for Ben, Cedric saves his awkward silence by walking over, grabbing the basketball he'd thrown, and handing it to Honey. Ben and Tom also grab their basketballs.

"Oh, I don't think I'll be good at it." Honey accepts the basketball from Cedric with a small shrug.

He smiles. "You'll probably be better than us. Here, Honey, just aim at the hoop and shoot it."

Honey looks at him like he's lost his mind. She turns to the hoop. Her hands mold around the ball like she's trying to shape it, like it's Play-Doh or something. But it's already a ball. All that's left is to shoot.

She lifts her arms—and shoots.

Ben, Cedric, and Tom all tense, holding their breath, eating their shirt collars as the ball arcs through the air.

It drops clean through the net.

None of them have ever made a three-point shot. Not once. Either they really suck... or Honey just pulled off the luckiest shot of her life.

***

I can't believe it! Ben thinks.

The entire Wolf Pack got brutally owned in H-O-R-S-E by a girl.

Honey drops buckets like she's Kobe Bryant. Ben is walking home in shame, still hearing those crows mock him from the power lines.

He pulls up his hoodie, as if that'll somehow hide his humiliation. But there's nowhere to hide. Honey is the Bucket Queen. They're nothing compared to her.

"That was fun," she says, walking beside him. "Let's do it again tomorrow?"

Ben glances at her. "Have you ever thought about joining the girls' basketball team?"

Honey flashes a puzzled expression. "No, why?"

Ben continues walking. "Never mind."

He tries to forget the total annihilation she served him and his best friends, but it'll haunt him forever. He can still hear the crows jeering as they reach his house.

He turns to say goodbye—but rubs the back of his neck awkwardly instead. *Great. How do you say goodbye to a girl?*

"Um...This is my house... I guess I'll see you later."

Honey smiles. "Hey, you just live across the street from me."

Ben's eyes go wide. "Really?"

"Yeah, me and my mom just moved to that house over there." Honey points at the house across the street. "We're neighbors, isn't that amazing?"

Ben laughs awkwardly. "Yeah, I guess it is."

"Well, I guess I'll see you tomorrow." Honey waves goodbye as she runs toward her house.

"Sure." Ben waves back.

Wow, she lives across the street.

A new girl. A cute one at that. In his art class too. And now, his neighbor.

Things might just be looking up.

All that's left is to show his dad the picture he drew. Maybe that'll make him smile.

Ben opens the door and enters his house. The first thing he notices is the TV on in the living room and his dad sleeping with a beer bottle in his hand. It looks like he is drunk again. He's been doing that a lot ever since Mom got sick from cancer. Now that she's dead, it's only bound to get worse.

Regardless, Ben decides to wake him up and show him the drawing. "What do you think of this picture, Dad? It's me, Mom, and you as wolves."

His dad barely glances at the drawing before pushing it away. "It looks stupid." He gets up out of his recliner and walks away.

To the kitchen. Probably to get another beer.

Ben stays frozen, the drawing still in his hands. He doesn't cry. Not yet. But his throat tightens, and everything inside him folds in.

He thought maybe—just maybe—today would be different. That his dad might smile. Say something nice. He thought the picture might help.

It doesn't.

He stares at the drawing for a few seconds more—then walks over to the trash can and drops it in. He was so proud of it earlier. Showing it to Honey. Laughing with the guys. Feeling like... like things might be okay again.

But they're not.

Still, he can't give up. Not on his dad. Not completely.

If Mom were here, she'd tell him to keep trying. She always believed people could change. That love was enough.

So maybe—just maybe—he can believe that too.

Tomorrow is another day. Maybe tomorrow will be better. Maybe.

But as he watches the empty hallway where his dad disappeared, it's hard to believe in anything. His chest aches in the place where hope used to sit. He tries to remember the sound of his mom's laugh. The way she used to ruffle his hair when he got something right. But it's fading. Blurring.

Like the drawing. Like everything.

Why did God have to take her?

Chapter 1- The Future

8 Years Later

Ben can't believe how messy his backyard is! Why did he let this happen?

All summer he kept thinking, *no one's going to see it anyway, so who cares?*

But yeah. That was a mistake.

Now, every time he steps outside, he's hit with a jungle of tall grass, vines strangling the white wooden fence, and wild bushes spilling in all directions. The whole thing looks less like a yard and more like an alien took a dump and forgot to clean up.

Determined to fix it, he grabs the weed whacker and gets to work. Hours pass in a blur of buzzing, chopping, and swearing. He yanks down vines, trims the grass, clears the fence. His brown overalls soak up sweat and dirt until they're nearly black in some places. He'll probably need new ones soon.

Still, he likes his overalls. They feel like armor. Comes with the territory when you spend your weekends elbow-deep in junkyards, digging for scrap. Most of the time he's just messing around—building gadgets that may or may not be useful. Yesterday was a jackpot. While hacking at weeds, he keeps glancing over at the gleaming pile of metal he scored. His brain's already turning over ideas.

The sun beats down, relentless. Sweat clings to every inch of him. He feels like a melted vanilla ice cream cone, except dirt's mixed in now—chocolate chunks, maybe. Gross. But thinking of it that way somehow makes it feel less disgusting.

Eventually, the backyard looks... well, *emptier*. The vines are gone, the grass is trimmed, and only two overgrown bushes and a weed-choked flowerbed remain. He gets to work clearing the bed. Maybe he'll plant something. Something colorful.

Too bad it's probably too late in the season. The neighbors' yards look like paradise compared to his.

As he stands there, trying to figure out what kind of flowers he should get, a familiar jingle drifts into earshot. Ice cream truck. He smiles. The kids are already screaming in the distance. *We all scream for ice cream,* right? And damn, he could use one.

He peers over the fence. Sure enough, there's a crowd of kids—and among them, someone he wasn't expecting to see.

Honey Barnes.

His heart stutters.

There's only one girl like her. Yellowish blonde hair pulled neatly back (he secretly misses the wild curls she had when they were younger), black-and-yellow-striped shirt, and brown overalls that match the dirt. Must be gardening, too.

He watches her laugh at something one of the kids says, and for a second, everything in him softens. But then—she looks straight at him.

Crap.

Ben ducks behind the fence. Grabs his pruning shears. Starts attacking the bushes like his life depends on it. The last thing he needs is for Honey to see the mess he's been living in. Her yard's a garden catalog. His looks like a disaster zone.

"Ben?" Her voice floats over the fence. "Hello, Ben, are you there?"

Well, no choice but to answer her now.

"Yeah, I'm here!" Ben slaps his forehead; he immediately regrets replying.

"Ben, I can't see you over the fence. Can I come in?" The creaking fence gate reveals she isn't waiting for an invitation.

"Oh, wait!" Ben yells, trying to stop her, but it's too late. She's standing in the open gate in full view of the mess: the old, rusted gardening tools he left on the ground, piles of sickly vines and scrap metal all over the backyard, and dirt and sweat all over his face.

Honey raises an eyebrow. "What are you doing?"

"Oh, nothing." Ben chuckles, brushing his hair with his hand.

"Are you gardening?"

"Uh, yes, I am. Sorry for all the mess."

Honey smiles. That same smile which always comforts Ben, but right now, it's doing the opposite. Surprisingly, she doesn't look bothered by the mess or the dirt on his face.

"What are you planning to put over there?" Honey points at the empty flower bed between the two bushes.

Ben shrugs. "I don't know. I was planning to put in some flowers."

"Flowers? Oh, that's lovely, but I don't recommend you plant them now. It's almost the end of August, and you know how the fall weather in Montana will be. You got a short timeframe to work with."

"Yeah, you're right. I guess I'm too late."

Honey chuckles. "Don't worry, there's always next year. Plus, you can always plant indoors. I also notice that you have some piles of scrap metal over there." She nodded at the other end. "Guess you scored good at the junkyard. What are you planning to make with them?"

"Oh, well, I always wanted to make a suit of armor shaped like an owl that I can wear. You know those fake owls they use to scare swallows away. I am planning to make an owl suit to see how many kids I scare during Halloween."

Honey laughs. "That sounds like a good prank. I can help you build the suit. I got the welding tools and everything."

"Sure."

Honey finishes the ice cream cone she got from the truck and points at the piles of weeds and vines that he pulled. "Do you mind if I take these weeds off your hands? I can take them to my house and burn them with the rest of my weeds."

Ben drops his pruning shear. "Yeah, sure. You can use my wheelbarrow."

"Hey, are you ready for the first day of school tomorrow?" Honey asks as they gather the weeds.

"Yeah, I'm honestly glad that this is our last year. No more school means no more Cougars." Ben smirks.

"When are you going to stop your fighting with The Cougars?" She rolled her eyes. "You guys have been fighting with each other ever since I've known you."

Well, Cougar Jack has been his rival ever since kindergarten. He would never forget the day back then when Jack beat him in rock-paper-scissors. Ever since, he'd been trying to beat Cougar Jack at everything.

"Well, if The Cougars stop being such jerks, then I'll stop."

"But will you ever stop, Ben? You tend to never give up on trying to defeat them. When are you going to give up?"

"Give up? I will never give up as long as they keep being jerks, then I will keep being a jerk to them."

Honey sighs and rolls her eyes again.

He knows what she's thinking—probably that he's being ridiculous again. But someone's got to stand up to The Cougars. If not him, then who?

He's seen how the world works. People with money and shiny reputations always get their way. Cougar Jack and his crew? Everyone listens to them. It's like they were born important. But kids like Ben? No one listens—unless he makes them. That's why he keeps fighting. That's why he and The Wolf Pack don't back down.

They finish stuffing the last pile of weeds into the compost bin.

"Speaking of never giving up," Honey says as they finish loading the weeds, "you haven't given up on your dad, have you? How's he doing?"

"I don't know. I haven't seen him all summer. He's probably out doing cross-country. He just took off one day and never came back home. I guess since I turned eighteen, he thought he didn't have to take care of me anymore."

Honey gasped. "You mean you've been taking care of the house all by yourself. How are you able to pay all the expenses?"

Ben shrugs. "Oh, my dad comes back from his trucking job to pay bills. That's probably the only time I see him."

"What do you do when he's gone?" Honey asks.

"I get by. I just run around doing chores for people and get paid. You know, handyman type stuff."

Honey's face has that concerned look. "Yeah, but how are you going to do that and go to school at the same time?"

"Don't worry, I have a plan. Plus, school is only temporary. After that, I'm going to college to become an artist. Once I get enough money to get out of this shithouse, that is. You and me, Honey, will be successful artists and become rich just like The Cougars. I guarantee that once we become rich and successful, then everything will be great in the world."

Honey looks at the ground. Her face has a mix of concern and deep thought.

What did I say to make her react that way? Is she imagining what I said? About being successful artists? If so, why does she look worried? His mind is churning.

"Ben, what happens if you don't become successful?"

"What do you mean?"

"Success isn't all that matters. You know I'll be happy even if you're not successful. I love you just the way you are, Ben."

"Yeah, but what are we supposed to do, live like poor people the rest of our lives?"

"Ben, we're not poor. As long as we have each other, then success doesn't really matter."

Ben stays silent.

Honey grabs the handles of the wheelbarrow. "Do you mind if I borrow your wheelbarrow for the rest of the day? I've also got a bunch of weeds at my house that I need to take care of."

Ben nods.

Honey lifts the cart and heads toward the gate. "Thanks, I'll see you later, okay?"

"Okay."

Ben waves goodbye as Honey slips through the gate. Once she's out of sight, her words echo in his head. Maybe she's right—maybe they don't need success to be happy. Just each other.

He used to believe that. But everything changed when his father left. That was the moment he realized something harsh and undeniable: in this world, only the successful survive.

That's why he pushes so hard—for Honey, for Tom and Cedric. He wants to protect them. To help them rise. Because if they don't, who will?

Even in nature, the pattern is clear. The strong survive. The weak get picked off. That's how it works, whether you're an animal in the wild or a poor kid in Montana. School taught him the same thing—history proves it.

Ben reaches for the chain around his neck. A fake diamond pendant shaped like a wolf glints in the fading light. He wears it every day. Cedric, Tom, and Honey each have one too. Whenever Ben makes a new friend, he buys them a wolf chain from the local mercantile.

Wolves survive. Wolves lead. And as alpha of their little pack, Ben's job is to protect them.

They're all he has.

If they left... he wouldn't be a leader anymore. Just a lone wolf. And a lone wolf is vulnerable. The kind that doesn't last.

Ben swallows hard.

He won't let that happen.

He can't.

Chapter 2- Ready for School

Cedric's POV, the busy cowboy

I can't believe what's happening to me right now. This feels like a dream! Cedric can't believe what's happening.

Edwin Sharp—his nemesis from the Cougars—is scrubbing his feet. And not just scrubbing. Vigorously. Like he's some girl with a foot fetish.

Cedric glances down. He's wearing a purple robe and a golden crown.

Am I a king?

Yup, definitely a dream. Edwin, dressed in a plain white robe to match his stupid white hair, must be his servant.

Cedric smirks. Dream or not, he doesn't want this one to end.

"Feel any better, my King?" Edwin looks up, all serious.

"Don't forget between the toes."

"I'm sorry, my King. Please forgive me."

Edwin gets back to work, scrubbing harder. Cedric leans back in his golden throne, smug as a bug in a rug—or in this case, a king in his ring.

Oh yeah. Don't wake up—

Buzz.

What the—?

Buzz.

Reality slams into him. No palace. Just his stankin' bedroom.

Buzz. The walls are wood, not gold.

Buzz. No throne—just a twin bed with a brown fur blanket.

Buzz. And instead of Edwin scrubbing his feet, his blue heeler is licking them.

Buzz. Christ, that alarm is gonna make him deaf—

Cedric tosses the blanket and jumps out of bed.

"Hey, Rusty, quit it!"

His old pal Rusty tries to lick his feet every morning because he's hungry.

Cedric presses the screen of his phone really hard to turn the alarm off. After the rude awakening, he feels like smashing his phone to the floor and kicking Rusty. It doesn't help that the alarm means it's the first day of school. He certainly doesn't want to be late for that.

He turns on the lights and blinks away the blurriness as his eyes adjust.

All his cowboy decorations on the walls come into focus. There are a few Charles Russell paintings of landscapes of the Old West and a cowhide rug on the floor, all in an attempt to make his room as western as possible.

He shambles over to the mirror next to his closet. Instead of a king's robe, he's wearing nothing except his boxers. Instead of a crown, only his messy mullet is at the top of his head. Cedric checks himself in the mirror very closely.

Man, it's a wonder why I don't have a woman yet. How come my six-pack abs aren't getting any love? That's what Cedric thinks to himself, but he's just deceiving himself. He shakes the fat of his belly. He really needs to lay off the fast-food burgers for a while, but he has no time for meal prep.

He grabs a plain gray t-shirt and some jeans out of his closet drawer and puts them on. He thinks he should have been more prepared for today, but he's been doing so much work on the ranch that he hasn't had time to go clothes shopping.

He's not the only one in this house that must go to school today; his little sister Sarah has to go as well. She is in the fifth grade, her last year of elementary school. She's already ten years old. Jeez, time goes by fast.

He remembered when he was that age; it was a good year for him. Probably not for his cousin Benjamin, though, because his mother died that year. He honestly feels bad for Ben because he heard his dad just left him to go do his trucking business. Now he's living alone.

Cedric wants to take care of the kid, but he's been so busy. Getting enough money to support his family's ranch is the top priority for him, whether he likes it or not. He hasn't talked to him much this summer. Hopefully today at school, he can talk to him.

Cedric grabs his trucker cap with the numbers 406 on it, puts it on his head, and runs to Sarah's room. She isn't a morning person, so he always has to wake her up. He's not a morning person either, but he has his job that gets him up early.

All the work he had to do at their ranch yesterday left him exhausted, plus he had to deal with his sister last night, fighting with her about who gets the last slice of the apple pie. Typical stresses a rancher has to deal with.

Regardless, he needs to get going. He opens the door and shouts, "Hey Sarah, wake up! Time for school!"

His sister ignores him and shifts her body to face away from him.

He walks over and pushes her. "Hey, wakey wakey. Eggs and bakey. It's breakfast!" Cedric keeps nudging her body.

Sarah shambles out of bed.

"Ugh! Why do you have to be so annoying?"

Cedric smiles and shrugs. "I'm just trying to be a good brother and wake my little sis up. It's not my fault that you love sleeping late."

Sarah just gives him a dirty look as he backs out of her room, waving for her to hurry up.

"Get dressed quickly. We're already late. I'll be waiting in the truck."

As Cedric runs down the stairs and into the kitchen, he sees his lovely mother sitting at the table eating cereal. She seems tired from the dark spots under her hazel eyes. In her nightgown, she just woke up too.

It's amazing she can keep a slim figure for her age, maybe because she's always active with taking care of the ranch and dealing with him and his sister. Still, she's been depressed since Dad died a year ago. She smiles, but Cedric can tell it's the smile she gives when she's bothered by something.

"Did you wake her up?" she asks.

"Yeah, she's stubborn as a mule, though." Cedric gives her a kiss on the forehead and walks to open the door to go outside.

"You know the only reason she is so stubborn is because you barely hang out with her—or me, for that matter. You're always busy with work."

"Well, who's going to make all the money around here? You certainly can't do it by yourself, Mom."

She looks back with a concerned expression. "I know, but there's a difference between being busy with work and avoiding your family, young man."

Cedric shrugs. "Time is money. Speaking of time, tell Sarah that if she doesn't come outside in the next five minutes, I'm leaving her."

Once outside, Cedric heads toward his pickup, a faithful 1995 Ford F-150 that used to be his dad's. It runs fairly well, and he made it work a lot yesterday. However, when he gets in and tries to start the engine, it doesn't turn on.

Assuming he may have a dead battery, he grabs the jumper cables from the back seat, hooks them up to his mom's car, and tries to turn on the engine again. It still won't start. While he is busy trying to figure his truck out, Sarah comes rushing out the door.

"What's happening?" Sarah looks at him, seeming puzzled.

"I can't start the truck."

Sarah rolls her eyes. "Oh, great. You know, I really should have stayed in bed."

Cedric gives Sarah a stern look. "Now you listen here. It's not the end of the world. We will be able to head out of here in no time. I just need to—"

Cedric tries to turn on the ignition again, but to no avail. He walks back to check the engine and shakes his head. "Yeah, I don't know what's the matter with it. I guess we'll have to wait for the school bus to come if I can't figure it out."

"Well, we shouldn't have woken up earlier than we had to."

Cedric ignores his sister and turns back to the truck. Then suddenly, he hears a honking noise. Turning around, he finds his friend Tom in his 2015 F-150 pulling up. The newer truck is immaculate compared to Cedric's. *He sure does take care of it*, Cedric thinks.

Tom gets out of his truck wearing his father's black leather jacket. He's trying to be like his father: a serious and dignified man. Cedric reflects on how much he has changed. He was serious and dignified ever since they were kids, but not like his father.

He's getting closer to being like his father every year that passes, even aspiring to be a police officer. Tom's father is a sheriff, but he's too serious and restrictive with Tom, Cedric would say. Tom is so focused on making his father proud that he doesn't like to mess around anymore. Cedric doesn't mind the change, but Ben hates it and often tries to get Tom to cause trouble like back in the day.

Cedric waves. "Hey Tom, what are you doing here?"

Tom hands Cedric a mechanical part. "I thought it was a good idea to hand you this before I head to school."

Cedric looks at Tom, puzzled, then looks back at the mechanism. "Oh, that's right. The new part for my tractor. I forgot about this. Thank you. My tractor has really been giving me problems lately, so this will do well."

Tom looks over Cedric's shoulder. "Is something the matter with your pick up?"

Cedric looks back at his truck and shakes his head. "Yeah, I can't seem to start the engine. I tried jumping it, but it won't turn on. I guess all that off-roading I did yesterday really wore it down."

Tom sighs. "Jesus, Cedric. You need to really take care of your stuff better. First it was the tractor, and now you have a problem with your truck? You're about as bad as Ben taking care of his stuff."

Cedric shrugs in embarrassment. "Well, me and Ben are related, so I guess it runs in the family."

Tom rolls his eyes. "You might not have enough time to figure out what the problem is. I can take you two to school if you want?"

"Yeah, sure. Thank you."

Cedric looks back at Sarah, who rolls her eyes as she takes the keys out of the ignition. Cedric hands her the part that Tom gave him for the tractor and the jump cables, which she puts in the truck before shutting the door.

On the way to school, all Cedric could think about is Ben's dad leaving him.

"Hey, Tom, have you heard that Ben's dad left him all summer to take care of himself? Why would he do that?"

Tom has his eyes fixed on the road. "They have a complicated relationship. It certainly wasn't okay for him to leave, but there's nothing anybody can do about it. Not even the police or my father can do anything about it either."

"I just really feel bad for Ben though. He's been trying so hard to please his dad ever since his mother passed away, but his dad just ignores him."

"Yeah, that's what years of neglect is like. Unfortunately, it seems like Ben doesn't want any help, so we can't force it on him."

Cedric's phone vibrates. Ben texted him.

Speak of the devil! Cedric thought, then he read Ben's text: **Meet me at the football field during lunch. I'm planning to have an important meeting.**

All Cedric can do is sigh. He already knows that this "important meeting" is probably about messing with The Cougars. Ben does this at the start of every school year. Ben is just obsessed with it at this point.

But like their motto says: "No wolf works alone." As a pack member, Cedric has to listen to his alpha. Even though his alpha is quite stupid. Cedric hears Tom's phone vibrating as well; he can only assume Ben texted him too.

Tom sighs. "Speaking of Ben."

Cedric shakes his head. "Mm, hmm."

Both of them roll their eyes. There's one thing about Ben that will never change: his stubborn determination to defeat The Cougars.

Chapter 3- Wolves vs. Cougars

It's lunchtime! Thank goodness because Ben couldn't sit in another classroom for another minute. All the new teachers start introducing themselves. Some of them were new, some of them Ben already had before. Some are nice. Some are just textbook, old school dignitaries that immediately want to start teaching them about the algebraic equation the very first day.

Some try to make every student stand up and participate in front of the class. Introducing themselves about who they are, what they did in the summer, and what they're planning to do after they graduate.

Ben hates it when the teachers have them pinned in front of class. Big deal, it's a small school, everybody knows who they are and that's the end of it. He doesn't want to know what the other students did during their summer breaks, and he knows that they don't care about what he did either.

At least it's lunchtime. He can have a break from all the chaos. He can also have a short time of playing little games with his friends, Cedric and Tom. The three of them are just hanging out on the bleachers at the football field.

Unfortunately, Honey isn't with them because she's part of the women's basketball team. She's the general manager of the varsity. Honestly, Ben thinks she should be on the actual court playing some ball by how much she beats him, Cedric, and Tom at H-O-R-S-E. She's a very busy girl though. Ben is glad to be dating her.

Ben can tell that Cedric and Tom are annoyed that he summoned them to the field but hasn't shared his plan yet. He can tell because they have been quiet ever since they got their food at the cafeteria.

Now they're munching away just staring at Ben with looks Ben's used to seeing every day. He's seen more frowns than smiles in his life and Ben is used to it at this point. But he's always hoping to turn those frowns upside down.

"Ben, what are we doing here? You better not be planning to force us to do some shady stuff," Cedric finally asks.

"Don't worry, this isn't about The Cougars."

"Then, what is it about then?" Cedric gives Ben a stern look.

"I will tell you later, when the two kids I volunteered show up to help me with my plan."

Tom raises an eyebrow. "Who are you forcing to do your biddings this time, Ben?"

Ben frowns at Tom. "I didn't force anybody to do my biddings, for your information. These two willingly volunteered to help me when I asked them. The only thing they asked in return was... well... is that I pay them."

"Oh, so you bribed them?"

Tom's humor hasn't changed one bit. That's the only thing his dad hasn't torn away from him, but Ben wishes he would be as enthusiastic about his plans as when they were younger.

Ben just frowns in reply. He's staying silent. He doesn't want to argue with Tom right now about what's right and what's wrong. He usually loses to Tom's arguments anyway. Tom always gives him facts and rules to prove his points.

Honestly, he should be a teacher or be part of the debate team. Tom would be a very good master debater. Even though he is a teacher's aide, Tom really isn't interested in that kind of stuff. He just follows what his dad wants him to do.

Ben hates seeing it. Seeing his friend become something he doesn't want to be. And it kills him that he can't stop it.

"Hey, Ben!"

Ben hears someone calling him from way down the bleachers. They are sitting way up high, so Ben has to tilt his head down a little to find his two volunteers that have finally arrived.

Slam Dickson Dolly and Baxter Rodriguez, also seniors, walk up the bleachers.

Slam waves at Ben with the widest smile Ben has ever seen from a human being. His optimism always makes Ben smile. He's like Honey if she were Native American... and a man. If she was a man, then Ben doesn't want to even imagine it. But if she was, then Slam would be it.

His hair is dark brown, very long. His signature tan trench coat. As far as Ben can remember, he has never seen that guy take that coat off. He's nicely dressed in black cowboy boots.

Ben can only assume that he just bought new clothes, but that old trench coat remains, something Ben has never seen him without, even in the heat of summer. Ben can't even imagine how he lives with that heavy thing on.

He's got tons of Native American bead necklaces on him, a dreamcatcher to boot. Ben's glad to see him wear the wolf chain he gave him. He's really an interesting fellow; it's a weird moment when he first met him. He's a nice guy though. He was willing to help Ben with his plan, so he must be a good guy.

And then there's Baxter.

Ben met Baxter when they both got sent to the principal's office last year for fighting with Cougar Jack. Ben barely knew the kid, but for some reason Baxter defended him, coming out of nowhere to give Jack a punch to the face. He might have knocked Jack out, but a teacher intervened. They both got sent to the principal's office. Unfortunately for Jack, he made a new friend.

Baxter doesn't look excited to be here. He always looks like that way, and his baggy black hoodie is as ubiquitous to him as Slam's trench coat. Ben doesn't really get how Baxter and Slam can wear such heavy clothing with this heat and not get suffocated, but at least Baxter is wearing dark brown jean shorts to let some air in. He also has a brown leather vest over his black hoodie with interesting Mexican embroidery.

Baxter always walks sluggishly with his hands in his pockets, which isn't surprising since his dad is like Ben's; never caring about him and ignoring him most of the time. Ben feels close to Baxter because of this. Even though Baxter hasn't opened up to him about it, Ben knows that he probably feels alone like him. That's why he wants Baxter to join the Wolf Pack as well as Slam.

As Slam and Baxter get closer to them, Ben looks back at Tom and Cedric. "See, here they come now."

"Well, would you look at that? You invited two indigenous kids to join our party. You're really trying to diversify our group, Ben," Tom quips.

"Hey, isn't that the kid who threatened to bomb the whole school last year?" Cedric points at Baxter.

"He didn't threaten to bomb the whole school," Ben frowns at Cedric. "Those are just rumors kids keep spreading around about him."

Tom frowns. "Ben, what sort of idea are you planning here?"

Ben waves his hand at Tom. "Just wait. I will tell you later."

Tom continues to frown, but Ben ignores him and gets up to greet Slam and Baxter.

"Hey, how is it going Ben?" Slam asks.

"Uh, good." Ben shakes Slam's hand.

"Ah, that's great to hear. I'm ready to get down to business. Like a secret agent planning to find his nemesis. How about you, Baxter?"

"Oh, Jesus Christ! Will you ever shut up? You've been talking my ear off for the last twenty minutes." Baxter frowns at Slam.

Slam rubs his head awkwardly. "Heh, heh. Sorry, my friend. I have the tendency to talk a lot."

"Psh, whatever, man." Baxter looks at Ben. "Just tell me what to do and pay me so we can get this over with."

Ben rubs his head, thinking, *So much for bonding today.* "Oh, right, okay." Ben grabs a small whiteboard he left on one of the bleacher seats, takes a marker out of the pocket of his overalls, and waves at Tom and Cedric to get up.

They roll their eyes but acquiesce.

"Alright, let's get started. As you all very well know, the girls' basketball team sells candy and has booths set up all over the school. I'd like to focus on the one at the playground area between the high school and the elementary."

Ben takes out a map of the whole school campus, including the elementary and the middle school. Ben's glad that they live in a small town, otherwise making this plan of his would be more confusing with a bigger area. He hates explaining things. That's why he unfolds the map over the whiteboard. He grabs the marker and circles where the elementary playground is.

"Why the candy booth at the elementary playground, specifically? You're not planning to steal their candy, are you?" Tom asks.

"That's exactly what we are doing, but we are not just stealing this candy for no reason. No, the reason is because Anna Sharp is running this booth."

"Why do you want to steal candy from Anna Sharp?" Slam asks with a confused look on his face.

"It's because Anna Sharp is Cougar Jack's girlfriend." Tom answered, frowning at Ben. "I thought you said this plan of yours wasn't going to involve The Cougars."

Ben shrugs. "Not directly, it isn't."

Tom throws his hands up. "Oh, come on! Now you're getting involved with his girlfriend as well? What's the matter with you?"

"Hey, now. It's not like I like to get involved, but it's a matter of payback."

"Psf, yeah, but I know there's going to be a bunch of little kids from the elementary that are going to be buying the candy from her stand. Do you seriously want to traumatize some kids just because you want to fight Jack's girlfriend?" Toms says.

"If that's what it takes, then yeah. Plus...um..." Ben pauses as he chuckles awkwardly. He knows he's blushing because his face is getting warmer. He stumbles when his friends look at him for more explanation. "Well, the main reason is because I need a quick date gift for Honey."

Ben half-expects Cedric, Tom, or even Baxter and Slam to yell at him after he says this, but all of them stay silent. That makes him want to hide underground even more. Ben looks down and fumbles with his fingers, acting like he did something wrong.

"Wait, you're dating Honey? Right on, man!" Slam's sudden burst is surprising to Ben. What's more frightening is when Slam goes and playfully punches his arm. "I knew you could do it. I knew you had the courage to ask her out."

Ben chuckles. "Actually, she asked me out."

Cedric's eyes go wide. "Wait, she asked you out? Wow, I wish a girl asked me out instead of being the opposite way around."

Baxter crosses his arms. "Psh. You gotta be kidding me. I can't believe I'm helping with a stupid Romeo and Juliet saga here. You better be paying me some good money for this."

Ben giggles. "Don't worry, you'll get paid well."

Tom raises an eyebrow. "Ben, if you're doing this to satisfy Honey, then don't. There're other ways to give gifts; ways that don't involve stealing."

"Yeah, yeah. I know... Anyway, my plan is to have me, Tom, and Cedric walk up to the candy booth. We will distract Anna. Meanwhile, Slam and Baxter will sneak around and steal the candy. Then, we will all leave and meet up here before we head back to class. Sound good?"

Ben looks up to find Cedric and Tom with their usual frowns, but Slam and Baxter both nod.

"Alrighty, then let's get to it. To the playground, Wolves!"

***

Minutes later, the five of them, the five hungry wolves ready to eat some candies, are hiding behind some bushes, waiting for their moment to strike, to grab a gift for the alpha female. She's not with the pack at the moment and it's a good thing she isn't.

Otherwise, she would kill Ben if she found out. But the alpha female is tending to another candy stand because she's also part of the basketball team. That leaves time for the males to go out hunting.

They're watching their prey, a female cougar by the name of Anna Sharp. She's tending to customers at the candy booth. A bunch of younglings surround the female cougar like she's a goddess giving them salvation, but Ben knows she's full of lies just like her mate.

"Hey, Ben. Doesn't this count as stalking?" Cedric looks at Ben.

"No, this isn't stalking. We're just imitating wolves, waiting for the right time to strike our prey."

Cedric raises an eyebrow. "Isn't that also called stalking?"

Ben gives Cedric a dirty look and turns back to watching the booth. There's nobody around, so it's a perfect time to strike. "Alright, let's go." Ben motions Tom and Cedric to follow him as the three of them grab their water guns and run up to the booth.

As they approach, Anna looks confused.

Ben points the water gun at her. "Alright, you listen here, little miss. Give us all your candy, and we promise we won't shoot you."

Ben looks back and sees that Tom and Cedric are not pointing their water guns at Anna. Ben gives them a dirty look, and they roll their eyes, but finally point their water guns at Anna. She doesn't seem fazed at all. In fact, she looks more bothered than anything.

Dang it! Ben thinks. *The plan didn't work!*

"Seriously, what are you doing, Ben? I can't believe Honey would ever date a dummy like you."

Ben growls. "Hey, you listen here! At least she isn't an idiot like you, dating a jerk like Cougar Jack!"

Ben raises his water gun, his finger sliding over the trigger as he takes aim. *I'm going to enjoy this*, he thinks, savoring the moment as Anna's eyes widen in shock. *Perfect*, he thinks. *Aim for the eyes.*

He relishes the thought of the burning she'll get from the pepper juice he mixed into the water guns. He starts to put pressure on the trigger, slowly, enjoying the anticipation, when—

"Hey, Ben! Step away from my girl. You already got one, haven't you?"

Ben can recognize that stinking voice from anywhere. Why does he have to ruin this perfect moment? "Jackass!"

"Uh, seriously? You keep calling me that, but in reality, you're the jackass, Ben."

Cougar Jack stands with his usual tagalongs—Larry and Edwin. Three more kids are with them, but Ben doesn't recognize their faces. So many come and go from The Cougars that Ben swears Jack must be paying them. Without the money, he'd just be another washed-up bastard.

Cougars aren't even pack animals—they're solitary by nature. But Jack doesn't get that. He thinks he can buy loyalty, buy friends. Ben sees right through it.

The only ones who've stuck by Jack's side are Larry Terry and Edwin. Ben can't stand any of them. He doesn't get why people like Jack, but somehow he's got half the school wrapped around his finger.

When Ben tried to grow the Wolf Pack, the only ones who joined were Slam and Baxter.

"I don't know why anyone would want to join a jerk like you, so I guess you did some sort of spell to force them to sign up." Ben points at the three new kids.

"Oh, you think I forced these guys to join me? No, it's because they know who's really successful at school." Cougar

Jack points to himself and smirks. "I will not ask you again, Ben. Step away from my girl, or else," Cougar Jack laughs as he and his posse pull out water guns, "we will have to water down your worthless trash!"

Cougar Jack laughs, and the rest of his posse laugh along with him.

All Ben sees is dark and his worst nemesis in front of him. A redness in Ben's skin makes it look like he got burned.

Burned from that stupid remark Cougar Jack made. It's always the same, Cougar Jack still thinks he's a worthless nobody, but Ben is determined to show him something.

Gun ready at Cougar Jack's eyes. A water gun full of surprise juices that will surely burn more than his stupid jokes. An arm suddenly grabs a hold of him.

"Don't do it, Ben."

Tom stops him. It's too late to stop him. He can't take it any longer.

"Oh, we're doing this." Ben looks back at Jack. "Hey, Jackass, you're not the only one who has added more people to his group."

Cougar Jack raises an eyebrow in confusion.

Ben waves his hand at Slam and Baxter, still hiding behind the bushes. Suddenly, they jump out and shoot their water guns at The Cougars. In the moment of confusion, Ben strikes, shooting water at Jack's eyes, momentarily blinding him as he yells out in pain from the pepper water. Anna runs from her booth, but candy is the least of his worries.

"Alright, Wolves, let's fight!"

Tom and Cedric roll their eyes again, but they charge with Ben, the three of them blasting away. Everybody is soon soaked, and some of their eyes are burning from the pepper in the water.

Ben runs at Cougar Jack, who is recovering from the shot to his eyes, and pounces at him before he can react. He pushes Jack to the ground and is about to punch him when he feels somebody holding him back. Ben turns and his eyes go wide.

Principal Jensen, looking furious, has an iron grip around Ben's arm. Anna is behind him. The female strikes unexpectedly.

Oh, great! Just when he had the opportunity to hit Cougar Jack in the face...

***

Ben and The Wolf Pack, including Slam and Baxter, have been sitting on one side of a big table in the teacher conference room for an hour. Cougar Jack and his buddies are on the opposite side. Looking at Cougar Jack's face for an hour is the worst punishment that Ben can imagine Principal Jensen giving him.

He has given a lot of punishments to Ben over the years, but this one takes the cake (or the piece of candy if you will). That's all Ben wanted in the first place, but Cougar Jack has to ruin it, doesn't he? Jack is just lucky that the principal is sitting between them. Otherwise, he would be slapping him and that stupid face of his.

"I can't believe that on the first day of school, I already have to deal with you guys."

Surprisingly, Principal Jensen isn't yelling like he usually does with them. He just sounds tired. Ben can see how tired he is. He'd heard the principal's son is facing cancer, just like his mom before her death. He wouldn't want the principal's son to face the same fate.

"You guys need to settle this beef, or else I will expel all of you and none of you are going to graduate this year, you got that?"

Cougar Jack offers his hand. "Hey, no hard feelings, Ben."

Ben just stares at it. He knows Jack doesn't truly want to make peace. He can tell that by his stupid smile, but for the sake of him getting out of this room, he shakes Jack's hand.

From Principal Jensen's expression, he doesn't believe this will be the end of their conflict either. "Okay, that will be it. Off you go. Don't cause trouble now." Principal Jensen motions them to leave.

The Cougars leave first, then The Wolf Pack, and Ben is the last one to the door, but Principal Jensen calls out to him. "Hey Ben, before you leave. I know you were the true source of the fight."

Ben looks down in embarrassment.

"You know, Ben, Jack is just going to continue harassing you if you continue letting yourself be harassed. So, please, Ben, just give up trying to beat Jack, because you're just causing problems for yourself."

Ben flashes an awkward smile. "Don't worry, Principal Jensen, I'll try to be good."

Jensen's face reveals he doesn't believe him.

Ben turns to the door, then stops himself and looks back. "Hey, Principal Jensen. Sorry about your son."

Principal Jensen looks up and raises his eyebrows.

"My mom had cancer too. I hope he gets better soon."

The principal looks at him, seeming confused, but then smiles and nods.

Ben turns around and heads out the door. He thought he was going to get away quickly, but he finds Tom, Cedric, Baxter, and Slam waiting for him, staring at him with angry expressions. Great, nothing he hasn't seen before. Again, he's used to it at this point. Ben just shrugs and chuckles uncomfortably.

"Looks like things haven't gone as planned. Don't worry, I'll make it up to you guys."

Tom and Cedric, as usual, roll their eyes. Ben worries about how Slam and Baxter will react; they look angry.

"Sorry I brought you two into this mess. Here..." Ben pulls out his wallet and retrieves two twenty-dollar bills. He holds one out for Slam, but to his surprise, he just smiles and shakes his head.

"There's no need to give me money, Ben. That was probably the most exciting experience I ever had." Slam laughs.

"You're not mad?"

"Mad? No, not at all. I'm actually glad you decided to take me in. I'll be happy to join The Wolf Pack..." Slam laughs again and pats Ben on the back.

Ben is so surprised by Slam's joy that he doesn't know what to say.

Slam walks away with a wave. "See you guys around. I hope your date with Honey goes well, Ben."

That is the happiest man Ben has ever seen. Despite all the stupidity he brought him through today, Ben is just in shock. He turns back to see Baxter staring at him with a malicious frown. He motions toward the money still in Ben's hand.

"I'll take my pay and his as well, since he didn't want it, then we're even."

Ben lets out a sigh and hands over the forty dollars. "Sorry I got you into this mess. You're welcome to leave. You don't have to join us if you want."

"Nah, I think I'll stay with you guys. You aren't half-bad."

Ben, Cedric, and Tom look at Baxter like he's crazy as he shambles away from them. Ben is surprised, but happy to get two new members.

He looks at the others with a shrug. "Looks like we got two new Wolf Pack members."

"Great, two more weirdos to join the party," Tom quips.

Ben ignores Tom's sarcasm and puts his hands on both boys' shoulders. "Let's just go back to class. I'm getting tired."

Cedric nods. "I agree. What are you going to do about Honey's gift?"

"I don't know."

"Well, lucky for you, I've got something," Tom says.

Ben looks on eagerly as Tom pulls a box of chocolates from his backpack and hands it to him. It's a simple box of chocolates, but for Ben, it's like Tom handed him gold. It was from the heart that counted. Ben is glad to have good-hearted friends with him. He hugs the box of chocolates like a teddy bear.

"Oh, wow. Thank you. How the hell did you manage to get one?"

Tom shrugs. "Well, I just went to a candy store and bought a box of chocolates instead of stealing it, you know, like normal people do."

Ben smiles. "Thank you."

Tom waves his hand and walks away. "Don't get too sentimental, kid."

Once Tom walks away, Ben and Cedric nod to each other and go their separate ways. Ben heads to art class, excited to see Honey there. He decides not to tell her about all the chaos he caused.

If she found out that he was trying to steal candy, he'd be in deep trouble. Especially since she's the general manager of the girls' varsity basketball team. She's the one who arranged for all the candy stands. He's praying for his life that she will not find out.

The Wolf Pack's unfortunate exploits are getting exhausting. Ben knows that it's mostly his fault. Being the alpha in the pack, you must do crazy things in order to survive and get to the top of the food chain, but no matter how hard he tries, he always loses. Every year, it seems like he and his friends are stuck in an endless loop of failure.

Things have to get better eventually, right? Ben thought. He sure hopes that will be the case. It seems he was always doomed to fail. His father's leaving is just proof of that. He just wishes that there would be some miracle. Some miracle from God that will help him. He doesn't know why God would treat him this way, but he just wants to know...

Chapter 4- The Miracle

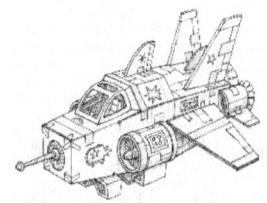

The bell rings, signaling the end of the day, and an end of imprisonment that the school keeps him in. Ben is just glad that this will be his final year of high school. No more school after that, unless he decides to go to college, but Ben is not sure.

He's not really sure what he wants to do with his life. All of his life was just him spending time having fun and playing games with his friends. All the teachers nagged him about goal planning and what his goals are after high school. Ben would always respond to his teachers that he wants to take art classes and become a successful artist, but in reality, Ben just doesn't know what he wants to do with his life.

There's no time to dwell on this, though. The final bell rings, and school is over for today. Ben rushes out of the classroom. He doesn't want to stay in the building for one moment longer, especially since Cougar Jack was in his last class: chemistry. The only chemistry he be doing with Jack is staying as far away from him as possible.

Ben zigzags through the hallways like a madman. Other kids burst from their classrooms like a bunch of animals escaping from a zoo. The cages are set free. All the wild animals escape. For the alpha wolf, he wants to get out of here. He has a date with the alpha female later today. No time for schoolwork.

Ben heard that Cedric's truck broke down. Ben wanted to give him a ride, but Cedric insisted that he and Sarah would just take the bus. Tom got to quit early for school because he has most of his credits. He's the teacher's aide for their biology class. That lucky son of a gun gets to quit early. He's lucky that he's smart. Unlike Ben, Ben is just glad that he's able to make it senior year. But Ben is happy for Tom though; he's a good man despite how much they fight with each other.

Ben passes through the school's main entrance before the stampede comes. He heads through the school parking lot to find his truck. He finally spots the only gray Toyota Tundra in the parking lot with the license plate reading: "DA HWLR." He calls his truck "The Howler" because of how much noise it makes every time he turns on the engine. The truck actually used to be his dad's, but he doesn't drive it very often because he's usually busy doing his cross-country driving.

Ben is about to put the key into the ignition and prepare his ears when suddenly, strange noises emit from a dark alley next to the parking lot, drawing Ben's attention. It sounds like someone getting punched.

He hesitates, then decides to get out of The Howler to investigate. Kids often smoke and make out in the alley because the place is hidden and rarely checked by teachers. Ben isn't sure why he's going into the dark alley despite knowing there's probably some nasty business going down, but his curiosity gets the better of him, and he peers into the shadows.

Anger boils within him upon seeing a little boy getting beat up by three older kids, a group of eighth-graders Ben recognizes. They often come from the middle school down the road to hang out at the high school for some reason. He doesn't recognize the little boy that they are beating up, though. The kid looks about the same age as Cedric's little sister.

"Hey, feather boy. Why don't you show us one of your tricks?" one of the bullies says.

"Yeah, come on, feather boy, defend yourself," adds another.

The bullies start throwing stones at the boy, and one hits him in the groin, dropping him to the ground. Ben winces in sympathetic pain and remembers the Cougars picking on Honey back in middle school. The bastards would pick on something so innocent like Honey is just messed up.

One of the bullies winds up for another stone throw and Ben races into the alley, arriving just in time to bat the projectile away and save the boy from another nasty bruise.

The three bullies' eyes go wide.

"Hey, why don't you pick on somebody your own size?" Ben shouts.

The bullies said nothing. Their only response is to throw another stone, and Ben falls to the ground in pain, grasping his own nuggets. He no longer needs sympathy to imagine what the smaller child feels. He's feeling it right now. "Ah... Ugh..." Ben gasps, struggling to catch his breath. "You—You'll pay for that, you little turd!"

Before he can drag himself to his feet, the boys run from the alley, laughing. When he finally gets up, the little boy stares at him wide-eyed. The boy gets up as well, wiping sweat from his face.

"Are you alright?"

The boy stays silent for a bit, but then he nods. "Yeah, I'm alright. Thank you."

The boy sounds like he's from the Middle East. He also has a blue head scarf he's adjusting to get the sweat off of his forehead. *Do those stupid eighth-graders think they can pick on a kid just because he's foreign? Man, that's just wrong!*

"What's your name, kid?"

"Uri."

"Uri? That's an interesting name. Sounds Middle Eastern."

"Yeah, it's Hebrew. What's yours?"

"Benjamin, but you can just call me Ben."

"Nice to meet you, Benjamin. I'll give you a gift as a token of my gratitude."

"Oh, you don't have to give me anything."

Uri seems to ignore Ben and runs past him and into a big, empty cardboard box in the middle of the alley. Ben scratches his head.

Why did he go inside a cardboard box?

Ben analyzes it. There's a bunch of kid drawings on the box of different animals. The word "Imaginator" is drawn in the middle of each side. There's a big red cone at the top, like

53

a kid trying to make a cardboard spaceship. Ben decides to go inside the box and see what the heck is going on. When he enters, he can't believe what he sees.

"What the hell?" Ben says under his breath.

It wasn't a cardboard box at all! In fact, it looks like the inside of a spaceship that he sees in sci-fi movies. Ben walks inside and looks around. Maybe he passed out after being hit by that stone.

It looks like he's in some sort of entryway with an open door at the other side. Rumbling noises come from there, so he decides to go in. Once inside, he sees this Uri kid, whoever he is, digging through a chest, throwing random gadgets behind him, forcing Ben to dodge out of the way.

"Now, where did I hide it?" Uri keeps digging.

Ben looks around at what must be the control room to fly this thing, based on all the random buttons, switches, seats, and the steering wheel in the middle of the room.

Uri seems to finally notice him. "Oh, you're here!"

Ben looks at him skeptically. "Who are you?"

"Oh, right. You must be confused about what's happening right now. I forgot you Earth humans are isolated from the rest of the universe." Uri giggles awkwardly and rubs his head in embarrassment.

"Isolated? What the hell are you talking about? Am I dreaming right now?"

"You're not dreaming. What you're seeing is real, only because you helped me. I usually don't let strangers inside The Imaginator unless I totally trust them."

"The Imaginator?"

"Yeah, that's the name of the space cruiser you're in right now. You must have a lot of questions right now."

"Oh, you bet. I'm still wondering if I'm dreaming or not." Ben continues to look around the ship, touching everything to see if it's real. He even touches himself to see if he's real. He looks back at Uri, who is smiling at him. "Who are you?"

"I'm Uri, prince of Zion, son of King Yadin, servant of Jehovah. I'm from The Old World."

"The Old World? Prince of Zion? What kind of trick are you pulling here, kid? You're just saying random names that don't make sense. You can't fool me." Ben crosses his arms and walks away. He knew this kid was full of it. He was about to leave when—

"Wait."

Ben turns around.

Uri has his hand out and a sad, almost longing expression on his face. He then looks down and sighs. "Fine, if you still don't believe me, then I guess I have to show you my special ability."

"Special ability?"

"Yeah, you Earth humans don't have special abilities. It's like a superpower. Wait..."

Uri digs inside the chest again, throwing stuff behind him. Ben dodges, again. Uri then takes out a wooden staff. Uri clasps his hands together, holding the staff, it looks like he's praying.

Ben just stands there waiting for Uri to show him this "special ability" of his. All of a sudden, Ben sees Uri's skin change. Orange and blue feathers sprout all over his body, including his face. They match the same orange and blue of his shirt and jacket he's wearing.

Ben gasps in shock, he can't believe what he's seeing with his own eyes.

Uri's form completely changes. He looks like a bird now. In fact, Ben knows what species of bird he is.

"Hey, wait a minute. You're an American kestrel!"

Uri's beak opens slightly, and his eyes perk up in what Ben assumes to be the avian equivalent of a smile. "It looks like you know your birds. I like birds as well. I've been studying different birds that live in your area."

Uri giggles as he flies around in his kestrel form. "This is my special ability, or superpower, or whatever you wanna call it. I can change into different forms of creatures. Pretty neat, huh?" Uri then suddenly changes back to human form and opens his arms wide with the staff, like he just showed Ben a magic trick. "Believe me now?"

"I can't believe it. I'm meeting a real alien." Ben puts his arm on his forehead making sure he doesn't faint.

Uri looks at him with concern. "Are you alright?"

"Why are you here?"

"What?"

"Now that I know you're an alien, I want to know why you came to this planet."

Uri looks down, his smile gone again. He sits on the floor, crossing his legs.

Ben decides to sit on the floor with him.

"It's a long story," Uri begins. "Remember that I told you that I'm a prince, right? The prince of Zion. Zion is where I'm from. It was a great place until..."

"Until what?"

"Until it got destroyed by an evil group of creatures called The Babylonians."

"The Babylonians?"

"Yeah, The Babylonians. They're also called the creatures of Babel. They're dangerous creatures; they're skilled fighters.

Unfortunately, they were able to destroy Zion. All that is left of it is rubble. The only survivors were my parents as well as a few others." Tears creep down Uri's cheeks as he tells his story.

"Where are they now?"

"I don't know. I got lost and separated as we escaped. I've been traveling to different planets to look for my parents. That's why I ended up here."

The trickle of tears grows to a raging torrent. Ben's heart sinks, remembering the last time he cried like that, when he lost his mom. It seems Uri has suffered through a lot, and now he's lost. Ben wants to help him.

Uri says that he's a prince, which means Uri's parents are a king and a queen. Maybe this is the opportunity that Ben and the Wolf Pack have been waiting for. If he takes Uri to his parents, maybe they'll reward him and his friends. *Yes! That will show The Cougars how successful we are!*

"Hey, Uri, I want to help you find your parents."

Uri's eyes go wide. "Are you sure?"

"Yeah, and I have some friends that can help you too."

"Really? I don't know. I don't want to be a burden on you and your friends."

Ben smiles and puts his hand on Uri's shoulder. "What? Of course not. You've travelled through space, so you're probably tired. You can stay at my house to rest. Then me and my friends can help you find your parents."

Uri gazes at the deck beneath him for several long moments. He looks like he doesn't trust Ben, but then he smiles. "Sure, thank you. I hope I'm not going to be a problem for you."

Ben gets to his feet. "You are not going to be a problem at all. I practically live in a house by myself anyway, so I'll be more than welcome to let you stay."

Uri gets up as well. "Okay!" Suddenly, Uri's smile disappears yet again. "What about my space cruiser?"

"Is your space cruiser heavy at all?"

"Nope, it's about as light as an actual cardboard box."

Uri knocks on the wall of his space cruiser. Ben is surprised at how solid the walls are when Uri knocks on them. It sounds like they're made out of steel, you will never think that the exterior of this spaceship is just a cardboard box.

"You got a unique ship, but good thing it's not heavy though. We can probably fit it on my truck bed."

"Alright!"

Uri jumps for joy and runs out of the space cruiser.

"Hey, where are you going? Do you even know where my truck is?"

Ben hurries after Uri, who's darting ahead like he owns the place, weaving between trees and cutting across patches of dry grass behind the school buildings. A few kids glance their way, but Uri doesn't slow down—doesn't even check if Ben's still following.

Ben jogs to catch up, breath puffing in short bursts, his mind spinning faster than his legs. *How the hell am I going to explain this to the guys?* He can already picture the looks on their faces—Cedric with his skeptical scowl, Tom trying to crack some sarcastic joke to make sense of it. A bird-boy alien with a stick? Yeah, that's gonna go over great.

But something tugs at him—underneath the chaos, the weirdness, the feathers and sudden responsibility, there's this buzz in his chest. Like this could actually matter. Like maybe—just maybe—they're about to do something real for once. Not another half-baked prank. Not some failed candy heist. Something that counts.

Chapter 5- Secret Betrayal

Baxter's POV, the mad pyromaniac

There's one thing Baxter hates more than anything, and that's friends.

What even is a friend in this cruel world? He really doesn't get why Benjamin and The Wolf Pack have been friends for so long. If he were them, he would leave the group and rely on himself instead of other people. However, working for The Cougars as a spy is worth the pay. He has this "contract," as he calls it, with The Cougars. He agrees to help The Cougars be a spy for them as long as they pay him according to what he asks.

Honestly, he would've denied the contract but rent in Montana has been high these days. If he didn't need the money, then he would just forget about being involved with this stupid "Cougars v. Wolves" beef going on. Plus, The Cougars are doing his homework for him to pass school so he can't complain.

He could drop out, but it's no use at this point. Especially since he got this far into school. He's surprised he made it to senior year, but it doesn't matter to him. He is just glad school will be gone soon. He'll be lonesome and won't have to deal with these stupid kids. Be a hermit for the rest of his life.

Baxter muses over the situation in his Ford Mustang on his way to "The Cougar Mansion," as Cougar Jack likes to call his house. It's a stupid name for a house, and who names their own home? It isn't even Cougar Jack's house anyway; it's his rich parents' house. He is one of the most spoiled kids Baxter has ever seen.

If he had that kind of money, he'd probably spend it all on fireworks and make the whole sky explode. Or he would spend as much gun powder as he wants to make himself some bombs to explode those broken down vehicles at those junk yards. What a waste of space for those junkyards if they just let the junk stay there. He thinks he's helping the junkyard by doing so.

His dad is an FBI agent, and he lets Baxter make bombs for research. His dad's friend owns a junkyard, and he lets Baxter test his bombs out. There's no trouble when he gets caught. If he does, then he would just say that his dad is an FBI agent, and they back off.

Baxter pulls up to The Cougar Mansion, gets out of his car, and heads to the backyard where Cougar Jack said to meet him. He finds Jack and his stupid friends hanging out by the lake. Baxter always wanted to have a chance to explode a bomb in the lake just to see how big of a splash it would make.

Jack and his buddies are on the dock in their swimsuits, some of them diving into the water, as a speaker plays loud rap music. Jack has his arm around his girlfriend, Anna, drinking a beer. Her white hair is frizzy and wet, probably because she's been swimming. However, she doesn't seem like she wants to be here.

Baxter doesn't care about her. If he was her, he would've killed himself already. Just tie a knot around his neck and throw him overboard if he was Jack's girlfriend. It seems like they're having a "good time," or what they think a "good time" is.

Baxter just wants to hear what Jack has to say to him. Nothing pains him more than parties and socializing. He's surprised there aren't any more kids here. He expects there will be more, especially considering how many people at school keep following Jack around like he's Jesus or something. The Cougars have so many people coming and going that Baxter doesn't even know most of the people who join.

Jack and Larry are laughing and teasing Anna and her twin brother Edwin about something. Both of them have bothered looks on their faces.

"Jeez, you two sure are twins. Neither of you can take a joke!" Larry laughs at the twins.

Anna and Edwin frown at Cougar Jack and Larry.

Jack looks like he is about to say something as well but stops and looks up at Baxter with that stupid smirk of his. Baxter gets why Ben hates it; he wants to punch that smirk off his face too.

"Ah, it looks like my favorite spy has arrived. How's the spying going? Have you found out any deep, dark secrets about Ben yet? Any secret files?" Jack laughs at his own joke.

"Nah, nothing so far," Baxter says.

"Ah, that's too bad. I really want to know how that kid spends his free time. He always wastes it trying to defeat me. It's embarrassing," Jack growls in disgust. "Honestly, I don't know what that Honey chick finds in him. She must have some bad brain damage."

"Hey, don't be rude!" Anna punches Jack in the arm.

"Hey, I'm just being honest, Anna. You of all people should know. You and her play basketball together..." Jack shrugs.

Anna frowns at him.

"So, Baxter, my friend," Jack says, ignoring her, "why don't you come and join us for a swim? It's the weekend, and my parents are out of town. Stay for a while, bud."

"Friend? Psh, man, you listen here. I'm not your friend, bozo. The thing between me and you is just business. The only reason why I'm here in first place is cause your stupid ass texted me to come to discuss something, so get to it or I'll be leaving!"

Baxter swipes the beer can that Cougar Jack was holding, sending it spinning to the ground spilling its contents.

Jack looks surprised for a moment, but his stupid smirk returns. "Hey, buddy, relax. Take a chill pill. I'm only trying to be friendly. Plus, the reason why I texted you is because I got your money..." Jack runs through his pockets and holds out three hundred dollars. "There, that's probably way more cash than what poor Ben gave you, and that's just a small portion of it. Keep doing your job and I'll give you enough cash to spend on whatever your pyromaniac-ass wants to buy."

Baxter grabs the money and walks away without saying anything.

"What? You just going to leave without saying goodbye?"

Baxter calls over his shoulder without stopping, "Bye."

He wants to get out of this place as quickly as possible. Nothing bothers him more than people, especially people like Cougar Jack. People like him prove to Baxter that you can't trust anybody in this world.

If you do, they will use you. He doesn't want to be used. His dad taught him that at an early age. He's a crazy man, but at least he knows how the world works. Hell, he's an FBI agent, so he knows the ins and outs of everything.

Baxter hates his dad, but at least he taught him how to survive. Everything he sees in the world today just proves what his dad taught him.

The Wolf Pack troubles Baxter, though. They have been loyal to each other for a long time, and they have been nice to him even though he just joined them. He doesn't get how they could be so loyal to each other. The Cougars have also been friends with each other for a long time, so that alone doesn't mean they're good people. Even if The Wolf Pack is nice to him, he expects that they will just stab him in the back and use him if they have the chance.

Chapter 6- Friends Are Loyal

Ben can't believe it!

An actual alien from another planet and he's driving him to his house. The alien kid's spaceship, which he calls The Imaginator, is in the bed of The Howler. For Ben's truck, it's not used to carrying such light luggage. The Howler is used to Ben putting loads and loads of scrap metal on its back like there's no tomorrow. But with the lightweight, Ben is zooming across the streets with ease as The Imaginator bounces around like crazy.

It looks like a cardboard box on the outside, but inside it's a whole different reality. It's like the TARDIS in Doctor Who, except Uri says that he can't time travel.

Dang it! Ben was hoping to travel back to the times when The Cougars defeated him and his friends.

He could tell his past self how to beat The Cougars. He and the Pack would have finally defeated them in those multiple basketball games. He would have finally gotten back to the time in kindergarten when Jack beat him at rock-paper-scissors.

Then maybe he wouldn't be such a failure, but he's in this present-self and it's beating him that he can't change it. He would have finally gotten to see her again. When his mom was still alive. Just to see her again and hopefully find a way to stop that stupid cancer...

He knows he can't go back, but at least he just wants to talk to her one last time. Ben tries to hold back the tears while he's driving.

When he pulls up to his house, to his surprise, Honey's at his door, leaning against the wall and looking at her phone.

"Who's that?" Uri blurts out.

"Wait here."

Ben gets out of the truck, holding his hand out to Uri to not move, then heads toward Honey. She notices him and she smiles her contagious smile.

Ben awkwardly smiles back at her.

"What happened to you?" she asks. "Did you forget we had a date? I've been trying to contact you for the last thirty minutes now."

Ben slaps his forehead. "Oh, dang it! Sorry I'm late. There's this random thing that happened."

"What random thing?"

"Hey, there! I'm Uri!" Uri appears out of nowhere between Honey and Ben.

Both Ben and Honey jump.

Uri offers Honey his hand. "Nice to meet you. You must be Ben's lover?"

Ben feels a sudden heat rise to his cheeks that matches the red blush on Honey's face. "Hey, I told you to wait in the truck!"

"Ben, who's this kid? What's going on, Ben?" Honey asks.

Ben shrugs and laughs. "Oh, this kid? That, I will explain later. I think it's best if we skip the date, Honey. We need to summon the Pack because I have to tell you all something important."

Honey squints and frowns like she always does when he mentions one of his hair-brained schemes. But this is the most confused squished face she ever made. It's like she's grown 20 years older by how her face is. Ben swallows hard and his heart thumps in his chest.

Oh, boy! How am I going to explain this one to everybody?

***

Ben yanks the last window shade down with a snap and double-checks the front door lock for the third time. The deadbolt clicks hard in the silence. He turns, pacing the length of the living room, fingers tapping against his leg, breath shallow.

The others are frozen.

Honey stands with her arms crossed, eyebrows drawn tight, eyes flicking between Uri and Ben like she's trying to solve a puzzle no one gave her the pieces to. Cedric slouches at the edge of the couch but doesn't take his eyes off Uri. Slam hovers near the back, one hand on the wall like he's ready to bolt. Baxter's expression is unreadable—half-bored, half-wary—but he hasn't said a word.

Uri, meanwhile, settles into the recliner like he's done it a hundred times, even though it still smells faintly of Ben's dad's old cologne. He runs his fingers along the frayed edges of the armrest, smiling calmly, like he's the host of this awkward little party.

Ben keeps glancing at the door.

"What the hell is going on? Who is this kid?" Cedric asks.

Ben shakes his head. "I'll tell you later, once Tom gets here."

Honey frowns at him. "You better have a very good explanation for why you dragged everybody here, and especially why you cancelled our date."

Ben hasn't seen her get angry in a while. Getting her angry isn't something he should be proud of.

Cedric looks at Slam and Baxter. "Sorry, he dragged you two into this mess?"

Slam shrugs. "Hey, it's okay. I had nothing to do today anyways, so this is great timing. Man, this is exciting! It's a pleasure to meet you, Uri."

Uri smiles at Slam. "It's a pleasure to meet you too."

"Please don't talk to the kid, man." Baxter frowns at Slam.

The doorbell rings, and Ben rushes to answer it, opening the door, grabbing Tom, and yanking him inside.

"What? Hey! Ben? What's going on?"

Ben silently leads Tom to the living room before letting go of his arm.

Tom frowns at Ben, then he looks around, cocking his head to the side when he finally turns to Uri.

"Hi, I'm Uri! Nice to meet you!"

Tom stares at Uri for a moment, then looks at Ben. "Ben, don't tell me that you're so desperate for money that you're holding a kid ransom."

Ben waves his hands. "No, no! Okay, look, I will explain myself. You guys will not believe this..." Ben steps over to Uri, puts his hand on his head, and pats it. "This little guy is an alien."

"You mean that kid is an illegal immigrant?" Baxter blurts out.

"What? No! I don't mean that kind of alien. I mean he's an alien from outer space. You know, from out of this world."

Everybody looks at him like he's crazy.

Ben sighs. "Fine, don't believe me? Uri, show them what you can do."

Uri nods and gets out of the recliner. He grabs his wooden staff and does that praying stance. Ben's friends just look at Uri, seeming confused. Suddenly, orange and blue feathers sprout on Uri's body.

Everyone jumps back and gasps in shock, their eyes wide as Uri changes into an American kestrel and flies around the room. Ben and his friends duck as he soars overhead, feathers shed as Uri flies. Then he changes back to his human form and lands next to Ben.

"Tah dah!" Uri giggles as he opens his arms like he did a magic trick.

Ben turns to look at his friends' reactions, and they all have that same look of shock. "See, I told you he's an alien." Ben crosses his arms with a cocky smile on his face.

"How's that even possible?" Tom walks up to Uri.

Uri shrugs and smiles. "It's like a superpower. I can shape-shift into any creature I want if I study it correctly that is. Then I can develop their unique characteristics as well. It's all thanks to this staff in my hands."

Uri suddenly shape-shifts into a house fly and zooms around The Wolf Pack before changing back and landing next to Ben again.

"Yeah, but how? It's physically impossible." Tom scratches his head.

"It's because of God that I'm able to do this."

"God?"

Uri smiles. "Yeah, with the help of God's spirit, I have this shapeshifting ability."

Uri shows his hand to Tom, which glows with a bright white light.

The Wolf Pack gasps in shock, even Ben. Ben hasn't seen Uri's hand glow before. What's going on? The power that's radiating from Uri's hand is immense!

"Interesting." Tom mutters as he examines Uri's hand.

"So, what are you? An angel?" Baxter chimes in.

"Oh, no. I'm not as perfect and powerful as an angel is. I'm just an imperfect human like you guys. The only reason I have this power is because my dad taught me the holy scriptures. I practiced what my dad taught me and put my faith in God." Uri closes his hands, cutting off the light.

"Wait, is that why you're always in that praying stance before you change?" Ben asks.

"Yeah, it's just something I do to ask Jehovah if he can help me with this ability."

Honey raises an eyebrow. "Jehovah? Who's Jehovah?"

"That's God's name."

Honey scratches her head. "God's name? I thought God's name is just God?"

"Psh. All this talk about God is killing me, man. There's no such thing as God. Whatever your dad taught you, it's certainly not going to work on us. You're just playing tricks on us, kid." Baxter says, crossing his arms.

"Yeah, that's kind of strange..." Uri starts looking around at The Wolf Pack. "I don't get how you Earth humans don't have any special abilities. Maybe it's because of how far away you guys are from the truth."

"Far away from the truth? What do you mean?" Slam raises an eyebrow.

Uri looks at Slam. "Oh, it's just that I think it's interesting you guys live on a planet that's so far away from any planet with life on it. This probably explains why you guys can't use powers, because your people haven't associated with anyone outside your world."

Honey looks at Uri wide-eyed. "Jeez, how far away did you travel to get to our planet?"

Uri shrugs. "I don't know, pretty far. Had to get away from a black hole for the first time. Boy, that was a fun one." Uri laughs, but The Wolf Pack just looks at him in disbelief.

"Why are you here in the first place?" Cedric asks.

"Uri's people got destroyed by an evil group called The Babylonians, and he got lost trying to escape," Ben answers.

"The Babylonians?" Tom raises his eyebrow.

Uri chimes in. "Yeah, The Babylonians. They are an evil group of creatures, and they are some of the most skilled warriors on my planet. Unfortunately, they decided to fight against my people, and they were too powerful for us." he sighed heavily. "The only survivors of my people are my parents and some others who managed to escape. I got lost trying to escape and ended up here." Tears well up in Uri's eyes as he tells his story again.

Ben walks up to him and puts his hand on Uri's back to comfort him. "And that's why we're going to help you find your parents?"

Uri looks at Ben and smiles, then wipes his tears away.

"We? What do you mean, 'we'?" Baxter blurts out.

Ben frowns at Baxter.

"Um Ben, can we talk to you for a second?" Tom waves Ben and the Wolf Pack toward the living room. They huddled together in the entryway just outside the living room entrance, leaving Uri alone.

"Ben, are you sure you want to help this kid?" Tom whispers.

"Of course, I'm sure. This kid has gone through a lot, and I want to help him," Ben whispers back, frowning at Tom.

"Are you sure we can trust this kid?" Cedric asks. "He might not be what he claims to be. He might be an evil alien himself, luring us into his ship so he and his alien friends can eat us."

"You have been watching too many sci-fi horror movies. Man, look at him. He's just an innocent kid," Ben says.

They peek in the living room, where Uri is sitting on the recliner. He smiles when he sees them. The Wolf Pack immediately ducks back in the entryway and huddles again.

"Psh, I don't trust that smile, man. I say we kill him before he kills us," Baxter whispers.

Ben frowns at Baxter. "No, we're not doing that. Listen, that kid is a prince. I didn't tell you this, but his parents are a real king and queen. This means when we take him back to his parents, imagine how much praise we're going to get. And hell, since they're royalty, they might even give us some rich gifts for helping their son." Ben chuckles and smirks.

Tom frowns at Ben. "It's always about riches for you, isn't it?"

Ben shrugs. "It's not always about the money."

Tom just rolls his eyes and sighs. "Uh, okay, listen. Even if we help this kid, I don't know if you guys remember that we have this thing called school. If we leave and travel with this alien kid to God knows where, what are we going to do about our parents and school, huh?"

Tom looks at Ben and the rest of The Wolf Pack, waiting for an answer.

Ben just sighs. "Look, we can figure that out later. I just really want to help this kid, man. And remember our motto: 'No wolf works alone.' I don't want this kid to work alone. So, are you guys with me, or are you guys with me?"

Ben put his hand out to all his friends. He also lifts up his wolf chain. The wolf chain to help remind him and his pack that they are loyal to each other, through and through. His pack members all look at each other and roll their eyes. One by one, they put their hands on top of each other. Ben notices that he's missing one hand, and that's Baxter's. The Wolf Pack stares at him.

"Uh, I can't believe I'm doing this." Baxter finally puts his hand on top of all of their hands.

"Alright, Wolves. Let's do this."

Ben nods and all his friends shoot their hands up in the air with him. They then walk into the living room. When Uri notices them, he looks at them with eager eyes.

"Alright," Ben says, "we all agree to help you."

Uri jumps for joy. "Alright!"

"But the thing is, Uri, we all have this thing called school and our lives are busy. So, we're willing to help, but only when we don't have school."

Uri shrugs. "Hey, fine by me. I'm just surprised you're willing to help. You're the only people through all the planets that I went to who are willing to help me. Are you sure you guys want to help?" Uri raises an eyebrow.

Ben looks at his friends, and they all nod at Uri.

"Sure, we all want to help!" Ben smiles.

Uri's smile grows bigger and bigger. His eyes well up again, but this time it seems to be tears of joy. Ben has never seen a smile so big in his life. It's even bigger than Slam's smile.

How's that even possible? Uri runs up and hugs Ben. Ben's eyes go wide as he doesn't know what to do with himself.

"Um, heh." Ben giggles awkwardly.

He catches Tom's raised eyebrows from across the room and shrinks a little under the weight of Uri's full-body hug.

What the hell just happened?

Ben's brain scrambles to make sense of it. They've got a shapeshifting alien sitting in his dad's old chair, hugging the life out of him like a kid on Christmas morning, and somehow, this still feels like the start of something huge. Maybe even good.

If they play this right—if they actually find Uri's parents—this could be it. Their shot. The Cougars wouldn't know what hit them.

But then he thinks about school. About Cedric's mom calling every fifteen minutes if he misses dinner. About Slam's mother. Honey's mom. Tom's strict-ass dad. All of Ben's friends have parents that actually care about them.

Ben exhales sharply through his nose. They're gonna need a damn good plan—and even better lies.

Chapter 7- Slam's Homie Life

Slam's POV, the clumsy Native

Life is always amazing and interesting. I don't get how people could be so pessimistic about life. If they could just meditate on the good that happened to them over all the bad in their life, everyone would be happier. The world would be a more peaceful place.

For example: Right now, I'm in a situation that could make some people frustrated. Me and my little twin brothers, Dunk and Shoot, are trying to carry a recliner inside our trailer home. The only problem is that the recliner is too wide for me and my two brothers to fit it easily through the narrow door.

Now to some people, they would rage, and their face would blow up like a balloon. They would fly into the sky, seeming to go upward, but then gravity humbles them, and they have to face the consequences as everything blows up in their face and they fall very hard.

But for me, I relish the challenge. I look at this situation as if I was still in my mother's womb and was coming out. This recliner is me and this house is like my mom when she gave birth to me...

Wait...

If I view it that way, then that means I'm trying to get back into my mother's womb... Okay, I'm not going to use that analogy anymore...

Wait...

What was I doing right now?

"Hey. Slam, are you even paying attention back there?"

Shoot's voice snaps me back to reality. I can always rely on my brothers, Dunk and Shoot, to wake me out of my daydreaming. I tend to think a lot, say a lot, and do-so-do on random things that are not important to what's happening to me at the moment. Man, I really need to stop doing that. Heh, Heh, but that's why I have my twin brothers to help me out.

"Oh, sorry! Heh, heh. I was daydreaming again." I rub my head. Now that I'm snapped to reality, I see that my brothers are trying the best they can, pulling and pushing the recliner through the door. They've made progress, hey look at that, but they only managed to get the recliner halfway through the door before it got stuck again.

"Ho ho! It looks like you guys got some real progress going. Good job." I gave my brothers a big thumbs up. They ignore me and continue to push and pull on the recliner.

"Oh, come on! I give up. This thing won't move." Shoot yells out.

I just smile. He's got a strong will but a short fuse. Good thing Slam—big brother extraordinaire—is on the case. Dunk gives up too and slumps to the floor, defeated.

Meanwhile, we're letting all the hot air out and the cold air in—literally and metaphorically. Literally, because it's snowing outside. Metaphorically, because my brothers are letting their fiery determination fizzle out and letting in the frosty winds of despair.

If we don't do something soon, we're gonna freeze our balls off.

"Woah, hey now, guys. Don't give up. You just have to view things from a different angle."

I walk up to them, and they look at me, seeming confused. Well, I guess I have to show them what I'm talking about.

"Here, help me turn this recliner." I motion Dunk and Shoot to help me. They get up from the floor and begin helping me reposition the recliner at a different angle. The recliner begins to loosen up a little through the door.

"Oh, yeah! We got it. Keep pulling."

I crack a smile through my exhaustion. Suddenly, the recliner finally moves through the door frame. Then, like a miracle from the Creator, it is finally inside.

"Go job. Now, let's go," I say as my brothers struggle carrying the recliner to the living room.

Once there, I see our mother standing and watching TV. I have to forgive myself for that stupid analogy of my mother's womb. Scratching that imagery aside, my mom sure is beautiful. She's wearing a nice white blazer and some slacks. She has to go to work soon at the tribal court. Her red lipstick is sticking out when she smiles at us.

"Oh, good. You guys finally managed to get that recliner in," she says.

I try to smile back at her, but I forget I'm too busy lifting a heavy recliner right now. I loose a little grip on the recliner, but me and my brothers manage to finally put it on the spot our mom wanted us to put it. We set the chair down with a sigh of relief.

"Ah, look at that! Now we're the strongest Indians in this reservation." I laugh, nudging my brothers.

They just look at me with deadpan expressions.

Guess they didn't find it funny. Oh well—I laugh anyway. I love my little brothers, but come on, can they at least crack a smile once in a while? Things have been rough since Mom and Dad split. That's why we ended up in this trailer with Mom— Dad's been drinking and getting violent too much. Now he's in county jail.

Mom wanted a fresh start, so we moved to another town on the reservation. It's not far, but we had to switch schools. Making new friends is no problem for me—I love talking to new people. My brothers, though, they're not handling the move well. Neither is Mom, really. I think they're all stressing way too much. If only they could focus on the good stuff and let the past go. I just want to see them smile again. Nothing gets to me like a frown.

I finally stop laughing because my stomach growls. Lifting that recliner did a number on me. Good thing I saved some school lunch for later. I dig into my left coat pocket and pull out the leftover tater tots I stashed away. It's pretty great that school offers free lunch—I'm gonna take advantage of it, considering how tight money is at home.

The tots are a little smooshed, and… wait, is that a hair? Eh, whatever. Adds a little extra flavor. I pop one in my mouth.

"Eww, that's gross!"

I hear my brother, Shoot, say. I keep chewing. "Hmm? What are you talking about, Shoot?"

"You're seriously eating that?"

"Yeah, I'm hungry. You want some?"

Shoot turns his head away from me, acting like he's going to barf. "No, thank you!"

I don't get what Shoot is talking about. These taters are still tasty. They could taste better if they were warm and fresh, but still, can't beat free food.

"Jeez, Slam, when are you going to wash your coat, honey? It's starting to smell." My mom says, plugging her nose. My brothers are plugging their noses too.

I looked at my trench coat. It's got so many stains from so many memories I had with it. Especially that big stain on the left shoulder. I was eating ice cream one time and accidentally slipped on a puddle. The ice cream went flying into the air and landed on my left shoulder.

Now I have a big stain from it, but I keep wearing it. Wearing this trench coat makes me look like I'm a detective or a magician. I love it and I'm not planning to take it off. Only when I take a shower and its bedtime is when I take it off.

I take a big sniff. "It doesn't smell bad at all. What are you guys talking about?"

"Man, what's wrong with you? Is your nose plugged or something?" Shoot shouts.

Slam shrugs. "Yeah, it must be. Or maybe you guys are smelling something else in the house? Maybe there's a rodent infestation? We should check to see, ma."

My mom shakes her head. "Oh, no. I know it's your trench coat. Just give it to me, Slam, and I'll put it in the washer."

I titter. "Hey, ma, I don't know. What if you put it in the washer and it shrinks?"

"Oh, it won't shrink. Just hand it over."

I back away from my mom who's trying to take my trench coat off me. "Sorry, but maybe another time, ma. Maybe tomorrow."

My mom frowns. "Oh, alright, but I'm going to wash that coat no matter what. Hey, are you guys going to close the door? We don't want any hot air out." Our mom points at the door we left open to get the recliner through.

I snap my fingers. "Oh, right. Hey Dunk, close the door, will you?"

Dunk nods and runs to the door, but pauses for some reason, looking at something outside.

"Dunk, what is it?"

Dunk turns around. "Someone's here."

I walk up to the door and realize who it is. "Oh, nothing to worry about, Dunk. It's just my buddy, Ben. Hey there, Ben!"

I wave as Ben's getting out of his truck. He waves back. What a nice guy.

Mom's always telling me I should make more friends at school, but that's easier said than done. I try, but people don't seem to want to be friends with me. Maybe it's because I talk too much. Heh, yeah, I do that a lot.

Like this one time in freshman year—I was talking to this girl at lunch about pizza. Who doesn't love pizza, right? Apparently, she didn't. I kept trying to convince her to like it, talking up the nice Italian bread and all the different toppings. I even listed every kind of pizza I could think of. But she just said no.

Her excuse? Too many carbs. She didn't want to get fat. Weird, right? The weird part is her not liking pizza. She shouldn't care about being fat. That's what I don't get about most people and their insecurities. If they don't try, then they'll never know. And I mean, come on! Everyone likes pizza!

Eventually, she got annoyed and stopped talking to me. Fine by me. I can't change people. Honestly, I don't even want to be friends with someone who hates pizza.

This reminds me of another story of when—

"Hey, who's here!" My mother suddenly breaks me out of my thoughts, and I come back to my senses.

"Oh, don't worry, ma. It's just a friend of mine picking me up for the hunting trip."

My mother walks up to the door. Ben waves at her.

"Slam, are you sure you want to go on a hunting trip with a bunch of kids you only met at the start of the school year?" My mother looks at me with concern.

I just smile. "Ah, don't worry. I'll be safe, trust me."

She puts her hand on my cheek. "Okay, I just don't want to lose you, honey. It's going to be very cold, so stay warm."

I continue to smile and put my hand on her shoulder. "I'll be fine. Plus, there's this kid—Wait..." I almost accidentally told my mother about Uri. The hunting trip is actually a coverup for spending Thanksgiving break traveling to outer space to look for Uri's parents. I hate lying. It's so hard not to tell my family about Uri and the fact that he's an actual alien from another planet, but I guess I have to lie to keep Uri safe.

My mother looks at me confused. "What kid?"

Oh boy, how do I get out of this one?

"Um, well. I'm talking about Baxter of course. Remember when I told you that he's an expert at burning things? A pyromaniac, I think it's called. He's also good at making bombs out of anything too. He's a real skilled survivor. You should meet him one day." I look at my mother's face, hoping she believed me. She frowns at me.

"Oh, that pyromaniac kid is also coming with you guys? You better keep your distance away from him. I don't trust him one bit."

"Heh, heh. Don't worry, I'll be good. I'll make sure that I come back in one piece."

Great, it looks like she fell for my lie. I wave goodbye to my mother and my two brothers... Wait a minute... Where's Dunk and Shoot? I notice my brothers are missing. I look back to see Dunk and Shoot messing around with Ben. Dunk is holding onto Ben's leg and Shoot has a big stick and is hitting Ben with it.

"Hey, stop that! Get over here!" Mother yells out but suddenly Shoot hits Ben in the head with the stick. Ben's face turns red with anger, and he grabs the stick out of Shoot's hands. Dunk and Shoot then run away as he chases them. He gives up when they go inside the house.

"Are you alright?" Mom asks Ben.

"Yeah." Ben rubs his head.

Ben begins walking to his truck and motions for me to follow him.

I turn around and wave goodbye to my mother one last time. I go inside Ben's truck and the both of us drive away. That face Ben made when Shoot hit him with the stick looked like he was about to kill my two brothers. It certainly did scare my brothers off because that's the same face our dad made when he was drunk and angry.

I heard from Ben's friends that he tends to get mad and act irrationally at times. In the truck, Ben's face is still red as he stares straight in front of him.

"Heh, heh. Sorry for my brothers. They're pretty rough with strangers sometimes."

Ben doesn't say anything to me as he starts up the truck and pulls away.

I try to break this awkward silence by switching the subject. "Hey, by the way, where's Uri?"

"He's on your shoulder."

I'm confused until I look over my shoulder and see a fly.

"Ah, I see! He's a fly. Your shapeshifting ability is quite interesting, Uri. I wish I had superpowers. I wish I could disappear like a magician, that would be an awesome superpower. How about you, Ben? What kind of superpower would you like to have?"

"Turn everything to gold."

Suddenly, a bright light appears between us, then dims to reveal Uri.

"Sorry, I don't think there's a special ability that can do that, Ben, unless you're Midas, but it would be cool if there was one like that." Uri smiles at Ben.

"That's too bad." Ben sighs.

Me and Uri just look at each other, shrugging.

I don't understand what's wrong with Ben. I think he's still mad at Shoot for hitting him on the head. It's probably best if I don't pester him, so I decide to stay silent for the rest of the trip and Uri follows suit.

I hope that Ben can control his anger, otherwise it will cause more trouble than good.

I'm going to help him look at the bright side of things, just like how I taught my two brothers today about looking at things from a different angle. I know about Ben's home life, and that's why I'm determined to help him.

Hey, that reminds me of that one time when—

Chapter 8- Flight Training

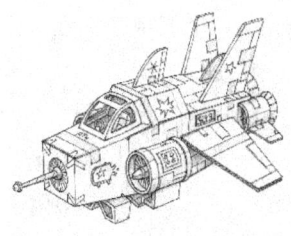

Every jigsaw puzzle can fit perfectly with the next puzzle piece and the next puzzle piece after that, and the next, and the next one until everything fits perfectly together and you have a nice full picture. A full beautiful canvas that you can show on display to everyone.

Right now, Ben is just trying to figure out what right puzzle piece should fit with who. Nothing degrades him more than trying to figure the right puzzle piece to put, or in this case, trying to figure out the right place to put a flower vase.

A gift from the alpha female.

Honey just gave him a bouquet of flowers as a dating gift, which is quite unusual because in custom it's usually the man who gives the bouquet of flowers, but in Ben's circumstance, Honey told Ben that his house looks a little bland. She didn't mean that to be an insult.

At first, Ben didn't understand what she was talking about. That's because he was only focused on the one puzzle piece, but then Honey showed him the whole beautiful canvas that soon all the individual pieces will go to make a beautiful picture. It all started back when Honey found him trying to fix his backyard and figuring out what kind of flowers he should put.

Unfortunately, that was before school. When it was summer, and the warmth of the sun was the only thing that kept those plants alive as they prepared to get killed by the snowy depths of winter. Ben has missed his chance to do anything outside once that frosted white stuff came out of nowhere. But on the bright side, Honey told him that he can grow plants indoors and take care of the interior of his house. That's what Ben is doing right now because boy, does his home need a touch up.

There's literally nothing on the walls, no decorations, not even family pictures because Dad keeps tearing them down. Every family photo probably reminds him of Mom's death. Ben can't blame his dad for taking the pictures down because he feels depressed just looking at them too.

Just another reminder of how happy they used to be. Now everything inside of the house looks bland and empty, kind of like his heart. Usually, Mom was the one to fix things, the one to clean it all up, but now that missing puzzle piece is gone, and Ben can't have her back. You can't have a full beautiful picture when one of the most important pieces is missing.

That's why Ben doesn't like spending so much time in the house. His dad doesn't take care of it either when he's usually here, and that's a rare sighting if he actually does show up. Ben hasn't seen him yet, and maybe that's for the best. Maybe not.

He keeps holding on to the false hope because Dad is also an important piece to the canvas whether he likes it or not. He's an important puzzle piece to fill in the beautiful picture that people call a "perfect household." It's a good thing he has his new alien friend to keep him company when loneliness covers him in a blanket.

Uri is just following him around the house, giving him orders on where he should put the flower vase. He's trying not to break the vase, so help him God, because if he breaks it, then he doesn't know how Honey would react.

Ben puts it on one of the tall shelves of the living room. Ben is on a step stool, balancing, making sure to not fall into the grave that is the living room floor. He looks down at Uri, wondering if it suits the alien prince's approval. Uri shakes his head.

"Nah, I still don't think it goes well in the living room."

Ben just grabs the vase and gingerly gets off the step stool. *So help me God if this vase breaks.*

"You know what? I give up. I'm just going to put it on the kitchen table."

Uri shrugs. "Okay, fine by me. It's your house."

Uri follows Ben to the kitchen as if he thinks he's going to get praised for having the idea to put it in the kitchen in the first place. Ben places it on the middle of the dining table. He breathes and smells the beautiful scent of Honey's gift.

Strangely enough, it's the same scent Ben smells off of Honey. Ben just smiles for a while, silent, imagining the beautiful time he had with Honey on their date. The way she smiles, the way she hugs, and the scent Ben smells off of her when they were embracing which Ben could tell, at that moment, that she was hanging around at her backyard garden. He's glad to have such a loving person. A person that is as colorful as the flowers she gave him, but Ben feels a little upset.

He's grateful, but now he feels obligated to give her something back. Those stupid chocolates weren't enough, he's not enough. He feels like he can give her more. He just wants to give her something valuable, maybe another plant, but a unique plant. Maybe a favorite indoor plant that she likes or maybe an unusual plant she has never seen before. Something alien.

"Hey, Uri. Is there a place, out in space, that you know of, that sells plants?"

"Yeah, I actually know a guy, but it's very hard to find him. Why you ask?"

Ben chuckles. "Oh, I'm just asking about a gift for Honey."

"Oh, I see. Well, I can take you to see him, if we can find him that is." Uri snaps his fingers. "In fact, this might be a good moment where I teach you and your friends how to drive The Imaginator."

"Teach us?"

"Yeah, this will be a perfect opportunity to do some space flight training with you guys, especially if you're planning to travel with me." Uri giggles uncontrollably.

Ben tries to match the same joy Uri is having, though he's a little nervous about driving The Imaginator. "Um... are you sure?"

Uri pats him on the back. "Oh, sure, I'm sure. This will be fun. I'll promise."

***

Imagine that you're first learning how to drive a car.

Nerves set you in, sweat maybe. There's excitement and also anxiety. You have full control of a machine that is as big as your mom's booty.

Figuring out the puzzle pieces of where you want to go.

If you're lost, then deal with the consequences, or deal with someone else's consequences when they make a stupid choice. Driving is just a massive table with scattered puzzle pieces, and you need to figure out how to fit it all together.

Now imagine driving your car into outer space.

That table has become more massive with more puzzle pieces to figure out. You may think you'll have more room, more freedom because there are no traffic signs, there are no cops to pull you over, but really you have to deal with the same things on the road.

Instead of driving on a small concrete road, you'll be riding the universal highway to bigger places. Bigger dangers, but also bigger more exciting adventures.

That's what's scurrying through Ben's distorted mind at the moment, but luckily an expert is sitting next to him, giving him instructions on how to drive his spaceship.

"Oh, for the last time. It's not a spaceship. It's a space cruiser."

"What's the difference?" Ben asks.

Ben wants the answers to everything that this little alien kid knows because this kid is the only thing that's keeping him from a life-or-death moment once he starts this spaceshi— oh, sorry— he means space cruiser to the unknown of the universe.

"Well, a space cruiser is just a smaller version of a spaceship. A spaceship can hold more things, including more crew cabins for people to actually live in if they want to. A space cruiser is smaller, and its only purpose is to travel and travel quickly."

Ben just rolls his eyes like he does with Tom when he gives factual debates. "Whatever, can we start already?"

"Okay, it's just like driving a car. First, put the keys in and start the ignition."

Ben does so, he sees all the buttons and switches light up on the dashboard. The engine is roaring like The Howler, though not as bad.

"Alright, push down the throttle slowly."

Uri orders like a drill sergeant and Ben obeys. Ben feels the sudden pressure of Earth's gravity. The Imaginator shakes when they go through the sky.

Blue.

Blue is the only thing Ben sees through the window, but then clouds blind him.

Then it was dark.

Dark and stars.

Outer space.

Stars are shining brightly at Ben acting like they want to be discovered and Ben does want to.

Though there's silence, the stars are telling Ben that there is something out there. Some other lifeforms out in the distance. Proof is sitting next to him, literally.

Uri smirks at him, knowing what excitement he feels because he's been nagging Uri for the longest time to take him out on a space adventure. He looks at his left where some of his Pack members are sitting.

They all haven't said a thing during take-off. They're probably half-excited, half-terrified like he is. Ben is mostly looking at Honey. She's grinning at him, not knowing the surprise that he has planned out for her. Ben blushes at the thought of it. He looks back at Uri.

"Hey, can we take our seat belts off?"

Uri looks confused. "Yeah, you can, but why do you want to do that?"

Ben shrugs. "Oh, I just want to see if I can float since there's no gravity."

Uri laughs. "Well, the thing is, there is gravity. I had this cruiser made with well-insulated multi-layered material that can make you feel like you're walking on Earth. It also helps keep radiation off, that's why we don't have to wear suits. As long as this cruiser keeps moving in a straight line, it will feel like we have gravity."

"Oh, so kind of like artificial gravity?" Tom asks.

"Yeah, exactly. Right now, we're still moving as long as the throttle is up. Does anyone want to drive next?"

"I guess I will." Tom and Ben switch seats.

They put their seat belts back on for another fast ride, and another motion sickness. Ben swears he needs a paper bag during these flights, but he smiles as he looks through the window. The stars, and the Earth's moon as they pass it.

Time passes, does time even matter when they're in space. That's what Ben is wondering as he watches each of his Pack members take turns driving The Imaginator.

They all practiced how to land as well. They landed on the different moons in their solar system. Uri had Ben take back the wheel to help him land on Saturn's moon, Enceladus.

"Okay, just stay calm. Land slowly. Keep a close tight on the wheel."

Uri instructs Ben as he pushes the throttle down. The Imaginator goes slower and slower until they finally land carefully on the surface of Enceladus.

"Okay, cool. We landed successfully. We can take our seatbelts off." Uri orders. The Wolf Pack obeyed.

Ben looks through the window, the surface of Enceladus is icy, bright, desolate, and bland, like Ben's house. Some craters are scattered about looking like a giant, like the Greek giant Enceladus, just walked on this moon. Fitting name.

"Hmm, interesting moon. Enceladus sure looks pretty. Pretty bland. Kind of like your house, Ben." Honey giggles while poking Ben.

"Hey."

"I'm just joking, Ben."

Uri giggles. "Yeah, I like Saturn's moon too. And it's a good thing we land here. Apparently, my friend is staying on this moon for some reason, and I want to find him."

"Wait? Your friend?" Cedric asks.

"Yeah, my friend. Remember what I told you, Ben, about my friend. I want to see him."

Uri winks at Ben, not suspicious at all. Ben then remembers what he needed to say. "Oh, yeah, right. Sorry, but me and Uri have to meet this friend of his for an important gift."

"Okay? Then what are we supposed to do? Just wait in this stupid box?" Baxter asks.

Uri shakes his head. "Oh, no. You guys can also explore, but we have to put on our space suits first."

So, space suits are on, out of The Imaginator they go. As soon as they step a foot out on the moon's surface, they start floating. All of them walk awkwardly, not used to the weightlessness. Baxter is the only one having fun, doing cool flipping tricks. Spinning and lifting big moon rocks like he just gained three times his own strength.

All of them ignore him. *Show off.*

"Alright, you guys can explore. Just make sure you stay close to each other and not too far from the cruiser."

Ben's Pack nods at Uri's orders. Ben stays close to Uri when he follows him to the direction of his friend. After walking a while, Ben sees a little hut structure made out of moon rock. There are green vines growing everywhere around the roof and on the walls. Uri points at it.

"That's where he's staying. Come on."

When they reach the hut, the hut looks empty inside. There are no windows, no doors, not enclosed at all. Ben doesn't think there might be a living being inside...

"Woo!"

Suddenly, a strange man, or Ben thinks it's a man, comes out of the hut like a surprise present, but instead of confetti, there's dirt flying everywhere. It's a good thing there's no gravity because Ben is sure that he would be blind by dirt in his face. Instead, it just floats slowly past him.

The crazy man looks like a caveman. He's wearing a dirty old torn up space suit like he got attacked by a space monster.

His green hair is a mess, all swiveled, twigs sticking out like he just got out of a forest, but there are no trees growing around this place. Ben doesn't know how he got those twigs, or how he got on this moon in the first place.

Ben sees no spaceship. The space suit he's wearing looks like an actual dress suit that businesspeople would wear, but it's all torn up and it's green like his hair. This guy certainly looks like he would get along with all the drunk people at the local bar.

The man is flying, floating above them. Surprisingly, all the twigs don't float off his hair. He finally lands. He grins at him and Uri. His teeth show a bunch of broccoli pieces stuck between them. Ben is glad that scent isn't a problem in these space suits, otherwise he would imagine how this guy would smell.

"Oh hoy there my fellow human beans! Why have you seedlings decided to come down to germinate with me?" The guy continues to grin.

Ben is not comfortable with this man. He starts backing away slowly from him. Uri is the crazy one and floats to him. He gives the strange fellow a handshake. "Oh hoy there! My name is Uri."

"Nice to meet you, Uri. My name is Lone Pine Joey. You must be the one who called me." Lone Pine Joey continues to shake Uri's hand while staring into Uri's soul.

Uri keeps smiling, despite looking uncomfortable. "Um, yeah. I'm Uri. This is my friend Ben. We're wondering if you got some plants that can survive harsh snow."

Lone Pine Joey twirls his crazy long green hair. "Oh, I got tons of plants that fit exactly what you are looking for. Just let me come inside my mansion real quick."

Lone Pine Joey scurries inside his hut. Ben tries to dodge him when he floats by. He doesn't want to get too close to him. He might eat his soul out. Only a few seconds passed. Rustling noises inside the hut, but then Lone Pine Joey shoots out of his hut like a string bean. He floats above Ben and lands next to Uri. He gives Uri a small packet of what seems to be seeds, or maybe something else. Ben sure hopes it's not something else.

Lone Pine Joey smacks the seed packet like he was smacking a newborn's bottom and hands it to Uri. "Here you go my friend. These seeds will grow some nice frosty daisies."

"Frosty daisies?"

Lone Pine Joey grins. "Yeah, frosty daisies. They can grow in the most harshest conditions, especially in the snow. In fact, they thrive in the snow. They prefer it than any other condition. The only catch with them is that they get extremely hungry all the time, so make sure you feed them lots of food, or else..."

"Or else what?" Ben asks.

Lone Pine Joey laughs. "You'll see..." Lone Pine Joey jumps over him and Uri, floating straight to his hut. Before going inside, he grins. "You'll see." He then laughs one last time as he enters his hut.

Ben and Uri just look at each other. Shrugging against the weirdness of this situation. They spacewalk quietly to The Imaginator where the rest of the Pack is waiting for them. They seem to be in the same spots where he and Uri left them, except this time Cedric is also doing flipping tricks with Baxter. *Two showoffs.*

"Wow, you guys haven't moved an inch. Did you guys even explore?" Uri asks.

Tom shrugs. "Yeah, we did, but there really wasn't anything around. Just some craters I guess, and that's it. Did you find your friend of yours?"

Uri nods. "Yeah, we did, and it was quite an interesting conversation, but he actually gave us something."

Honey says. "Really? What?"

Ben smirks at her. "You just have to find out."

Honey chuckles. "Oh, I see. Well, I love surprises so I can't wait."

Ben motions at Uri. "Well, let's get going then."

They get inside The Imaginator, taking their space suits off. Uri, this time, takes the wheel as he drives the cruiser back to planet Earth.

After they land in Ben's backyard, Ben says his goodbyes to his Pack members as they leave his house, but Honey stays. She's been looking at Ben with anticipation ever since Ben told her about the gift.

She says. "Okay, I waited long enough. What's this gift you want to give me?"

Ben smirks. "Oh, nothing. It's just in here." Ben takes out the seed packet.

Honey looks at Ben confused. "A seed packet?"

"It's not just a seed packet. My buddy is a gardener, and he gave us some seeds. Apparently, these seeds can grow frosty daisies." Uri says.

Honey scratches her head. "Frosty daisies? Never heard of them?"

Uri grins. "Yeah, they're a unique flower from another planet. My buddy said that they can grow in the hardest conditions, especially snow."

Honey smiles. "Oh, interesting. Thank you for the gift, Ben."

He blushes. "No worries."

"I'll go and plant these right away. You guys have a goodnight."

Honey waves goodbye and walks out the door. Ben loves to see her smile. Now he can rest more easily.

***

Honey is in her house, in her pajamas as she plants the seeds in a pot and waters them. She puts the pot on the kitchen counter. She yawns, but before she heads out the kitchen, she stares back at Ben's gift one last time before going to her bedroom. It's a thoughtful gift Ben has given her; she's smiling the way through sleeping.

Sleep tight little girl. Don't let the bed bugs bite…

Cling

Clong

Clang

Honey wakes up and jolts her head up with the sudden clunking noise. It sounded like it came from the kitchen. Honey looks at her clock. It's 2:03 am. Three hours have passed since she started sleeping. She was hoping for some sweet dreams.

Cling

Clong

Clang

The noise again. Honey knows it's coming from the kitchen. It sounds like a dish. Could it be mom? A burglar?

Honey grabs the flashlight on her nightstand. She walks downstairs. Whoever it is, they are going to pay for waking her beauty sleep.

She rounds the corner to the kitchen.

A mom?

A burglar?

A plant?

Her eyes go wide. A plant is digging through her fridge like it owns the place. The stems, the leaves, the whole flower is blue and white, except it's huge, and it even has a mouth. The monster flower is using its leaf hands to gather food and swallow it whole. This whole flower is blue and white, reminds Honey of frost. Frosty daisies.

What kind of gift did Ben give me? Is this a prank?

The flower monster suddenly turns its ugly head to her; she freezes like the flower just put a spell on her. She feels leaves around her feet. She looks down. The flower is trying to capture her.

She immediately jumps out of the flower's gasp. She breaks out of the flower's freezing spell.

She ducks under and crawls on the floor. She knows there's knives in a cabinet, but they're next to the beast. The plant is senile to what she is doing. It really wants to grab her, caress her, choke her... eat her.

Some of the flower's leaves catch Honey off guard. Leaves start wrapping around her legs.

The leaves are freezing her body; she can't move again. She tries not to scream; her mom is probably still sleeping. She can handle this beast by herself. She just needs to dig through the cabinet.

She grabs a random frying pan. She has no time to think. The plant is going to consume her.

She whacks the flower head good, beating it as many times as she likes.

Never has she wanted a flower dead, but this is not a flower at all, it's a monster. The frosty leaves are still freezing her legs, but she continues to beat down until she knows it's dead.

The frosted leaves let go of her. The flower retracts. The bud was all smooched. Blue goo spurts out all over the floor and on her clothes, but Honey continues to smash.

I want it dead.

The flower finally stops moving. It's just in pieces. The only thing she's worrying about is getting the flower out of sight and cleaning the mess before Mom finds out.

She quickly grabs pieces of dead flower and throws it inside the fire stove in the living room to burn it to ashes. She grabs a mop and a bucket and cleans the messy goo spill the flower made.

That's when her mother shows up...

Honey pauses. She stares at her mother, not knowing what to say to her.

Great, and I didn't even have a chance to shower.

"Uh, Honey. What happened?"

Her mother groans as she turns on the kitchen lights, revealing Honey with the mop in her hand and some goo on her. She has been caught.

She's frozen, even though that flower's dead. She's frozen, not from frosty leaves, but from her mother's stare.

"Honey, why are you mopping the floor so late at night?" Her mom gasps. "Is that blood on you? Did somebody broke in? I heard a lot of noise."

Honey giggles awkwardly. "Yeah, somebody broke into our house and attacked me when I was getting a midnight snack. Luckily, I killed him before he could do anything to me. I'm cleaning his blood."

Her mother breathes a sigh of relief. "Oh, that's good to hear that you're okay, sweetheart. You used those self-defense moves that I taught you, right?"

"Yes, ma."

"Oh, that's good. I taught you well. Though I would have liked it if you screamed for help. I could have just killed him in an instant and gotten rid of his body myself without yourself getting hurt and having the evidence on you."

"I'm sorry, ma, but I just want to fight for myself for a change."

Her mother frowns. "Do you understand, Honey?"

Honey sighs. "Yes, ma, I understand."

Her mom sighs too. "I'm sorry, Honey. It's just that I don't want you to get hurt, that's all. Especially with how many past enemies I have. By the way, that guy that attacked you. He didn't look familiar to you, did he?"

"No, he didn't."

"He didn't have any scars or marks on his body that you can see?"

"Ma, I'm pretty sure he wasn't a past enemy of yours. If he did really want to kill you, he would have gone straight for you. Instead, he was digging through the fridge for some reason."

"I guess that's true. But still, just to be safe, I'm going to keep watch the rest of the night. You and I are going to stay in the living room. I guess you burned the body because I can smell it."

"Yes, I did, but I want to take a shower."

"Okay, but be quick. I'll make sure that there is no sign of other intruders." Her mom takes out her pistol from her sleeping robe.

Honey rolls her eyes. "Suit yourself."

"Hey," Her mom grabs her shoulder. She can see her mom try to smile, despite knowing the pain she probably feels. "I love you. I don't want to lose you."

Honey smiles too. "Yeah, I know."

Honey already knows she's safe, especially knowing her mom's past and that Glock pistol in her hands. Honey yawns. Step by step, she heads to the shower.

"Sleep tight little girl. Don't let the bedbugs bite." Dad used to tell her that before heading to sleep when she was a little girl.

Well, she's not so little anymore. She doesn't want to be like her mother, like her father. They raised her so she could not be like them. To be paid killers, even though they decided not to do that line of business for a long time, the past still haunts them. Honey doesn't want to hurt people, she wants to heal them.

She knows that may sound weird in her mind after she just whacked a flower monster to death, but still. She decides to close her eyes, on the couch, in the living room, next to her crazy mother, next to a fire.

Sweet dreams.

Sweet dreams.

That's all she wants. One thing is for certain, even though she is trying to get it rid of her mind, she's going to kill Ben once she wakes back up for that gift.

***

Sweet dreams. Sweet dreams.

Ben had the sweetest dream ever. Him and Honey, sitting under a tree. Flowers everywhere, a big garden. Both of them laughing. Honey's smile was as bright as the sunshine.

That's the life Ben wants, the feeling he wants to keep forever, but then the doorbell rings to ruin the joy.

Someone's ringing the doorbell a bunch of times, like they want to annoy Ben and get punched in the face for waking him up.

Ben groans and rolls out of bed, almost stumbling down the stairs while he sees Uri still fast asleep on the recliner. He walks past Uri and opens the door.

The sunshine blinds him once he opens, but his eyes adjust to reveal a beautiful woman before him. A nice morning surprise.

Ben smiles. "Hey, Honey. How's it—"

Smack!

Ben gets stunned. The most painful sting he has ever gotten from a honeybee. He didn't know why he got stung, to piss the bee off, but he's just preparing for another one. He's blocking his head as the bee, the queen bee, the alpha female, stares at him with the intent to strike again, he's sure.

"Ben, what the hell were those seeds?"

Ben gulps. "Um... I don't know. You didn't like them?"

"Didn't like them!? They almost killed me, Ben! I almost got eaten by a big flower monster. Luckily, I managed to kill it on my own, but what the hell was that? Some kind of joke?"

Ben laughs awkwardly. "Oh, it wasn't at all, I swear. I just— I just thought it would have been a good gift. Turns out to be a monster, I'm sorry."

Honey groans. "No worries. I forgive you. I'm not mad at you at all." Honey kisses Ben on the cheek. "I love you. Thanks for the gift anyway."

Honey just walks off and waves goodbye leaving Ben in a trance, frozen in time, like Honey put a frozen spell on him when she kissed him.

What just happened?

He rubs the sore spot on his cheek that Honey punched and then kissed later. He really doesn't get women. They're the one creature that he will never understand. First they hit you, and the next they kiss you and say they love you.

"Hey, Ben. Are you alright?" Uri has finally woken up.

Ben stutters. "Yeah... I'm fine."

"What was that all about?"

"I don't know"

Ben will never know. All he can do about it is just move on, he guesses. At least his girlfriend still loves him, despite that stupid gift. It turns out Lone Pine Joey tricked him. He knew he shouldn't have trusted him.

Ben knocks Uri on the head. "Why the hell did you take me to see that guy?"

Uri rubs his head. "Oh, you're talking about Lone Pine Joey? Yeah, sorry. I don't know what's up with him. He's the one that gave you the seeds, not me."

"Pff, whatever, man."

Chapter 9- Plan for Another Planet

School is over, thank goodness. Ben is not sure he could take another antagonizing hour of school, so he's thankful it's finally over for the day. It's the start of Thanksgiving break. They have two days off from school, plus the weekend. He told his friends to meet him at his house to discuss their plan to go to outer space and look for Uri's parents.

Uri could have just gone out to space to look for his parents on his own, but he decided that he wanted to stay with Ben at his house and wait for him and The Wolf Pack to find enough time to help him. Ben doesn't get why Uri is willing to wait for them, especially through this Montana fall weather of snow and cold.

Boy, it's getting cold and for his sake he's glad that Uri is willing to wait for them because he wants to get out of the cold as soon as possible this Thanksgiving break. Going to a warmer planet would be nice.

In Ben's truck with Slam and Uri on their way to his house, Uri is in his fly form on Slam's shoulder. It's all too astounding to believe, but Ben hopes helping Uri will change his and his friends' lives for the better. He's tired of them always being unsuccessful and being defeated by The Cougars. Maybe helping Uri will turn things around.

The Howler's engine ruffles to a stop when they finally arrive at his house, the rest of the Wolf Pack are waiting for them, evidenced by the cars parked in front of his house and the lights on inside. He gave Tom a house key so they wouldn't have to wait outside. It's not like he doesn't trust any of his other friends, but Tom is the most responsible one.

When they get out of The Howler, Uri suddenly turns back to human form. Ben opens the door to his house and enters with Slam and Uri tailing behind him. He goes to the living room to find the rest of his friends already there.

"Wow, all of you are here already. I'm surprised."

"Yeah, well," Tom says, "you should know by now that every time you call us to come together to discuss a plan, we all come rushing. We all know that you're just going to force us to come if we don't." He looks like he doesn't want to be here.

Looking around the room, Ben can see that everybody else doesn't want to be here, either.

"Oh, come on, you guys. Don't you want to help Uri find his parents?" Ben frowns while rubbing Uri on the head.

"It's not like we don't want to help Uri, Ben. It's just that we all have more important things to do than waste our time going to God knows where out in space to look for his parents. And we still don't have the slightest idea where they are, by the way." Cedric raises his arms.

"Wow, I can't believe you guys."

"Listen, Ben," Honey says in a calming voice, "we are all just worried about your willingness to help Uri when we don't even know any of the dangers of this mission. Plus, Uri says that there's evil creatures that are after him. If we travel to outer space, there's a chance we might meet them. What are we supposed to do then?"

Ben smirks. "Ah, don't worry about that. If any evil creature tries to hurt Uri, we can fight them."

"Are you serious, Ben?" Tom asks. "Did you not hear what Uri said? The evil creatures that are after him are a bunch of crazy warriors with superpowers. Look at us, Ben. We Earth humans aren't born with superpowers. How are we able to protect Uri when we don't have special abilities ourselves?"

"Actually, I wasn't born with my special abilities." Uri chimes in.

"Wait, you weren't?" Tom raises an eyebrow.

"Yeah, in fact, nobody in the entire universe is born with special abilities. They all had to learn them."

Ben looks at Uri wide-eyed. "Well, now you tell me! Wait, is there a chance that we also can learn special abilities?"

Uri rubs his head in embarrassment. "Well, I'm not sure if you Earth humans can have special abilities because I haven't seen any with them, but we might as well try."

Ben stares at Uri. "Good, so that means you can teach us?"

"Well, I don't think I can. I'm just learning to use my powers myself, but maybe a teacher from another planet can help you guys learn how to use special abilities."

Tom raises an eyebrow. "Yeah, but isn't that going to take a long time?"

"No, not at all."

Uri darts across the living room, weaving between chairs and piles of books, and stops at the cardboard spaceship sitting smack in the middle of the floor. Ben's barely sure how it even fits there. The Imaginator's too big for any other spot.

Uri's back a moment later, clutching something rolled tight in his hands. He drops it on the dining table and unfurls it slowly, the paper cracking and creasing like it's survived a dozen adventures.

Ben leans in, eyes tracing the faded lines and smudged sketches. The map looks ancient—edges torn, colors faded—but it's packed with swirling planets and twisting orbits, like a wizard's treasure map for a space quest.

"Alright, where did I write it?" Uri asks, scanning the map.

There're two planets drawn on Uri's map that Ben finds interesting. The names of the two planets are The Old World and The New World. What's striking Ben is the names that are written on these two planets like Zion, Babylon, The North, and The South.

"Hey, wait a minute. What are those planets? 'The Old World and The New World'? They got some strange names." Ben points at the map.

Uri starts scratching his head. "Yeah, it's interesting that you point those two planets out because those were the first two planets to ever be discovered in the history of the universe."

"Oh, really? The first two planets to ever be discovered, huh?" Tom raises an eyebrow at Uri.

"Yeah, in fact it's interesting that your planet is called Earth because that was also the name of The Old World before it came to be called The Old World. The Old World used to be where the Kingdom of Zion dwelled until it got destroyed. The Old World used to be called Earth, and it was the only planet that Jehovah created to have life on it." he paused for a moment. "Literally every belief out there in the universe is based on this planet. Every creature lived on it including the first humans, Adam and Eve. The first humans were supposed to take care of all the mammals, birds, reptiles, and sea life. They lived a happy life until they disobeyed God and then God caused everyone to speak different languages. Then..."

Tom leans back. "Then, what?"

"Well, some races decide to head out and move to new planets because of the overcrowding, the violence, and just the opportunity to want to explore and conquer different areas. That's how the other planet, The New World, got discovered. After The New World got discovered, people wanted to explore more. So they went to new planets to live, some races decided to stay and make a new life there creating new colonies."

"Other planets?" Honey mused.

"Oh yeah, but there are so many planets out there in the universe that it's hard to know which ones have life on it or not, so The League of Nations decided to establish a system to keep track of the different colonies that established themselves on new planets as well as keeping track of the nations in The Old World and The New World."

"Who are The League of Nations?" Slam asks.

"They're an organization that tries to unify every nation out there that they know. There are still a lot of planets that have life on them that The League of Nations doesn't have a track of and most people don't know about. The universe is a big place with so many planets that it's hard to keep track. Again, I'm surprised that I was able to find your planet Earth because it was the farthest planet I've ever been to."

"Hey, I have a question for you, Uri. What is the king of The South and the king of The North? I see that written on your map." Honey asks.

"Oh, that. The king of The South and the king of The North are titles given to the nations that are the most powerful in the universe. Right now, the king of The South dwells in The New World and the king of The North dwells in The Old World. The king of The South and the king of The North despise each other. One thing you need to know about the nations of the universe is that every nation is striving to get on top of one another. That's why there are so many wars."

When hearing Uri's stories, Ben has an eerie feeling. He looks at his friends; they are all quiet and seem starstruck by what Uri said. What Uri said about the history of the two planets sounded almost similar to their planet Earth's history. Ben is a little curious, and nervous at the same time, to visit these nations for himself to see if they are similar to Earth's nations. He wants to learn more, but he has to help Uri first, and he has a plan.

"Hey, Uri. Can you show us planets of where you think your parents might be?"

Uri points to three planets that are grouped together. "I think my parents might be on one of these, but they are all far away. The closest one is a planet called Sweetopia."

"Then that's the planet we should head to first." Ben smiles.

"It will take us a couple days on a normal ship to travel there, but my space cruiser isn't normal." Uri smiles, pointing to his cardboard spaceship.

"Psh, yeah. It's certainly not normal. Then again, I don't know what you aliens consider normal." Cedric says, staring at The Imaginator.

Uri laughs. "Well, in a normal ship, it would probably take us two days to get there, but The Imaginator can take us there in only two hours." Uri leans on his box, looking confident.

"Holy! Only two hours? Two days and two hours is a major difference. How the hell is it able to get there so quickly?" Cedric asks.

"Two words; super speed." Uri giggles.

Ben frowns, eyes narrowing. That giggle feels like a challenge. He doesn't fully get what Uri means, but if it means getting there faster, he's all in.

His mind races—planets spinning in his imagination, strange creatures lurking in alien forests, places no one on Earth has ever touched. A grin tugs at the corner of his mouth.

If Uri can really find someone to teach them these special powers, maybe this is it—the break they've been waiting for. Ben's chest tightens with a mix of hope and excitement. For the first time, the impossible feels close enough to reach. Maybe, just maybe, his pack will rise to the top. Maybe he'll finally have a reason to keep going.

Chapter 10- New Planet

Nour's POV, the angry feline

Strange... Strange

That is how Nour would describe the situation that he and his comrades are in. He never realized a planet with life on it could be so far away. When they traveled they never thought to find a civilized planet in the far reaches of the universe.

In fact, they had to escape from a black hole to get here and they never have done that before. Nour is not sure how far they went. The only life he knew was back home, in the nation of Mizraim, on The Old World, in his own galaxy, the Fruit Galaxy. He knows that there's other galaxies that support life.

Like the far far away Skyriver Galaxy that those Jedi people dwell. Nour thought he would end up in that galaxy by how much they'd been traveling. He's honestly getting tired, and he knows his comrades are getting tired too.

That's when they decided to land on this random planet that they detected life on. He wonders how the creatures living on this planet can survive living in a place so desolate, without any contact with other planets. He gnaws on his whiskers. He's fumbling his paws.

Nour ponders this while looking at the sunset. There seems to be only one sun in this planetary system. Only one moon, as far as they saw, is revolving around this planet. It's a perfect balance of gravity and weather. This planet is perfect for life. The inhabitants that live here must be lucky to live far away from the known existence of the League of Nations.

Nour knows there's inhabitants on this planet because they just found a random village. He's just waiting for his brother, Nader, and his friend, Antar, to return with information about the village they found.

Nader decided that Nour and the others would wait until they came back. It always pains Nour when his brother gives him commands even though he's supposed to be the leader of the group. It's okay though because his brother is the smartest cat he knows. He probably knows best. Still, his brother giving commands irks him.

"Jeez, what the hell is taking them so long?" Sebastian throws his paws up in the air, letting fly the two playing cards he's holding.

Nour can always rely on Sebastian to vocalize the things he is thinking. They're waiting in their spaceship, Battleship Lion. Nour likes to call their spaceship "BS Lion" because lions are a whole lotta of BS. Nour hates lions. This ship is full of BS too: there's so many things wrong with it. It is a sack of junk, but at least it gets them from one planet to the next.

Nour looks around the table in the galley of the BS Lion at the four other crew members playing Tarneeb. Well, they were playing Tarneeb until Sebastian decided to throw his cards up in the air like a crazy cat. Sebastian's red fur is sticking out of the top of his head, looking like his head is on fire.

There's no way they can put his fire out. Once Sebastian gets going, there will be broken down chairs and tables, and even some people dead, at the end of it all. Tito tries to calm his brother down, but it doesn't seem to be working.

Even though they're both shorthair cats, the brothers' furs are completely opposite of each other. Sebastian's dark gray fur all over his body is frizzy and crazy, but what stands out about him the most is his red fur that sticks out at the top of his head like he's burning, and the gray fur is the ash covering his body.

Tito, on the other hand, has a personality and coloration that's opposite of his brother. He is a kind and peaceful-natured cat. His green eyes are sticking out of his white cloudy fur. Nour can always tell what's written on Tito's face because he's always expressive. Right now, Tito's eyebrows are down, which tells Nour he is worried.

"Hey Sebastian, quiet down. They're probably going to be back anytime soon."

"Pff, come on, Tito! You said that about a million times already!"

Sebastian stares at Tito almost looking like he wants to kill his brother. Tito's head shrinks, probably nervous. The Albion people can get angry at times, Nour knows that from the experience of these two brothers.

"Hey Sebastian, can you just stop your bickering? We're trying to play here,"

Ginger's tiresome voice chimes in as he looks back and forth at the two brothers. He has always been a loyal friend of Nour's. As a sand cat (Felis margarita), he is the tamest of all Nour's friends.

He is their navigator, but Nour is not sure how he's going to navigate out of this one. Ginger sounds tired, which is very reasonable because they all have been stuck in the BS Lion traveling for four months now. Plus, Ginger is the pilot and has been driving BS Lion for them, so it's understandable to Nour that he just needs a break. There's a beer bottle next to him as he drinks it.

Sebastian just throws his remaining cards on the table. "I don't want to play this bloody game anymore! It's getting too boring now. Hey, Nour, are they back yet?"

Nour gets back to his senses after Sebastian calls his name. He keeps looking back through the window next to him. Nader and Antar are not here yet, and that's making Nour antsy. They landed the BS Lion in some weird, wooded terrain. It's snowing outside the window.

It's certainly not like the desert of Misr back home. It's extremely cold, and the breeze is making them shiver. BS Lion is not that well insulated. It's too bad the heating unit doesn't work in BS Lion. They need to fix it quickly, but they don't know how.

"Dang, if Nader and Antar don't show up soon, then I will go to the cockpit and drive us out of here." Sebastian shivers.

"Yeah, the heating unit is having problems right now and I don't know why." Ginger scratches his head.

"Well, you better do something quick, otherwise we'll be freezing to death." Sebastian frowns.

"Well, I may be an expert on flying ships. As for fixing them, you need to ask Antar for that." Ginger says.

"Pff, well they better show up or I swear." Sebastian growls.

"Hey, how come you two are freezing up? You, shorthairs, are built for this weather." Nour raises an eyebrow at Sebastian and Tito.

"Well, it's been a while since we've been to Albion. We've been too used to the warmth of Misr for so long. But we'll get used to it quickly here in a minute." Tito says, shivering.

Nour looks up at Ebo, another friend. He is sitting on the galley deck looking through the window opposite the others.

"Hey, Ebo, are they here yet?"

Ebo looks over at Nour, his yellow eyes contrasting his dark fur. "No, not yet." He looks back at the window. Ebo is a young tomcat, a juvenile Bombay from Bharat.

Nour knows it might sound racist, but he can't tell Ebo apart from any other Bombay cat. They're all just black to him, there are no unique characteristics about them that help him tell them apart. Ebo's red cloak with the logo of their group is all that sets him apart.

The logo shows a cat's face—one eye swollen and wrapped in a bandage. Nour draws it himself. To him, it isn't just a picture; it's a symbol of survival—a cat beaten but still standing after fights with cruel creatures.

117

That's why he forms The Ferals. When people hear the word "feral," they think of wild, uncontrollable animals—chaotic and undisciplined. But Nour knows better. He's been feral once, not by choice but because of the life he's forced into.

Now, with the help of his comrades, he's different. He wants to reach out to others like him—those who feel lost and broken—and show them there's a way back. That's how they find Ebo, a young black tomcat with the same wild look Nour once had. Nour is determined to protect him, to give him a chance at something better.

Suddenly, Ebo's ears shake, and his head follows.

"Oh, wait! I see them coming!"

"Finally!" Sebastian yells out, rolling his eyes.

Ebo runs up to Ginger and prostrates himself. "They will be here soon, master."

"Oh, for the last time, don't call me master. Just call me Ginger. We're friends, alright?" Ginger sighs.

Ebo giggles. "Sorry, Ginger."

The ramp at the entrance of BS Lion hums as it opens, and they all run to it. There, Nader and Antar enter the ship in heavy coats, but they are still shivering.

"Jeez, what took you guys so long?" Sebastian blurts out to Nader.

Nader remains silent as he walks past the inquisitive Sebastian and heads toward Nour with an unamused expression.

Nour can't tell if the news is good or bad from his face. Nader has been dignified and straight-faced lately, but he hasn't always been that way. Back when they were kittens, Nader was always happy, but as he grew older, his personality completely changed.

Nour knows that he's half-robotic, his half right side is made out of the finest bronze of Misr from Bubastis. But still, even with his bronze mechanical side, he could at least try to smile. His cybernetic augmentations changed him.

Soon, he will become a full kitty robot if he doesn't have a little fun. Nour just wants to see his brother smile again. Especially after that incident... Nothing has truly been the same after that.

"Have you gotten any information about this village?" Nour asks.

"Yes. It took a long time, but that's only because Antar and I found some pretty interesting things," Nader says as he pulls what looks like a scroll from his bag with his robotic foreleg and starts analyzing it with his robotic eye.

Nour then looks at Antar. "تصلحه ممكن. مكسور السخان؟" (The heating unit is broken. Can you fix it?"

Nour has to talk to Antar in Arabic because he can't speak English. Antar was born and raised in Misr. He can understand English, he's just so stubborn to speak no language except his native tongue. Antar leans on a wall when he gets inside, pawing at the icicles on his ears. His nose is full of frozen condensation.

"أيوة. (Yes.)" Antar nods slightly. Being a sphynx, he has no fur. He's probably suffering from the cold more than the others as he's shivering violently.

Nader turns back to Nour. "I think we should head to the galley and get warmed up before I give you any info, because there's a lot we need to talk about."

Everyone nods in agreement, so they head toward the galley.

In short order, they were finally able to fix the heating unit, thanks to Antar's help. They're at the galley table, Nader looks them over, scroll in his paw.

"Now, before I begin telling you guys what we discovered, I want to show you this."

Nader unrolls the scroll on the galley table, and Nour instantly recognizes a map. He begins analyzing it but is confused. There are a lot of places with a lot of words, seeming to be a map of the planet they're on, and he sees a lot of nations on this planet. There's Canada, Brazil, China, South Africa, and Egypt.

"Hey, Nader, what's going on? Why are you showing us this map? These places have some weird names." Nour looks at Nader with one eyebrow raised as he points at the map.

"Dude, that's the map of this whole planet." Nader says.

"Really? Interesting." Ginger chimes in.

"Yeah, do you guys realize what planet we've discovered?" Nader points through the small window in the galley to a clear view of the village they found.

Nour and the others look at Nader like he's crazy and shrug.

Nader sighs. "Huh, you guys seriously don't know anything about planets, do you? Look around you, through the windows. There are trees everywhere. This place is perfect for life. The people that live here are lucky. They're fascinating creatures." Nader continues to point his silly paws to the window at the strange village.

"Oh, really? And what is this place called?" Nour asks.

"Earth."

"Is that seriously what this planet is called? Earth? Pff. Doesn't look like a wondrous planet to me. Why would they name their planet after the ground?" Sebastian blurts out.

Nader slaps his paws on his forehead. "Uh, I can't believe you guys don't know anything about civilizations. Especially you, Tito. You read books more than any of us. You must know stuff like that?"

Tito giggles. "Well, I know somewhat about it. I only read a little about what the Holy Scriptures say about civilizations and how people live, but this planet does seem interesting."

Tito scratches his head, looking between the map and the actual planet through the window.

Nader suddenly grabs the map out of Tito's paws. "Well, this planet has been lived on for a very long time. This map just proves it. At the top of the map it says Earth. Remember what the Scriptures say about the history of The Old World and how it was originally called 'Earth' too. God created the earth and all the different creatures. It's claimed that that's where we originated from."

"Pff, yeah, well, that's just what the 'scriptures' say. I'm not going to believe that." Sebastian argues.

"Well, whatever you believe, this planet is interesting," Nader insists. "In fact, Antar and I discovered that the village we found is indeed a human village called Silvertown, and it's in the land of Montana, which is part of a nation called The United States of America. What I found interesting though is when Antar and I tried to introduce ourselves to a couple of humans, they panicked and ran away from us. This proves my

121

theory that these Earth humans haven't met anybody outside their planet before."

"Is there any other species besides humans here?" Nour asks.

"Yeah, there sure is, but the interesting thing is that other species can't talk here, or at least not the ones we've encountered."

"Can't talk? What do you mean?" Ginger chimes in.

"It seems nothing else can speak. Just whistles and growls. In fact, I don't think they're sentient because when Antar and I tried to speak with some, they didn't even seem to notice us talking to them and just passed us by."

Nader scratched his half-robotic head as he looked at the map.

Meanwhile, Nour and the rest of The Ferals stare at Nader like he's crazy, until Tito speaks up.

"Hm, that is interesting. I think we should explore some more of this world before we make any assumptions."

Nour just shrugs. "Yeah, I think you're right, but let's just make things clear here. The only reason why we're even here in the first place is because we are looking for Uri. I say we should explore some more of this human village we've found, but this time we're all coming."

Nour looks Nader dead in the eye after he says that. He's not going to let his brother make their plans when he's the leader.

Nader just frowns at Nour.

"Fine," Nader relents, "but we need to be careful. That means we shouldn't interact with any of these Earth humans until we find Uri."

Nader looks around at all of The Ferals. They all nod in agreement.

"Well, it looks like we got a plan here," Nour concludes. "I say we shouldn't waste a minute and go back to this human village to look for Uri right away."

Nour looks at all of his friends as they begin putting on some warm clothes before heading to the winter bliss of this strange planet. They tread through the snow. The village a cat vision away from them.

Nader is in the front taking the lead. Meanwhile, Nour is at the back of the line. Keeping close and keeping warm. Keeping safe as well.

Nour doesn't know what dangerous creatures are going to harm him on this planet. But he just wants to keep his comrades safe. It's his top priority.

Nour takes out a picture from his pocket, his favorite picture of a white female cat, her eyes are as green and sparkly as her green dress.

Nour always keeps a picture of her to remember her by. He's going to find Uri no matter what it takes, because he doesn't want to lose another important person in his life again.

Chapter 11- Paradise Earth

Nour's POV, the angry feline

Humans are fascinating creatures. Some call them intelligent monkeys. While some consider them to be too overpowered for their own good. That's why other creatures try to do everything they can to get away from a human's control. That's either by controlling them instead by striking fear in them, if that's even possible, or you can just try to run away from them, if that's even possible as well because they live everywhere.

That's why Nour is not surprised that they found a human village on this random planet they found, which is apparently called Earth. Every creature is trying to be on top of the food chain, and humans are always on top. So that's why Nour wants to be careful.

Nour remembers the things that Mommy Susanna taught them, through the Scriptures, about how humans and other creatures came into existence. How God ordered the humans to watch over and take care of the other species.

Nour knows, throughout history, humans have done a terrible job at obeying God's command. Now it seems like everywhere Nour goes, no matter what planet they land, there's always violence in some way or another.

Nour sure hopes this planet will be much different. This planet Earth will be destiny hopefully in a universe full of darkness. He hopes this Earth will be a paradise, a paradise Earth.

Walking through the small human village, nothing special seems to be happening so far. There's literally nobody around. They saw a few vehicles, that to be cars, driving on the roads, but that's about it. There're also some houses, some human buildings that look like regular human buildings on their home planet. Nour is still looking for the treasure inside this dull wasteland.

"Jeez, it already feels like we're skirmishing through half this village, and we still haven't found anything interesting at all! These Earth humans must live boring lives!" Sebastian blurts out.

"Well, granted. It looks like it's nighttime, so these humans must be diurnal. They're probably going to come out once the sun comes up, which means we should hide once we see the moon go down, so we don't end up confronting them." Nader walks beside Nour, looking around.

"Why can't we just take over this village while we have the chance? These Earth humans won't expect a thing." Sebastian chuckles and smirks.

"What's with you and trying to conquer everything?" Ginger blurts out behind Nour.

"Hey, I guess it's just the Albion in me." Sebastian shrugs and continues smirking.

Ginger just rolls his eyes. "Uh, whatever. Just try to keep it down," Ginger looks around nervously. "We don't want any Earth humans to wake up and catch us."

"Pff, I don't think any of these bloody humans can catch us. What are they going to do with us? Kill us? We're The Ferals, we can take down a few worthless humans."

Sebastian activates his special ability, and red arrows paint over his body.

"Hey, now. Turn off your ability." Nader frowns at Sebastian. "Ginger is right, we don't want to cause any commotion. Even though it's dark out and there's no humans around, we still need to be caut—"

"And besides," Nour interrupts, "the only reason why we're here is to catch Uri. We'll worry about conquering later, so stay quiet."

"Pff, okay, fine. Since you're so determined to catch this kid anyways." Sebastian walks defiantly. "Hey, why do you even want to catch this kid in the first place?"

"Because that kid is a friend."

"Yeah, but you know that Bast and Sekhmet will try to execute all of us if they find out we're not serving them anymore and left," Nader says.

Nour knows that already, but he knows his brother is only trying to warn him and protect him, like he always does. That's what Nour is trying to do with Uri, he's trying to protect this little Zion boy from the dangers of the universe. He promised Angel he would protect their friends. He doesn't want to lose any of them.

Sebastian surprisingly has nothing to add.

Even though Sebastian is a good friend, Nour finds his interruptions annoying. He is a good fighter though and most importantly a good friend. Nour just hopes he doesn't do anything crazy that might cause trouble.

Nour suddenly notices something in the corner of his eye, a building flashing colorful lights and standing out from the rest of the dull structures.

"Hm, I wonder what that building is?" Ginger says.

"I don't know, let's check it out." Nour begins running.

"Hey, don't try to get too close to it."

Nour ignores Nader and continues running toward the building. When they get close to it, Nour realizes that the lights are coming from a neon sign that reads Silvertown Bar.

"A bar? Like a pub? If that's what this place is, then finally we're getting into something exciting!" Sebastian chuckles as he runs toward the entrance of this "bar."

"What are you doing? Stop, Sebastian!" Tito chases after his brother.

"God damn it." Nader says under his breath as he chases after them.

"Should we go too?" Ebo asks Nour.

"Nah, let them go. Let's get back to searching."

Suddenly, screaming emits from an alleyway near the bar. Nour runs toward it, and the rest of his friends follow him. There, he finds something terrible. A female human is being assaulted by a male human, who seems drunk by how much he's staggering.

"You stupid woman, give me what I want!"

The drunk man yells as he shakes the woman violently. She is crying and trying to escape from this man's grip, but he's too strong.

That bastard! Nour is so angry at what he's watching right now! What does that bastard think he is trying to do assaulting such a— ^^$^%$&$%$$%...

What... What the heck happened? My vision turned red for a second and then... What the hell's happening?

Nour is breathing heavily. Hyperventilating.

Now his vision is back to normal. His whole body is numb. He tries touching himself to see if he can feel. When the numbness goes away, his fur is wet for some reason.

He's looking down...

Blood...

Nour's fur has blood on it.

He looks behind him.

The drunk man is lying on the ground, dead in a pool of blood and with scratches all over his body. Nour looks up at the others, who are staring at him wide-eyed. The woman is breathing heavily and panicking as she sees the dead man in front of her and Nour covered in blood.

"Are you alright?" Nour walks toward the woman.

She screams. Runs away from him. Passes Nour's friends and heads out of the alleyway.

Oh, great. Why did I do that?

"What the hell happened?" Nader yells as he turns the corner. He stops and stares at the dead man. "Oh, great! Nour, why?"

"I... I don't know."

"God damn it! Ah..." Nader looks around in a panic. "Let's just get out of here!"

Nour and his comrades sprint away from the chaos he caused. Killing that man was reckless, but the man deserved it for attacking that woman. Nour hates how the powerful always prey on the weak.

At first, Nour was excited to find this planet—he thought they'd found their destiny. He hoped Earth's inhabitants would be peaceful. But now he sees Earth is just as violent as every other world they've known.

He prays those violent humans haven't found Uri yet. If they have, Nour will show them what real violence means. It's a shame he has to kill, but he will if anyone threatens Uri or his comrades.

Chapter 12- Tom's Case

Tom's POV, the police boy

"Education is the first thing you should be worrying about right now."

That's what Tom's dad tells him almost every day during his senior year—how he needs to join the Montana Law Enforcement Academy and become a deputy sheriff, just like him. But Tom doesn't want that. What he really wants is to join the Army. He never says this out loud because whenever he tries, his dad just scolds him. Tom hates to admit it, but he's afraid of his dad. A serious, proud man who seems to love his job more than his wife and son.

Tom doesn't know why his dad is dragging him along on a case. Someone was murdered at the Silvertown Bar last night, and his dad insisted Tom come along to get a taste of real deputy life. It's the start of winter break, and Tom was supposed to meet his friends to prep for their trip to planet Sweetopia. They spent all fall getting ready, and now it's almost time. All that's left is escaping this nightmare with his dad.

As they pull up, Tom sees police cars everywhere. It was probably chaotic last night, but now officers block a crowd of onlookers. Tom hates this bar—there's always sketchy stuff going down around here.

His dad kills the engine, and they get out. Tom follows him to a familiar face: Officer Juan Shelby. Middle-aged, clean-cut, and always trying to impress the ladies. Tom knows Shelby's a creep—he talks about women nonstop and has more porn magazines in his office than a convenience store. Tom's surprised his dad tolerates him at all, let alone watches football with him. But apparently, Shelby's good enough to keep around. It's like Batman and Robin—dad's Batman, Shelby's the pervy Robin.

"Hey, Sam! What's up, bro?" Officer Shelby smiles. He tries to make his dad do a fist dump with him.

Tom's dad just walks up to him. "What happened here?"

Officer Shelby scratches his head. "Uh, well, I don't know."

His dad raises an eyebrow. "You don't know?"

Officer Shelby laughs. "Well, it's just a strange situation we have here."

"Strange?"

"Yeah, it's strange. Let me just get started by telling you about the dead man. His name is Steve Cornillieus Rubin, age thirty-five. He died from excessive bleeding from a bunch of scratch marks on his neck and back, but then there's this strange bit. The witnesses claimed that 'seven alien cats' were the ones that killed him."

"What? Alien cats? What the hell are you talking about?"

Officer Shelby raises his hands. "Hey, hey. Just listen to what I have to say here because it's a real doozy. Here's what all the witnesses said." Officer Shelby hands Sam a piece of paper. "Some people at the bar said that they saw three cats wearing clothing like that of ancient Egyptians. They suddenly appeared at the entrance, and they started talking. They then looked like they heard something and ran out of the bar. A few minutes later a woman ran in yelling that a talking cat killed a man. Some decided to go out of the bar, and they saw seven cats coming out of an alleyway, all wearing what looked like Egyptian clothing. They went into the alleyway and found the body." he shook his head. "The woman claims that Steve was trying to rape her when a strange cat showed up and killed him. She panicked when the cat talked to her and ran out of the alleyway."

"What kind of story is that?"

Officer Shelby waves his hands innocently. "Hey, hey, don't get mad at me. That's just the stories all the witnesses told me."

Sam shakes his head. "I don't believe it. It's probably some hooligans, and the woman is working with them. The people at the bar were probably just too drunk and thought they saw cats. Maybe they had masks on. Did you think of that?"

Officer Shelby rubs his head. "Yeah, that sounds like a more logical explanation. I talked to the coroner a few minutes ago. He said another possibility was that he was attacked by a grizzly bear based on how deep the claw marks are on him. That's the only big animal we can think of. We've been searching around for any tracks."

132

Sam scratches his chin. "Hmm, yeah, that's also another possibility. Certainly more logical than alien cats. Especially with how many reports we're getting of bear sightings."

"Yeah, I think so too, but I don't know Sam. The coroner also said that the claw marks were on the exact right places to instantly kill this guy. They're not random slashes, like a bear's, it's like some expert assassin killed him."

"Well, I guess that leaves the possibility that the woman is working with some hooligans then."

"Yeah, but you know, I only live two miles away from here. Me and my wife got woken up in the night by some strange noises in the woods next to us. I looked out the window and saw a strange glow. I'm afraid to say this, but maybe their stories are true. Maybe some alien cats from outer space came to Earth."

"That's ridiculous! I don't want to hear any of this. The Silvertown Police Department has no time for silly tales. Where's the coroner? I need to talk to him."

Shelby chuckles awkwardly. "Well, the thing about that is that the coroner is not here. He's on vacation in Mexico."

"Oh, yeah. That's right. I forgot. Wait, who did you talk to then?"

"Well, about that. There's somebody I like you to meet. There's an exchange coroner from Mexico. In fact, he's a buddy of mine," Officer Shelby yells in Spanish to a random officer standing by. It looks like another Hispanic guy with a thick mustache. "I would like for you to meet my buddy, Emmanuel Abasto, he only speaks Spanish."

Sam shakes Emmanuel's hand. "Nice to meet you."

"Hola."

Sam raises an eyebrow at Officer Shelby. "How are we going to do this if he doesn't speak a word of English?"

"Don't worry, I can translate. My buddy here is very good at analyzing bodies, dead ones, but especially women's bodies." Officer Shelby smirks and nudges Emmanuel.

"Sí, me encantan los cuerpos."

Sam sighs. "Uh, jeez. I got no time for this. Just tell me what you know."

As Tom's dad argues with Officer Shelby and with Emmanuel, Tom considers the story of the 'seven alien cats' killing the man. Uri said he and his people were conquered by creatures called The Babylonians. If the cats the drunk men and the woman saw were them, then Uri is in trouble. Tom walks over to Officer Shelby and sees he's holding a bunch of drawings of these supposed 'alien cats.'

Tom taps Officer Shelby's shoulder. "Hey, excuse me. Are those the pictures you drew of the cats? Can I see them?"

Officer Shelby turns his head. "Uh, yeah sure."

"Don't even bother, son! There's nothing to prove here!" Tom's dad says.

Officer Shelby hands Tom the drawings anyway and continues to argue with his dad along with Emmanuel.

Tom examines the drawings. Officer Shelby isn't the best drawer in the world, but Tom already can tell the cats he drew certainly aren't normal. They look like beasts with fangs, though the witnesses may have exaggerated. Tom takes a picture of the drawings anyway, so he can show them to Uri.

"We're done here," his dad says. "No point wasting any more time. Come, son, I'm taking you home."

Tom gives the drawings back to Officer Shelby and follows his dad.

"Hey, wait a minute. Aren't you coming over to my house to watch some football?" Officer Shelby yells out to Tom's dad.

"Yeah, no thank you. I got better plans."

"Oh, come on. Emmanuel is going to be joining me too. He makes some good enchiladas."

"Sí, enchiladas."

Once Tom's dad hears the word "enchiladas," Tom can see his eyebrows go up. Tom knows how much his dad loves enchiladas. It's probably his only weakness. The man is trying his hardest to have a serious expression, but he just looks like a kid trying to hold back his excitement.

"Okay, fine. I'm coming to your house."

He waves goodbye and walks quickly to the police car. Tom follows suit.

He wants to tell his dad about Uri and the possible truth of the 'alien cats,' but he promised not to tell anybody. He wants to make his dad proud of him, but he remains silent. He has made a promise to a friend.

Yet, his mind is conflicted. In a back and forth spiral between if or if not. No time for that now.

He needs to talk to Uri first to make sure these 'alien cats' are the alien gang that's after him.

***

Nour never thought he would return to the alley where he killed the Earth man, yet there he is.

Nader wanted to go back to that bar, but why? He reasoned they should just check the area again, but for what?

Does he want to make peace with these Earth humans?

Nader should know you can't make peace with humans. All humans are the same. Even on another planet, they're still violent creatures.

Nour didn't question his brother's motives though, so here they are, except weird-looking Earth soldiers are roaming around, or he thinks they are Earth human soldiers? He guesses they are soldiers by the black armored vests and yellow badges they're wearing.

"Those must be the human soldiers who protect this village. That is some weird-looking armor they're wearing," Sebastian whispers.

"Hmm, must be bullet-proof vests they are wearing, which means that Earth humans must love their guns here." Nader stares at one human soldier.

Sebastian frowns. "I think guns are too overused. Just another human invention that other creatures overly rely on back home," Sebastian chuckles and turns on his ability, red arrows cover his body. "I think arrows are better projectiles. We can take over this human world easily if that's the only weapon the soldiers carry, especially since you said these Earth humans don't have any special abilities."

Nader rolls his eyes. "Yeah, well, good luck. I just have to warn you, even though they don't have special abilities, there are billions of them living on Earth. Are you sure we can take down billions of Earth humans?"

Nour looks at Nader wide-eyed. "Wait, did you say billions?"

"Yeah, seven billion to be exact. I haven't seen so many humans living on a single planet before, which just proves even more that Earth is unique."

Nour raises an eyebrow. "Jeez, these Earth humans must reproduce quickly then. We definitely can't handle billions of humans."

Nader looks back at Sebastian. "Yeah, plus, they don't only have guns here. They have other weapons that are even more powerful. Even though these humans don't have special powers, they make up for it with their genius. I read some Earth human books about the technology that they use here, and I'm surprised by the complexity of the machines they make. These Earth humans' are the smartest I've ever seen of any creature in the universe. It's lucky that these Earth humans don't have special powers. Otherwise, they would probably take over the entire universe."

"Damn it." Sebastian looks frustrated. "Why do humans have to be so powerful?"

Nour couldn't agree more; humans are just too over-powered, especially these Earth humans. Nour can't believe how smart they are. These Earth humans are probably even smarter than the other humans throughout the universe. This makes him want to find Uri more quickly and get out of this abomination of a planet. Nour turns around and looks at his friends.

"Alright, I think Nader's right. It's more logical for us to not associate with these humans at all, especially if there are billions of them. It would be very stupid to try to conquer them. Besides, we're only after Uri, so let's find him and then get off this cruel planet. We can figure out how to destroy it later, after we get home and gather more troops."

Tito has a concerned look. "That's not a peaceful way, Nour. Have you not learned from the Bible? We can't fight violence with violence because it will only lead to tragedy."

Nour smiles at Tito's peaceful nature. It's appealing. It reminds Nour of his sister.

"Don't worry, I'm not planning to destroy this planet. We just need to consider all our options."

Tito raises an eyebrow. "Well, I sure hope that your thinking won't lead you to make a bad choice."

Nour just smiles at Tito and looks back at the rest of his friends. "Alright, I think we should split up so we can scout Silvertown better. Me, Tito, and Sebastian will be in one group. Meanwhile, Nader, Ebo, Ginger, and Antar will team up. If you find Uri or any evidence that Uri is here, contact me immediately. We all got our comms?"

They nod back to him, then split up in separate directions.

Chapter 13- The First Confrontation

Now where is Uri anyway?

Ben told him not to wander far while he got ready to go. Uri has been traveling to random places while he's busy, and he can't keep track of the kid.

Right now he's just sitting in The Howler at the side of the road near a cow pasture. Cows mowing at a distance. Ben is just enjoying the warmth of the rare winter sun. Enjoying it while it lasts because he knows that it won't last long and there will be a blizzard the next day. Uri told him that he wanted to get some fuel for The Imaginator before they headed out to space and said he would be back soon. What kind of fuel does The Imaginator take, anyway? It's just a cardboard box, but a spaceship at that. There's only one way to find out.

"Hey Ben, I found the fuel, but I need your help!"

Ben jumps when he hears Uri's voice next to his ear. He looks over his shoulder and sees Uri in his house fly form. Jeez, he needs to get used to seeing a talking fly. "Jesus, you scared the crap out of me."

Uri, in his fly form, rubs his head. "Sorry. I found the fuel for The Imaginator. Now all I need is your truck."

"Okay...." Ben looks skeptically at Uri. "What kind of fuel does The Imaginator take anyway?"

"I'll show you," Uri says.

***

"Animal crap?"

Ben yells out on the way back to his house. There's a pile of literal cow crap in the bed of The Howler. Flies are buzzing all around in the cab, and Ben is not happy. He tries to swat the flies away as he pulls his shirt collar over his nose to block the scent.

"What kind of fuel is that?"

Uri, in his human form, also covers his nose. "Hey, it's a pretty efficient fuel source. Well, that's what my dad said."

"I need to tell your dad that it's a bad idea when we find him."

"Yeah," Uri agrees, sounding depressed, probably worried about finding his parents.

Ben tries to smile reassuringly. "Hey, don't worry. We'll find your parents."

Uri smiles back. "I sure hope so."

"Hey, you said that your dad taught you how to use your special abilities. He must be a good teacher."

"Yeah, he's quite the teacher."

"Is there a chance that he can teach me and my friends how to use special abilities if we find him?"

"Yeah, but that's a big 'if'". Don't worry, I know there's probably going to be a good teacher in Sweetopia that can teach you guys."

"If we don't meet your parents first, that is."

Uri grows silent, and Ben decides to follow suit, the air between them thick with unspoken thoughts. He won't admit it—maybe not even to himself—but the biggest reason he wants a special ability is to impress Honey. He pictures it clearly: his friends, each with their own powers, standing strong against alien threats. Heroes of Silvertown. That would finally show The Cougars who's really in charge.

When they reach Ben's house, he jumps out, fumbling for his keys. His fingers freeze. The door is already ajar. The handle dangles loose in his hand. A cold rush of fear slithers down his spine.

He nudges the door open, heart pounding. Uri slips in behind him, silent as a shadow. Once he enters inside, a big mess on the floor welcomes him.

"Somebody broke into my house," Ben whispers because he doesn't know if the thief is still there.

A faint rustling from the far side of the room makes his blood run cold. He ducks into a narrow closet near the door and grabs the bat he keeps hidden there. Without a word, he motions Uri behind him.

Slow, careful steps toward the noise. The floor creaks beneath his weight, each sound magnified in the heavy silence.

Ben edges around the living room entrance and freezes. Two cats—strangers—rifle through his dad's CD collection.

One's black, sleek, moving with unnerving grace. The other is much bigger, spotted like a leopard, but it's the mechanical legs that grip Ben's attention, humming quietly as they shift.

The bat slips from his trembling hands.

"Jeez, who lives in this place? He must be somebody old because nobody uses CDs anymore. What do you think, Nader?"

Did that black cat talk?

"You'll be surprised, Ebo. People still use them. I guess these Earth humans still use them too."

And did his robotic-legged friend talk as well? What the hell is going on? These aren't normal cats! How did these cats break into my house? Wait a minute. These guys aren't—

"Wait a minute, I think I heard someone come inside this house." The robotic-legged one says.

The two cats suddenly seem to notice Ben and Uri, who are staring at the two cats wide-eyed. They're having a staring contest with each other. A long silence...

Suddenly, the black cat rushes toward Ben, leaps up, and lands on his face. He tries to get the black cat off but fails. Blinded, Ben stumbles outside with the hissing mass of fur and claws.

***

Uri's chest tightens. He thought those feral cats were behind him—his past finally left in the dust. But the shadow returns, darker than ever. The Ferals have tracked him to Earth. And now Ben's caught in the middle.

Fear spikes. Uri wants to freeze, but he can't. Not this time.

A metal leg clicks forward, pointed straight at him.

"Oh, no you don't! You stay here!"

Uri immediately uses his ability to make stones appear out of nowhere, he grabs his sling, and slings the stones at the cat's robotic leg. The stones have sharp edges stabbing through the robotic leg and driving him back against the wall.

It would be very painful if it was his actual flesh, but with something artificial the pain is fake.

He detaches his artificial leg, but Uri shoots out stones again.

The cat tries to dodge, but one of them strikes his leg. Not his artificial one. Very painful this time.

Uri is sure because the cat can't move. He's holding his fleshy leg, trying to stop the gushing blood. Uri immediately runs away.

"Hey, get back here!" Nader cries out as he struggles to move.

Uri feels bad. It pains him also to see Nader bleeding. He doesn't want to hurt any animal, but he's never going back. He's especially never going back to his home nation ever again. It's all darkness he's leaving there.

***

Ben continues to struggle to get this black cat off his face, dropping to roll on the ground. To his surprise, this black cat finally gets off after a few rolls, and he gets back up. He starts wiping black fur off of his face, trying to spit out the hair that he accidentally swallowed, and realizes he's outside in his front yard. He looks back at this strange black cat.

"Okay, who the hell are you?" Ben points his fingers at the black cat.

"Darkness." The cat laughs like a maniac.

Darkness?

Great, Ben doesn't know what this cat is up to. Suddenly, he sees his surroundings turn black. He panics and looks at his house, but it's gone. Everything is gone. All he sees is black.

What the hell is happening? Wait a minute...

If this cat is an alien, then that means this is his special ability.

Oh great, I'm dead meat.

Ben suddenly gets punched out of nowhere. The ground feels more attractive than the sudden sting in his stomach. He screams in agony.

He wonders how he can stop this cat's ability, but it's no use. He can't defeat him. If only he had a special ability. Just then, he has an idea.

Ben takes out his phone and turns on its light to see where this black cat is, but that idea doesn't work because he still can't see anything. He then gets punched again.

"He, he. Nice try Earth human, but physical light doesn't work."

Physical light? What does he mean by physical light? Light itself is not physical. Ben doesn't know anymore. This cat is just playing with him at this point. Ben just starts walking backward in a panic. Suddenly, a random face appears out of nowhere next to him.

"Boo!"

Startled, Ben falls to the ground. The face looks like the cat, except it's huge, and it is laughing maniacally.

"Well, I had my fun. I guess I have to kill you now."

Wait, what? Kill me? Ben panics, trying to figure out another idea to get him out of here. *Come on brain, think.* It's no use...

Suddenly, the huge face stops and looks confused. Then, to Ben's surprise, his creepy face disappears. Ben looks all around him and the darkness disappears. He can see his surroundings again. Everything is back to normal, but what happened?

He gets his answer. The black cat is on the ground all bruised and beaten up. Ben looks over to see Uri staring at the cat with malicious eyes, breathing heavily, like he's scared too.

Uri turns his gaze at Ben. "Let's get out of here!"

Ben points to The Imaginator that's next to the front door. "What about The Imaginator?"

"Let's take it, quickly!"

Ben and Uri grab The Imaginator and put it in the bed of The Howler with the pile of cow manure. Ben doesn't care, so long as they get out of here quickly. He and Uri quickly get in and drive off.

The Imaginator was just outside the front door of the house. He shouldn't have decided to put it there. That's probably why they decided to barge into his house. He thought since it looked like a cardboard box, nobody would've noticed anyway. Bad choice on his part, but no time to dwell. Luckily, they escaped alive.

"Are you okay?" Uri asks.

"Am I okay? Are you okay?"

"I am. I'm sorry."

"It's okay. Who were those cats anyway? Are they those Babylonians?"

"Oh, no. They look like they could be from Misr."

"Misr? Well, whoever they are, let's just get my friends together. I think it's time we head out to space."

They nod to each other, relief settling in Ben's chest. He glances around, grateful both he and Uri made it out alive. Honey's absence is a small comfort—if she'd been home, he'd have dragged her out too. That black cat who attacked—his moves were sharp, precise. Ben's stomach twists with doubt. Could he really keep Uri safe? Without powers, he and the Wolf Pack might just slow Uri down.

For now, getting Uri somewhere quiet feels urgent.

Chapter 14- A Space Adventure

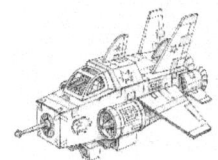

Ben decides to drive Uri to his favorite quiet spot in the middle of the woods near town. He calls it "The Wolf Den" (Don't judge him). It's so isolated, nobody will find them there. Not even those cats. He hopes not.

He loves it there because it's usually where he and his friends hang out and goof off to keep their minds off the problems in the world, but he isn't taking Uri there to goof off. After the encounter with those cats, he told his friends what happened and asked them to meet up.

He doesn't understand how those little kitty cats are so powerful. Uri wasn't kidding when he said that there's dangerous creatures after him and his people. He can't believe he almost got killed by a little black cat. Ben doubts he's strong enough to protect Uri, but for now, he can take Uri to a safe place.

Uri looked worried on the drive. Ever since they encountered those two cats, he's been silent, which is odd for him because he usually talks Ben's ear off about all the space adventures he's been on.

"Are you alright?"

Uri just stares nervously at the road in front of them. "Yeah."

"Okay." Ben holds tight on the wheel. The Howler is shaking, which isn't helping his nerves at all. They are not far from The Wolf Den though. He finally sees two trucks parked at the side of the road: Cedric's and Tom's. They've finally made it.

Ben parks behind his friends' trucks and gets out, motioning for Uri to follow. They follow a little trail that he and his friends made to get to their hideout. A little hut made out of branches that sticks out like a sore thumb among the trees. The rest of the Wolf Pack are already gathered around it, and Honey runs toward him with a mixed expression of fear and concern.

"What happened? Are you guys hurt?" She grabs hold of Ben's arms.

Ben blushes and gives an awkward smile. "Nah, we're okay."

"Who destroyed your home?"

"I don't know. Some strange cats. Uri says that they are from his planet."

Honey looks at Uri. "Are those cats the Babylonians that conquered your people?"

Uri shakes his head. "Oh no. These cats are from a different nation. I know them, they call themselves 'The

Ferals.' They are from the nation of Misr. The nation of Misr are also enemies of Zion, but I don't know how they are able to find me."

"Yeah, and I'm pretty sure they're going to be waiting to destroy us if we go back." Ben says.

"Oh, that means that we probably shouldn't go back to our homes for a while then, huh?" Honey keeps holding onto his arms as Tom walks up.

He looks at Uri. "By the way, your kitty friends decided to kill a guy at the bar for some reason. Now the whole police force is investigating it, including my dad. Here's some pictures."

Uri looks at Tom's phone and rubs his chin. "Yeah, that's them alright. I'm not surprised. They've probably scouted the entire town even before we even encountered them." Uri fidgets with his hands. "And they're probably going to destroy the entire town, and it's going to be my fault." Uri looks at all of them. "I'm sorry I brought them to your planet. I think it's best that I leave and take care of things on my own."

Ben shakes his head. "What? No. We're going with you."

"Um, Ben," Tom looks at Ben cock-eyed, "I think Uri is right. They've killed a man, and they've almost killed you. I think it's best that we let Uri go and take care of things on his own. I mean, look at us. We don't have any special powers to protect him with."

Ben frowns at Tom. "That's why we're going to Sweetopia to learn special abilities so we can—"

"I don't know," Uri interjects, his eyes downcast. "The Ferals are also very skilled like the Babylonians. I don't think you guys can defeat them. Sorry, Ben, but I have to work alone. It always has to be this way."

Ben smiles. "No, it doesn't. It doesn't because that's not the wolf way. You're part of The Wolf Pack now, and 'No Wolf Works Alone;' that's the motto. I'm going with you. "

Ben raises his wolf chain to Uri, who remains silent as he looks up with a shocked expression on his face. Then he smiles.

"Thank you."

"Well, if you're still willing to go, then I guess we are too," Tom says, and the rest of the group nods in agreement as they hold up their wolf chains as well.

"Are you serious?" Baxter blurts out, shaking his head. "Uh, I can't believe it. Fine, then." He also holds up his wolf chain.

Uri looks at all of them cock-eyed. "I don't know why you all want to go with me now that The Ferals found me," Uri's smile returns, "but I appreciate it."

"Hey, no worries," Ben says. "Shall we get going then? Honey and I probably can't go to our houses now."

Uri nods. "Yeah, now is a great time." Uri looks at Tom. "Did you guys bring the things we need for this trip?"

Tom nods. "Yeah, all the emergency med kits and other things we need are in all of our backpacks."

"Great! Let's get The Imaginator ready and we'll be off."

***

Earth, the living planet.

The planet that is only known to man, Earth man, to have life. Earth, a beautiful planet. One of a kind from all of its neighbors in its system. From all the other stars in the Milky Way Galaxy. It's very unique like its inhabitants. A bunch of crazy lifeforms. A two-legged creature called a human. Who can blame them for being crazy when they've been stuck, isolated on their own planet. Isolated from the truth, not knowing what their outside world is like.

It's amazing, to Uri, how these Earth creatures can live without knowing. Knowing their purpose. That's what hopefully he's going to help The Wolf Pack with.

He's sitting comfortably on his seat, waiting for his Earth friends to sit down as well as they pack their luggage. They don't know it yet, but they're going to realize the truth, the truth of the universe and how it came to be.

"Alright! We're ready for takeoff," Uri announces in an excited tone.

Ben and his friends buckle up their seats. He's sitting next to Uri, who is behind the wheel, looking over with joyful and eager eyes. Everyone else seems to be wondering how they got wrapped up in all this. Ben still can't believe he's not dreaming; they're actually with an alien in a cardboard-box-looking ship going to outer space to another planet. He's excited and nervous at the same time.

"Ready?" Uri asks.

They all nod.

"Then let's go!" Suddenly, Uri pushes down the throttle.

A sudden force pushes Ben back in his seat as the blue sky fills the windows. As they rise through the atmosphere, The Imaginator rattles, but as the blackness of space and the distant stars fill their view, it becomes still. The moon grows larger in the window, and the Wolf Pack stares in amazement as they pass by it.

Uri looks up at Ben with joyful eyes. "We've finally made it to outer space. Just wait until I turn hyper speed on, and we'll really have an adventure."

Ben smiles at Uri. "Hey, you don't mind if I take the wheel?"

Uri looks at Ben cock-eyed. "Sure but be careful. I know I have been teaching you to drive The Imaginator, Ben, but I don't think you're ready for hyper-speed yet."

"Oh, come on. Why not? I can handle hyper speed."

Uri frowns. "Okay, I'll give you the wheel and you can drive with hyper-speed on. Just make sure you take a good grip on the wheel."

"Um, are you sure it's a good idea?" Tom asks.

Uri just smiles at Tom. "Oh, I'm sure. I need to teach you guys how to drive at hyper speed anyway just in case we encounter The Ferals' ship or a ship from the Babylonians."

Uri gives Ben the wheel, and The Wolf Pack hold onto their seats tightly. Ben doesn't know what his friends are worried about; he's a good driver. They've seen him drive The Imaginator before when they were practicing. He's honestly surprised by how simple it is to drive a spaceship. It's almost like driving a car... Almost.

He grabs the wheel from Uri and braces himself. "Alright, Uri. Let it rip!"

Uri pushes the throttle as far as he can to the fastest speed possible. Immediately, a big force pushes them back to their seats and they can barely move. Ben looks at the window and all he can see is a bunch of flashing lights. He squints as he tries to hold the wheel as tightly as he can.

There's so much force pushing him back that it's kind of hard to take hold of the steering wheel though. Just the mere speed they're going is making it very loud to hear anything. He sees Uri pull the throttle a little bit and The Imaginator goes a little slower, but there's still a lot of force that's pushing him against the seat. At least he can hear.

"How much longer do we have?"

Ben looks at Uri.

"About an hour left!"

An hour? He has to deal with this force on his bones for an hour?

Oh, boy!

Chapter 15- The Prince Has Been Found

Nour, the angry feline

Where is Uri anyway?

Nour, Tito, and Sebastian have been scouting the human village for the last five hours or so. It's daytime, so more Earth humans are roaming about now. They're just hiding in a bush next to a building. Some kind of market is happening because Nour sees humans coming and going out of this building carrying bags of food.

They've been walking, avoiding humans as much as possible and peeking through windows to find Uri. No luck so far. Surprisingly, none of the humans seem to notice them. Nader had said other animals on Earth aren't even sentient.

Hard to believe, but if it's true, to these Earth humans they're just ordinary, silent cats. Still, Nour warns everyone to stay away from these humans—they might come after them because of the bar incident. Nour catches Tito's worried glance.

"Nour, I just hope that you and Sebastian don't do anything barbaric. I don't want both of you to hurt yourselves or even hurt these humans around us."

Sebastian growls. "Pff, why do you care so much about these humans? I think they are nothing special to the humans that we meet on other planets."

"Yeah, but do you realize these Earth humans have something very different about them than other humans?"

Sebastian rolls his eyes. "Yeah, they're so lame."

"Lame? They're not lame. They got some very complex brains."

"Yeah, but what bothers me is the fact that other animals on this planet don't talk. What's up with that?"

Tito scratches his head. "I don't know, it must be because they don't have a highly developed cerebral cortex."

Sebastian raises an eyebrow. "Cerebral cortex?"

"Yeah, a cerebral cortex is a part of your brain that helps you think, to problem solve, to have a conscience. I don't think other animals on this planet have a complex cerebral cortex."

"Yeah, well I don't think these humans have complex brains either. I mean look at them..." Sebastian points at the Earth humans that are just walking past them. "They're not even paying attention to us. They're like robots. Not only that, but they don't even have any special powers. I mean come on! That's so lame! Hey, Nour. What do you think?"

"I think you guys should be quiet and start looking around for Uri."

Sebastian rolls his eyes again. "Okay, fine. Since you're so determined to find this stupid kid."

Finally, after a few minutes of silence and Sebastian not talking his ear off this time, Nour suddenly hears a buzzing noise. Nour looks down and realizes that it is his watch. He reads on the screen to show him who's trying to contact him; it's Nader. He immediately answers Nader's call.

"What happened? Have you found anything yet?"

"We found the kid."

Nour gasps in shock. "Wait? You found him? Where is he? Did you catch him?"

"No, me and Ebo didn't manage to catch him. There was an Earth human with him."

"Wait, an Earth human kidnapped him?" Nour growls.

"Well, I don't think he kidnapped him because it looked like he wanted to go with the Earth human. That kid is more clever than I thought. I think we need more than the two of us to catch him."

"Wait, what do you mean? Isn't Ginger and Antar with you?"

"Nah, the four of us decided to split up into pairs so we can cover more ground. That was a bad idea."

"Yeah, no kidding. Just tell me where you guys are."

"Well, I don't think we should meet up here. He's long gone from us anyway. Let's just meet up at the spaceship and discuss what we can do from there."

"Alright, I will call Ginger and Antar myself. We'll meet up at BS Lion."

"Alright, see ya."

Nour turns off his phone.

"Wait, did they find them?" Sebastian blurts out.

"Yeah, they did, but they lost him."

Tito raises an eyebrow. "I'm surprised they're able to find him. Well, I guess this means you are planning to stay on this planet for longer then, huh?"

"Yeah, but for not too long. I need to call Ginger and Antar, then we're going up to the spaceship to discuss a plan."

***

Back on the BS Lion, in orbit, Nour hopes the Earth humans don't spot them, though it shouldn't be possible with their cloak enabled. The Ferals gather around their galley table. Nour doesn't know how many times they've discussed plans here.

He remembered back when Angel was with them, they used to have tons of discussions about how to execute their plans. Whether planning to visit a strange planet or planning how to make their job better, they had a lot of good conversations here.

He grabs a picture out of his robe pocket; the picture shows a white female cat wearing a green dress. Nour doesn't know what he's going to do without Angel...

"Hey, Nour! When are we going to discuss this plan of yours already?"

Nour snaps back to his senses at Sebastian's voice. He fumbles to put the picture back in his pocket.

"Right, sorry. Now that we have finally found Uri, I say we should split with half of us trying to catch him. Meanwhile, the other half will stay on BS Lion to look for any intruders."

Ginger looks at him cock-eyed. "Come on, you think another ship will be this determined to travel so far just to catch a human kid."

"Well, I mean we've done so and I'm sure there are other creatures out there that are as determined as us. I'm just trying to be safe here."

Nader also looks at Nour cock-eyed. "Yeah, well the safe thing to do is to not try to capture this kid in the first place. You know how powerful he is. Plus, we compete with other powerful creatures that want this kid too, like the Babylonians, and they're willing to kill anybody who's in their way."

"Well, we just have to kill them first. We're way far ahead from capturing Uri than they are, and I like to keep it that way."

Tito looks at Nour with concern. "Nour, you shouldn't let your emotions cloud your judgment. I know you want to protect Prince Uri, but you're doing it the wrong way. Let's try to confront Uri calmly and then tell him the reason why we're after him."

"Pff, we already tried that before, but yet he still ran away from us."

Tito shakes his head. "That's because we weren't patient and tried to rush things."

"Oh, come on! How can I be patient when we have other gangs on our tails? How about you tell them to be patient and see what happens."

"Honestly, I told all of you for the hundredth time that we shouldn't bother with this kid. It's not worth the effort of chasing him around all over the place. Even though the price on this kid's head is worth a lot, why even waste our time?" Sebastian blurts out.

Tito looks worried. "Sebastian, do you have any love at all? We're not after this kid for the money. We're after him because he's our friend. Don't you remember that he's King Yadin's son? We have to continue to search for Prince Uri, not for the money, but for King Yadin's sake."

Sebastian rolls his eyes. "I'm sorry, but we've been chasing this kid for so long that I'm tired of it. Right, Antar?"

"صحيح. (Correct.)" Antar says.

Sebastian smirks. "See this is what I like about you, Antar. You never say much and just do things. You can at least speak one word of English though."

"لا. (No.)"

"Well," Nader chimes in, "for the sake of everybody, I think me, Ebo, Antar, and Tito will try to catch Uri. Meanwhile, the rest of you try to be on the lookout for any strange spaceships coming."

Nour frowns at Nader. "Hey, why not me? I should go with you."

Nader shakes his head. "Nope, for the sake of all our safety, you should stay."

Nour rolls his eyes. "Okay, fine, but if you come back without Uri, then I'm going too."

Nader shrugs. "Fine by me." Nader looks at Ebo. "Come, let's find this kid, wherever he is?"

Ebo's not paying attention because he's looking at his phone until his ears perk up. He suddenly jumps and turns on his teleportation watch.

"Right, let's go!"

Ebo says, stammering. Nader just rolls his eyes and turns on his teleportation watch too.

"Alright, let's get going then."

Nader nods at Antar and Tito as they also turn on their teleportation watches and there's a bright light shining around each of them as they disappear, leaving Nour, Ginger, and Sebastian on the lookout for any evil ships. Ginger and Sebastian immediately go to the navigation board without saying anything.

Nour stares through a window at Earth for a while. This planet, a paradise? Why did he think it would be a paradise planet before? He's always too optimistic when discovering new things. His naive kitten-self would have loved the dream of traveling the whole Fruit Galaxy with his friends...with her. But all hope is lost with her gone.

He takes out his picture of Angel. The beautiful green dressed molly who always brought sunshine in his life...now gone.

What I'm going to do without you, Angel?

If only you were still with us, then you would see how much we've accomplished since you've been gone.

We've done so much, but yet why don't I feel happy?

Our friends don't seem happy, either. Your loss wasn't the easiest thing to deal with, but you told me to stay happy no matter what. It's very hard without you. Maybe that's why the rest of our friends aren't happy?

Maybe they miss you as well. That's why I never want to lose somebody I love ever again.

I can't let those evil creatures capture Uri, because I made a promise to you, Angel, that I'm never going to let any of our loved ones be harmed.

As for right now, I must—

"Hey, Nour! I'm getting a signal." Ginger says.

"Really? Where?"

"About a kilometer and a half away."

"So close? Why didn't we detect them sooner?"

"Hey, were you even paying attention?" Sebastian yells out.

Ginger shrugs. "Hey, hey. It isn't my fault. The ship must be able to avoid passive detection. Only mercenary ships can do that."

"Mercenary ships?" Nour runs toward the navigation system. "If it's a mercenary ship, it must be after Uri."

"Why the hell do you have the sensors on passive? Man, no wonder you can't detect anything." Sebastian frowns at Ginger.

Ginger frowns back at Sebastian. "Hey, listen. I didn't think we would find a ship way out here. Plus, we're cloaked. Active sensors would make us easier to detect." Ginger scratches his head and looks back at the navigation system. "I don't know why anyone would want to travel this far for a kid anyway."

"He's not just any kid, he's King Yadin's son." Nour looks at Ginger. "Can you contact this ship and ask why they're here?"

Sebastian looks at Nour cock-eyed. "Why would you want to do that when you can just blast them right now?"

"Yeah, but that would cause a lot of mess. We don't want the people of Earth looking up at the sky and expecting anything."

Sebastian rolls his eyes. "Okay, fine, but I hope you're not planning to compromise with a bunch of mercenaries. Tell them if they don't leave, then we'll have no choice but to blast them."

Ginger just rolls his eyes. "Well, I'm not going to tell them that. Just keep quiet and let me do the talking."

Nour and Sebastian sit down, arms crossed in defiance. Meanwhile, Ginger tries to contact the mercenary ship. Suddenly, there's loud beeping sounds and the screen of the navigation system flashes.

"Aw, finally. Got them..." Ginger mumbles under his breath as he turns on the microphone of his headset. "Hello? Hello? This is BS Lion. Please respond."

Suddenly, from the speaker, Nour hears a loud raspy voice. "Hey! What do you want? If you don't get out of our way, then we'll blast ya!"

Ginger does not react, unlike Nour and Sebastian, who are itching to blast the mercenaries' ship to smithereens.

Ginger continues, "We're here to guard this planet from any intruders. Please say what you're doing here, or I must ask you to leave."

The raspy voice speaks again, but this time in a calmer tone. "There's an important thing we're after, and we think that it might've landed on your planet accidentally. Have you seen a strange-looking cardboard box anywhere?"

Once the mercenary says that Ginger looks back at Nour with wide eyes. It's clear why they're here.

"Ah, you see that?" Sebastian asks. "They are after Uri. Just say the command, Nour, and I'll blast these bastards into oblivion."

Nour shakes his head. "Nah, I got a better plan. Tell them that we want to board their ship and team up with them to capture this 'important thing' they're after."

"What? Why do you want to do that?" Sebastian blurts out.

"Hold on. I'm not planning to compromise with them; I'm planning to kill them."

Ginger sighs. "Jeez, what's up with you two?"

Nour raises an eyebrow. "Well, you heard what he said. They don't want to negotiate, so let's just trick them into thinking that we want to team up with them, then once we get into their ship... we kill them."

"I can't believe I'm doing this." Ginger mumbles under his breath. He turns the microphone on and starts speaking. "Are you guys looking for Prince Uri?"

"What? How do you—?"

"We already caught Prince Uri, and we have him right here. I know you guys are mercenaries, so let's make a little deal, shall we?"

"Alright, what the hell do you want?"

"How about you let us into your ship first before we discuss anything."

"Alright but bring the kid with you. I want to make sure you're not bluffing."

"Alrighty, then. See you soon," Ginger says before turning his microphone off and putting his headset down. "I hope your idea works. We're entering into enemy territory."

"Yeah, yeah. Just be prepared, alright."

Nour turns on his teleportation watch. Ginger rolls his eyes before doing the same. Sebastian readies his, and they all nod to each other before everything suddenly turns pixelated.

Reality returns to normal and Nour finds himself in what looks like a spaceship cockpit with Ginger and Sebastian next to him. Both are staring at a bunch of buffalo, who are just staring back at them.

They're Alkebulan buffalo (Syncerus caffer) from their home planet The Old World. Nour has no animosity toward the Alkebulan buffalo race, but he knows that these are evil mercenaries.

He's analyzing all the buffaloes in the cockpit. About 30 head in all. Some got broken horns, grated teeth, and disgusting foul.

Nour is trying to hold his breath and plug his nose of all the stench he smells. Damn his sensitive cat nose.

They just stare at each other for a while until one of the buffaloes speaks. He seems to be the leader because he's wearing a golden crown, unlike the others.

"Hey, I thought you said you had Prince Uri with you? I know I shouldn't have trusted you cats of Misr!" The buffalo leader says.

"Well, I guess you buffalo know where we are from as well," Nour responds.

"Of course, I recognize your Misr ship from any other ships in the universe. You cats think you're smart, don't you? You don't have the prince with you. You're lying."

"Well, I guess we don't need any introductions then. If you cows don't leave this place, then me and my friends have no choice but to slaughter all of you and once we slaughter you, we're going to feast on your meat."

"Slaughter us?" The buffalo leader laughs. "Man, you predators try to use every tactic you can use to scare us herbivores, don't you? Look at you, you're just three puny house cats." The buffalo leader and all of his friends laugh.

"Let's just get this thing over with, shall we." The buffalo leader looks at three of his henchmen. "You three, take care of these puny cats, will ya?"

His henchmen start walking toward them. Nour heard what the buffalo leader said. It's always the same. Every enemy that they've encountered said the same thing, that he and his friends are just a group of puny house cats. Well, Nour guesses he has to prove these buffalo wrong as he did with every enemy they faced by killing them all!

Nour charges at the buffalo leader giving him only a moment of surprise to motion to his three henchmen to attack. Ginger uses his sand ability to cover the buffaloes' bodies. The three buffaloes are surprised and try to break free from Ginger's grasp, but he wraps his sand around their necks and chokes them to death.

The buffalo leader is surprised as he sees Nour turn on his fire ability and continue to charge at him. When Nour gets close to him, the buffalo leader dodges at the last minute before he can scratch him. Nour looks back and sees the buffalo leader just standing there.

The buffalo leader has a burnt mark on his right shoulder. *Almost got him.* Nour looks over on his left and sees Sebastian and Ginger fighting off with the other buffalo. He looks back at the buffalo leader.

"Okay, I just about had it! You puny house cats think you can destroy us? Well, how about you try this!"

The buffalo leader charges at Nour with his horns. Nour begins to charge toward him too, but that was his biggest mistake. Nour realizes how fast the buffalo leader's going. He tries to dodge him, but then he gets smacked by one of his horns.

Pain erupts near his stomach as he falls to the ground. His vision blurs.

He tries to get up, but the pain is too much, and he falls back, realizing he is bleeding heavily from a stab wound. That buffalo bastard got him good.

The pain is too... he can't get... he's starting to... he can't... he can't—%$%$&$&%&%...

What the hell is happening to me? My vision turned red all of a sudden. What is this strange sensation? It's the same thing I felt before. I... What is it?

He doesn't feel pain anymore. The stab wound, it's gone. He looks at his body and it's glowing a bright red. He doesn't know what this power is or where it came from, but it's helping him.

I feel so powerful!

"What the hell?"

The buffalo leader gasps. He sees the buffalo leader just staring at him looking terrified.

"How the hell did you get The Predator's Eye?" The buffalo leader backs away slowly.

"Predator's Eye"? That's what Nour keeps hearing creatures call it. He doesn't know what to call it himself, but it's giving him more strength. It's kind of odd. He doesn't know where it came from, but he's gonna use it to destroy this buffalo bastard!

Nour immediately charges at the buffalo leader. He is so shocked that the bastard can't even move. Well, it just makes it easier for Nour, he guesses.

Nour finally jumps, aiming for the buffalo leader's neck. He slashes with his claws and immediately jumps away.

Nour moves so quickly that he's just a blur of fur and claws racing across the buffalo's neck.

Suddenly, his vision turns back to normal. He notices his heavy breathing starts calming down. He looks back to see the buffalo on the ground, not moving, in a growing pool of blood. Did he kill him? Good. Now it's time for him to help Ginger and Sebas—

"Aw!"

Nour yelps in pain. The spot where that wound used to be is starting to hurt again, but the wound is not there? He's feeling dizzy. His vision blurred again. Oh, great. He needs to—

***

"So, can you tell me exactly what happened to him?"

Uh...what? Nader is that you?

"I don't know. It was the same thing that happened to him a few times since we even found out about it."

Um...what? Tito?

"So, What do you think it might be? Some sort of spirit that's possessing Nour?"

Ginger?

"I don't think an evil spirit is possessing him, because we all know that Nour doesn't practice magic, and certainly we don't either. The Devil's Eye is a thing that a creature has when their feelings get the best of them. The Devil just uses it to his advantage, and it makes it look like they're some insane overpowered monster, which in reality, they're not."

Uh...what the hell is Tito talking about?

"Well, Nour hasn't been himself lately ever since Angel died. He's gone mad ever since. I think Satan is using this to his advantage and making Nour want to go on this wild goose chase to capture Uri."

Nader? What the hell are they talking about?

"Well, the only thing we can do now is try to persuade Nour the best we can to make him stop this. It's up to him though if he wants to stop. You know how stubborn he is though. Let's just hope and pray to God that there's the slightest bit in him that wants to make the good choice."

Tito? Okay, what's going on?

"Oh, wait a minute. I think he's awake." Nader says as Nour opens his eyes. He has a soft blanket over him and is lying on one of the galley couches of the BS Lion. He looks over to see all his friends around the old galley table playing cards. He rolls out of the couch and lands on his paws. All his friends are staring at him.

"Oh, it looks like the beast finally woke up," Nader drawls.

"Hey, Nour, how are you doing?" Tito says, looking at Nour all concerned.

"I'm fine. What happened?"

"You had one of those episodes where your eyes turned red, but somehow it got worse. We saw your whole body glow red this time, Nour," Ginger chimes in.

"Nour, this thing you're having, The Predator's Eye, or The Devil's Eye, is getting serious now and it's affecting your whole body. You even passed out, which didn't happen before," Tito says.

"Pff, well, whatever this thing is, it helped save my life. By the way, what happened after I passed out?"

"We took care of the rest of those buffalo mercenaries while you were out. Stole their stuff and blew their ship to smithereens." Sebastian blurts out.

"Good, and why are you four here? Did you capture Uri?"

Nour looks at Nader, Tito, Antar, and Ebo intently. Nader shakes his head.

"Nope. In fact, according to the tracker, he's not even on Earth anymore."

"Wait, what? What do you mean?"

"I mean that his cruiser moved. It's off Earth and it's heading somewhere."

"Where? How come you guys let this happen?"

"Well, we couldn't tell you guys earlier because you were too busy fighting."

"Oh, dang it! If it wasn't for those stupid buffalo bastards, we would've seen his stupid cardboard… Er…" Nour suddenly feels pain in his head.

"Nour, calm down. Your anger is getting the best of you and it's not good for your health." Tito puts his paw on Nour. Nour ignores him and looks at Nader.

"Er...Do you think possibly that Earth human is with him too?"

Nader shrugs. "Possibly, but all I know is that he's traveling somewhere."

"Where?"

"I don't know, but we're making sure that he's on the radar, so we won't lose him."

"Good, let's just continue chasing him. Er..."

"You know, Nour. You should rest. Your mind and your emotions are hurting you right now." Tito puts a soft blanket over Nour.

"Fine, fine."

Nour walks back to the couch. His friends may be right. He shouldn't be letting his emotions get the better of him, but he has no time for that. He has a prince who is in trouble and needs saving. He just needs to rest a little and only a little.

He's going to get back up soon. There's no time for rest.

Wherever Uri is going, he's going there too. Whatever beast tries to hurt him there, he's going to kill them.

Chapter 16- Sweetopia

"Ok, you can turn it down, now! We're getting close," Uri says.

Thank God!

Ben cannot take another minute of it. He slowly pulls the throttle down. Slower and slower The Imaginator gets, and he feels like he's getting lighter and lighter until it finally stops. He can finally breathe again. As he tries to catch his breath, he looks back at his friends who are also trying to catch their breaths. They're frowning at him. He just laughs awkwardly and shrugs.

"Well, that was a fun ride."

Tom, who is sitting closest to him, punches his arm. "Ben, what the hell was that?"

"Yeah, at least grasp the wheel tighter next time or something," Baxter chimes in.

"Hey, I was grasping it as hard as I can."

"Ben, you literally had your eyes closed most of the time, and you were steering like a madman!" Cedric says.

"Yeah, well why don't you try to drive this thing next time and see what happens?"

"Guys, be quiet!" Honey says, pointing at the front window of The Imaginator. "Look, we're here."

In front of them is a little pink planet. The pinkest thing Ben has ever seen. Ben can't tell how small it is compared to Earth, but it's tiny just by looking at it. Ben has to squint to analyze more detail. Pink clouds swirl over the surface.

"We finally arrived at Sweetopia, ladies and gentlemen!" Uri cheerfully yells out.

"Man, it's a small planet. I know you mentioned that it was small before, Uri, but I never imagined it being this small. It's like the size of Pluto." Slam uses his hands to try to measure Sweetopia.

"Well, if it's the size of Pluto, then would it even be considered a planet at all," Tom mentions.

"Okay, let's not get into a fight with what's a planet and what's not, alright?" Ben rubs his forehead.

"Wait, you Earth humans get into universal politics too?" Uri raises one eyebrow.

"Universal politics?" Tom asks.

"Yeah, that's a universal political issue among the nations of the universe. They're trying to debate what's an actual planet or not."

"Well, it looks like politics never change no matter what planet you go to," Tom says.

"Let's just stick to the plan, shall we?" Ben looks at Uri. "Uri, can you take the wheel? I'm done driving this thing."

Uri nods. "Sure, I'll land." Uri grabs the wheel out of Ben's hands.

Tom looks at Uri puzzled. "How do you know where to land?"

"Oh, it's simple! I just set up a destination on the UPS to help us get to a landing station on Sweetopia that's nearby."

"UPS? Do you mean the delivery service? What are you talking about?" Tom asks.

"It stands for Universal Positioning System. It's a neat device to help navigate to other planets."

"Oh, like a GPS, a Global Positioning System, except Global is switched with Universal. Jeez, everything is universal in this place." Tom scratches his head.

Uri laughs. "Man, you Earth humans really are isolated, are you?" Uri continues to laugh as they all just look at him puzzled. Uri ignores them as he looks ahead. "Alright, it's time to land this ship already. Prepare for landing!"

Ben holds onto his seat and prepares to land on the strange planet. His nerves are kicking in. He's half excited and half nervous to land on a planet with actual lifeforms on it. He wonders what they'll be like. Uri says Sweetopians are friendly and welcome any visitors unless they're rebels or crooks.

They enter the atmosphere of Sweetopia, and the whole cruiser starts shaking. Pink clouds fill the windows.

Suddenly, turbulence stops, and the clouds dissipate to reveal a colorful apple-shaped piece of land surrounded by a pink sea. The whole apple is like a rainbow, except the stem is completely dark at the top. A complete contrast in colors, but the island is striking, nevertheless.

Ben can see the pink waves coming towards the land like a swirling strawberry milkshake that they serve at the ice cream trucks back home, and the space cruiser is swirling toward the land with the same vigor.

As they get closer to this apple island, they see a small little town with every color of the rainbow on it. Even the surrounding forests and mountains are colorful. The whole landscape looks beautiful.

Uri begins to turn The Imaginator left and right as they get closer to this town. Other ships soar by them. There's a big area with a lot of spaceships on it, looking like an airport. As they get closer, Ben sees two weird-looking, colorful lizard creatures running up and waving lights at them. Uri hovers The Imaginator and lands slowly next to them.

"Hey, wait a minute! Those are velociraptors!" Ben points at the two colorful lizard people.

Uri smiles. "You guys know what velociraptors are? Hmm, interesting, I didn't realize dinosaurs live on your planet. I didn't see a single one, so I just assumed that they didn't live on Earth."

"They used to live on our planet until they went extinct millions of years ago. Now there's just fossils of them," Tom says.

Uri looks at Tom cock-eyed. "Wow, that's kind of odd. Dinosaurs are still alive and roaming about on other planets. It's strange to hear that they're extinct on your planet."

"Yeah, but these look way different. They're all colorful and seem way too friendly." Cedric scratches his head. "I mean, look at them, they're smiling and waving at us."

"Well, I mean we're not sure what the velociraptors on Earth look like either." Tom offers. "We only could tell based on their fossils. Maybe this is what they truly look like on Earth too."

Cedric cocks his head. "What? You think they look like something out of a kid's dreamland?"

"Maybe."

"I don't care what they look like," Ben says with a smile. "These are aliens we're talking about. I wanna talk to them, let's go."

"Um, Ben…" Uri says. "I think it's best if you let me do the talking, because this is the first time I've seen them too. I don't know how they communicate or what language they speak. I don't know if they're friendly or not. Just let me talk with them first."

"Okay."

The Wolf Pack all grab their backpacks full of supplies as they follow Uri out of The Imaginator and into the strange world. Outside, Ben takes in his surroundings. The sky is like swirling strawberry milk too as Ben just wants to grab a big straw and drink it. The clouds are as fluffy as cotton candy. This whole place smells like candy. *Man, this place does seem like a kid's dreamland.*

As they are looking around, the two colorful velociraptors walk up to them. One of them has brown skin like he got dipped in chocolate and came out a chocolate lizard. Alien-looking antennae on his head. They start flashing lights.

The other has light blue skin, like the ocean, with neon green splotches and a matching crest on his head. Both are wearing silver vests and carrying spears, looking like ancient guards. When they walk up to them, The Wolf Pack has to look down because they're so short.

Uri waves. "Huh hoy there! How's it going?"

The blue raptor walks up to Uri. "Good! What planet did you guys come from?"

Ben gasps in shock.

These raptors talk?

Honestly, he shouldn't be surprised because they're aliens. It doesn't matter, anyway. What matters is that these weird-looking raptors can speak, and one of them can speak English. Uri turns around and looks at The Wolf Pack.

Uri looks back at the two raptors. "Well, I'm from The Old World. From the nation of Zion. My friends here are from planet Earth."

The blue raptor looks at Uri cock-eyed. "Wait? From Zion? No way! Uri, is that you?"

"Oh, you know who I am?"

The blue Sweetopian smiles. "Yeah, I used to work with your dad, but it has been a very long time. I don't know if you remember me, Uri, but I'm Blueberry Ocean. I remember you when you were just a baby."

Uri's eyes shot up. "Wait, you used to work with my dad?"

"Ha ha, yeah. Your dad used to come to Sweetopia a bunch of times before he... wait a minute..." The blue Sweetopian looks at Uri skeptically. "What are you doing here, Uri? I heard what happened at Zion. Is someone chasing after you?"

The blue Sweetopian and his chocolatey brown friend grew tense.

Uri giggles awkwardly and waves his hands at both of them. "You guys got nothing to worry about." Uri points at The Wolf Pack. "I'm completely safe because I have my friends here to protect me."

The raptors look up at The Wolf Pack.

"Are these humans brothers?" The blue Sweetopian looks at Uri skeptically again.

Brothers? What are they talking about? Ben wonders.

"Nah, they're non-believers, but they're good people. In fact, they want to learn more about special abilities. I'm trying to find a good teacher for them."

Non-believers? What a minute!

Are these two raptors part of Uri's religion?

That seems odd.

Ben hasn't expected raptors to believe in God, but he also didn't expect to find a civilization of them on an alien planet, so oh well.

He just wants to learn about special abilities. He doesn't care what kind of teacher Uri finds for them, as long as he can teach them how to protect him and learn some cool tricks.

"Oh, I see. It's nice to see more people want to learn more about the truth. I know a good teacher, if he has time, that is. Our overseer, Jegu The Great Candymaker, can probably teach them. He's an older brother and has more experience." The blue Sweetopian looks at his chocolatey brown friend. "Hey, Chuck, can you show them where Jegu's house is?" Chuck nods. The blue Sweetopian looks back at The Wolf Pack. "I'm Blueberry Ocean by the way. This is Chuck The Chocolate

Monster. Before I let you guys explore, I have to ask for your IDs. Sorry, it's Sweetopian policy to keep track of who comes and goes on our planet."

Wait, IDs?

Uri didn't tell them that they needed to bring their IDs in outer space.

Oh great, what are they supposed to do now? If they didn't bring their IDs, then what does that mean? That they're not legally binding citizens of the universe?

Uri nods. "Oh, okay. I have my ID, but unfortunately my friends here live on a planet that's unknown to the League of Nations, so they don't have IDs."

Blueberry Ocean nods. "Oh, is that right? Well, that's no problem. Our overseer, Jegu, can help them get registered. Chuck can take you to see him. It's nice meeting you all. You guys have fun."

"Yeah, you too..." Uri waves goodbye to Blueberry Ocean as he just walks away.

As Ocean walks away, they turn to Chuck. He doesn't say anything and motions for them to follow. They all shrug and do so, taking advantage of the opportunity to look around.

The houses of the Sweetopians look like small colorful cottages. A market is happening, and Ben can smell it as they go through a crowd of Sweetopians. A bunch of Sweetopians walk around them, velociraptors of different colors and sizes. They all have feathers on them, and some sharp claws, and some sharp teeth when they smile.

Ben gets spooked at first with those razor-sharp nails that could slice him to pieces if they wanted to. Except they all smile and wave at The Wolf Pack.

Man, Ben thinks, *these raptors are very friendly.*

They're very different from people on Earth, that's for sure. If only the raptors from Jurassic Park were that friendly, then Ben wouldn't have nightmares as a kid when he watched that movie.

"Man, this place sucks," Baxter grumbles.

Ben glares at him. "What do you mean? We just got here."

"Yeah but look around you. It's like some little girl's dreamland and the people are too friendly. I don't trust them."

Cedric shakes his head. "Oh, really, too friendly for your violent ass? Well, that's too bad."

Baxter grinds his teeth. "Hey, you shut up, cowboy, before I knock your teeth out!"

Cedric rolls his eyes. "Yeah, violent is right."

"Shut up!"

"Jesus Christ, will you just quit it?" Tom looks back at Baxter. "We're on a strange planet with alien people. We don't know their customs and beliefs. It's probably best if we don't do anything stupid or cause a scene."

Baxter frowns at Tom. "Pff. Well. I'll tell you what's stupid. What's stupid is the fact that we're in this situation in the first place."

Ben frowns. "Hey, now. You all agreed to come with me. You didn't have to come."

"Well, I wanted to come with you."

Ben raises his eyebrows when Honey chimes in. She smiles at him.

"It's good that you want to take care of Uri after all he's been through, Ben. I want to help him too."

"Yeah, I want to help Uri as well," Slam chimes in as he smiles at Ben. "I'm like you, Ben: I feel bad for Uri after hearing the stuff he's been through. I want to travel with you guys every step of the way. It's going to be a fun adventure."

Ben smiles at Slam's and Honey's comments, then looks back at Baxter. "Ah, you see? Slam and Honey know what they're talking about. I don't know what you're on about."

Baxter just shakes his head. "By the way, where is this lizard taking us? I don't trust him one bit."

Uri smiles at him. "Oh, don't worry. We can trust him. He's a brother. He's part of the brotherhood of Zion. He serves Jehovah just like me."

"I don't care if he's part of your religion," Baxter says. "I still don't trust him. I mean, he hasn't said a word to us at all, and we're just here following him?"

"Don't worry, it's probably because he's just shy. I'll walk up to him and ask him where we're going."

Uri runs up to Chuck and says, "Hey there, Chuck."

The raptor turns, his antennae flashing.

Uri seems confused, then he smiles.

"Oh, I see!" Uri slaps his forehead. "So that's how you speak. I should have known when I saw you had those antennae."

Wait? So that's how this raptor speaks? He speaks through his antennae? Interesting. Strange, but interesting. It's going to be a challenge though because Ben can't understand what those flashing lights are and he's pretty sure his friends can't either. Chuck's antennae start flashing again at Uri.

"Oh, I see. Let me tell my friends here."

Uri then starts running back to The Wolf Pack. Wait, Uri understands what he said? Does he understand raptor?

"So that explains why he can't talk." Uri smiles, pointing at Chuck. "I should have known that because he had those antennae. Whenever you see a creature that has antennae like that, that means that they can communicate using a certain code with flashing lights."

Tom looks at Uri cock-eyed. "Oh, like Morse code? Is that how the raptor speaks?"

Uri smiles at Tom. "Yeah, there's a universal code that can be communicated with everyone. My dad taught me some of the code, so that's how I was able to understand him."

"If that's the case, then I can translate it as well." Tom rubs his chin.

Cedric looks at Tom cock-eyed. "Wait? You know how to translate Morse code?"

"Yeah, it's quite simple to understand." Tom looks at Uri. "What did he say to you, anyway?"

"Oh, just that we're getting close to Jegu's house." Uri points ahead of them. "It's just a few minutes away."

"Good, I want to see who this 'Jegu The Great Candymaker' is anyway." Baxter blurts out.

They follow Chuck for a few minutes, reaching the edge of the settlement.

Ahead is a little white cottage. A cottage that seems like it came from medieval times. Its roof looks like it's made of straw, weathered and golden. As they get closer, a sweet, marshmallow scent drifts through the air. With that smell, the cottage almost looks like a giant toasted marshmallow. Chuck steps up to the door—rough and crumbly like a graham cracker—and knocks.

Suddenly, Ben feels something strange on his ankle. Before he can look down to check it, he gets swooped into the air. He hears his friends screaming.

All around him, his friends are hanging upside down, just like him. Chuck is the only one who's still on the ground. Ben realizes there are long, black things wrapped around their ankles. It's strange because they smell just like dark chocolate.

"Hey, what's going on here? See, I told you we shouldn't have trusted these colorful lizards! Now we fell into their little trap!" Baxter yells out, trying to swing out of the dark chocolate strings.

Chuck seems as surprised as they are, then he looks at the white marshmallow cottage and flashes his antennae.

Another chocolatey-brown velociraptor steps out of the cottage, looking much older. Ben notices patches of gray in his fur—and wait, hair? The raptor sports a black afro. Ben never imagined velociraptors could grow hair like that.

Then he sees the dark chocolate tendrils wrapped around him—they're connected to the raptor's long, twisting mustache. This must be Jegu, The Great Candymaker. Ben never thought he'd be attacked by a velociraptor wielding a chocolate mustache, but here he is.

The old Sweetopian's eyes perk up as Chuck's antennae continue to flash, then he says, "Oh, I see."

He sounds like an old man. The old raptor places Ben and his friends safely on the ground and releases their ankles. His chocolate mustache shrinks to a normal size. Ben didn't even know velociraptors could grow facial hair, let alone hair made out of chocolate. Is it even considered hair at this point? Ben doesn't know anymore.

"I'm so sorry I attacked you guys. I never expected to have new visitors here on Sweetopia." The old Sweetopian says in a grumbling voice. He smiles at them, then turns to Uri. "I also never expected to see you here, Uri. What are you doing here? I heard what happened to Zion. Are you in trouble?"

Uri rubs his head awkwardly. "Yeah, but don't worry. My new friends here helped me out. You must be Jegu The Great Candymaker?"

The old raptor nods. "Yes, I am. Pleased to meet you all." Jegu looks at The Wolf Pack, seeming puzzled. "Who are these humans, and how did you meet them?"

"They're from a planet called Earth. They're the main reason why I've come here, Jegu. I need your help teaching them how to use special abilities."

Jegu tilts his head at The Wolf Pack. "Teach them how to use special abilities? But don't they already know how to use them? I mean, they look young, but they seem old enough that they already know how to."

Uri shakes his head. "No, humans on their planet don't have special abilities. In fact, none of the inhabitants on their planet do. That's why I want to bring them to you to see if you can teach them. Can you help us, please?"

Jegu stares at The Wolf Pack, seeming to examine them or maybe thinking they're a weird bunch of hooligans, which is not far from the truth.

There's a long, awkward silence, and Ben's body is sweating from all this awkward staring.

Suddenly, Jegu shrugs. "Yeah, why not? And I know the perfect place to train them, too."

Chapter 17- What Are Your Dreams?

"Alrighty, it's time to get the hanky-panky started," Jegu says to The Wolf Pack in a nonchalant tone.

He's flanked by Uri and Chuck in a big, open field interspersed with colorful rocks and surrounded by a colorful enchanted forest. The smell of the trees is like the smell of sweet syrup. Ben tries to look around where he is if he can. That is because everywhere his nose goes there's always a splash of that sweet syrup smell from those colorful trees. This planet sure is colorful, and the people are too.

Speaking of—

"Hey, what's with you Sweetopians and being so nice?" Ben asks Jegu.

Jegu smiles. "Oh, we're nice, huh? Well, that's good to know, thank you. We try to be nice to visitors as best we can."

"'Jegu The Great Candymaker'? I need to ask, what's with the cute names? I find your Sweetopian names to be interesting, from 'Jegu The Great Candymaker' to 'Blueberry Ocean' to 'Chuck The Chocolate Monster.' Why do all of you have cute names?" Slam asks.

Jegu laughs. "Oh, you think our names are cute, huh? Well, that's great because they're supposed to be cute. They're supposed to distract our enemies to make them realize that we're not a threat. Unfortunately, some creatures in the universe don't think we're so nice. They try anything to make people believe that we're evil."

Honey looks at Jegu cock-eyed. "Wait, really? People think you're evil? But there's tons of people greeting us kindly, even though we've just arrived on your planet."

Jegu laughs. "Yeah, well, some people don't seem to think so, and it's understandable because the universe is full of violent people. It's kind of hard to trust anybody anymore. That's why a special ability is good because it will help defend yourself from evil creatures." Jegu looks at Uri. "Uri knows that firsthand. It is the main reason the kingdom of Zion was destroyed in the first place. Again, I'm sorry about what happened to Zion, Uri."

Uri looks down. "It's okay."

Slam speaks up. "That's why we want to learn to use special powers, Jegu. We want to protect Uri from those evil creatures like The Babylonians."

Jegu smiles. "Oh, really? Well, that's good to hear, but I have to warn you. You are taking a big risk here. There are very dangerous and skilled creatures out there in the universe. That's why my people and I will take over to protect Uri. Meanwhile, I will help you learn to use special abilities— if you can, that is."

Ben smiles. "We're ready."

"Very well, the first step in learning how to use special abilities is..."

Jegu pauses. The Wolf Pack waits in eager anticipation. Ben is sweating really hard. He's leaning, trying to prepare for the big news of what Jegu is going to say, but the old velociraptor is just staying silent for some reason. What a minute. Is he asleep?

Sure enough, snore sounds are coming from him. His eyes closed. Uri that's behind Jegu taps his shoulder.

"Um, Jegu."

Suddenly, Jegu wakes up. He jumps, coughing like an old man.

"Uh, I'm sorry, what was I going to say?"

"You're going to mention to them the first step of learning how to use special abilities." Uri says.

"Oh, yeah. That's right. Well, the first step of learning a special ability is dreams."

The Wolf Pack looks at each other, everyone seeming confused.

"Dreams?" Baxter blurts out.

"Yeah, that's right, dreams. What are your favorite things to do? What do you want to be? What do you believe? In order to even have a special ability, you need to establish your identity and what you want to be. This is the main foundation of a creature's special power."

"Psh, man, this is stupid. I already know who I want to be, yet how come I don't have some strange superpower?" Baxter crosses his arms.

Jegu shrugs. "I don't know, it must be because you people of Earth don't know anything spiritual."

"Don't know anything spiritual? What is that supposed to mean?"

"It means that you're only focused on the physical things you see, and you don't know the things unseen. You can't physically see what your dreams are, but you have that vision in your mind that you want to succeed at. That's why the only way you can get a special power is by visualizing your dreams. You guys look like you're of the age of adulthood, so visualizing your dreams is very important. Come on, do so, and see what happens."

Ben just looks at his friends wondering if they know what Jegu is talking about because he doesn't and seems like his friends don't either judging by their faces. They stay silent until, all of a sudden, Slam snaps his fingers.

"Oh, I see now. Man, I meditate all of the time, so I know what to do." Slam says, nodding.

He clasps his hands together and bows his head like he's praying, similar to Uri before he uses his special ability.

Then, all of a sudden, a bright light appears around Slam, and they all gasp. When the light disappears, all The Wolf Pack's eyes go wide.

Slam's clothes changed to a black top hat and a tuxedo, looking like an old-school magician. He laughs as he takes a good hard look at himself. He then takes his top hat off and it suddenly becomes large. He does the most peculiar thing and jumps inside it, then suddenly it disappears.

"What the hell?" Baxter mumbles.

"Wow, I can't believe it! It actually works!"

The Wolf Pack all jump and turn to find Slam emerging from his hat behind them.

"What the heck is going on here?" Baxter frowns and points at Slam. "How the hell did you do that?"

Slam just shrugs. "You know what, I have no idea myself. I just did what Jegu said in visualizing my dream. I always wanted to be a magician, and then suddenly, poof!" Slam takes his big top hat, makes it normal-sized, and puts it on his head. "Man, this is neat. It's like I'm making my dreams come to life. This is amazing!"

He jumps around and plays with his top hat, making it large and small. He then makes a bunch of top hats appear and goes through one of them and comes out another.

"Hm, that kid has got some imagination." Jegu says.

They all look down at him.

"How's that even possible?" Baxter asks.

Jegu shrugs. "He just did what I told him. He visualized his dream, and it looked like it came true for him." Jegu's head bobs as he follows Slam, who's going through all of his top hats like a madman. "I gotta say, it's a pretty weird dream to have, but I'm not here to judge."

"And you guys can do it too," Uri chimes in. "Come on, visualize the dream you have. Something that you always want to become. Come on!" Uri uses his ability to turn into a kestrel, and he starts flying around, laughing.

The Wolf Pack just look at each other. Tom closes his eyes for a moment, then suddenly his whole-body glows like Slam's did. When the glowing stops, Tom is wearing golden medieval-style armor. The armor is so immaculate that the sun is reflecting on it. Ben covers his eyes, but everyone gasps as Tom makes a sword and shield appear out of nowhere.

"Hmm, a soldier, huh?" Jegu examines Tom. "Hm, I can see that you are the type of person who likes to protect and defend the people he loves. Is that correct?"

"Um, yes, sir."

Jegu smiles. "Well, Tom, it looks like you're a very mature and grown-up man. Very good if you want to become successful at your special abilities."

Tom nods.

Jegu looks back at the rest of The Wolf Pack as they all try to use their heads and visualize what they want to be. Ben finds it more difficult than he expected. He doesn't really know what he wants to do when he grows up. It's really hard because all of his life, he just wanted to have fun with his friends and become rich like The Cougars. *Come on, brain, think!*

It's very hard to think when you're hungry. Ben's tummy is rumbling. He hasn't eaten anything ever since they left Earth. Now he's hungry and it doesn't help that they went through the Sweetopian village and all he could smell was the beautiful food that these nice Sweetopians were making at their shops.

Suddenly, he sees another glow coming from his friends.

It is Honey.

The glowing around her body stops and she's wearing a cute yellow dress with colorful flowers all over. She has a flower crest on her head. She snaps her fingers and suddenly a bunch of flowers come out of nowhere out of the ground.

"Ah, beautiful, Honey," Jegu says. "I can tell that you want to become a healer, is that true?"

Honey nods and smiles at Jegu. "Yeah, I really want to become a nurse. I also want to have a big garden as well."

Jegu smiles. "Ah, I see. You're a precious young woman. You'll be a good wife one day."

Honey blushes, and Ben does as well.

He tries to push down the embarrassment and concentrate.

Suddenly, Cedric's body glows, but when it fades, he's wearing the same old clothes. However, he has a lasso in his hands, and he starts swinging it doing tricks with it. Going through it like a dog going through a hoop.

Jegu looks over. "Ah, interesting, it seems your attire didn't change at all, young man. Well, Cedric, you must be very good at using ropes and doing whatever you're already doing, because it looks like you already have what you want, you just want to build more skills around it."

Cedric smiles. "Yeah, well I don't really care about standing out and being all fancy with it. I just want to keep it simple."

Jegu smiles and nods. "And sometimes simplicity is the best."

Suddenly, Baxter's body starts glowing, then fades to reveal a straw sombrero that is as big as Baxter's ego and a black and red poncho that is covering his shoulders, making him look like a big tortilla chip. He takes a good look at himself and smirks. He snaps his fingers, and a bunch of bombs appear around him. He starts throwing the bombs up in the air and they explode.

Ben covers his ears from how loud the explosives are.

"Jesus Christ, man! Why did you do that?" Cedric yells out.

Baxter just ignores him and laughs. "Oh, man. This is neat! Now I can create any bomb I want."

Baxter starts jumping around and starts exploding bombs everywhere.

Jegu just stares at Baxter as he is running around. "Hm, that kid has quite an explosive personality."

Now that Baxter has found his special ability, Ben's the only one who hasn't.

Come on brain, think.

Ben tries to focus on one thing at a time—what he wants to do with his life—but his mind keeps jumping between ideas. He wants to help his friends, but that's too vague. How does he turn that into a real dream?

Rrrr.

Great, his stomach's growling again. He can't think straight when he's this hungry. All he can picture is a juicy hamburger.

Rrrr.

Drool starts to form.

Suddenly, a bright flash blinds him for a moment. When the light fades, a hamburger is floating right in front of him. Finally, food! He grabs it and devours it.

When he looks up, Uri, Jegu, and Chuck are watching him—completely baffled.

"Hmm, it seems like your passion, Ben, is food. Are you a chef or something?" Jegu asks.

"Nah, I'm just very hungry." Ben laughs awkwardly.

"Hmm, well your first ability is always the thing you're most passionate about, but it seems like you are passionate about a lot of things, Ben, which is very good for a young man like you, because it's good to be enthusiastic to try a lot of things." he paused. "However, it could also be bad in a sense that you want to do so many things that you can't choose, which leads to procrastination and hesitation. I can see that based on how long it took you to think about a dream, Ben."

Ben laughs awkwardly. "Yeah, well. I just got a lot of things in my head. It's just I'm afraid of failing."

Jegu just gives a grin. "Ah, don't be so hard on yourself. You're young! I mean, look at your friends here…" Jegu turns around and nods toward the others, who are trying out their individual abilities.

"You see, they have their own passions, their own goals they want to accomplish." Jegu looks up at Ben and has one of his claws around his mouth like he's going to tell Ben a secret. "But just wait and see what's going to happen to them in just a few seconds."

Just a few seconds after Jegu speaks, Ben looks over and sees his friends' powers vanish all at once. Like a wolf pack suddenly scattered, each member looks confused and lost.

Slam, the new and naive pack member, is the first to notice. His clothes shift back to normal, and the top hats he made disappear.

Tom, the dignified wolf, watches his golden armor fade away—along with his sword and shield. What once shone brighter than the sun now looks dull and lifeless. Without his armor, Tom doesn't know how to defend himself.

Honey, the alpha female, loses her beautiful flower dress—the one the alpha male always admires. Still, she looks striking, even as she walks cluelessly over the same dirt that once bloomed flowers beneath her feet.

Cedric, the alpha male's best friend, swings his lasso confidently—until he realizes he's swinging nothing.

Baxter, the Mexican wolf, sees his poncho, sombrero, and even the bombs he created start to vanish into thin air.

Baxter frowns and looks at Jegu. "Hey, what's the big deal here, old lizard? Why did my power suddenly disappear?"

Jegu shrugs. "It's because you haven't done the next step yet."

Baxter raises an eyebrow. "The next step? What next step?"

Jegu smiles. "Well, you can't expect to accomplish your dreams instantly. You need to put in the effort and practice so you can accomplish your dreams."

Baxter crosses his arms and looks to the side. "Psh, man, isn't that great. It looks like you can't have everything in this place too."

Jegu giggles. "Well, you can't expect life to give everything you want, but what will help you to accomplish your dream is to have confidence and be hopeful." Jegu points his claws at his head. "You see, your powers come through here: in your mind. Some creatures say that the physical things you see is all that matters, but it's what you don't see is the most important source of your powers. Putting faith into what you don't see will help you endure and work hard to continue to try and see if you actually can do it. Your mind is your biggest weapon."

Tom looks at Jegu intently. "What should we be doing now? Just continue to learn what we can do to help our powers?"

Jegu nods. "Exactly! You have to keep learning. Trial and error. There are so many ways in which you can learn from. You can learn from books, you can have someone personally teach you, or with technology these days, you can also learn from watching videos. There're tons of sources to learn from. Just be careful and make sure you don't blindly follow every source you read or hear. You need to make your own assessment and make your own decisions. I will try to guide you in the way you should walk, but you need to have time to do things by yourselves and learn things on your own. You guys got that?"

The Wolf Pack just look at each other. They all then look at Jegu and nod.

"Good, well off you go then. There's a library in our village and there's tons of our fellow Sweetopians who are nice enough to teach you, so don't be afraid to ask them for help. I'll be in my cottage, so if you need me, you know where I am." Jegu looks at Uri and Chuck, who are standing next to him. "You two, I actually need to discuss something with you guys. Will you come with me?"

Uri and Chuck nod. The three of them wave goodbye to The Wolf Pack who all look at each other.

Ben knows that they're all thinking the same thing. Now that they know they can use special powers, this motivates them to want to learn more. Learn more about who they are, what they can do, and how they can accomplish it. Their eyes are now wide, open to the possibilities. Now they seem end-less.

Ben's hands fidget as he watches his friends light up with new powers—eyes wide, smiles breaking out like sunbeams.

Laughter bubbles up around him, and the air feels electric with possibility. Yet, a knot tightens in his chest. His own dream feels blurry, like a distant echo he can't quite catch.

But the moment shimmers with hope. They've unlocked something real—something that could change everything.

Still, Ben's gaze flickers to Uri, steady and serious. The weight of their mission presses down: keep Uri safe, find his parents. The Ferals—deadly, skilled—and those whispered Babylonians loom like shadows they're not ready to face. They're raw, untested.

Ben shakes the thought away for now. Hunger gnaws louder than fear. If his power's just making food appear, maybe that's not so bad—at least not yet. Tomorrow's problems can wait. First, he's headed to the Sweetopian markets. Because right now, he's starving.

Chapter 18- Recipe

A human walks down a dirt path—but it's not dirt at all. It's made of crushed cookie crumbs. On this planet, you *can* eat everything, though it's not wise. If everyone did, there'd be nothing left. Like any land, this place needs care and cultivation to grow more sweets—more sweets means more food for more creatures. Every creature plays a part. Ben wonders what his role is here, how he can help.

Mmm, this food is good.

Sweetopians aren't just kind—their food is delicious. Taking a break, Ben visits the local market and indulges in the rich, sugary treats. Everywhere he looks, colorful trees and plants grow, bursting with the sweetest fruits in the universe, or so a Sweetopian told him. This place feels like a kid's dreamland—you can eat all the sweets you want and still have plenty of open land to play. Surprising, considering Sweetopia is much smaller than Earth.

What's more surprising is how happy the Sweetopians are, despite their struggles. They aren't recognized by the League of Nations—their planet is too small and too sparsely populated. Without registration, they lack protection, leaving them vulnerable to ruthless gangs who prey on unprotected worlds. So, the Sweetopians defend themselves.

Ben hates seeing the powerful bully the weak. It reminds him of Uri's stories about the Kingdom of Zion, destroyed by ruthless enemies. It's not fair. Ben vows to protect Uri and the Sweetopians if any threat comes. Knowing he and his pack now have special abilities only fuels his determination.

If only he could figure out his own dream. Then maybe he could unlock a new ability—something better than just making food appear. What kind of power is that anyway? Jegu told him it's wise to stick with what he knows for now. Mastering one ability is better than confusing himself with many. Jegu insists every power is special, even food-making, and believes Ben can use it in ways he hasn't imagined. Ben doesn't fully see it yet but trusts Jegu's experience.

As Ben walks, he spots Tom nearby, scribbling furiously on a large whiteboard. Ben doesn't understand the words he's writing but moves closer to ask. Next to Tom lie a sword and shield. Sweat and dirt streak Tom's face, but he keeps writing without looking up. Ben raises an eyebrow.

"What are you doing?"

Tom doesn't stop writing.

"I'm making a step-by-step plan."

"A step-by-step plan?"

Tom finally stops writing and looks at Ben.

"Yeah, since Jegu says that our special abilities connect with our dreams, then that means a step-by-step plan would probably help."

"Help? Nah, listen." Ben points at Tom. "You're only wasting your time, Tom. You need to stop writing and start doing."

"Man, you really don't know how to make plans, do you? No wonder every time you have a plan to defeat The Cougars, it always fails."

"Hey, they don't always fail. Some work."

"Yeah, that's only because you're lucky. You need an organized plan, Ben. Otherwise, what are you going to do if an unexpected thing happens to your plan?"

"I'll just make a new one, duh."

"Yeah, then you'll be wasting your time thinking of a new plan on the spot instead of just preparing beforehand with your first plan."

"Why would I need a plan for a plan? Sorry, it doesn't make sense to me, Tom."

Tom just sighs and rubs his nose. "Ben, just think of a step-by-step plan as like a recipe. Your special ability is to make food appear out of thin air, right? You can make a step-by-step plan to master that ability by just looking at different recipes of foods you like, instead of just grabbing random ingredients and hope for the best."

Ben stays silent for a while.

A step-by-step plan is like a recipe.

He guesses Tom is right. Knowing him, he can't make anything good just out of his head, so he guesses he'll get a recipe, and he knows exactly what type of recipe he wants. Ben smacks his hands together.

"Ah hah! I know exactly what kind of food recipe I want."

"What?"

"Cotton candy."

"Cotton candy?"

"Yeah, think about it. Cotton candy is very colorful and fluffy. Nobody would expect it to be used as a weapon, but once they touch my cotton candy, it sticks to them, and they can't move. It's genius."

"Well, it's not the first food I would have thought of to be used as a weapon, but I guess it might work."

"I'm going to ask Jegu to give me a cotton candy recipe."

"Well, I'm just curious on how it's going to turn out for you. Good luck."

As Ben is about to walk away from Tom, he suddenly turns around.

"Hey, Tom."

Tom is about to get back to writing but looks back.

Ben smiles at him. "Thank you."

Tom quickly goes back to writing. "Sure."

Ben turns around and runs toward Jegu's cottage, determination sharpening his steps. Maybe this food-making ability feels like a dead end, but thanks to Tom's recipe idea, he's ready to make it work—turn it into a weapon to protect Uri.

A heavy cloud of doubt had settled over him earlier, watching his friends' powers flare while his felt so small. But now, something flickers inside him. His brain might feel useless sometimes, but it's still his. If he can find the right recipe, if he can learn to master this, maybe he can prove himself after all.

***

The big, soft marshmallow house is right in the alpha male's sight, but he's not hungry—plus, someone lives there. It belongs to a strange old brown velociraptor named Jegu. Ben's hoping to get a cotton candy recipe from him if he has one. From what Sweetopian villagers say, Jegu is called "The Great Candymaker," and this marshmallow house is where he makes all his sweets.

Ben wants to know more about this odd velociraptor. He only knows that Jegu oversees the whole Sweetopian village and is Chuck's father. That's about it. Now, standing just inches from the graham cracker door, Ben's ready to find out more.

As soon as he opens the door, a strong rush of candy scent hits him—much stronger than outside. The inside feels hollow, like a regular cottage, but the walls are sticky to the touch. Ahead is a large living room with a big couch and a TV. Next to the TV, an old lizard wearing glasses is reading a book.

Ben doesn't say a word. He moves quietly toward Jegu, like a stalker watching prey, and leans over to peek at the book. The print is too small for Ben to read.

"Oh, how nice of you to drop in, Ben. What do you need?"

Ben jumps. *Dang it. I got caught.* "Oh, nothing. I just want to know if you have a cotton candy recipe." Ben chuckles awkwardly. He knows his face is probably red like a cherry on a sundae, but he waits for Jegu's response.

Jegu laughs. "Oh, I see. Well, good thing for you is that I have tons of cotton candy recipes and I also have a machine for it as well. I'll be glad to teach you how to use it."

Ben smiles. "Thank you."

"Sure, just let me get done with my studying of the Holy Scriptures and I'll help you."

Holy Scriptures?

So that's what he is reading.

Ben should have guessed the book was religious—Jegu is part of Uri's faith. Uri told him the Holy Scriptures are called the Bible. At first, Ben didn't think much about Uri being religious, but since arriving on this strange planet, his curiosity has grown.

He's been wondering about their God, Jehovah, especially since his mom died of cancer. That loss left a hole filled with questions he can't shake. Why did God take her away? What's the meaning of life if we're just here by chance? The things school taught him about evolution only deepened the confusion. If life is random and ends in death, then what's the point?

Ben's been searching for answers—trying to unravel life's mysteries—but so far, he's only found more questions. Maybe Jegu can help. Ben feels lost on his own, hoping this Great Candymaker holds some kind of wisdom.

"Umm..." Ben stutters before he speaks up. Jegu stops his reading and looks at Ben. "Hey, I want to know, why do people die?"

Jegu chuckles. "Oh, wow. That's a deep question. Why do you want to know that?"

"Well…" Ben stutters again. "I just want to know why God took my mom away to heaven. My mom taught me that God is loving, but if he is loving, then why did He allow my mom to suffer?"

"Oh, wow. I'm sorry to hear about your mom, Ben. That's sad. I lost my wife and son to death; it was very hard for me too."

"Your son?"

"Yeah, I used to have two sons. Chuck is one of them, he's the oldest. He loved his younger brother so much. It was very hard for me and him to cope over his death as well as the death of my wife when both got into that spaceship accident."

"I'm sorry."

"Nah, don't worry. It was nobody's fault. It was just that they were at the wrong place at the wrong time. Time and unexpected events overtake all of us no matter who we are. That's what the Holy Scriptures say, but the Holy Scriptures also give us hope for the future. I like to show you something. Notice what it says here at Revelation, chapter twenty-one, verse three and four…" Jegu takes his Bible book and flips some pages. He gives Ben the book and points at a section of words. "'God… will wipe out every tear from their eyes, and death will be no more, neither will mourning nor outcry nor pain be anymore. The former things have passed away.' So, Ben, what feelings do you have when hearing these words?"

Ben says. "Well, they give me peace, they give me hope that God will take care of things."

Jegu smiles. "Exactly, but you notice that it says no more death and no more pain. This scripture talks about a future hope that us servants of Jehovah have. It's the hope that the whole universe will be a paradise and our loved ones will be resurrected and we will get to see them again. How does that make you feel?"

"Good, but it sounds too good to be true."

"You know, I agree with you, it does sound too good to be true, but I want to tell you something Ben. Why did you come with Uri to this planet?"

"Umm, because I felt bad for Uri. I saw that he was a good guy, and he had these cool powers. Knowing that it's possible that I can have special powers too was the reason why I came here."

"But yet, you barely know who Uri is, yet you still want to help him. Why?"

"I don't know, because I know he is a good kid and I love him and I have hope that I can become successful in protecting him."

Jegu smirks. "Ah, you see. It's hope that's driving you. That's what drives us servants of Jehovah to keep on working despite the powerful creatures that are against us, like The Babylonians. In order to build that hope, though, you need God's word. How about you try reading the Holy Scriptures and see if it answers your questions."

Jegu taps the Bible, motioning Ben to take it. Ben, however, shakes his head. "Uh, I don't know. This is all new to me. I'm not sure if I trust it."

Jegu shrugs. "Hey, that's fine. I'm not going to force you to do something you're not comfortable with. How about I look for that cotton candy recipe for you?"

"Uh, yeah sure. By the way, what's up with your hair? I don't think velociraptors can grow hair." Ben points at Jegu's funky afro.

Jegu chuckles. "Yes, you're right. Velociraptors can't grow hair. In fact, this is not hair at all. It's fake hair made out of chocolate. I just love wearing it. Come on, take a piece and taste it for yourself."

Jegu takes a piece of his afro and eats it. Ben grimaces at the sight of it. Still, he's curious. He cautiously takes a piece out of Jegu's afro. It looks like hair, and it even feels like hair. But the smell gives it away as chocolate. Ben closes his eyes and smells it, so he won't puke afterwards. He takes a bite. Ben's eyes shot up.

"Hey, not bad." Ben grabs another tiny piece.

"Aw, you see. Things are not so bad once you try them. That's kind of like reading the Bible in a way."

"Really? How is that?" Ben asks.

"Well, when you look at the Bible, it doesn't look very appetizing to read, does it? I mean look at how thick it is." Jegu takes hold of his Bible for Ben to analyze. "But if you take just a simple piece of it, like you did with my hair, then you'll see how good it is." Jegu hands Ben his Bible again.

Ben flips through the random pages of this thick ancient book. This Bible has seen some wear and tear over the years. Some of the cover material is peeling a little, but this might be an answer Ben is looking for after all the things he learned. Ben tries to smile at Jegu, showing his consideration.

"Thank you. I'll read some time."

Jegu smiles. "Hey, no problem. If you got any more questions, just ask."

Ben nods and they head toward the kitchen.

He's got a recipe now to help guide him with his new skill, his new special ability, and an old velociraptor trying to teach him how to operate a cotton candy machine.

He also has something to help guide his life, the Bible.

He's not sure if it can help him. But perhaps? He's tried to look for answers about life ever since his mother passed away. If it's true, if he is able to see his mother again, then that would be a dream come true, but that just sounds too good to him.

Chapter 19- The Ability Struggle

Mothers are always the best when it comes to cooking the most delicious meals, grandmas too. Ben has an Italian grandmother from his mom's side. She would make the most amazing Italian dishes when they visited her house. Ben would be afraid of how her grandmother would react right now as he struggles to do the simple task of making cotton candy.

He tries to put some different mixed flavors in the cotton candy sugar. When he puts the sugar in the spinner head, the heat turns the sugar into random strings of fairy floss. Ben twirls his stick around and collects all the cotton candy.

He takes a bite. It's certainly good for food, but is it good for a weapon? Ben throws the stick with the rest of the trash. There's a gigantic hill of sticks behind him. He's getting tired of making cotton candy now. He's wondering if he can make other types of confections. Maybe chocolate.

He knows that Jegu's son, Chuck, is an expert on chocolate. With the name "The Chocolate Monster", he must be a good fighter as well. He could probably teach Ben how to fight with his cotton candy, and maybe teach him some new candy recipes. For now, Ben wants to take a rest. He's been stuck in the kitchen all day and needs a breather.

Ben stares at the big pile of sticks one last time. He's not sure if this food making ability is useful. His other pack members are probably already accomplished with their abilities. The only thing he can do is make candy. There's just no use.

He takes a brisk walk on a random cookie crumb road. Where this road will lead him, he doesn't know. Hopefully to see his friends. To laugh with them.

He expected to see a colorful raptor come up to him, to say hi. To smile at him, giving him the joy that he is worthy to keep on going. Instead, he sees nothing. Not even a tree or a bush. It's all flat with a cookie crumb path that leads to somewhere.

There's a sudden green in the corner of his eyes. A random raptor hiding behind bushes for some reason.

Ben gets close to this brown velociraptor, and realizes that it's Chuck, the expert chocolate maker himself. It's a good thing he spotted him.

An unusual sight Ben is seeing, though. He doesn't know why The Great Candymaker's son is hiding behind a bush. Ben gets closer to the peculiar raptor.

"Hey, Chuck. What are you doing?" Ben shouts.

The raptor jumps in a frenzy. Those antennae are flashing a million miles per hour that Ben can't even understand. He just looks over Chuck. There's a giant strawberry orchard behind him. Rows and rows of colorful berries.

In the middle is a random raptor that is as pink as this strange planet. The raptor looks like a female; she has a strawberry crown on her head.

Beside this pink raptor is another female, a human named Honey. That female human Ben could stare at all day if he wanted to. Especially with that strawberry crown she's also wearing.

She's talking and giggling with the pink raptor. They don't seem to notice him and Chuck.

"Who's that pink raptor, Chuck?"

A little pink forms on Chuck's cheeks. He looks down shyly, not saying anything with his flashing antennae. Ben is putting two and two together to take a full picture of the puzzle piece and realizes— *Chuck is being a peeping Tom.*

Ben giggles. "Oh, I see. You like that raptor, don't you?
Chuck nods.

"Why don't you talk to her?"

Chuck immediately shakes his head "no."

"Oh, come on." Ben pushes Chuck out of the bush and into the open. His pink crush finally spots him, and so does Honey.

The pink raptor smiles. "Oh, hi there Chuck. Why have you guys dropped by?"

If Chuck wasn't blushing now, his face is practically a cherry on top of a chocolate sundae, and the chocolate sundae is melting. Chuck's whole entire brown body is shaking and shrinking smaller than it has before until he couldn't take it anymore and runs away. Ben gets blown off as Chuck runs past him.

"What was that all about?" The pink raptor says.

Ben swears that he's going to kill Chuck for leaving him in an awkward situation. Now Ben's lover, the alpha female of his pack is just staring at him like a fool. Ben laughs awkwardly and shrugs. He immediately runs away, following Chuck the best he could.

***

Never thought being inside a big marshmallow would make him feel safe, but Jegu's cottage is a perfect place for Ben to relax and reflect on what he should do with his food making ability. Chuck is sitting right beside him, contemplating life. Whatever thoughts a brown raptor has, Ben doesn't even now, but they both needed to catch their breath after running for a while.

The running actually helped Ben. Help get his struggles out of him. The very need to get all his frustration out running helped him stay silent, reflect on why he's here in the first place.

He's here to help Uri, not himself. This ability needs to help Uri.

Ben looks at Chuck, the young brown raptor smiles at him, quiet. He never thought he could relate to an alien raptor before, but Chuck is just like him in a strange way. Now hearing the story from his father about how his mother and brother died is completely sad. Loss brings loneliness, and loneliness brings sadness.

Ben can tell Chuck's smile is of trying to hide the pain, covering it up with fake joy. Ben tries to match his smile.

"Hey, who was that pink raptor? What's her name?" Ben asks.

Chuck blushes, but he grabs a nearby piece of paper and pen. He writes something down and hands it to Ben. The paper reads: Strawberry Shores.

"Strawberry Shores, huh? That's pretty. I know she likes you."

Chuck doesn't even flash his antennae in response. Instead, he just looks down. Ben scratches his head as always when something awkward occurs.

"Hey, uh, where's your dad?"

Chuck writes on the paper again and the paper reads: Out teaching people.

"Oh, I see." Ben nods.

He understands. Jegu must be a very busy raptor based on how much Ben has seen him running in and out of his cottage. According to what he has heard, Jegu is an overseer, and overseers are very busy people and have busy roles in the Brotherhood of Zion. Ben finds the servants of Jehovah to be very interesting ever since he first learned Uri is one. He wonders if he can learn something from Chuck.

"Hey, Chuck..." Ben pauses, and rubs his head again. "Um, I don't want to be a bother, but I wonder if you can help me with making chocolate. I found this cool chocolate cake recipe that I want to make."

Chuck smiles and writes on a piece of paper: *Yeah, sure. Glad to help!*

Ben says. "Thank you."

So, they're in the kitchen. They cleaned all the cotton candy mess and moved to a different kind of mess. This time, with chocolate. He's having a fun time with The Chocolate Monster himself, even though he's struggling a lot with the recipe.

One moment almost blew up the whole oven and they had to extinguish the fire before Jegu's cottage would actually become a burnt marshmallow. Still, they laughed and played like kids on a kid-filled planet full of imagination until the beautiful pink sky turned dark as black licorice.

The day is over, night is beginning. Ben loves it when it is nighttime. The smell of the air is different. The smell of sweets in the day turns into the smell of dark licorice at night. To some, the smell of black licorice may not be as welcoming, but Ben kind of likes it. It takes him back to when he used to draw pictures with his smellable markers, black licorice was one of the marker scents.

He looks up at the Sweetopian moon. The only moon that's orbiting the planet. It's just a gigantic cheese ball. The yellowish cheesy moon stands out in the black. Nothing around this planet makes any physical sense, but it's not supposed to. For the Sweetopians, it's the imagination, it's the things spiritual, the things that you can make with your mind. That's what he remembered Jegu teaching. That's what he should always remember when practicing his ability.

But tomorrow is another day. The cheesy moon is telling Ben to go to sleep. Ben helps Chuck clean the kitchen, but before saying goodbye. Jegu appears as Ben sees him walking toward the cottage.

"How's it going Ben?" Jegu yells out.

"Good." Ben replies.

Jegu's black chocolate mustache and afro are as perked and fluffy as they could ever be. He smiles at Ben. "Oh, that's good. How's the progress with your special ability going?"

Ben shrugs. "I'm progressing, that's all I have to say."

"Well, that's good. At least you're getting better."

"Yeah..." Ben nods. He pauses for a brief moment, scratching his head. *Should I tell him?*

"Hey, Jegu."

"Yes, what is it?"

Ben pauses again. "Um... Well, I have been reading the Bible you gave to me."

"Really? You have? That's wonderful. And what do you think about those scriptures I recommended to you?" Jegu asks.

"They're very encouraging, thank you. I'm just wondering if you got some more."

Jegu laughs. "Oh, I definitely do have some more, but to make it easier for you and me, how about I give you a book that us Brotherhood of Zion use to study the Scriptures. It's called Insight on the Scriptures." Jegu looks at his son. "Hey, Chuck. Go into my office, will you please?" Chuck nods and goes inside the cottage. "I think you will find the book to be quite interesting, Ben. I can give you mine."

"Thank you."

"Sure, by the way, has any of your friends shown interest in what you're reading?"

Ben shakes his head. "Nah, not really. Just me."

Jegu nods. "Oh, okay. Well, I'm just glad to see you and your friends here. It may not feel like it, but you and your friends have been a lot of help for us Sweetopians. Please tell your friends that. In fact, let me just tell them myself. You're going to the bunkhouse, right?"

"Yes."

"Good, let me come with you. I want to tell all of you something."

Chuck finally arrives with the book in his claws and hands it over to Ben. Ben takes and looks at it. A big thick green book. Ben hates reading, especially books that are as thick as this. It's like reading school textbooks, but the thing is Ben is actually enjoying what he is reading. It's strange, he never thought of himself as a researcher, but Jegu has got him hooked on the Scriptures.

"Shall we get going? Chuck, you can come with us." Jegu says.

Ben and Chuck follow Jegu toward the nearby bunkhouse that Jegu keeps for visitors. That's where he and his Pack have been staying for the last five days since they arrived here. They get inside the bunkhouse made out of the same marshmallow material as the cottage.

Ben just loves feeling the squishy walls before heading in. It's oddly satisfying to the touch, but not too much touching before he decides to head in. His pack members, including Uri, are lying around on their bunk beds. Honey is the first one to notice them. She grabs a hold of Ben's arms.

"Hey, Ben. Had a fun time today?" She asks.

"Yeah."

She smiles. "Oh, that's good. How's the progress of your ability going?"

Ben shrugs. "It's getting there, but still trying to figure it out though."

Honey nods. "Yeah, me too. I'm still trying to figure out how the plants grow in this colorful environment. It's interesting. They are not like the plants on Earth. Never thought candy canes could grow on trees. By the way, what were you and Chuck doing when I was with Strawberry Shores?"

Chuck's face is red, but Ben chuckles. "Oh, that? That was nothing. We're just goofing off."

Honey analyzes Ben up and down like a nurse giving a checkup. "I can see that." She chuckles. "It looks like you had a fun time in the kitchen."

Ben is wondering why Honey is checking him out until he looks at himself. All his clothes, from his dark hair to his jean shorts, are covered in chocolate goo. It has been a fun day. Ben laughs at himself. "Yeah, I guess I have. I'm going to take a shower now."

"Wait, hold on." Jegu interrupts Ben's focus on the shower. He and his Pack look at Jegu intently. Jegu coughs before he speaks. "I'm sorry to interrupt you like this, but I would like to invite all of you to a special gathering we Sweetopians are having at the village center."

Tom looks at Jegu cock-eyed. "Special gathering? What for?"

"Oh, it's just a fun gathering I planned for guys. I enjoy all of your help with me and my village. Plus, I can see your efforts in trying to learn your special abilities. All of you are making good progress. That's why we're having a special gathering. I hope you guys can come."

Ben and his Pack members look at each other before answering. Ben finally blurts out. "Sure. We'll come."

Jegu smiles. "Oh, glad to hear it. It's going to happen tomorrow night, so be prepared. I hope all of you sleep well."

"Yeah, you too." Ben waves goodbye.

After Jegu and Chuck say goodbye, his pack chat amongst themselves. As for Ben though, the shower is calling his name. The only shower in the bunkhouse will hopefully be the only time that Ben will have to use it because cold water doesn't help the chills. Still, it's a nice home.

A home away from home.

But as long as he's with his pack, then he knows he's not alone.

Chapter 20- Ability Accomplished

Tom's POV, the police boy

Even after spending six days on Sweetopia, it's still strange to Tom that there's an actual planet, besides Earth, that has life forms on it. It doesn't get much weirder than a bunch of colorful talking velociraptors, or he sure hopes it doesn't get much weirder.

He doesn't know what other strange specimens there are throughout the universe, and to be honest with you, he doesn't really want to find out, but with Ben's stubborn insistence on always having an adventure, he feels he doesn't have much of a choice.

Tom thought Ben was out of his mind the first time he trusted Uri. Some strange kid shows up with a weird ability and a cryptic backstory, and Ben just... believes him. Tom didn't get it. Still doesn't. But he came along anyway—mostly to keep Ben from getting himself killed.

At first, this whole "special powers" thing felt like a joke. Ben was eager. Too eager. Tom expected disappointment, maybe a dramatic meltdown. What he didn't expect was standing here, summoning a damn sword out of thin air like some knight from his childhood fantasies. A sword. And a shield. Real. Solid. Heavy.

He's just walking on a random path right now, eating some colorful strings grown from a random tree he picked.

He still can't believe everything is edible around here, and it tastes good too.

Earlier, Jegu told him the others had gone through the same thing—figuring out their abilities, struggling with them, growing into them. He told Tom to head to the open field just outside the village. Said it was time for the next step. Tom didn't need a detailed explanation. He knows knights. He's been obsessed with them since he was a kid—swords, shields, chivalry. He always said he'd join the Army one day. Something about protecting people makes sense to him. Feels right.

The field is empty when he gets there. Just him and the wind rustling through the tall candy grass.

Then—he freezes.

Something shifts. The air. The pressure. A weird sensation crawls over his skin, like the world's holding its breath. His senses spark, alert. Something's coming.

Before he can move, a burst of heat slams the ground beside him—an explosion of light and sound. The shockwave throws him off his feet, and he crashes into a jagged pile of rocks.

Pain rips through his arm as he scrambles to sit up, cradling it, wincing through gritted teeth.

"Hey, come out, you idiot! I know you're here."

"Hmm, nice to see that you got senses too, police boy!"

Baxter is standing on a branch of one of the colorful Sweetopian trees over Tom.

"Err..." Tom growls. "You could have killed me, you bastard!"

"Psh, don't get angry. I didn't intend to kill you. That was only a test bomb. I was testing to see if you got skills, police boy, and it looks like you do."

Tom frowns at Baxter and holds his right arm. Baxter just smirks and chuckles. How did Ben make friends with this kid, anyway? Tom tried to get information from the kid on who he is, but he's very discreet. Tom never trusted him.

Baxter's smirk changes to a look of surprise as one of his legs starts jerking. He grabs his leg, but it keeps moving, then he flips over in mid-air, hovering in the air and bouncing around.

"Hey, what's the meaning of this? Get me down!" Baxter tries to pull his leg, but it's making him swing into the air like crazy.

"That's what you get, 'Mr. Inferno'."

Suddenly, Cedric emerges from a bush nearby. His hands are moving like he's holding onto a rope, but there's nothing there.

"Hey, cowboy! Get your stupid lasso off of me!"

Cedric shrugs. "Why would I do that? You're just going to throw bombs everywhere like a madman, anyway."

Baxter crosses his arms. "Fine, then. If you're not going to let me go, I'll do it myself."

Suddenly, Baxter pulls out a hunting knife from his pocket. A knife so big that it could be considered a sword.

Jeez, this kid had a knife this whole time?

Now Tom's trust levels are lowering to near the bottom. He could have stabbed him in the back before. Tom's lucky that he has a special power to protect himself with, but Baxter has one too and can throw bombs everywhere.

This kid's a maniac!

Cedric's eyes go wide. "Hey, what are you doing, you idiot?"

Baxter cuts through the invisible rope and crashes head-first to the ground. He rubs his head in pain after he lands. Groaning and moaning. Tom doesn't even feel bad for him. It was his own choice.

Cedric rolls his eyes. "Man, you truly don't have any brain cells, do you?"

Tom just shakes his head and inspects his arm. It's covered in scratches, but in moments, they disappear. He doesn't feel any pain either. However, he feels something on his right leg and looks down to find a vine wrapped around it. Wait a minute, this is—

"Are you alright?"

Tom looks back to see Honey. The vine disappears.

Tom nods. "Yeah, I'm alright. Where's Ben?"

Honey shrugs. "I don't know. The last time I saw him was when he was in the kitchen of Jegu's cottage."

"Yeah, he's coming. I just met him a few seconds ago."

Tom raises his eyebrows when he hears Slam's voice, but Slam is nowhere to be seen. Tom looks down to find a top hat on the ground, and Slam pops out of it. Tom and Honey jump.

"Oops, sorry." Slam rubs his head. "I didn't mean to scare you guys. Man, this ability is cool! I can go everywhere I want to in an instant."

A bunch of top hats appear around Tom and Honey. Slam just jumps into one and out of another. Suddenly, most of the top hats disappear, leaving only one. Slam jumps out of it and lands on his feet. He picks up the hat and puts it on his head.

"I'm a magician now."

"Oh, great. Just make sure you don't appear next to me, or I'll blow you up." Baxter points at Slam.

Slam rubs his head. "Heh, heh. No problem."

Tom raises an eyebrow at Slam. "You said you just met Ben a few seconds ago. You must know where he is?"

Slam nods. "Yep, in fact, he's already here. He's just waiting for all of us to be here so he can attack us with his ability. Isn't that amazing? Now all of us have special abilities."

Tom nods, then processes Slam's words. "Wait, what did you say?"

Suddenly, Tom senses something above them. He looks up and all he sees is a big pink thing coming down toward them. Oh, fantastic. You know, he really shouldn't have given Ben the recipe idea. Tom and Slam stand dumbstruck as Cedric, Baxter, and Honey try to run away. There's no escaping this one, they've helped Ben and now they have to face the consequences.

The cotton candy hits all of them.

Tom tries to dig his way out of the sticky mess. He finally reaches the surface and pokes his head out. He looks around and sees the rest of his friends poking their heads out one by one, like gophers. He then looks at the top of this massive mountain of cotton candy and sees Ben sitting on top with a mischievous grin.

"Hey, get us out of here, will you?" Baxter yells out.

Ben shrugs. "Sorry, I can't. You just have to eat your way out."

"Psh, I got a better idea."

Tom wonders what Baxter is planning to do until suddenly he sees a bunch of bombs surrounding them.

"Wait, no, stop!" Cedric yells out.

Tom can't believe Cedric hasn't learned yet.

There's no stopping stupidity.

Tom is just preparing for his fate as a massive explosion erupts, sending pink stuff and The Wolf Pack flying everywhere. He doesn't know where he's going to land.

Is it heaven? Is it hell? Is this how he dies?

Unfortunately, he doesn't die, even though he really wants to right now.

Tom lands on a soft pile of cotton candy, from one pink mess to another. Everybody else seems to be in the same sticky situation.

"Hey, are you serious? Get me out of here!" Baxter yells.

Tom turns around to see Baxter stuck to a tree with cotton candy, wriggling like a fly in a web. Good, for the sake of every creature in the universe, let him be stuck.

"Hey, Tom! Look at me!" Ben yells as he puts some cotton candy on his upper lip like he has a pink mustache. "Hey, Tom! I'm your dad!"

Ben then does an impression of Tom's dad, pretending he's holding a pistol and shooting it. Honey, Cedric, and Slam laugh at Ben like he's the funniest comedian the universe has ever seen.

Oh, great. I'm surrounded by a bunch of idiots!

Chapter 21- The Next Step

Uri, Chuck, and Jegu. The three alien musketeers.

One of them a human, the other two a strange subspecies of velociraptor. Three aliens walking down the cookie crumb path.

Then—splat!

A huge pink substance flies towards them. They try to escape, but they don't because they too are in a trap of helping the Earth human named Ben just like his pack is. It's too late for them. They have to deal with him now.

They get covered in sticky cotton candy. They try to move, but they move stiff. Uri starts tasting the cotton candy off of his body.

"Hey, not bad."

Uri smiles. But Chuck and Jegu just glare at all the mess The Wolf Pack created. All the Pack members are covered in cotton candy trying to move the best they can. Jegu just has to laugh.

Jegu thinks The Wolf Pack are an interesting bunch. He hasn't seen a group of humans like The Wolf Pack before. Never in his many years of traveling across the universe has he seen such interesting creatures. He guesses the Earth human race are a bunch of interesting individuals too. He laughs to himself.

"Hmm, it looks like they are ready for the next step."

Chuck and Uri just look at Jegu confused.

***

After some time, they all manage to clean off the cotton candy and line up next to Jegu's cottage. Jegu is standing in front of The Wolf Pack with Uri and Chuck, looking them over.

"Well," Jegu finally says, "now that you have yourselves cleaned up and it looks like you've mastered your abilities... er... sort of. Now, it's time to tell you the next step." Jegu pauses for a moment, all of them are just looking at him intently. "You must help others."

Baxter raises an eyebrow. "Help others?"

"Yes, help others. I know you've helped us Sweetopians out gratefully, without using special abilities. But now that you know how to use your powers, it's up to you whether you want to use your powers to help others or use them to help yourself. I have to warn you, though. If you choose to use your powers for your own gain, then it will help you become more successful, but later, you'll regret it. So, what are you going to choose?"

Ben smiles. "Pff, obviously we're going to use them to help others. That's what we came here for."

Jegu smiles. "That may seem obvious to you, but there are tons of creatures in the universe who feel the same way as you, but the temptation was too strong for them, and they succumbed to their own greed. I know you guys don't want to be Christians and I won't force you but remember this: If you encounter any challenges that test you and tempt you to do what's bad, try your best to do what's right."

Baxter rolls his eyes. "Yeah, yeah. We know. Why are you telling us this, old lizard?"

"The reason I'm telling you this is because there's an evil beast my people call The Blob. It dwells inside The Veggie Forests, and it keeps on attacking our village."

Tom asks. "Wait, The Veggie Forests?"

Jegu nods. "Yes, The Veggie Forests. These trees that you see near this town are actually vegetable trees. It's bark and everything tastes like broccoli or any vegetable you can think of."

Tom rubs his chin. "Hmm, interesting, and this 'Blob' lives inside these forests?"

"Yes, actually it came from an area that's called the Stem of Darkness. You probably saw a little black stem part of the land when you first landed here. That's the Stem of Darkness where all the dark creatures dwell." he takes a deep breath. "When our people first established this planet 40 years ago, this land wasn't as colorful as you see it today. This may come to a surprise to you, but there's multiple islands on this planet

226

and each island has a piece of land that's dark where these dark creatures dwell. We don't know where these creatures came from, but it's our job as Sweetopians to make sure these dark creatures don't destroy this land and make it as dull as it can be."

Slam snaps his fingers. "Oh, I see. So you want us to help you destroy these things?"

"Yes, in fact, The Blob just attacked the village center this morning and now we can't have our social gathering I planned. We need your help to defeat it. It's your decision if you want to help us, or you can just leave and do whatever you want."

"What? Of course, we'll help you." Ben blurts out.

"Yeah, we don't want to see your nice village get terrorized. We'll totally help you." Slam chimes in.

Jegu nods. "Thank you, it's great to hear that you guys want to help us, but it's easier said than done. You'll soon find out just how hard it is to do good." Jegu looks at Chuck. "Chuck is going to lead you to where we detected The Blob. Uri is coming with you as well. This is a test to see if you can actually use your powers to defeat a real evil creature. I'll be staying in the village just in case The Blob comes here while you're gone. May the holy spirit be with you guys because you'll definitely need it."

We'll definitely need it?

The Wolf Pack exchanges uneasy looks. Jegu's words shake them more than they want to admit. They're not sure what The Blob is, or how they're supposed to beat it—and honestly, they don't know why Jegu is trusting *them* with this at all.

But Ben… Ben believes.

He doesn't know what this evil creature looks like or how powerful it is, but he has faith in his friends. Faith that they can pull this off together.

Faith.

It's strange, hearing himself think that word. He used to hate it. After his mom died, he swore he'd never use it again.

But then Jegu gave him that Bible. Told him there was a paradise Earth. Told him he'd see his mom again.

Now, *faith* feels different—because it's not blind anymore. It's tied to something real. To *truth.*

Ben never even knew God had a name. But now he does. Now he understands what Uri means when he talks about truth—not just facts, but *spiritual truth.*

That's what these powers are built on. That's what all of this is connected to.

And maybe… just maybe… his friends will see it too, when they come face-to-face with the evil creature called The Blob.

He hopes they will.

He'll find out soon enough.

***

The Wolf Pack and Uri follow Chuck the best they can as he runs and jumps through the colorful forest that smells odd like broccoli. Broccoli is definitely not a sweet food, and certainly doesn't smell good as Ben covers his nose when following Chuck.

The whole environment of this vegetable forest seems eerie to Ben; it's like they're inside some witch's stew pot.

Steam is coming out of random spots on the ground. The ground smooches with every step they take, making it harder for them to dodge and navigate every morsel coming their way. A flying string bean, an exploding carrot. Ben has seen it all now.

Despite the tense moisture, like a ninja, Chuck easily jumps over a big old celery log that was in the path. Meanwhile, The Wolf Pack and Uri barely even get over the log before they see Jegu running again.

"Jeez, does this raptor ever stop? He's barely looking around," Baxter yells out.

"Well, it looks like he knows where he's going, so just try to keep up with him." Uri says.

Ben is falling behind the group. He's just distracted by the surroundings, looking around for any creatures, hopefully not evil creatures. He tries not to fall too behind, keeping eye distance away from his Pack.

"Ben."

A quiet whisper comes out of nowhere. Ben jumps.

"Ben."

Ben jumps again.

Who was that? Sounds familiar?

The bushes to his left rustle. Ben flinches, heart jumping. He stumbles back a step just as someone bursts through the branches.

"Jesus Christ, Honey. You scared me."

Honey puts her hand over her mouth and chuckles. "Ulp, sorry Ben."

Relief floods him—it's not a monster. Just Honey. But something feels off.

He expected her to be way ahead, chasing after Chuck. Yet here she is, popping out of a bush like she's been dropped from a tree.

Ben studies her, trying to make sense of it. Twigs poke out of her tangled hair. Bits of leaves cling to her hoodie. She looks like she's just wrestled with the woods—and lost. But somehow, she still looks like Honey. Still beautiful, in that wild, sun-kissed way she's always had.

The sight pulls something old and familiar out of him— memories of scraped knees, dirt under fingernails, and Honey always ahead of him, climbing trees barefoot. She hasn't changed. Not really. He realizes he's been staring.

"Honey, what are you doing here? I thought you went on ahead of me." He finally asks.

Honey smirks. "Oh, I just decided to fall behind, for me and you to be alone together..." she sways her hips seductively at Ben and wraps her arm around his neck. "To be private, to make love to you." She kisses him.

Ben blushes, he can't believe this is happening to him. Honey, alone, and she wants to make "love" to him. Ben wants this to keep on going, but he shakes his head.

This is wrong.

He immediately pushes her away.

"This is wrong, Honey. I can't do this. What's gotten into you?"

All of a sudden, a brown spear comes straight for him and Honey like a rocket. Ben immediately ducks away.

As for Honey, she gets hit...

Ben screams out loud, but then he gets confused.

"What the?"

He says under his breath. Blood doesn't come out of Honey. A bunch of black goo comes out of her.

What the hell is going on?

All of a sudden, Honey starts changing form. Honey isn't Honey anymore. Her body twists, warps—melts.

Ben freezes. His breath catches in his throat. In a matter of seconds, she's no longer Honey at all.

Something huge and shapeless towers in front of him— slick, black, and pulsing like a living shadow. The monster oozes upward, stretching as tall as the Sweetopian trees, its body shifting and churning like boiling tar.

Ben scrambles backward, palms scraping against the dirt. The creature lunges, rippling toward him with terrifying speed.

Then—

Chuck bursts through the trees.

Without hesitation, he charges straight at the thing. His claws flash in the moonlight. He slams into it with all his weight—

But the blob splits in half, letting him pass right through.

By the time Chuck skids to a stop and turns, the creature has already sealed itself back together.

Ben's heart pounds.

Is this... the Blob? The one Jegu warned them about?

The name fits—an ever-shifting, living mass of darkness. And the smell... it hits Ben's nose all at once. Thick, sharp, and strangely familiar. Black licorice. Just like the scent that drifts through the Sweetopian nights.

This blob opens its mouth, or what Ben assumes is the mouth, and roars, raining spittle on his clothing. *Great, I just cleaned those.*

"Ben!"

Ben glances over his shoulder. The real Honey is there—wild-eyed, out of breath, twigs tangled in her hair. She grabs his arm and pulls, trying to drag him away from the monster towering in front of them.

Behind her, the Pack leaps into action.

Baxter hurls a handful of summoned bombs toward the creature, but the Blob slithers aside with unnatural speed. The explosions echo uselessly across the field.

Ben swallows hard. If Chuck hadn't seen it coming... he'd be gone. Obliterated.

Jegu taught his son well—how to sense danger before it strikes.

Ben didn't feel a thing.

Now, Uri, Chuck, and the rest of the Pack are circling the monster, fanning out across the clearing. Chuck winds back and hurls a chocolate spear with force—but the Blob catches it mid-air and swallows it whole.

Not a scratch. Worse—it grows. The Blob swells in size, its body rippling, stretching, pulsing with a sick, hungry energy.

Then, without warning, it launches a burst of spear-like tendrils in every direction.

"DOWN!" Uri shouts.

They all dive, scattering for cover behind nearby boulders. Sharp, gooey spikes thud into the earth around them, sizzling where they land.

As everyone takes cover, Baxter yells out. "What the hell is that thing!?"

"Chuck says that's The Blob. Apparently it tried to tempt Ben with his sexual desires." Uri responds.

Ben blushes, but he frowns. "Well, isn't that just wonderful!"

Cedric asks. "How do we even get rid of this thing? The dark power of this creature is immense."

Uri shrugs. "Chuck says that he doesn't even know. It seems like if you try to get close to it, it will have a psychological effect on you like it did with Ben."

Tom growls. "Well, it looks like we can't even shoot at it either if it keeps on throwing million projectiles at us."

"Well, we can't just wait here!" Baxter says. He looks over at Tom who is lying next to him behind a rock. "Hey, make one of your shields and give it to me."

Tom raises an eyebrow. "I'm not giving you anything."

Baxter lends his hand. "I've got an idea. Just give me one of your shields."

"No!"

"God dammit! Just give me a shield so we don't die!"

"Alright, fine!" Tom makes a shield and reluctantly hands it to Baxter.

Baxter summons a bomb, the most powerful bomb he can ever make. He runs toward The Blob with the bomb in his hand, blocking the creature's projectiles with the shield as he closes in.

The closer and closer he gets to this creature. The darker he feels.

For ounce, Baxter actually feels scared. Afraid for his life. The first he ever felt this way, and hopefully the last.

Suddenly, the Blob opens its mouth and he throws the bomb inside.

The creature explodes, bursting into tiny pieces and creating a huge mess.

Everyone ducks for cover. Baxter lays in the middle of the clearing, covered in Blob goo. The others stare at him in shock as they emerge from hiding.

"What the hell kind of idea is that?" Ben walks up to Baxter to help him off the ground.

Baxter also thought it might have been a stupid plan, but at least it worked. Baxter just shrugs at Ben after he helps him off the ground. "I don't know."

"Well, I'm just glad you're alive." Ben pats him on the back and hugs him.

Baxter's eyes go wide when Ben surrounds his arm around his shoulders, like a father giving a hug to his son for a good job. Baxter has never felt a hug ever in his life, not even from his father.

But unlike fear, it actually feels nice. Baxter doesn't know what this nice feeling is, it feels weird. Baxter immediately tries to push Ben away. "Hey, what are you doing? Stop hugging me."

Ben let's go and chuckles. "Sorry."

Baxter grumbles and backs slowly away from Ben.

Even though he hates to admit it, he likes the hug, but he knows that his face is red as he puts his hoodie over his head.

There's a reason why he wears it. To hide the embarrassment, to hide the pain.

Ben gets his attention off of Baxter when Cedric taps him on the shoulder.

"Shall we get going then?" Cedric asks.

Ben nods. "Yeah, let's tell Jegu that they don't have to worry about the Blob anymore."

Chapter 22- The Social Gathering

Civilization is near in sight of the beautiful hazel eyes of Ben.

We're here! Oh yeah baby!

The Sweetopian village has never looked so immaculate with its rainbow colors and the sunsetting behind it. Ben, Uri, Chuck, and his Pack got good news to spread to the Sweetopian masses. The good news of freedom, freedom from the monster that once terrorized but won't terrorize no more.

The Blob has been defeated!

Those words have been sticking in Ben's mind and are bouncing around through his skull. Full of energy, full of life, full of vigor.

Ben has no problem following Chuck through the woods unlike the others who are stuck behind like they're being tugged away on a leash, forced to come with Ben and his adventures. The only three who seem to have the same vigor are Uri, Slam and Honey. They follow Ben, smiles and laughter.

Chuck's antennae light up. ".- .-.. -- --- ... - / - .... ..-.."

"Chuck said that we're almost there." Uri translates.

As Chuck gets done with his flashing code, he resumes running until they reach the edge of the village. Ben can already smell the sweet goods the villagers are making. Ben's tummy starts rumbling, looking to be fed. He's exhausted and he's sure the others are exhausted as well.

A crowd of moving colors is a blur in front of Ben, but then he realizes that it is a crowd of nice Sweetopians waiting for them. Jegu is with the crowd, and they all have party hats on.

"Ah, hoy there travelers! Have you guys defeated The Blob?" Jegu yells out.

"Does this answer your question?" Baxter says. He shows Jegu his clothes that are drenched in the Blob's guts.

Jegu's eyes go wide. "Oh, my. You fought tough, haven't you?"

"Well, it was a very quick fight, but we defeated The Blob in the end." Tom says.

As soon as Tom finishes his sentence, the crowd of Sweetopians cheer. Confetti comes out of nowhere. They hug Ben and his Pack, including Uri and Chuck. Now Ben and his fighting buddies found themselves in another battle situation, the battle to escape the hugs. Baxter is the one who seems to actually fight with the hugs, he tries to push all of them away, but the hugs are a powerful creature that can take over everybody.

"Congratulations on your first spiritual battle with a monster! I'm so happy for you guys. You trained well." Jegu compliments.

Slam smiles. "Oh, it wasn't that bad. We didn't do much really. It's a shame that we can't have that social gathering you planned, Jegu. We would have loved it."

"About that. We tried to rebuild the village community center. Unfortunately, it's going to take some time, but not to worry because I've decided to have the party at my cottage. It's big enough. Plus, we'll be having the party outside anyways. We invite you guys to come."

Apparently Jegu wasn't looking for a response because literally he and the crowd of Sweetopians pushed Ben and his Pack to the journey of partiness.

***

There're more people than Ben expected. Practically the whole village has arrived. He would have never guessed all the villagers cared about them, or at least thought of them. All the Sweetopians are laughing and talking to one another. Uri is part of the joyful crowd, meanwhile Ben and his Pack are standing awkwardly in the middle.

Even though nobody is actually looking at them, Ben still feels like a hundred eyeballs are staring, watching every move he makes. *Damn my social anxiety.*

All of a sudden, music blasts through the speakers—and Ben's worst nightmare begins.

Dancing.

Dancing, of all things. An unfortunate family trait passed down from his dad, who somehow managed to win over Ben's mom with moves so cringey they probably broke the laws of physics. If only Ben had inherited that same shameless confidence. But he doesn't. So he stands there, frozen, while colorful raptors bounce and groove all around him.

The music is *loud*. Not just loud—planet-shaking. If they had blasted this during the Blob fight, it might've exploded from the sound waves alone. Instead, the only thing exploding is Ben's eardrums.

At the DJ booth, a Sweetopian bobs his head like he's trying to exorcise demons. Around him, raptors lose themselves in the rhythm, flailing joyfully, totally ignoring one another.

Uri and Slam dive into the chaos, caught up in the energy.

Ben feels a tug on his shirt. He turns—and there's Honey, grinning.

"Join me on the dance floor, Ben!" Honey asks.

She doesn't wait for a response. Her hand grabs his, pulling him into the glowing swirl of light and sound. It's supposed to be magical, hypnotic, but Ben resists every step. He doesn't move. Doesn't sway. Doesn't care for the spell of lights and beats.

Honey doesn't give up. And she's not the only one. Other Sweetopians push his Pack mates toward the dance floor like it's a mission. Even Chuck, who's lingering near Strawberry Shores, gets nudged into the pit by her.

"Come on, Ben! Dance with me."

Honey grabs him by the hands, and she does a dance serenade with him. Ben looks at her eyes, her beautiful smile, and for once... He's happy.

Everything is going well. Until Ben feels exhausted and can't move anymore. Honey has been worrying him out with her moves.

What a woman.

Ben thinks to himself as he rests on a random bench near the dance floor.

He's drinking water. He never thought water was so sweet before.

Honey has gone off somewhere. To somewhere Ben doesn't know, but he's glad that he escaped the dance torture. The rest of his pack is resting with him.

"Alright everyone, it's time for dessert!" Jegu yells out.

He's near a large table decorated with all sorts of sweets, but then out comes a big cake, the biggest cake Ben has ever seen. The ones pulling this massive cake are Honey and a few others. The cake is a big castle. The castle pastern has frosting words that read: Thank You Wolf Pack!

It was kind of a cute cake. Too bad he has to devour it now. There're decorative statues on each of the castle towers that look like wolves. There're six wolves, representing him and his friends.

Jegu hands Ben a knife.

"The alpha goes first." He says.

Ben takes the knife and does his first slice until somebody pushes him. Ben stumbles and lands headfirst into the cake. He can hear everyone around him gasp.

A face-full of frosting, some even got into his nostrils. The castle is ruined and he's the fallen soldier.

Ben looks at the culprit. The alpha female puts her hand over her mouth, acting surprised, but he can see that little smirk under her hand telling him that she did that on purpose.

"Oops! Sorry Ben. My fault." Honey lends her hand.

This woman has another thing coming to her. Ben grabs her hand, but instead of pulling himself up, he pulls Honey into the cake depths with him. Another gasp of shock comes from the crowd around them, but—

"Food fight!"

Jegu yells out and throws a pile of cake at his son. Chuck chucks a pie back at his father.

Oh, boy. What did I start?

Immediately, he and Honey get back up as they see some Sweetopians trying to throw food at them.

A food battle begins. Everyone is throwing food at each other. A wild free-for-all. Some are flipping tables and chairs to protect themselves. Not a bad idea.

Ben hides himself behind a table. He totally lost Honey. He needs to make a plan on how to defeat these raptors if he's able to survive this battle. He assumes Chuck and Jegu are not on his side. He needs to regroup with his Pack, then figure out a plan from there.

Now that he's hidden, he's trying to look around for his Pack, if that's even possible. It's hard to see through all the flying cakes.

Suddenly, he feels a tap on his shoulder. He jumps a little when Honey appears out of nowhere.

She smirks. "How did you like that cake?"

Ben shrugs. "It wasn't bad," He smirks. "But I swore it tasted like strawberry and I thought I saw one of your hairs in it as well."

Honey blushes and chuckles. "Yeah, sorry. I had the idea of making the castle cake. Jegu and Strawberry Shores helped me."

Ben laughs. "Oh, I see. Well despite it being a joke, I liked it anyway. Thank you."

He gives Honey a hug, but not long after this embrace, comes trickery. He secretly grabs a piece of cake off the ground and merges Honey's face with it.

He immediately runs away from the alpha female that's cursing him like a storm. He continues to run despite getting hit by some sneaking Sweetopians. He hears somebody calling him. Tom is yelling behind a table.

Ben rushes to him like a puppy to its owner. Being saved, being reunited with his Pack once again. They always find a way to be together.

"Jesus Christ, man. Why did you do that for?" Cedric asks.

The rest of his boys are staring at him like he caused World War 3 to happen. Ben shrugs. "What? It ain't my fault. Honey had this planned all along."

Tom frowns. "Well, whoever planned it, I guess we just have to deal with it."

Slam smiles. "Oh, come on you guys. This is fun. What are the chances we get to do this at the school cafeteria back home?"

"Pff, yeah. If we do this at the school cafeteria, they would expel us for sure." Cedric says.

Ben frowns. "Nevermind school. We got a war with a bunch of raptors to deal with. What would you say is going to be the best strategy, Tom?"

Tom shrugs. "I don't know. It's going to be almost impossible. I don't know what side Uri is on, but if we find him, then we can up our chances of winning. It looks like your food making ability is finally useful at a time like this, Ben. We can use it for an endless supply of amo, but that still gives us a slim chance of surviving this thing."

Ben shrugs. "Either way, we're going to—"

Ben gets interrupted by a sudden female. The angry female jumps on him and pins him face down on the cookie crumb dirt. He tastes the cookie crumbs. Not bad actually. He looks behind at the bitter female that's ready to break his arm at any moment. Karma time.

Ben tries to get out of Honey's grasp, but Honey has him pinned down so hard like an assassin ready to end his life. *Jeez, where the hell does she get this strength?*

Honey grabs a random pie from the amo supply they have. Ben recognizes the flavor. It's pecan pie, Ben hates pecan. Why did she choose that one?

Honey slams the pie in his face. The immediate taste of that dull pecan makes Ben spit it out. After choking for a while, Ben looks at Honey. She has that smirk on her face again.

"Yeah, serves you right." She says.

Ben chuckles. "Hey, man, I'm sorry. Can we have a truce?"

Honey laughs. "Sure."

She finally lets go of Ben. He is finally free to live another day thanks to his merciful girlfriend. Now that she's here, his Pack is complete. Ben grins. "Okay, it looks like all of us are here. Is everybody ready?"

Tom nods. "Ready as we'll ever be.'

"Alright." Ben points towards a bunch of Sweetopians hiding behind a table. "Wolves, let's go!"

Immediately, he and his Pack charge at the Sweetopians. They do so with pies and cotton candy. It's time to do what wolves do best, and that's fight together.

***

Ben laughs with his Pack and Uri as some Sweetopians are cleaning all of the mess from the craziness. Ben and his Pack helped clean a little until Jegu says. "No, it's okay. Me and my friends will clean the rest."

Ben still wishes he could have stayed and help some more, but Jegu's persistence forces him and his Pack on a trail back to the bunk house.

When they walk back, they walk back slowly because of how stiff their clothes are and how sore their muscles are. Still, they laughed with each other, getting themselves cleaned up, and heading to bed.

As his friends take their beauty sleep in the cozy marshmallow, Ben just stares in silence, contemplating the night he had. Never knew that raptors could have so much fun, especially raptors that believe in God.

He's actually thinking about joining the Brotherhood of Zion. These servants of Jehovah are his kind of people. His Pack may call him crazy, but he's actually planning to ask Jegu what he can do to join the work these people are doing.

Every face he looks at from these Jehovah's servants are always happy, joyful. Ben wants to join that happiness... He's finally found it.

Chapter 23- Evil Comes Back

Nour's POV, the angry feline

Er... Where the hell are you going, Uri? Why won't you let me protect you? It's for your own good. Er... Jeez, when is this headache going to end?

"Nour, are you alright?"

"Yeah."

Tito and the others play cards around the big galley table, their laughter and chatter filling the room. Meanwhile, Nour lies on the galley couch, waiting—waiting like time itself stretches into an eternity. He can't stop thinking about the kid who's been slipping through his paws for months now, like a stubborn thorn stuck deep in his side.

They left that strange planet called Earth a few days ago, and honestly, Nour is relieved to be away from its chaos. Now, all he wants is to find Uri. He can't wait any longer. Uri has to be on another planet by now—but who knows what kind of creatures live there? Friendly? Hostile? Nour's mind jumps to the worst-case scenario every time.

He glances at his friends, casually shuffling cards as if none of this matters—that Uri might be in danger, somewhere out there. Frustration burns inside him. Without another word, Nour pushes himself up and heads for the cockpit, where Ginger pilots the BS Lion through the stars.

"Hey, Ginger. Has your tracker detected Uri yet?"

"No, it looks like he might have used super speed again. Wherever he is going, he must be very determined to get there. My tracking device isn't the most accurate thing in the universe, but it's accurate enough to tell me the general area where his space cruiser might be. Wait a minute..." Ginger looks over at a bright red light flashing on the detection screen. "I've found him."

"Wait, you found him? Where?"

"I don't know, some sort of planet. I'm looking over the information right now..." Ginger taps the tracker screen. "Strange, all it's giving me is the name."

"What's the name?"

"Sweetopia."

"Sweetopia?"

"That's what it says. There are no records from the League of Nations about this planet. It must not be registered."

"Do you know how to get there?"

"Yeah, I got the UPS set up already."

"Good. How far away are we?"

"Not that far actually. Only twenty minutes away."

"Only twenty minutes? Now you tell me!"

Nour runs back to the galley and slams his paws on the galley table to make all of his comrades' playing cards go flying into the air. "We found Uri's ship!"

Nader looks at Nour cock-eyed. "Really? Where?"

"Sweetopia."

"Sweetopia?"

"Sweetopia?" Tito asks. "Isn't that the planet that just has a big community of velociraptors living in there?"

Nour glares at Tito. "How come you know about this planet?"

Tito chuckles. "Well, I only know it because I heard that our dad's friend, Jegu, lives there."

"Wait, really?" Sebastian blurts out.

"Yeah, remember when our dad told us about this new congregation that his friend Jegu is helping to develop? He said there's a lot of interest over there on Sweetopia."

"Jegu? Why does that name sound familiar?" Nour rubs his chin.

Tito smiles. "Well, that's because he's one of King Yadin's best friends too."

"Jegu? Well, if a lot of them are servants of Jehovah, then that probably means that they're nice. We don't have too much to worry about then." Nader looks at Nour specifically as he says this.

Nour just frowns. "Yeah, well let's just go over there and see what it's actually like. If they are nice, then they will have no problem telling us where Uri is."

"We're almost there! Prepare for landing!" Ginger yells through the ship's intercom.

The Ferals suddenly rush and put their seatbelts on. Nour just rushes to sit on the couch that he's been lying on all day. He holds on for landing. If they finally manage to find Uri, then this whole mission will be all over with.

Nour sure hopes he won't have problems finding Uri here after finding out from his friends that most of the creatures that live there are servants of Jehovah. They ought to help them find Uri, but he still has an eerie feeling again that something might go wrong.

Besides, even if this planet is full of good people, Nour knows that there are tons of bad creatures that are after Uri, and he doesn't want these nice people who live in Sweetopia caught in the crossfire. After all, it isn't their fight. It's only Nour and his friends' role to catch Uri. Uri is just a boy, and the universe is full of dangerous creatures.

Suddenly, BS Lion starts to shake, and Nour holds on to a handle above his couch. After a while, the shaking stops.

"Alright, we made it through the atmosphere," Ginger says through the intercom.

The Ferals all let go and unbuckle their seatbelts. Nour heads over to the cockpit again and looks through the window to see a very colorful planet. Nour can't believe how pink the environment is.

"Hm, very colorful planet." Ginger remarks.

"Yeah."

"Let's see, there's a landing spot around here some-where."

As they get closer to an area with other ships grounded, two colorful velociraptors wave flares at them. Ginger lands near them. As The Ferals disembark, the two colorful velociraptors approach, smiling and waving at them.

One has red skin and the other, pink. The pink one might be a female from its slighter build, but Nour is only assuming. Nour knows that in the bird world, the males are usually the colorful ones, the females are the not-so-colorful ones, and the raptors are part of the bird family, but both of them are colorful, so Nour isn't sure.

"Welcome to planet Sweetopia. Where did you guys come from?" The pink one asks. It sounds like a female voice, so Nour guesses he might have been right.

Tito waves. "Greetings. We're from The Old World. From the nation of Misr. You haven't happened to see a ship that landed here that looks like a cardboard box, would you?"

The pink one raises an eye ridge. "Cardboard box? I don't know, we get a lot of weird ships here, but none of them look like cardboard boxes. Hey, Stewy, have you seen a ship like that?"

The red one shakes his head. "Nah, sorry, I haven't seen one before, Strawberry."

The pink one also shakes her head. "Hm, sorry we can't help you, but you're welcome to visit our village and walk around. There's probably somebody there that knows where a cardboard box spaceship is."

Tito starts, "Thank you, have a good—"

"Who's in charge of this village?" Nour interrupts.

The pink one, whose name is apparently Strawberry, looks at Nour, seeming confused. "Sorry?"

"Is Jegu in charge of this village?"

The pink one smiles. "Oh, you guys know Jegu? You must be brothers?"

"Yes, we are."

"It's nice to see you. Welcome. Yes, Jegu is our overseer. He usually is at his cottage. Here, I can take you to meet him if you like?"

"That would be great, thank you."

"My name is Strawberry Shores, by the way, and this is Chewy Stewy." Strawberry Shores looks at Stewy. "I can help these guys out by myself, Stewy. You can help others."

Stewy nods. "Sure."

As Stewy leaves, Strawberry motions her claws at Nour. "I just need you guys' IDs first. Sorry, it's regulations. Then I can take you to see Jegu."

Nour looks back at his friends. His comrades look at him expectantly. Nour knows what his friends are thinking; that he doesn't trust these Sweetopians one bit, and they would be mostly right.

It's not that he doesn't trust them. These two Sweetopians who greeted them seem to be nice, but Nour just wants to know if they are hiding Uri or not. The Ferals hand their IDs to Strawberry Shores. Strawberry checks them and hands them back.

"Great, you can follow me, and I will take you to Jegu's cottage."

The Ferals walk behind Strawberry Shores as she takes them on a journey through a colorful town. Literally, every face they pass by, Nour sees smiling faces. Nour doesn't understand how these people can be so joyous when they live in a universe surrounded by wickedness.

Nour was once that happy, he was once a part of these joyful people. Isolated from the rest of the dark universe, being ignorant from the outside world, pretending it is okay, but in reality it's not.

Time and time again is proof that they all live in a dark universe, slaves to those on the top of the food chain. These raptors that are smiling and waving at him are a reminder to him of how his life used to be with Angel, but the colorful life of these Sweetopians is just ignorance to the dark reality of the actual universe.

His brother is another reminder of the dark reality as his robotic face looks at him blankly. "I know what you're thinking."

Nour looks at Nader cock-eyed. "Oh, you do?"

"If you think you can find Uri by tearing this place apart, then I think you're not going to find Uri at all."

"Tearing this place apart? Who says I'm going to do that? Sure, I don't trust these raptors, but I'm just making sure that they are not hiding Uri. If they're not, we'll leave them be, but if I find the slightest hint that they're hiding Uri, then prepare yourself."

"Nour, please don't," Tito says.

Nour ignores him and walks up to Strawberry Shores who looks at him keenly.

"All of my friends want to split up and look around your village, if you don't mind. They think it's pretty interesting. I still want to meet Jegu though."

Strawberry smiles. "Sure."

Nour signals to the others and they all split up, merging with the crowd of villagers. Nour continues to follow

Strawberry Shores toward the edge of the village. Once there, Nour spots a white cottage nearby.

"We're almost there."

Nour follows her toward this white cottage. As they near, Nour sees a brown Sweetopian who seems old based on patches of gray hair on his fuzzy black afro. Nour didn't even know that velociraptors could grow hair. He assumes that it must be Jegu. The raptor turns around and looks at them.

As they approach, Nour examines Jegu's features. He feels like he recognizes the old velociraptor from somewhere but can't put a paw on where. Tito said that Jegu knows his dad, so Nour might have met him, but he doesn't remember.

"Jegu, this new visitor wants to meet you. He says he knows you," Strawberry says.

Jegu looks at Nour skeptically. "Ah, yes. How can I forget about you, Nour."

"So, you do remember me?"

"Oh, I do. One of Alfred's students. What do you want?"

"You haven't happened to see a cardboard box spaceship land here, have you?"

"A cardboard box? No, I haven't, sorry." Jegu looks away from Nour. "Now, if that's the only thing you want, then off you go."

Okay, kind of a rude answer. Nour grows suspicious. "Oh, I see. You haven't happened to have seen a human kid walking through your village? He was the one who was riding in the cardboard box."

"A human kid? Now, that's very unlikely. There hasn't been a human on this planet for years now. I'm sorry, my feline friend, but I guess you have the wrong planet."

"Oh, I see. Well, may I have your permission to search your village to see if the human boy is actually here?"

"Pff. It's very unlikely a human boy would get past my security, but you're welcome to try. Just don't go to the wooded areas; there's a strange beast that's terrorizing our village, and it's roaming in the woods."

"Oh, I see."

Nour knows that Jegu is full of bull. He's trying to hide something, and Nour knows what he's hiding. He's hiding Uri from him, and his words and reactions tell Nour all he needs to know. Nour turns on his phone speaker.

"Ferals, destroy the village."

Jegu and Strawberry Shores immediately assume fighting stances. Suddenly, a loud boom comes from somewhere in the village, and smoke rises from one of the buildings.

Good, it looks like his friends obeyed his order. Nour looks back at Jegu and Strawberry, both staring at him with fear in their eyes.

"You Sweetopians really think you can lie to me. I could see through your deceptions from the start." Nour also assumes a fighting stance. "Now, tell me where the kid is, or you will see your village completely destroyed."

Jegu says nothing, attacking with his mustache. Nour dodges the attack and immediately shoots fireballs at Jegu, which he dodges.

Nour catches a strange scent—dark chocolate—wafting from Jegu's mustache as he attacks. Chocolate? Is that mustache actually made of chocolate? Weird. Well, if that's the case, maybe it's time to turn this chocolate raptor into a steaming cup of boiling hot cocoa.

Strawberry Shores stands frozen nearby, wide-eyed and horrified. Too bad she's here—Nour's about to roast her overseer into a molten mess.

He summons every ounce of power and unleashes a blazing inferno from his nostrils. The fire rushes forward, crackling and hungry, ready to consume Jegu. But just inches away from his face, something impossible happens: Jegu's form melts into a puddle of shimmering goo. The flames don't even touch him.

Before Nour can react, a glint flashes behind him. He ducks just in time—wham!—a massive candy sword swings down where his head was seconds before. Jegu's carrying the sparkling weapon in his mouth, the sugary blade glittering like a deadly jewel.

Nour's heart pounds. If that sword hits him, it won't just cause pain—it'll be a sweet death worse than diabetes. *What the hell is going on? Is he really trying to kill me?*

Suddenly, a large explosion catches Jegu off guard.

Nour thought the Sweetopian people were going to be nice and tell him where Uri is but guess not. *That's it! I about had with these stupid—%$&%&%$%$&$%...*

Oh, yes. This power. My vision. Red. I know I shouldn't, but... I have to... It's the only way to get what I want.

Jegu seems to panic. "You really think you can be counted as a brother when you are relying on the Devil's power? Well, I'm not going to let you destroy my village."

"You shut up! You think I'm evil? I hate cocky liars like you! You know, I really thought you people of Zion were cool. I was glad to be part of the servants of Jehovah until she..."

Until she died. Nour will never forget that day when his beloved Angel died. Now he can't trust anybody anymore, not even these servants of Jehovah.

Jegu takes up a defensive stance.

He's going to shred this old lizard—

Wait. A bomb!

A bomb rolls toward Strawberry Shores, behind Jegu.

Nour runs past Jegu and pounces on Strawberry, pushing her away from the bomb, narrowly avoiding the subsequent explosion.

Nour lays over the female raptor, his body protecting her. He looks back at Jegu and gets up, breathing heavily...

I'm sorry... Why... Why do I have to be such an idiot?

Nour runs away. Not saying a word. Guiltiness weighing heavily on him...

***

Jegu's eyes narrow as the pieces click into place—now he sees exactly what Nour was aiming for. Nearby, Strawberry Shores stumbles toward him, trembling. She presses against his side, shoulders shaking as silent tears trail down her mouth like quiet rivers.

Jegu's gaze lingers on her, then drifts to where Nour disappeared—gone, swallowed by shadows. The weight of loss settles deep in his chest. He remembers the younger version of Nour: a fiery spark, full of hope and fierce loyalty to Jehovah. But now... something darker has twisted him.

Jegu reaches out, resting a steady claw on Strawberry Shores' back, grounding them both in the storm of what's become.

255

"Are you alright?"

Strawberry nods.

"Good. Come with me. We need to make sure that everybody is safe."

Chapter 24- Village Destroyed

Oh yeah, baby!

Ben swings back and forth on a bright, colorful licorice vine dangling from a candy tree. It feels like the perfect day to monkey around—if only his friends were here. But he's alone. He doesn't know how he got here or why, but the vine is fun, so he keeps swinging.

Then, something shifts.

The vibrant trees around him start to darken, their colors fading like a sunset swallowed by shadows. Even the pink cotton candy sky dims, turning an eerie shade. Night? Ben isn't sure. Before he can think it through, the darkness begins to swallow everything, and Ben's heart races as he breaks into a run, desperate to escape.

Ben.

Somebody's calling him.

"Who is it?" He tries to respond, but the voice keeps calling his name and the darkness is closing in on him faster and faster.

Ben.

Ben.

Ben.

"Goddamn it, Ben! Wake up!"

Ben wakes up to a loud Cedric who is shaking him out of his bunk bed. Ben tries to get Cedric to let go of him.

"What the hell is going on?" He asks Cedric. Cedric doesn't give him an immediate answer. The rest of his pack, including Uri, are already up and at/'em like the whole bunk house is on fire.

"Ben, we need to get out of here!" Honey screams, terror in her eyes.

Ben chuckles panicky. "What do you—"

Bang! Boom!

What sounded like bombs were immediately heard in Ben's ears. The screaming outside sure isn't helping the case. *What the hell is going on?*

Ben quickly puts some pants on and heads outside with his friends.

As soon as he opened the door, his eyes couldn't believe the scene in front of him. Smoke. Fire. What was once a beautiful, colorful village with amazing homes, now looks like burning hell.

Sweetopians are running around, screaming. Some of them are using their water abilities, trying to put out the destruction the best they could.

What happened? Did another beast come?

All of a sudden, he spots Chuck, all bruised up, fighting with a cat. The cat has gray fur with orange arrows covering his body. The cat is making spears like Chuck is with his chocolate, and they're throwing spears at each other. *Could that be one of The Ferals?*

They have come, and Uri is in great danger now. Chuck sees them and motions them to run away with Uri.

"Come on, Ben. Let's go." Tom yells at him.

He's trying to pull Ben away, but Ben just stands in shock. He looks at all the Sweetopians trying to save and get their friends out of their burning homes. *How could someone do such a thing? They didn't deserve this!*

He is so upset. He charges at the stupid gray cat like a bull ready to finally end the evildoer. The gray cat avoids Ben like it was just air. Ben accidentally trips and lands face first into the cookie crumb dirt.

"Man, who the bloody hell is this guy?" The gray cat blurts out.

Ben immediately makes cotton candy above the cat. *How about you taste this kitty?* The cotton candy was inches away from touching the cat's fur, but then Chuck unexpectedly pushes the cat away and the cotton candy lands on the ground instead.

What the hell are you doing Chuck? Ben doesn't understand why Chuck pushed him away, but Chuck resumes fighting the evil beast himself.

Ben is frustrated. He again charges at the cat, but then this time Chuck intervenes, putting a wall of chocolate in front of Ben. *Why are you doing this Chuck? It's like he doesn't want me to help him?*

Ben just has to choke in frustration while his raptor friend gets beaten up by the cat. Chuck is a good fighter, but it's clear that the gray cat has more skills. Each spear Chuck throws at him, the cat throws three times more until... *No!*

Ben is afraid this might happen. The chocolate wall finally disappears in front of Ben, but it's too late to save Chuck. *God damn. Why didn't you let me help you?*

Now Chuck is lying on the ground, two spears are pierced through his skin, sticking out of his back like two antennae.

Ben quickly rushes over to see if he's still alive. He checks the pulse. Good. Still breathing.

"Man, what a helpful friend you are, human? It seems like you just got in the way of your buddy. Now pay the consequences kid." The gray cat laughs.

Who does this stupid cat think he is? Ben just stands there. He can't believe it. Why would somebody attack such innocent creatures like the Sweetopians? This cat bastard! If only he were here sooner, then he would tear this Feral bastard apart for even trying to—^*%^%^%^%^%^%...

What the hell... What happened?

I saw red all of a sudden and blacked out.

Now I can see clearly...

What happened?

The first thing Ben sees in his vision is the gray cat again, but he isn't laughing. It is all bruised from head to claw. There is even blood on his fur. He's shaking.

Ben finally realizes he has the cat pinned down with his left arm. As for his right arm—well—Ben feels a slight tug.

He looks over. *Uri?*

He is holding onto his arm. Uri has saved him from whatever that was.

The boy looks at him, all frightened, and then continues to look around. A few Sweetopians, as well as his friends, are looking at him with similar expressions.

Ben doesn't even know why they are looking at him like that. Still, he let go of the gray cat. It doesn't even attack them, just runs away terrified. Not to be seen again hopefully.

"What happened?" Ben says as he looks around for an answer.

"You just got The Devil's Eye," Jegu says. He appears out of nowhere next to Chuck who has vines wrapped around his body, being healed by Honey.

Strawberry Shores is with them too; she looks at Chuck like she's going to lose her love. Jegu approaches Ben.

"The Devil's Eye?" Ben asks Jegu, waiting for another response.

"What happened to him?" Honey asks. "We just saw him get angry, and his eyes turned red."

Jegu nods. "Ah, yes. That's exactly what happens when you let your feelings take you over. Satan tries to take advantage of this, unfortunately."

Ben cocks his head at Jegu. "Excuse me?"

"Let me explain. There's this thing called 'The Devil's Eye,' or some creatures call it 'The Predator's Eye,' because of how strong a creature gets when they use it. It makes your eyes become abnormal. Remember when I told you about your special abilities being based on the things you don't see physically, the things spiritual?" he sighs. "Well, sadly, Ben, now that you and your friends know about this, it looks like the Devil is trying to tempt you and make you rely on your own feelings. This is exactly what happened to Nour when I fought him."

"Oh, come on! That's ridiculous," Baxter says.

"You may think it's ridiculous. I'm not going to force you guys to believe in God but know this: If you try to use your special abilities for selfish reasons, you're going to end up like Ben here."

Tom rolls his eyes. "Isn't that just great? I've never expected that our abilities would also be our weaknesses."

Uri looks at Jegu. "Wait, you fought Nour? Oh, great. That means all of them are here."

Jegu nods again. "Ah, yes. And seems like they're continuing to destroy the village as we speak. Still searching around, looking for you. Now that one of them knows where you are, he's probably going to tell the others. There's not a chance you guys will be staying on this planet. All of you should leave quickly."

Tom looks at Ben. "Ben, let's just not get involved anymore, this is too dangerous."

"Tom is right," Jegu says. "I think it's best that you leave Uri with us and let us protect him. You should go back to your plan—"

"No." Ben interrupts. "If Uri is staying with you guys, then I'm staying with you guys too."

"What? But why?"

"Because Uri is my friend, and now you servants of Jehovah are my friends too."

"What? Ben, are you insane? Did you not see what one of The Ferals did?" Tom points toward the Sweetopian buildings that are on fire.

"Yeah."

Cedric grabs Ben's shoulders. "Seriously, that's all you're going to say? 'Yeah'? Why do you want to protect this kid so much?"

"Because he's a friend."

"But The Ferals are going to kill you!"

"Don't worry. I'm sure Jehovah is going to help us."

"Jehovah? Oh, don't tell me these guys manipulated you." Baxter rolls his eyes.

Ben frowns at Baxter. "They didn't manipulate me. It's my choice. I want to join the Brotherhood of Zion. I want to serve Jehovah. Never have I been so happy in my entire life ever since..." Ben pauses, trying to hold back his tears. *Ever since my mom died, I have never been so happy in my entire life.* He knows he found the truth, hopefully his Pack has found it too.

Tom rolls his eyes. "You know, that's the problem with you, Ben. You never seem to give up."

Ben just smirks.

Good, it looks like they are still loyal to me.

He lifts his wolf chain.

"Jeez, that smirk is almost as bad as Jack's. You're lucky I view you as a brother too." Cedric lifts his wolf chain.

Tom sighs. "Your determination is going to be the death of me, I swear." Tom lifts his wolf chain as well.

Honey smiles and raises her wolf chain. "Hey, I'm here for you, Ben. I just hope that 'Devil's Eye' or whatever it's called doesn't hurt you."

Ben chuckles awkwardly. "Don't worry."

"Hey, I'm all in for it too. This is the most exciting experience I have ever had in my entire life." Slam laughs as he raises his wolf chain.

"What? Are all of you insane?" The Wolf Pack looks at Baxter when he says that. Baxter rolls his eyes. "Uh, Jesus," Baxter mumbles as he lifts his wolf chain.

"What? But why?" Jegu looks at The Wolf Pack.

Tom shrugs. "I don't know, ask Ben. Our friend here is the main reason why we're even in this mess to begin with."

"Hey, all of you were willing to come too."

"Yeah, yeah. Just get over here so I can kick your ass."

"Hey."

Ben tries to get away from Tom as he tries to hit him.

Jegu looks confused but laughs. "I love all of your enthusiasm. Fine then, if you all want to protect Uri so much, you can take him to your planet. I think you can protect Uri better than we can, but I think you could use some help, so I'm sending Chuck, Strawberry Shores, and Blueberry Ocean with you guys." Chuck's eyes pop up. "They will help you improve your abilities, which you'll need if The Ferals ever come back to attack you. Me and my people will try to fend them off the best we can. Hopefully, that will give you enough time to prepare."

Ben smiles and nods. "Okay."

Tom rolls his eyes. "Wow, no questions asked. Just willing to jump off the edge. See, this is what I love about you, Ben."

"Shut up."

Ben jumps on Tom and pushes him to the ground, where they wrestle like a couple of playful boys.

Honey just rolls her eyes. "Oh, brother."

"Hey, that looks like fun. Let me join in." Slam jumps on Ben and Tom.

Tom shouts. "Hey, what are you doing?"

The Wolf Pack continues to fight with each other. Jegu, along with Uri, Chuck, and Blueberry Ocean, just look at The Wolf Pack with puzzled expressions.

"Man, these Earth humans are the most interesting creatures I ever met." Jegu laughs.

"I don't mean to question you, Jegu, but why would you let them go with us?" Ocean looks at Jegu intently.

Jegu smiles. "Because, Ocean, these Earth humans taught me something. Ever since I met them, I'm reminded that there are creatures out there in the universe that are actually good, and they need to know the truth. You see what they did? Even without knowing if they're able to use special abilities, they still tried to help Uri. These Earth humans showed what it truly means to have faith, and they need to know the truth. That's why I'm sending Chuck, Strawberry, and you to teach them. Because every single one of them needs to know about God."

Ocean looks at Jegu cock-eyed. "Really, every single one? Even the hot-headed one?"

They look toward Baxter, who has a bunch of baby Sweetopians running around him. He is sitting on the ground, looking pissed, but he doesn't do anything, just watching over the baby Sweetopians as the adults take care of business.

Jegu nods. "Especially the hot-headed one. All of them need to know the truth. We've been hiding the truth for far too long now. We need to share it with the ones who need it more than we do: those who don't know Jehovah."

***

The Wolf Pack lands on Earth under a heavy night sky, the ground blanketed in fresh snow. Uri, Chuck, Strawberry, and Ocean step off The Imaginator, pulling their coats tighter against the sharp Montana chill. Ben's breath puffs out in white clouds as a cold breeze cuts through the air, making him shiver.

They've got only a week left of winter break before school starts again, but arriving before Christmas means they'll get time with their families. Ben thinks back on their trip—the lessons, the new powers they've begun to understand. He knows he still has a long way to go, especially when it comes to controlling his anger. If they ever face The Ferals, that will be the key to winning. Hopefully, Chuck and the others can help him grow stronger.

Chuck and his Sweetopians stand nearby, their colorful skin almost glowing beneath their cheerful sweaters. The three of them look right at home in the winter night, while Ben pulls his coat tighter and looks ahead, ready for whatever comes next.

"Man, I'm glad I'm back on Earth." Tom stretches.

Ben smiles. "Ah, you see. That wasn't so bad."

"Yeah, well wait until I get home. My dad is probably going to kill me because I've spent all of my time hanging out with you guys."

"Pff, your dad can suck it."

"Yeah, well, Ben, how about you tell that straight to his face?"

"..."

"Exactly."

"I hope you make it out alive." Honey chimes in.

"Well, we'll see. I probably should go now. See you all at Christmas."

"Wait, you're not planning to hang out some more? There's still two days left until Christmas Eve," Slam says.

Tom shakes his head. "Nah, if I hang out with you chumps any longer, I swear my brain will fry."

Ben frowns.

Chuck's antennae flash. ".- ..-. - . .-. / -.-. .... .-. .. ... - -- .- ... ..-- .."

"Chuck wants to know if you guys want to train your abilities after Christmas?" Uri says.

"After Christmas? Probably. It depends if my father lets me or not. I guess I will find out. Wish me luck."

Cedric follows Tom. "I have to leave too. This trip was nice, but I don't know what my sister and mom did when I was gone. Guess I will find out. See you later."

Cedric and Tom wave goodbye as they walk together into the woods. The rest of them huddle together next to The Imaginator, which is emitting a surprising amount of heat for a cardboard box.

"Oh, yeah. Back to the Montana cold. The warm Sweetopian weather was nice, but this is what I call heaven," Slam says as he shivers.

Baxter raises an eyebrow. "You're nuts."

"I know." Slam laughs.

"Man, I agree with the police boy. I can't hang out with you chumps any longer, I'm leaving."

Ben reaches his hand out to Baxter. "Hey, what about tomorrow?"

"If I'm not dead by then."

Ben just looks at Baxter puzzled as he walks away.

Slam speaks up next. "Yeah, in all seriousness, I should probably leave as well. My family is probably worried about me. Ben? Honey? Can one of you drive me to my house? I could walk, but I want to save my energy for tomorrow."

Honey nods. "Sure, I can take you to your house. Ben can take the rest to his house. I think our homes will be safe now that The Ferals aren't here anymore."

Slam snaps his fingers. "Ah, that's right, you guys can finally get back to your homes safely, which leaves more time for us to prepare for whenever those Ferals come. Hey, Chuck, Uri, my alien friends, it's been a pleasure to go on an adventure with you. Hopefully, there's more to come."

Strawberry smiles and waves. "Yeah, hopefully. You guys take care."

Slam and Honey wave goodbye.

Ben looks down at Chuck and his buddies. "Hey, when do you guys think The Ferals are going to be back?"

The raptors cock their heads, then Chuck's antennae flicker momentarily.

Ocean translates. "Chuck estimates that it's going to be five weeks until The Ferals realize Uri's gone. Don't worry, our people are going to do the best they can to distract them, I'm sure. I'm just worried that it's going to be sooner than that. Those cats are determined. Are you sure you and your friends can defeat them?"

Ben smiles. "Oh, sure I'm sure, but first let's get some sleep. I'm tired."

Ben motions them to follow him to his truck. The Howler will have some new guests to transport. Ben doesn't know when The Ferals will be back, but he knows he will be ready for them. He'll be training to use more of his ability to defeat them.

He would be lying if he said he wasn't anxious about this whole situation, but he trusts Chuck and the others to teach them.

Most importantly, he trusts in Jehovah.

Chapter 25- Back On Earth, Back On Work

Sarah's POV, the annoying sister

Sarah feels like she's been waiting forever in Cedric's truck.

Her brother is finishing up in the hardware store. He promised they would go horseback riding after this. She wishes he wasn't always so busy with work and had more time to hang out with her and their mom.

While Sarah is waiting, a boy from her class walks up and knocks on the window of the truck. Sarah rolls it down.

The boy shuffles with his hand, looking down. There's sweat on his face as he stutters, "W—Will... Will you go out on a date with me?"

Sarah sighs.

This isn't the first time boys from her class asked her out on a date. All the attention the boys in her school give her is annoying. She doesn't like to hang out with the kids in her school. She prefers to spend time alone. The only people she likes to hang out with are The Wolf Pack and her brother Cedric. She thinks most of the kids her age are immature and prefers to hang out with the older kids.

She doesn't want to go out with the boy and wants him to get off her back. Sarah has an idea of how to get rid of the boy.

"Hey, kid. What's your name?"

"B—Brian."

"Brain? Okay, Brain, let's go somewhere private. I want to tell you something."

Brain immediately smiles and nods.

He probably thinks she is going to kiss him, but she has another idea. She leads him to a tree they can hide behind so nobody will be watching what she's going to do. Once there, Brain already has his lips out, preparing for a kiss.

Sarah doesn't want to do this to the kid, but she has to if she wants him off her back. There is a little pond right behind Brain. Even though it has been getting warmer, it's still cold out, and the pond has a few ice chunks in it. The water is still going to be cold. Sarah almost feels bad that she's going to do this to the kid, but hey.

When Brain leans in for a kiss, Sarah pushes him into the cold pond and runs away with a mischievous grin on her face. She suddenly sees Cedric coming out of the hardware store. Perfect timing!

Cedric looks at her with a puzzled expression. "Where the hell did you run off to?"

She doesn't answer.

As the soaked boy emerges from the pond, Cedric's eyes grow wide. Probably by now, he realizes what happened. *Dang it! I thought I drowned him.* She's just preparing for how her brother is going to respond to her.

Cedric chuckles a little. "Oh, I see. It looks like another kid asked you out again."

Sarah rolls her eyes. "Just shut up and get back to the truck. Let's ride horses already."

"Hold on, I need to put up some fence posts I just got. Then we can leave."

"Then can we ride horses?"

"Nah, probably not. There's still some work I need to do."

"Hey, you promised!"

"I'm sorry, Sarah, but I can't be having fun all the time. You just stay at home and wait. It's not going to take long."

"Pff, you always say that, but then you always come back a million hours later."

"Whatever, just get in the truck."

***

Going back home is never a good thing. There always seems to be something bad happening while they are at the house, even if it's a little inconvenient. With more problems, comes less time Sarah has with her brother.

She is sitting next to him while he's driving the truck, staying silent, but Sarah is planning to bother Cedric the whole day. Luckily, they're having a family Christmas gathering tonight, so Cedric has no choice but to be with the family. She can't wait to see all her relatives gather in one place, from Uncle Ernie to Grandma Alex...

Actually, Sarah wouldn't miss Grandma Alex. She's the most annoying grandma in the world, but that's not what Sarah wants to think about at the moment.

As soon as they arrive at the house, though, she sees another relative of her's who has already arrived.

You gotta be kidding me? Why's he here?

Sarah is sometimes excited, but mostly annoyed seeing Ben at their house. It's mostly annoying because every time Ben is at their house, it's always a mischievous plan he wants Cedric to do, which brings even less time for Cedric to hang out with her.

He needs to fix a few fences on the property first. That's why they even went to the hardware store in the first place, but Cedric should have also bought a stapler gun so she can use it to staple Ben to a post so they wouldn't have to deal with him until family dinner tonight.

As soon as her and Cedric get out of the truck, Sarah realizes that there's a strange kid with Ben. The strange kid looks about her age, but Sarah doesn't recognize him. The kid is wearing a funky blue headband. *What is that funky headband for?*

The kid is laughing and petting their dog Rusty while they walk toward them.

"How's it going Ben?" Cedric shakes Ben's hand.

"Good."

Cedric looks at the kid. "Who's this kid? Is he a lost relative of yours?"

Ben shakes his head. "Oh, no. This is my friend. His parents don't care about him, so I'm taking care of him for the time being."

"Oh, that's sad. What's your name, kid?"

The kid offers his hand to Cedric. "Hello, I'm Uri."

"Uri? Nice to meet you." Cedric points at her. "This here is my sister, Sarah."

"Hello." Uri smiles at her and offers her his hand, she shyly shakes it.

Suddenly, their mom steps out of the house, wearing her well-worn cowboy hat. Rusty bolts toward her, tugging at the frayed hem of her jeans. She playfully shoos him with the hat, then launches into a game of tug-of-war. After tossing a stick for Rusty to chase, she turns to Uri with a skeptical look, like he's the odd one out among the familiar faces.

"Why how do you do, Ben? Who's this kid with you?" She asks.

Ben replies. "Hey, Mrs. Coy. This is my friend, Uri. He wants to join us for the Christmas gathering."

"Oh, really? Welcome, Uri. Everyone is family here. By the way, where's your dad, Ben? I've been trying to call him multiple times, but he's not answering."

Ben chuckles. "Well, that's because he's still gone on his truck-driving business to Colorado."

Their mom frowns. "Oh, you gotta be kidding me? That man is as stubborn as a mule. I swear once I see his ass, I'm going to punch the living dickens out of him for not taking care of his son well. I seriously can't believe he keeps leaving you alone. You're always welcome to stay at our house when he's gone. You're part of the family."

Ben waves his hands defensively. "Oh, no. Don't worry about it. I'm okay."

"Are you sure?"

"Yeah, I'm fine."

"Okay..." Their mom finally turns her gaze toward her and Cedric. "Hey, Cedric. After you finish putting the fence posts up, can you help with Christmas decorations please? Sarah you too."

Both her and Cedric let out a heavy sigh before saying. "Yes mother."

After their mother goes inside the house, Ben asks. "Hey, can I help?"

Cedric nods. "Sure. Hey, Sarah, feed the horses real quick before helping mom."

"Ugh, fine." Sarah slouches as she heads to the barn.

"Hey, can I help you?"

Sarah hears a voice say. She turns around and sees that it's the strange new kid that Ben brought with him. He smiles at her with a desire to become her friend, but Sarah knows better. She doesn't trust boys at all, especially whoever this funky kid is.

"Yeah, you can stand in a corner and not bother me at all, that would be great."

Uri gives her a thumbs up. "Okay, cool."

When Sarah works in the barn, that's literally what he does. He's just sitting in a corner, staring at Sarah as she feeds the horses.

Sarah frowns. "Okay, this isn't going to work at all. You just look like a creep. Turn around."

"Okay."

Uri turns arounds, but still Sarah is bothered. No matter how hard she's trying to focus, the boy is still there.

"Okay, this is not going to work either. If you're just going to sit there like an idiot, you mind as well help me."

"Okay, what do you need help with?" Uri asks.

"Just help me carry the alfalfa into the barn please."

Immediately, Uri runs out of the barn, and he comes back with so much alfalfa that Sarah could barely see the stupid kid carrying it. *Jesus, how is this kid carrying so much?*

"Hey, man. That's too much! I was going to drive the four-wheeler and carry it in the wagon. I just needed you to help me put it in the wagon."

"Oops, sorry." The kid giggles as he plops the alfalfa down. "Will this be enough?" He asks.

"It's more than enough. We only got four horses in this place, but you got enough to feed a whole corral."

"Oops, sorry."

"Whatever, just let me feed the horses by myself. You've done enough."

Sarah grabs a pitch fork as Uri stands there, smiling at her, all goggly eyed like the rest of the schoolboys do. She just tries to ignore him while she's feeding the horses. *I swear if this kid tries something, I'm going to kill him.*

"Hey, I gotta ask, how do you speak to your horses?" Uri blurts out.

She looks at him cock-eyed. "I'm sorry, what?"

"I mean, I know that other animals don't talk on your planet, but still, there's gotta be some way you Earth humans communicate with other species because how do you know how much alfalfa each individual horse needs?"

"What are you talking about? You can't talk to animals. I just know how much each horse needs based on how active they are, or what condition they are in, depending on what it is. Each horse is different, they can't speak to me, I just know either with body language or something else."

"Hmm, interesting."

Uri starts analyzing the horses like they are some strange creatures he hasn't seen before. He's checking everything out like he's a veterinarian. *Who the hell is this kid?*

"Hey, you're pretty strange, kid. Where you from?"

"Oh, me? I'm from the nation of Zion. It's on a planet called The Old World. It's very far from your planet."

Sarah can't help but laugh at what Uri said. *Is this kid serious?* "Man, you're weird. Let me guess, you don't have horses on your planet."

Uri nods. "Oh, we do have horses, except they talk unlike the horses you have here on Earth. We can talk to them. I really need to take you to another planet to see one."

Sarah continues laughing. "Oh, yeah, sure kid."

She has had enough of this blabbering about talking horses. She just ignores Uri and gets back to feeding the horses, but then—

"Hey, I'm curious, tell me about this 'Christmas' you Earth humans celebrate." Uri blurts out.

Sarah looks at Uri cock-eyed. "What do you mean? Don't tell me you seriously haven't heard about Christmas."

Uri shrugs and shakes his head.

Sarah sighs. "It's a holiday that we celebrate every year to commemorate Jesus' birth and where we get together with family and give gifts to one another. It's an amazing holiday. I seriously can't believe you haven't heard of it. You really are strange."

"Jesus' birth?" Uri laughs like she just told him a joke.

"Why are you laughing?"

"Oh, sorry. I just think it's funny how you Earth humans, despite how isolated you are from the rest of the universe, still know about Jesus. Jesus is a well-known person across the universe, but do you know who Jesus actually is?"

Sarah shrugs. "Yeah, he's God's son, isn't he? He died on the cross for our sins."

Uri laughs again. "Wow, that's truly interesting. I'm learning more about you Earth humans every day. Tell me more about this 'Christmas' and how you celebrate it."

"Well, we decorate our homes with lights and stuff. We put a tree in our living room and put lights on it as well. Mom puts some gifts under the tree. She claims that it comes from Santa Claus, but I'm old enough to realize now that it's actually her."

"Hmm, that is interesting. What about that star you put on the tree? I seen some people put stars on their trees, what does that mean?"

"Well, that star represents the star that guided the three wise men to baby Jesus."

"Oh, I see. But that's strange though."

"What is?"

"I've read the Holy Scriptures on the account of Jesus' birth many times and never does it mention 'three wise men' or this 'Santa Claus' that you said. Where did those beliefs come from?"

"The hell I care."

She's getting annoyed with this boy's questions. After the horses have been fed, Sarah grabs her saddle out of the tack room as well as all the other riding equipment and places it on her horse Pearl.

"Are you going to ride?" Uri asks.

"Yeah."

"Cool, I want to ride too."

Sarah pauses when trying to put a halter on Pearl and looks at Uri cock-eyed. "Are you sure you know how to ride a horse, 'Mr. Alien'?"

Uri nods. "Yep, I rode all the time back in my home nation."

"Okay, but you're not going to be talking to the horse when riding please."

Uri giggles. "Oh, no worries, I won't."

"You can ride on that horse over there, his name is Scrappy."

After Sarah finishes saddling up Pearl, she helps Uri saddle up on Scrappy. When they start riding, Sarah is surprised at how well Uri can ride. His posture is well-centered and balanced. He's very relaxed and very careful with the reins and leg movement. Sarah tries to make Uri stumble by going a little faster and faster, but Uri is keeping up with her no problem.

She grumbles. "What, how are you doing this?"

"Doing what?"

"Keeping up with me."

Uri shrugs. "I don't know. I told you before that I already know how to ride."

"Yeah, but your posture, your feet, the way you handle the reins, just everything looks good. Who the hell taught you?"

Uri chuckles. "Oh, thank you. My father, King Yadin, taught me everything I need to know. He used to own tons of horses."

"King? Okay, you're just making things up now. You're just trying to impress me, aren't you? Your father's not actually a king. Just who the hell are you?"

"I'm Prince Uri, son of King Yadin, from the nation of Zion, a loyal servant of Jehovah."

"Oh, just shut up! Who the hell are you really?"

"I just told you."

Sarah growls and rides Pearl straight back to the barn in frustration. *I need to get away from this kid.* She rides and rides, further and further away from Uri. She swears if he ever comes close to her, she's going to—

Bang!

The second Sarah gains consciousness, she doesn't know what happened in the last few seconds, but everything is dizzy. Her vision is blurry. The ringing in her ears is like a hundred bombs let off at once. He can hear a hundred voices, see a hundred faces, all calling her.

Calling her to wake up.

Sarah.

Sarah.

Sarah.

"Sarah, are you alright?"

Sarah can finally hear somebody, a familiar sound of her brother. Sure thing that's the first person she saw, but then she realizes that there's another hundred faces staring at her. All of her relatives are around her, staring at her, like she just died.

Oh, great. This is not how I wish Christmas Eve to be.

280

Rusty, their blue heeler, is licking her face, but then she pushes him away.

"Hey, Sarah. Can you see me?" Cedric says as he pushes two fingers in front of her face.

Sarah immediately swats Cedric's fingers and frowns at him. "Yes, I can see you, you moron, and I want to punch you in the face."

Cedric smiles. "Oh, good. It looks like she gained consciousness."

Their mother is there too. She looks at Sarah, rubbing her head gracefully. "Oh, my goodness, Sarah, you nearly scared the dickens out of all of us when you fell off of Pearl like that. Why were you riding so crazy and so fast?"

Sarah growls. "I don't want to talk about it. I was just really angry, that's all."

"Well, you really need to be careful next time. You're lucky Ben's new friend, Uri, found you like this and called us."

Sarah's eyes shot up. *Oh, great. That kid.* Uri is behind her mom. He smiles at her when she looks at him. She quickly turns her gaze away from Uri and gets up. "Well, I'm fine. That's all that matters. Anyways, can we get this party started? Why are all of you just standing around for?"

Her crowd of relatives just walk toward the house after seeing she's okay. Sarah follows them with Cedric and Ben by her side. All of a sudden, she sees Ben turn around.

"Hey, Uri. Aren't you coming with us?" He says.

Cedric looks back which leaves Sarah looking at the strange kid as well. Uri gulps when she looks at him, and chuckles. "Um, I'm sorry Ben, but you don't mind taking me back home?"

"Are you sure, don't you want to have fun with us?" Cedric asks.

"Well, I think I already had my fun for today. Plus, Sarah already told me about what Christmas is like, and some of its traditions go against my conscience. Just take me home, will you please."

"Alright." Ben looks at Cedric. "I'll be back."

Cedric nods and waves goodbye to Uri and Ben. Once Uri is finally gone, Sarah smiles. Another boy gone, two times in one day, that's just too much for her. Though Sarah kind of finds Uri to be interesting.

Weird kid, but interesting, nevertheless. The hell she cares, she's just going to have fun with her family and that's all that matters to her.

Chapter 26- Training Begins

Ben, Uri, Strawberry Shores, Blueberry Ocean and Chuck arrive at The Wolf Den after Christmas. The rest of The Wolf Pack is already there, faces flushed with cold and eyes heavy with exhaustion. Ben feels the weight of tired muscles in his own limbs but catches the eager sparks in his friends' eyes— they're restless, ready.

They move toward the training ground, breaths visible in the crisp air. Ben's heart pounds with a fierce determination. Each step fuels him—the need to master his power, to be ready. Uri's safety hangs in the balance, shadowed by the threat of The Ferals.

Nearby, Chuck and his Sweetopian allies exchange confident glances, their colorful skins glowing faintly in the dim light, a reminder that they're not alone in this fight. The Pack tightens, ready to face whatever comes next.

Ben looks at the three Sweetopians with eager eyes. "Okay, you guys, teach us what you know."

The three Sweetopians look at each, but then Blueberry finally says. "Actually, we're hoping that Chuck will take the lead in teaching you guys. Us two are just here for the ride."

Chuck's legs start shaking pervasively when his Sweetopian companions urge him on. Chuck shakes his head.

Strawberry smiles at him. "Oh, come on Chuck. I know you can teach them. You got more knowledge than the both of us combined."

Tom raises an eyebrow at them. "Um, how is Chuck going to teach all of us if he doesn't even know how to speak?"

Ben says. "It's okay. Uri can just translate what he's saying."

Uri tugs Ben's shirt. "Actually, I thought of a better idea."

"Really, what?"

"Well, while you guys were gone for Christmas, the four of us thought of buying a translator mask from the Intergalactic Market."

"I'm sorry, a what now?" Cedric scratches his head.

Strawberry elaborates. "A translator mask. It's a neat new device that was created so creatures that speak different languages can understand one another, including Morse code. All we have to do is put the translator mask on Chuck, and hopefully it will translate what Chuck is saying."

Baxter rolls his eyes. "Well, isn't that just convenient? Where is this translator mask anyway?"

Ocean answers. "It should be coming in a package soon. I bought one online from the Intergalactic Market, and hopefully they're willing to ship it this far away to Earth. Man, it's amazing what you can do with online shopping."

Tom looks at Ocean cock eyed. "Intergalactic Market? Wait, hold on. You aliens have online shopping? What, you never told us this. I assumed you aliens just had swords and arrows. Man, I didn't realize you guys had the interwebs."

Uri laughs awkwardly. "Well, we 'aliens' basically have everything you Earth humans have. It depends on what planet you're on. Some creatures just live with old technology or nothing at all."

Tom rubs his chin. "Hmm, interesting. When is this 'package' gonna come?"

"Oh, not that long. Actually..." Uri looks at his phone. "Right now? Um, you guys might need to back up a little bit."

All The Wolf Pack look at Uri confused, then look up at the sky. A small dot comes right toward them. Ben suddenly realizes it's coming right toward them fast!

The Wolf Pack all back up as the package hits the ground with a loud crash, sending a bunch of dirt and dust into the air. Ben covers his eyes until the dust goes away, then stares at the 'package.'

It's a small, metal, egg-shaped vessel with a bunch of unintelligible writing on it. Ben can't tell if the writing is English or an alien language. He can only understand the big font that says Intergalactic Market. The thing opens and reveals a small cardboard box that also says Intergalactic Market.

"Man, I really shouldn't have ordered for same-day shipping. It arrived so quickly that it broke the ground. Oh well, what can you do?"

Ocean laughs awkwardly. The Wolf Pack just look at him puzzled.

Uri waves his hand at Chuck. "Hey Chuck, lend me one of your claws. I need help opening this box."

Chuck uses his claws to open the box, shredding it into pieces. Uri starts to take out something wrapped in bubble wrap, opening this to reveal a black mask that looks like it has a speaker inside of it.

"Here you go, Chuck. Put this thing on. See if it works."

Uri hands the mask over to Chuck and he puts it on. His antennae flash, and yellow, waving lines move on the mask, but only strange static noises come from the speakers. Chuck moves a knob on the mask and tries again.

"Hello... Hello... Can you hear me?" He says through the mask.

The translation is a little staticky, but clear enough.

"Hey, it works!" Slam blurts out. "Right on. You sound like one of those text-to-speech robots."

"Yeah, but a little chippy though. It's still good for what it's worth." Tom chimes in.

Ben smiles at Chuck. "Hey, Chuck, what should we do to improve our abilities?"

"Well, we should begin by doing combat training. I'm going to fight each of you individually. I know you work well as a team, but I need to test to see how you fight alone. This is not only going to show me how well you can fight, but it's also going to show me what your individual needs are so that you can improve."

"Alright, who do you want to fight first?" Tom asks.

"I'll go." Baxter walks over to Chuck. "Finally, we're getting into something fun. Come on, you brown lizard, let's do this."

Chuck nods. "Very well, then."

There is a cold silence of Baxter and Chuck staring each other down. The rest of them are just spectating. Suddenly, Uri blows a whistle, and Baxter charges at Chuck with enormous speed, making a bunch of bombs appear out of thin air.

He shoots them all at Chuck, who dodges all of them. Baxter immediately makes another bomb in his hand and tries to hit Chuck with it.

The bomb, inching closer and closer to Chuck's face, but then—goo. Once a brown raptor, turns into a chocolate goo. Baxter's eyes go wide.

Suddenly, a bunch of chocolate goo falls on Baxter, covering his entire body. Only his head is not covered as he tries to move around, but the chocolate goo starts to harden.

Baxter growls and growls like a lion wanting to be set free, but then—sharpness. A sharp object is felt by Baxter's head. Baxter gulps. He turns his head. All there is a bright light. A brown raptor shining bright with power. It scares Baxter a little.

"Hey, what the hell happened? Chuck was moving so quickly that my eyes almost couldn't keep up with him," Slam says.

"Hey, you're glowing just like Uri does." Ben points at Chuck.

Chuck nods. "Yes, the glowing that you are seeing is the spirit of God helping me. It's called the holy spirit."

Honey smiles. "So that's what it is?"

"Yes, Jegu told you that your abilities are based on the spiritual things you see and not on the things you see physically. If you guys want to protect Uri, then you need to have the holy spirit to help you. The Ferals are very skilled at fighting, they're even more skilled than I am. The only way you can have a fighting chance is if you train hard and I'm not talking physical training, but spiritual training."

Cedric looks at Chuck cock-eyed. "What? How can we do that?"

"Just like you did when you first tried to accomplish using your abilities. You guys try to learn as much as you can from reading books and other information to develop your skills. The same goes for when you develop your skills in gaining the holy spirit, and by developing that you need the Holy Scriptures."

Ben scratches his head. "The Bible?"

"Yes, but not only that. You also need the expert and that's Jehovah who's the expert. I'll help you along the way, but always remember God is there to help too."

Baxter frowns. "Man, that's ridiculous. God doesn't even exist."

"You say that, yet you're the one who's stuck, and you didn't even see where I was going."

Baxter growls.

"The thing is, we got school too, and work. How do you expect us to train our abilities?" Cedric blurts out.

"I'm well aware that all of you have busy lives. That's why I recommend that you manage your time wisely. You should probably use your free time to practice your abilities, but you should also be using the time you have at work or school." there was a quick pause. "Once you read the Holy Scriptures, you will suddenly realize just how much you can apply what you learned on a day-to-day basis just from the scriptures alone. In the meantime, I'm going to teach you as much as I can today, and hopefully, you can apply it and use your own time to teach yourselves."

"Yeah, but what happens when The Ferals get here?" Honey blurts out.

"I don't know when The Ferals are going to be here, but I predict that they are going to be back in a few weeks or so. Maybe even longer. Until then, I'm going to train you as much as I can. Don't worry, I know you guys can do it. I know how smart you humans are, but still. If you can't manage to become better in the short time we have, then me and my buddies here are going to try to protect Uri ourselves as best we can."

Ben smiles. "Ah, don't worry. With God's help, we can become better in no time."

"I love your enthusiasm. Well, let's get right to it, shall we? Tom, you're next."

As Chuck gets his chocolate goo off of Baxter, Ben starts to feel a little anxious. He knows that he and his friends are going to be busier than ever, but he's confident that they are going to master their abilities and hopefully take down The Ferals. He is confident they will be successful.

Chapter 27- Secret Agent Carlos

This is the story of **Secret Agent Carlos Rodriguez** (the toughest FBI agent to ever live). He just got a call from his boss: a murder at The Silvertown Bar. The local police are stumped. Nothing was stolen, and some witnesses swear they saw "strange cats." The case was too weird for them, so it landed with the FBI. Carlos got the assignment because they think Catman and his gang—Carlos's longtime nemeses—are behind it.

Catman is Carlos's worst enemy. Silent and deadly like a cat stalking at night, Catman kills without mercy, then disappears before anyone can catch him. Carlos has chased him for years. His boss told him to give up, but Carlos never quits. He lives by three rules:

1. To never give up
2. Never show your weaknesses
3. Don't trust anybody (especially women)

The third lesson is the most important for Secret Agent Carlos. Trust doesn't exist in this world and that's why Carlos isn't married. Secret Agent Carlos has seduced many women in his life, so many women that he accidentally made a woman pregnant and now Secret Agent Carlos has a kid. This happened eighteen years ago, the kid is much older now and Carlos doesn't have to take care of him anymore (thank goodness).

The kid's name is Baxter Rodriguez, he almost looks just like Carlos but honestly not as handsome as dad. Carlos has been training his son Baxter how to fight even from infancy. His son may not be much of a good fighter like his father will ever be, but at least Carlos taught him how to survive in this cruel world. Carlos may have neglected his son a little bit and left him to live on his own a little bit, but at least Carlos taught him how to survive and his neglect is at least a lesson to his son that you can't trust nobody (not even your father). It's just how life works, especially in Carlos' line of work as an FBI agent, you can't trust anybody to do the work for you. Everyone is an enemy to him. He sees the worst in people.

Right now, Carlos is riding on a horse. He could've driven in a car, but that's not a challenge for Secret Agent Carlos. He prefers riding on horseback just like his ancestors did, or he even would just run on foot. Secret Agent Carlos is getting old and doesn't have as much back strength as he did when he was young, so that's why Carlos is riding on horseback and not running right now. He remembers when he was younger, he could run thirty miles, without resting, and that was nothing to him. Now he could barely run ten miles without collapsing. This damn asthma.

Besides, Carlos needs to save up his energy because he is heading to the supposed "Secret Lair" of Catman. They sent Carlos alone to check the place out. Secret Agent Carlos is almost there, so he makes the horse slow down a bit, so he won't make too much noise. Carlos quietly got off the horse and tied the horse to a tree.

The supposed Catman's Lair looks like an old abandoned factory building about 5 stories high. It looks like it hasn't been used in a while and it's vacant, but Carlos uses his binoculars to scout the area first before deciding to get close to it. Sure enough, Carlos sees hidden cameras covered with vines. Carlos thinks there might be some traps set around the building, so he's going to be careful before heading in.

Be careful?

Carlos thought to himself. *Why would I ever have the thought about being careful?*

That wasn't his way of doing things. Sure, that's what his boss always tells him, but Carlos doesn't usually listen to his boss anyway.

He's going to do this his way: BRUTE FORCE BABY!

Carlos uses his super speed and just runs straight to the building. There were traps set, but Carlos was too fast, and he was able to dodge them left and right. Bear traps, bombs, nothing is the match for the Mexican Stallion.

***

In his hideout, Catman stood before a big table surrounded by his henchmen—a rowdy bunch of cats. Some lounged calmly, others darted around, scratching posts, hissing at each other, grooming fur, and hacking up furballs. Catman sank into his throne—a recliner smothered in cat hair and crumbs. He took a deep sniff. The room smelled of cat poop and dust—exactly how he liked it. A slow grin spread across his face as he puffed on his catnip cigar.

He chuckled darkly. "Alright, henchmen, listen up. Silvertown is just the beginning. Soon, the whole world will be ours—overrun by fun-loving cats. Humans? Gone."

Scratching his scruffy, patchy beard, he unrolled the blueprints of Silvertown across the table. "Here's the plan: we move underground, through the sewage system. When I say go, I'll toss smoke bombs to blind the town. That's your cue—scratch their arms, puke on their legs, bite their fingers, cover them with your scent. Then I'll activate my laser. Anyone it touches will have their human genes replaced with cat genes—fur will sprout, and they'll be walking on all fours. Genius, right? How did I not think of this sooner?"

He was in the middle of revealing his evil plan, but—

Boom!

A big explosion. The entire building collapses. Catman is lying on the ground coughing from all the dust. He looks up to see Secret Agent Carlos, his worst nemesis, standing in front of him.

All of his henchmen are on the ground covered with debris from the explosion, Catman expects that his cat henchmen are already dead. Catman looks at Secret Agent Carlos with malicious anger.

"Curse you Secret Agent Carlos! I just want to make the whole world a safe place by turning every human into a cat, but you just had to ruin it, did you?"

Carlos laughs. "Turn every human into a cat? Man, that's the most stupid plan I have ever heard."

"I wouldn't expect a government-working idiot like you to understand. It's better than what the world governments are doing right now. I'm just trying to make the world safe and turning everyone into cats it's the safest thing to do."

"You're a simple-minded fool. Trying to take over a whole town is one thing, but trying to take over the whole world is just pure stupidity. It's over for you, Catman. You're not going to molest anybody's cats any longer. Ever surrender or die!"

Catman laughs. "Pff, I'd rather die, but I'm not losing without a fight. Come here you bastard! I'm going to tear you to shreds!"

That's the only thing Carlos likes about Catman, he doesn't want to give up. *This is going to be a good fight!* Carlos thought to himself.

Catman suddenly charges at Carlos, and Carlos charges at Catman. Catman raises his fist to punch Carlos, and Carlos does the same thing. When their fists collide, the sheer force from their fists causes a big air explosion that blows all the entire debris of the abandoned building.

None of the building remains except with Carlos and Catman, they are the only ones that remained. They are both lying on the ground. Carlos suddenly gets up, but Catman is still lying face down on the ground. Carlos walks up to Catman, Catman looks up at Carlos.

"Just kill me already."

"Will do."

It looks like Carlos has finally defeated Catman. Carlos points his pistol at him...

Bang!

Carlos just stands there, but then suddenly he feels a winch of pain and he falls to the ground. Carlos hasn't felt this kind of pain before, there are barely any scratches on his body. It's definitely not asthma.

It might be internally. Carlos thinks.

He is going to see the doctor after this. He calls his boss to pick up Catman's body for him, and then he gets on the horse to head to the hospital.

***

Carlos Rodriguez is at the Silvertown Hospital. His son, Baxter, is there with him. They are both sitting in the doctor's office waiting to see Carlos' results from the biopsy. The only reason why Carlos has his son here is because there's a chance Carlos might die. If that's true, then he wants to tell his son some things before he dies. The doctor finally arrives, and he sits at his desk.

"I'm sorry to say this, Mr. Rodriguez, but you got stomach cancer. Sadly, due to so much fighting you've done throughout your years, it seems to be terminal. Based on my diagnosis, you have five weeks to live. Sorry..."

The doctor was expecting Carlos to be very sad by this, crying like a baby, and he will be secretly grinning from the inside like he does with the other patients after he tells them that they have a terminal illness. The doctor couldn't believe how much his patients paid him just to try to see if he could cure them. It's such a good way to make money. But instead, he sees Carlos jumping for joy, like a kid that received a present on his birthday.

"Why are you so happy?" The doctor asks.

Carlos laughs. "I don't want my enemies to be the reason why I die, so knowing that I only have five weeks to live means I can die happy. Hah, hah! Yes, I'm not going to die from enemies' hands! Woah!"

Carlos begins to jump up and down. Baxter just sits there bothered. The doctor is so star-structed that he can't speak, and so the doctor just decides to take Carlos to a hospital room. Carlos just wishes to stay at the hospital for the rest of his life and asks to be alone. So the doctor leaves him alone, but Carlos wants his son to stay. When the doctor leaves, Carlos looks at his son.

"I want to tell you something before I die."

Baxter rolls his eyes. "Pff, what?"

"Don't be saddened by me dying, son. Stay focused on all the training I taught you to do throughout the years."

"Pff, ok? What is this supposed to be? Some last words of encouragement before you die? I know you don't care about me at all, dad. The only time you come to the house is to train me in these stupid lessons."

"Yes, that's because you shouldn't trust me at all, son. All the training that I taught you, let that be a lesson for you that you shouldn't trust anybody in this world, not even your father. Only trust yourself, son."

"Yeah, yeah. I don't care. Now, are you gonna die already or what?"

"Son, I love you."

"Pff, whatever man! I'm leaving! I'm actually going to be relieved when you're gone!"

After Baxter gets out of the room, he sighs in annoyance. His dad doesn't care about him at all, the only reason why his dad hangs out with him at all is to train him. Now that his dad is going to die, he is actually relieved because now he doesn't have to worry about his dad coming out of nowhere just to train him and just to leave the house leaving Baxter on his own to take care of himself. Baxter is applying what his dad is teaching him. Baxter doesn't trust his dad, and he doesn't trust anybody in the whole universe!

He walks through the hospital on his way to his car so he can drive out of there and never return. Before he gets out of the hospital though, he hears a familiar voice.

"Hey, Baxter!"

Baxter knows who that voice is, he almost just wants to ignore it and walk away, but he turns around to face that person. It is Honey, she is an intern nurse at the hospital. Honey is in a nursing scrub as she walks toward Baxter, smiling. *What the hell does she want?* Baxter thought to himself.

"Hey, Baxter. I just wanted to stop and say how sorry I am that your dad has that terminal illness. If you need any help, I—"

"I don't need your pity."

Baxter just walks away. He doesn't get people like Honey.

Why is she so nice to me and people in general? Why is The Wolf Pack so nice to me?

Baxter doesn't get it, but he doesn't think about it too much as he quickly gets in his car and drives off.

Why did my dad treat me this way all my life and why does he have to be an asshole and die now?

Baxter sheds a tear, but he quickly dries it away as he continues to drive.

Chapter 28- Date Curfew

Honey's POV, the loving flower girl

Honey can't wait to get off work. She and Ben haven't had a proper date since their space trip three months ago, and tonight is finally their chance. Spring has arrived in Montana—snow's melted, the air is warmer, and Honey's already dreaming of planting flowers in her backyard.

There's been no sign of The Ferals lately, which is both a relief and a mystery. Honey isn't even sure if Ben still likes her—they haven't had a moment alone since she asked him out. Maybe they've just been too busy, but now they've made time. She hopes the date goes well. She's scared Ben might hate it—and worse, that he might shut her out for good. She wants him to open up, to share what he's feeling.

Ben's quiet by nature, but since the Sweetopia trip, he's been even more withdrawn—maybe from all the intense training. Honey knows what it's like when someone won't open up, when they leave without a word. She just wants a chance to say goodbye if it comes to that.

Ben texts that he's watering his grass, so when Honey gets home, she heads straight to his backyard across the street. But instead of grass, she finds Ben watering himself—drenched in sweat from training with Chuck and the others. He doesn't notice her approach, so Honey grins, ready to surprise him.

"Hello there, gardener!"

Ben jumps and turns around.

"Honey? Man, you scared me." Ben is all wet, wide-eyed, and blushing.

Honey just laughs. "Ah, why do you worry so much, Ben?"

Ben just rubs his head, embarrassed.

"Anyway, we should probably hurry because the movie starts in only thirty minutes."

Ben nods. "Alright, let's take my truck."

"Um, actually, Ben, how about I drive. You're probably tired from training. I can drive, no big deal."

"Fine. Just let me take a shower first."

After that, Honey walks to her car with Ben beside her. She hopes this date goes well.

***

"Well, that sucked."

Ben says as he eats his ice cream with Honey. They're at a table next to an ice cream shop amongst other patrons. Some who also went to the movie theater are amongst the crowd, but others are either families or people going on dates just like they are.

Honey looks at Ben cock-eyed. "What? What do you mean? That ending was really good."

"Pff, I'm not talking about the ending. I'm talking about the part of the movie when they defeated the monster."

"Why do you think that part sucked?"

"Man, I don't know. Just the way they defeated that monster doesn't seem right to me."

"You mean sparing its life?"

"Exactly: sparing its life for what? So can it just go over to another place and destroy it too? God, see why I don't like fictional movies like that. It doesn't make any sense to me."

"Well, Ben, they're called fiction for a reason. They don't apply to real life."

"Yeah, well, whatever."

Ben continues to eat his ice cream. Honey grows silent. This is exactly the right time for her to open up with him. Honey gets a little nervous, but she starts to speak up.

"Hey, Ben..." She wants to tell Ben how she truly feels about him, but she hesitates before speaking.

Ben stays silent, but she has his attention.

"Ben, I want to talk about our relationship. All this time, we've been busy with school, work, and training our special abilities, which is all good, but Ben. I could see over the past few months you haven't been acting like your normal self lately."

"What do you mean?"

"What I'm trying to say is that you need to relax a little."

"Relax a little? What do you mean?"

"I mean that you've been only focusing on trying to get your special ability better. It seems like you neglected time spent with your friends, including me. And Ben—We've not been on a date since forever, and the only times we've ever hung out was when all of our friends got together just to train."

"Yeah, that's because we don't know when those Feral bastards will come back. I'm just trying to prepare us for when it's going to happen."

"I think you're preparing too much, Ben."

"Preparing too much? There's no such thing. Didn't Chuck tell us that we should try to prepare as much as possible for when The Ferals come?"

"Yeah, but he also told us that we shouldn't over-worry ourselves either. I can see that's what you are doing."

"Worried? You're the one who shouldn't be worried. When school is over and we finally defeat The Ferals, we all can have enough time to spend with each other. You'll see."

Honey knows this isn't what Ben truly feels.

"Ben, you know the reason why me and my mom moved here?"

"Yeah, I know the story."

"Well, I'm going to tell you again. Ben, the reason why we had to move was because my dad committed suicide. We had to leave because we couldn't bear the pain we felt..." Honey sheds a tear. "I felt dead inside because I wasn't able to save him. Ben, I want to save you. I know that you feel bad because your dad left you, but I'm here to help."

"I know that."

"Do you truly know that, Ben? Because you've been ignoring me and the rest of our friends over the past few months now. Ben, just say what's on your mind and we'll—"

"Okay, it's getting late. We should head to bed."

302

Ben gets up out of his chair and starts to walk away toward her car. He had already eaten his entire ice cream cone, and so did she. She just sighs in defeat. She gives up trying to make Ben confess and gets in her car to drive them home.

When they arrive, Ben quickly kisses her on the cheek. "Bye."

Ben walks quickly toward his house, and she just watches him go—like her dad did when she was little. He left for work that day and never came back. She never knew how much pain her dad carried, but now she can see Ben is feeling something similar. She loves Ben so much... just like she loved her father. She can tell he's hurting, and all she wants is a chance to help him. To save him. Every life matters. No one should have to feel this lost.

Why does everyone seem so sad?

Chapter 29- Time To Hide

Nour's POV, the angry feline

They're back on this messed-up planet after searching Sweetopia for Uri. Ginger's tracker on the BS Lion showed that Uri moved back to Earth—for some reason. Nour thinks it's probably because of that Earth human who kidnapped him. That human is likely trying to mess with them. But Nour won't fall for it. That kidnapper thinks he's smart, but Nour and The Ferals aren't a group to be messed with. So Nour decided they should check out that Earth human's house—after capturing some Sweetopians and holding them hostage.

That overseer, Jegu, was a tough raptor to beat, but Nour managed to capture him along with some others. Nour figures that Earth human probably went home with Uri in tow. He knows what they're planning. He tried to get Jegu to spill the plan to keep Uri away, but the stubborn old raptor stayed silent. Doesn't matter—they're here now. Nour and his friends are hiding behind bushes next to the Earth human's house, scouting the area.

Sebastian yawns. "Man, this is getting boring now. Why are we just waiting around? The Earth human's house is right there. Let's just barge right in and attack him."

"Well, we don't know if the Earth human kidnapper is even in there with Uri," Nour says.

"Well, the Earth human's vehicle is right there." Nader points at the truck. "But that still doesn't mean he's actually in there. And besides, we don't want to deal with those Earth human soldiers, so it's best if we just scout the area for now."

Sebastian rolls his eyes. "Pff, you think I'm scared of some wimpy soldiers. I just want to get my revenge on that Earth human for nearly killing me. He nearly killed me with the same 'Devil's Eye' power as you do, Nour. I need payback."

Nour just shakes his head. "I don't want to take any chances."

"Pff, alright then."

Nour and The Ferals continue to wait until they suddenly see a door open. Sure enough, the Earth human comes out with Uri and three other raptors. Nour's prediction that the Earth human kidnapper and Uri will be here is correct, but Nour didn't expect that three Sweetopians would also be with them?

"Wait a minute? They have three Sweetopians with them? Isn't that just great? That chocolatey brown one was the one I was about to kill as well." Sebastian blurts out.

"If that's the case, then we need to figure out a good strategic plan for this. Let's get back to the ship." Ginger chimes in.

Nour shakes his head. "No, let's follow wherever they're going."

Nader looks at Nour cock eyed. "Nour, you can't be serious? Three Sweetopian are with them now. Who knows what other creatures are helping them? You know, it would be a good idea to think things over."

Ben, Uri, and the raptors get in the truck that's parked in front of the house and drive away. Nour jumps out of the bush and tries to follow the truck.

"Hey, what are you doing?"

Nour is not going to let this vehicle get out of his sight. He is going to follow where this vehicle is going and hopefully take Uri out of the hands of that Earth-human kidnapper. His friends are tailing him. Nour is going to catch Uri no matter what it takes. If he has to kill that Earth human kidnapper and those Sweetopians that are with him too, then so be it.

***

Uri and the raptors are sitting beside Ben as he drives to school. Surprisingly, they haven't seen any signs of The Ferals yet, but Ben is still looking and preparing. There's supposed to be a field trip today in science class, where the teacher is going to take Ben's class to Silvertown Park to study native plants.

Ben is not sure how he is going to hide the raptors and Uri while he is at school, but he's sure he'll figure something out. He always does, right?

"Don't get scared, but The Ferals are here," Chuck says in his robot voice.

The eyes of Ben and the others' go wide.

"How do you know that they are here?" Uri asks.

"I'm feeling bloodlust coming from somewhere, and I can only assume that it's them. I've been feeling a little bloodlust ever since we left the house."

Ben looks at Chuck cock eyed. "You know, I've been feeling strange ever since we got out of the house too, but I didn't know what it was."

Ocean smiles. "Ah, good, your trained conscience is developing."

"Trained conscience?"

Strawberry chimes in. "Yes, a trained conscience helps you distinguish between what's good and what's bad for you just by sensing it. You can sense badness happening right near you."

"Oh, that explains everything."

"What should we do now?" Uri asks.

"Stay calm, it looks like they're just following us," Chuck says.

"Why aren't they attacking?" Uri asks.

Chuck shrugs. "Probably because they're in the public where people can see them. I know how the cat species work; they just wait patiently until they find the opportunity to pounce."

Uri bites his nails. "Oh, great. This is just fantastic."

"Don't worry, I have a plan. Me, Strawberry, Ocean, and Uri are going to shape shift into something small and hide in Ben's backpack."

"Great, what am I going to do?" Ben asks worriedly.

"Just stay calm and act like everything is normal. You're going to carry us and, hopefully, they won't notice. I'll be prepared to protect you guys just in case they attack us."

Chuck turns into a chocolate bar, and Uri uses his ability to transform into a fly. Meanwhile, Strawberry Shores becomes an actual strawberry, and Blueberry Ocean turns into a blueberry. Ben carefully puts them all in his backpack, with Uri buzzing in after.

Ben tries not to look suspicious as he opens the school's front door and slips inside. He lets out a quiet sigh of relief— The Ferals don't seem to suspect a thing. But there's a problem: he and The Wolf Pack have a science class field trip coming up, which means they'll be outside—an open invitation for The Ferals. He needs to warn his friends, and hopefully, Chuck's plan will work. If The Ferals do attack, Ben's ready to protect Uri no matter what.

Chapter 30- Field Trip

Baxter's POV, the mad pyromaniac

At Silvertown Park, The Wolf Pack waits with the other students on their field trip. Unfortunately, Cougar Jack and his annoying crew are here too—but at least they keep their distance. If they got any closer, a brawl would probably break out.

Baxter couldn't care less which side he's on, but to keep his spying low-key, he figures he might have to fight with The Wolf Pack if things heat up.

Honestly, he can't wait for school to be over so he never has to deal with The Cougars or The Wolf Pack again. He just wants to be alone, doing whatever he wants. His awful dad will be gone soon—thanks to that cancer diagnosis—and finally, Baxter can live for himself, staying as far away from people as possible.

Mr. Fleming, the science teacher, stands in front of the class. trying to calm everyone down, but the kids keep on goofing around. "Alright everyone, be quiet!"

The students keep being loud, but slowly they start to calm down.

Mr. Fleming coughs before he speaks. "Alright everyone, the reason why you are on this field trip is not to goof around, but to study the different native plant species in our local area. You must look for different native plant species and write down the different characteristics of each plant. It's sort of an educational treasure hunt. Each of you must pair with another person. The first three pairs to find five native plants and write down their characteristics will get extra credit in the final semester. You are off."

Immediately, every kid tries to pair off with their best friends. The Wolf Pack pairs off amongst themselves Ben pairs with Honey and Cedric with Slam, leaving Baxter and Tom to pair with each other. *Oh great, I have to be partners with the police boy.* Oh well, he's the smart kid anyway, so Baxter guesses he will have to partner up with him. Baxter walks up to Tom, who is standing next to the science teacher.

"Hey, police boy. You and me, partners."

"Sorry, Baxter, but I'm the teacher's aide. You have to team up with somebody else."

Well, ain't that a load of crap. Baxter frowns and looks around. It looks like everyone already has partners. *Great, it looks like I have to work alone again.* This always happens, but Baxter is used to it. He prefers this way because he hates partners.

"Hey, Mr. Fleming. Baxter doesn't have a partner," Tom says.

Oh, great. Why did you have to open your mouth, police boy?

"Oh, okay…" Mr. Fleming looks around. "Hey, Jack, come over here!"

You gotta be kidding me? Why did he call Jack's name? Cougar Jack walks over to Mr. Fleming.

"Hey, Jack, work with Baxter, will you please?"

"You gotta be kidding me, teach! I'm not going to work with this asshole."

"Baxter, language! It's your only option. If you don't want to partner up with Jack, then you can walk over to the bus, and I'll fail you."

Baxter looks over at Ben, who just looks at Baxter, seeming puzzled. Oh, great. This isn't helping him with his spy dealings. Baxter hesitates to speak, but then he sighs in annoyance.

"Fine, just don't get your dirty hands on me like you do with your girlfriend, creep."

Jack frowns. "Excuse me?"

Mr. Fleming frowns. "Baxter."

"Fine, I apologize. Let's just get this over with."

Ben nods at Baxter, probably out of respect for him giving Jack a hard time. Baxter just sighs in relief, and they walk out of sight of the others.

Jack smirks and shakes his head playfully. "Man, oh man. Your acting skills are on point. Ben didn't expect anything."

"Whatever, let's just find these stupid plants."

"That's what I like about you. Always discreet and eager to get things done. By the way, how's the spying going?"

"I'm making progress."

"Well, it sure does look like it." Jack takes out cash from his pocket and gives it to Baxter. Baxter accepts the cash.

"I like that cap. It got that good Native American style on it. How much do you want for it?"

"I'm not giving you anything."

Jack gives him more cash, and Baxter gives him the hat. Jack is lucky that Baxter needs the cash to make himself a special bomb or he wouldn't accept the cash and give him his baseball cap. The stupid idiot thinks he can manipulate him with his money, but once school is over, Baxter is planning to never deal with The Cougars again.

Jack jerks a thumb at the park behind him. "We should hurry and find those native plants quickly before Ben does. Come on, I know where to find them."

Baxter sighs as he follows Jack through the park. Before the field trip even started, Ben told The Wolf Pack that The Ferals were here and that the raptors and Uri were hiding in his backpack. He warned them to be on the lookout.

Baxter regrets even going along with The Wolf Pack and protecting that strange alien kid. If he'd known it would get this messy, he never would've agreed to spy for The Cougars. Now, no matter how much they pay, he just wants out. If protecting an alien is part of the deal, he's done. He also doesn't get The Wolf Pack's loyalty—they've been friends since they were kids. Baxter wouldn't trust anyone that long; eventually, someone betrays you. And this Slam kid? He's only been with them a few months but already diving into their crazy adventures.

Jack suddenly notices something weird ahead. Baxter can't help but laugh. Looks like Ben's trap worked—Larry and Edwin are stuck in a huge hole Ben dug. Ben had been pestering Baxter, Cedric, and Slam for a week to help dig it. He even used his ability to make cotton candy at the bottom for a nice soft and sticky landing. Jack sighs as he watches his two buddies struggle in the sugary mess.

"Wow, it's amazing that you guys are even part of my group."

Suddenly, Baxter pushes Jack in the hole. The hat that Jack bought from Baxter falls on the ground. Baxter picks his hat up, puts it on his head, and walks away. Baxter can hear Jack yelling at him.

Baxter gives Ben credit. He may not be the smartest kid in school, but he has some clever ideas. Baxter decides to find Ben and Honey. Ben planned for The Wolf Pack to meet together in an area where the science teacher and the rest of the students won't see them. Tom might be the only one who's not going to meet up because he's stuck with being the teacher's aide.

Ben said he expects The Ferals are still watching them. If they ever appear, they'll attack. Ben wants to lead The Ferals away from Uri as much as possible, so he has Tom hold onto his backpack that has Uri inside.

Chuck and his raptor buddies are in Ben's pocket so they can help. Baxter just wants to see what The Ferals really look like.

Do they look like evil cat assassins, or do they look cute like the Sweetopians?

Whatever they look like, Baxter wants to fight them to see if they truly are skilled fighters.

When Baxter finally arrives at the meeting place, Slam and Cedric are already there. So is Ben, who smiles at Baxter like he's glad to see him. Baxter doesn't get how Ben, with all of the problems with his dad leaving him, could be so joyous. Ben trusts his friends for some reason. If Baxter was him, he would just trust himself with all the crap he's been through.

"Hey, Baxter. How's it going? Did my plan work?"

"Yeah, they're all trapped."

"Oh, yeah. That will teach them."

Ben offers Baxter a handshake, which he awkwardly accepts.

Honey asks. "Plan? What plan?"

"Oh, nothing."

Ben, Cedric, Slam, and even Baxter all smirk mischievously. Honey just rolls her eyes.

"Do I even want to know?"

Suddenly, Ben takes a chocolate bar, a strawberry, and a blueberry out and it turns into Chuck and his buddies. The Sweetopians look at all of them after they change forms.

Ben looks at Chuck intently. "Are you sure this plan of yours will work, Chuck?"

"Yes, just make sure you let me do the talking when they arrive."

"Pff, if they arrive." Baxter rolls his eyes.

"You wanna talk?"

All of them jump in surprise when they hear a strange noise coming from somewhere. Some bushes move behind them and The Ferals emerge, standing just a few feet away from them.

Baxter barely heard anything, yet all The Ferals were just a few feet away without them noticing.

One of The Ferals has an Egyptian-looking crown on his head, who Baxter assumes is Nour, their leader. Pff, he doesn't look that tough, more like a small house cat. The Ferals are not attacking them surprisingly, they are just standing there quietly. Then this cat with the Egyptian-looking crown starts speaking.

"Where did you hide Uri?"

Chuck frowns. "If you think we're going to give his location away to you evil cats, then you assumed wrong."

Nour's face turns angrier than it was before, and he growls.

"Er, why are you helping these Earth humans, you Sweetopians? If you don't tell me where Uri is, then I'm going to kill all of you!"

Does this tiny cat really think he can kill all of us? Baxter laughs. "Man, seriously? These puny cats are what Uri is so scared of? Man, this is going to be a piece of cake."

Baxter charges at Nour, looking to hit him.

"No! Stop!" Chuck yells out to Baxter, but it's too late.

Nour dodges Baxter's punch like it was nothing and hits him in the stomach. The punch is so powerful that it pushes Baxter away and he falls to the ground, clenching his stomach in pain.

That punch was more painful than most of the punches Baxter's dad landed on him. *How is this small cat able to punch that hard?* Baxter gets on his knees, still holding his stomach.

Chuck was about to defend Baxter, but then a random spear came after him. He barely avoids it.

"Oh, no you don't. I'm the one who's supposed to finish you off." One of The Ferals says, the gray one with the orange arrows covering its body.

Nour completely passes Chuck and charges at Baxter with his claws out. *Oh, s**t. What did I start?* Baxter ducks his head, just barely avoiding an inch of claw slicing his hair.

Nour lands on the ground softly, while he's still just trying to recover from his stomach pain. *Damn it! Why can't I move? Come on, you're tougher than this.*

Baxter looks around and seems like everybody is busy fighting with the other cats. It looks like he's alone fighting this beast. Working alone, as always.

Baxter prepares for Nour to come at him one more time. Is this how he's going to die? All alone to this stupid cat? He thought so. Baxter breathes, his last breath as the cat is close, but—

What the hell? What is he doing?

Ben dives between them.

Nour scratches Ben's back but stops and backs off. Ben screeches in pain, and Baxter just stands there in shock.

"What the hell is wrong with you? Stop helping me! Help yourself, God damn it!" Baxter sheds a tear. "Why...Why are you helping me?"

Ben smiles. He doesn't say anything and just hugs him...

Baxter doesn't know what to think. It's the first time he ever had someone care about him. He doesn't know why Ben and The Wolf Pack are nice to him. Baxter feels guilty as he realizes how much good they have done for him. He realizes what friendship means at that moment. His dad was wrong, trusting and making friends with people will not make you weak.

Ben steps back and wavers, and Honey runs up to grab him. This is bad, Baxter can see how big of a scratch is on Ben's back, blood is seeping through his clothes. It's like a bear scratched him. How powerful are these cats? The Ferals and the others just stand there in shock. Baxter knows what he's going to do. He's going to protect his friends!

Baxter uses his ability and makes bombs appear around all The Ferals. They are so in shock that they almost don't realize that there are bombs around them.

Baxter then snaps his fingers, and the bombs explode. Luckily, they were just silent smoke bombs so the students and teacher wouldn't hear them.

After the bombs explode, Baxter immediately turns to Ben.

"Let's go!"

Chuck turns into a chocolate bar and his two buddies turn into fruit. They go into Honey's pocket. Baxter, Honey, Slam, and Cedric try to carry the hurt Ben and escape as quickly as possible away from The Ferals and to where their class is.

***

Cougar Jack's face burned as he flailed, trying to climb out of the sticky cotton candy pit. Edwin and Larry were tangled beside him, their clothes drenched and clinging. Around them, laughter exploded—kids pointing, whispering, snapping photos. Jack caught sight of Anna smirking, her phone raised, filming every humiliating second. Her friends giggled behind their screens, taking selfies with the spectacle in the background. Jack's fists clenched, but his sticky hands made it useless. He spat out a curse, eyes burning with fury. Ben had outsmarted them all—and Jack swore he'd make him pay.

"Hey! Stop taking selfies and get us out of here!" Jack growls.

"Oh, I'm sorry, Jack, but..." Anna sticks her lips out playfully while holding her bicep. "I can't lift you. You said I'm too weak, remember?"

Anna and her girly friends laugh. Jack continues to growl.

"Hey, Anna. For reals, stop taking pictures." Mr. Fleming blurts out.

Anna and her friends finally put their phones away in their pockets, but they still giggle as they watch some students try to pull Jack, Edwin, and Larry out of the hole with a rope.

"Yeah, this is definitely Ben's doing." Tom says, looking down at Jack.

Mr. Fleming frowns at Tom. "You weren't involved in this, were you?"

Tom shakes his head. "You have to understand, Mr. Fleming. Ben has a mind of his own. I can't keep track of him. Not even Ben can keep track of himself."

Mr. Fleming raises an eyebrow.

Tom can tell that Mr. Fleming doesn't believe him. Tom just awkwardly chuckles and rubs his head. *I swear I'm going to kill Ben after this.* Just when Tom thought of this, his friends finally arrived. Tom is surprised to see Ben hurt.

Baxter and Cedric are carrying Ben on their shoulders.

What the hell happened?

Mr. Fleming sees them and is surprised to see Ben hurt. Mr. Fleming's face starts fuming.

"What happened to you guys?" Mr. Fleming looks at Ben. "Why do you have a big scratch on your back?"

"A bear attacked me."

"You gotta be kidding me? I told you guys to stay where the park is, not wandering alone in the forests! We need to get you medical treatment, quickly!"

"Don't worry, Mr. Fleming. We can take Ben to the hospital." Honey says.

Mr. Fleming nods. "Alright, get on a bus, quickly."

Honey and Cedric carry Ben on their shoulders to the school bus leaving Baxter and Slam. Tom is there, he walks over to Baxter and Slam.

"What happened?"

Slam looks at Tom. "We'll explain later when we're alone. We've finally met them."

"Oh, I see."

The three of them stay silent.

Baxter doesn't know what he's going to do with his relationship with The Cougars as he watches the teacher, and some students try to lift Jack, Edwin, and Larry out of the big hole. All he knows is that he's not going to help them any longer, the spying jig is over.

Baxter is with The Wolf Pack now; he has true friends that he can trust.

Chapter 31- Honey's Mom

Ben and Honey aren't in the hospital long. Ben has a big bandage on his back, and the doctor says the scratch will be healed in a few days. The scratch was very painful and still stings. All Ben wants to do is rest. The Ferals are probably not going to attack them again, at least not after a while. This will give Ben time to figure out a way to defeat them.

One thing that's bothering Ben is why didn't some of them fight. Considering The Ferals are very determined to catch Uri, they didn't all attack. Instead, some were just standing there. Could it be that they think he and his friends are weak and are not worth their time? Well, if The Ferals think that he and his friends are weak, then he's going to show them they are wrong. Ben is going to show The Ferals that messing with a kid like Uri isn't right, and he's going to do whatever it takes to take them down! He's going to—

"Ben, let me help you." Honey gets under Ben's shoulders, helping him walk.

He doesn't say anything but lets her help him walk to the parking lot.

"Man, what you did was risky, Ben. You could've gotten yourself killed."

"That wouldn't be the first time." he shrugged.

"I'm just glad that The Ferals didn't kill you and Baxter. I'm sorry I didn't help you quick enough. I didn't know what to do at that moment. Everything went so fast, and we were just standing there."

"Hey, don't worry about it."

"I'm more worried about you, Ben. Let's just hope The Ferals don't attack us again."

"Yeah."

The only thing Ben is mad at is himself because he wasn't strong enough to go against The Ferals. Ben is going to make sure he gets stronger so he can defeat them. Not even with all that training he did, it still wasn't enough to even defeat one of them.

Honey called her mom to pick them up from the hospital, and they waited near the parking lot. Ben has only met Honey's mom a few times. Ben is kind of nervous about seeing Honey's mom, especially with the situation he's in. He doesn't know what she thinks of him, but he hopes it's good. He doesn't want her mom to think he's not right for Honey.

Ben looks up at the sound of an engine, only to find Tom's truck pulling up.

Tom stops and opens his window. "Hey, you two. Need a ride?"

Honey smiles. "Thank you, but we're just waiting for my mom to pick us up."

"Oh, okay."

Suddenly, a fly buzzes around Ben and Honey.

Ben could only assume it is Uri.

Tom nods toward the fly. "I'm going to leave Uri with you guys. I'm sorry, but I'm too busy doing work with my dad, and I'm not willing to find out what my dad's reaction is going to be when he sees Uri."

"It's okay, just make sure you keep an eye out for The Ferals," Honey says.

"I will. See ya."

Tom drives off, and Uri lands on Ben's shoulder.

"Hey, Ben. Are you alright?" Uri asks.

"I'm fine."

"Oh, man. I should've joined you guys. The Ferals are too powerful, Ben. You guys should probably let me leave and—"

"No, you're staying here."

"But—"

"You got nothing to worry about, Uri. I don't think The Ferals are going to attack any time soon. Besides, we've promised to do this together." Honey interrupts Uri.

"Oh, alright." Uri looks around. "By the way, where's Chuck, Strawberry, and Ocean?"

"They're in my pocket," Ben says.

"They can't talk when they're in their food forms, but we did have a chance to talk to them at the hospital when nobody was around," Honey says.

"What did they say?" Uri asks.

"They told us how sorry they were that they didn't do better at helping defend us from The Ferals. We also told them not to worry. Everything happened so quickly." Honey says.

Which is why Ben is going to train even harder now that The Ferals are here. Suddenly, they see Honey's mom driving toward them and Uri stops talking. Honey's mom pulls up to them and opens the door. Honey and Ben get in the backseat of the car.

"Hey there, Ben. Are you alright?" Honey's mom looks at them with concern.

"I'm fine. Thank you."

"Ben, you better be safe and not act recklessly in the woods, now. Especially around bears. You guys should probably bring bear spray with you now, alright?"

Ben just awkwardly laughs.

"Don't worry, I'm not going to act recklessly around bears again."

Honey's mom looks satisfied with Ben's answer, and she drives them back to their homes.

"Thank you, Mrs. Barnes," Ben says as she drops him off.

Honey's mom smiles. "Woah, hey now! Where are you going? Come to my house and stay for dessert. I made apple pie."

"Um, sure." Ben is always awkward when people are nice to him because he doesn't know what to say or do.

Soon, Ben, Honey, and her mom are outside on the backyard patio eating apple pie with vanilla ice cream. They have a fun time talking and laughing. Uri buzzes around, with Honey's mom none the wiser. After Ben eats his pie, he decides to say goodnight and go home for some sleep. They all say goodnight, and Ben heads toward his house.

On the way, somebody calls out to him.

"Hey, Ben! Wait."

Ben turns around to see Honey running toward him. She stops and seems about to say something but pauses for a moment and looks down. "Ben, I'm just here to tell you how sorry I am that our date didn't go so well yesterday. I'm sorry that I was so pushy trying to make you express your feelings...um..."

Honey pauses again. She's looking down like a puppy who feels guilty. All Ben does is smile. Man, this girl does worry a lot. That's what Ben likes about her because she's just like him. He steps forward and kisses her before she can say anything else.

After kissing her, he immediately runs to his house out of embarrassment.

Ben doesn't want to hear Honey's reaction right now, so he rushes inside his house before she can say anything. After Ben closes the door, he breathes a sigh of relief and lays on the floor.

Man, I love that girl.

He wouldn't know what to do without her.

***

Nour didn't know what to do when that human kidnapper protected his friend like that. He thought the humans were selfish creatures, so why did that human kidnapper just protect his friend?

Before he could process that, the kidnapper's friend made smoke bombs appear out of nowhere. Nour thought these Earth humans didn't know how to use special abilities.

What the hell is going on?

"Are you seriously just going to wait near this human's house until he gets here?" Nader looks at Nour cock eyed.

"Yes."

"Man, just give it up, Nour!" Ginger blurts out.

"يلا بينا! (Let's go!)" Antar exclaims.

"See, even Antar is tired, man. Let's just get out of here."

"No, I still need to find out if this human kidnapper has Uri or not."

"You know the human kidnapper has a name, right? As well as those other friends of his." Nader says.

"Pff, Ben? Sounds like a very kidnapper name to me. What are the names of his friends again?"

Nader scratches his head. "Well, based on eavesdropping on their conversations during their rendezvous, I know the crazy one that you tried to kill is Baxter, the female is Honey, the one wearing an Earth soldier jacket is Tom, the one with the leather boots is Cedric, and the one with the long messy coat is Slam."

Nour raises an eyebrow. "So there's six of them in total?"

"Correct, if you're excluding Uri and the Sweetopians that are with them."

"Man, those stupid Sweetopians. They're probably the ones who've been teaching these human bastards how to use special abilities. If it ain't for them, getting Uri would've been a piece of cake."

"Nour, they seem like nice people. How about we just talk to them?" Tito chimes in.

"Talk to them? Are you serious? I'm not talking to any of these human bastards. If one of them shows up, I'm going to kill them, no questions asked. You got that?"

All of his friends stay silent. Nour doesn't know what to do except wait near this human's house to see if he will come back. He knows little about the human kidnapper and his friends other than their names.

"Man, I don't think anybody will show up at this point. Let's just get out of here." Sebastian complains.

"No, wait a little while longer."

Suddenly, a car parks close to Ben's house. Three humans get out, and Nour recognizes two of them: Ben and Honey. There's another human who looks like Honey, except she's older. Nour can only guess she is Honey's mother.

"You gotta be kidding me. Uri's not with them." Nour growls.

Ginger asks, "What are you planning to do now?"

"We're going to attack them and force them to tell us where Uri is."

"What?" Nader asks. "That's a stupid plan. We don't want to have those human soldiers to show up."

"Fine, we'll wait until this Ben human gets in his house, then break in and quietly attack him."

Ebo raises an eyebrow. "How can you 'quietly' attack somebody?"

"Dude, we're cats. It's in our nature. Just shut up and wait."

"This plan of yours is not going to work," Nader says.

"Oh, shut up. You always say that."

"Because it's always true."

"No, it's not."

Nour and Nader argue for a while until Ginger interrupts them.

"Hey, guys, look! This Ben human got out of the house, and now he's walking alone."

Nour looks up as Ben stops and Honey runs toward him. Nour angles an ear toward them and hears them talking about a date. *Is this the human kidnapper's mate?* Nour ponders. They kiss...

Nour's heart feels like it might stop as he is reminded of Angel.

"Man, it's always strange to me to see how humans show their affection," Sebastian says.

Nader raises an eyebrow. "What? You want to see them lick each other?"

Sebastian smirks. "Hey, I wouldn't mind that."

"Okay, forget that I even asked."

"Look! They finally separated. Ben is alone now. Should we break into his house?" Ebo looks at Nour intently.

"No, leave them be."

The Ferals all look at Nour wide-eyed.

"What? What do you mean? You're not going to attack him?" Sebastian raises an eyebrow.

"I'm going to find another way to find Uri."

"What do you mean?"

"I know why..." Nader drones.

"It's because those two humans kissing each other reminds you of Angel, doesn't it, Nour?" Tito asks.

Nour takes out the picture of Angel from his sleeve pocket. "He's just like me." This Ben risked his life trying to protect his friend, and he seems to be in love with this female. Maybe Ben is trying to protect Uri, just like him.

Nader raises an eyebrow. "Well, what are you going to do now?"

"Ben and his friends are nice humans, but they don't realize the danger involved. There's a bunch of powerful creatures out there in the universe that are after Uri. If those creatures find this planet and they find Uri here, they will kill them."

Tito raises an eyebrow. "But isn't those Sweetopians teaching them how to use special abilities?"

"Pff, it doesn't matter. They're only just learning how to use their abilities. They won't be able to face the powerful creatures in the universe. They will get killed trying."

"So, what are you planning to do?" Nader asks.

"I don't know. I'm going to figure out a plan to get them to hand over Uri without us fighting each other. I'm going to find a way to negotiate with them."

Nader rolls his eyes. "Well, hopefully, you can finally make a successful plan for once."

"Oh, shut up. Let's just get back to the ship."

Chapter 32- Cut The Bridge

Baxter's POV, the mad pyromaniac

Baxter heads toward Cougar Jack's house, "The Cougar Mansion." A place where kids follow a rich, insecure douche-bag named Jack that has a way of manipulating people. Baxter can't believe he was one of those people, out of all the things he believed and stood for. With his dad on his deathbed, his final days. Baxter came to believe that he can't trust anybody.

He's determined to tell Cougar Jack that he isn't working for him anymore. There are actual good people in the world like The Wolf Pack, whom he can trust. He finally knows what friendship is, and it's not what he's doing with The Cougars and it's definitely not what his dad taught him over the years.

When Baxter finally arrives, he finds Jack, Anna, and the Cougars lounging around near the lake shore like a bunch of fish frying.

329

When Jack sees Baxter, he smirks. "Hey, there's my bomb-loving friend. Wow, you really did a good job at the school field trip today. It seems like Ben fully trusts you now. That means I can manipulate him whenever I want."

Baxter's heart thumps in his chest. All his life, he resisted trusting people so he wouldn't be used by anyone, but that's what Jack has been doing all this time.

Jack gives Baxter a huge stack of cash, but he immediately throws the money back at him.

"You can keep your cash and shove it right up your ass! I'm never going to work for you again. The Wolf Pack are far nicer than you'll ever be."

Jack looks shocked. For once in his life, Cougar Jack is actually silent.

Baxter walks away.

"Fine, then!" Jack finally shouts. "If you want to be friends with a loser group like The Wolf Pack, then you can just rot with them. See how much money you can make with them!"

All The Cougars laugh except Anna.

Baxter flashes his middle finger as he leaves. He wants to punch Jack in the face, but he struggles to control himself. He just wants to get in his car and drive out of here. He knows which people he can trust.

They are unselfish, caring, and their egos are not high as mountains. Baxter knows which lunch table he's going to sit at during school tomorrow.

***

Ben is finally relieved. He is all healed up now from that scratch on his back and he wants to train again. After school, Ben tells his friends to meet him at The Wolf Den and rushes to the parking lot. Just when he is about to get in his truck, someone calls out to him.

"Hey, Ben! Wait!"

Baxter rushes over and says, "Hey, I got something to tell you."

Ben is taken aback. Baxter doesn't normally want to talk, so Ben is curious to hear what he wants to say.

Baxter trips over his own words for a moment before blurting out, "Ben. I'm sorry, man, but I've been a bad friend all this time…"

"It's okay."

"No, it's not okay. Listen, I've been hiding a secret… I was paid by Jack to spy on you."

"What?"

"I was paid by The Cougars to be a spy for them. This whole time, I've been a fake friend, but when you risked your life for me, I realized what a true friend is. I'm sorry, man. Please forgive me."

Ben is dumbfounded but mostly feels betrayed. "No."

"What?"

"Why would I forgive you, asshole?"

Ben gets in The Howler before Baxter can say anything. He doesn't even want to hear what else the stupid betrayer has to say.

How could he? All this time, how could he?

He drives off, looking at the rearview mirror at the betrayer before driving even faster. The betrayer had desperate eyes, but he doesn't trust those eyes anymore. They're sickening to see now. He's not going to let this stop his training though because he has other friends to worry about.

Friends that won't betray him... hopefully.

Chapter 33- What!?

Ben's temper is about to boil over by the time he arrives at The Wolf Den. He keeps trying to forget what Baxter said to him, but it's too much of a pain to bury.

Damn it! Come on, brain, focus.

The others are already there waiting for him, plus the Sweetopians and Uri are with him in their disguised forms.

After the aliens resume their normal forms, Ben says, "Chuck, let's fight."

Chuck looks at Ben like he's worried about him. "Are you sure, Ben? I overheard what Baxter said to you. You don't have to—"

"Oh, forget about it! Fight me."

"Alright."

Chuck and Ben prepare to face off. Meanwhile, the others gather around to spectate. When Uri blows his whistle, the fight begins, and Ben immediately uses his special ability and makes food of different kinds all around him.

Chuck shoots chocolate from his mouth, but Ben dodges. He picks up a pineapple he summoned and throws it at Chuck but misses as well.

Chuck forms a sword out of his chocolate and charges.

Ben summons a crusty baguette to defend himself.

Ben thinks he's doing a good job holding his own, then Chuck changes into a chocolate goop and disappears.

Ben uses his conscience, feels Chuck appear behind him, and raises the baguette to parry the raptor's sword, but Chuck gets a hit on him with his tail, sending him tumbling forward.

Ben's mind a swirl of frustration thinking about Baxter's betrayal, and he shouts as he flings handfuls of sticky cotton candy at Chuck, sticking him to the ground. He then charges and swings his baguette, his vision going red as he pummels the trapped raptor over the head with blow after crumbly blow.

"Enough, enough!" Chuck yells, holding up his empty claws in surrender.

"Wow, good job, Ben!" Slam shouts.

The others remain silent, looking concerned. Honey narrows her eyes at him.

Ben looks down to avoid her accusatory glare, struggling to catch his breath. He takes a step toward Chuck to apologize, but the raptor only shakes his head and backs away.

Now they're all lying around laughing and having a good time. Well, except for Ben. He just watches his friends have fun, while he's still soaping about what he just did to Chuck.

Man, this stupid anger. Why can't I control it?

Slam jumps for joy. "Oh, yeah! This is just perfect! We all did it."

Ocean nods. "Yes, all of you did. You guys made good progress in developing your powers."

"Yeah, now if those cat bastards ever come, we will all be ready to shred them into pieces." Ben grins, but all of his friends just look at him with concern.

"Ben, remember what I told you? We're here to defend, not kill. We're here to defend God's name and protect Uri. We're not here to kill them just because they are more powerful than us. Violence is only going to make you use The Devil's Eye again." Chuck says.

"Yeah, Yeah. I know."

Ben knows that, but Ben is just so angry at what The Ferals have done to Uri that he wants to do to them what they did to Uri. Those stupid cat bastards deserve to die for what they've done. Ben walks away from Chuck all defiant. He goes to a nearby tree so he can rest. Meanwhile, Honey walks over to Chuck.

"Chuck, I'm afraid of what Ben is going to do. You know what he's like after you taught him over these past few months."

Chuck nods. "Yes, he's a very determined young man, but he's also stubborn. I've been trying to figure out how to teach

335

him to control his anger, but I'm afraid he might make a bad mistake."

Tom scratches his head. "Yeah, he has been off lately. I mean he is stubborn, but he's been acting more stubborn than usual."

"Yeah, I don't know what's got into him today. Must be the reason why Baxter's not here." Cedric blurts out.

Slam raises an eyebrow. "By the way, where is Baxter?"

Tom shrugs. "I don't know, Ben won't tell us."

Chuck nods. "Baxter is also another one I'm afraid of making a bad mistake too. The both of them are the same and can't control their anger. When The Ferals ever show up, all of you need to make sure that Ben and Baxter don't get out of hand because if they do, then I'm afraid things are going to get messy."

Tom nods. "Don't worry, we got an eye on them both."

After their training, The Wolf Pack as well as the Sweetopians and Uri have been just hanging around at The Wolf Den discussing plans on how they can face The Ferals when they meet them. Ben is still sitting alone next to the tree until Honey approaches him.

"Hey, Ben. You got a minute?" She asks.

Ben nods. "Yeah, sure."

"Hey, are you alright?"

"Yeah, I just got a little angry, that's all. I'm trying, I'm really trying."

Honey puts her hand on his cheek. "I know you are. It's kind of hard when unexpected things happen, is it? Especially when it involves a friend. Chuck already told me about Baxter and what he said to you."

"I just can't believe it, Honey. Why would he betray us?"

Honey leans on him. "I know, I know. I feel a bit upset too, but we should always remember that he did not only hurt us, but Jehovah as well. Remember Chuck showed us a scripture at Proverbs chapter nineteen, verse eleven. It says: 'The insight of a man certainly slows down his anger, and it is beauty on his part to overlook an offense.' Continuing to dwell on somebody else's hurtful actions are only going to hurt you, but if we let go and let Jehovah take care of it, then we'll feel much better."

Ben nods. "Yeah, I guess you're right."

Ben and Honey embrace themselves in a hug while watching the others talking and laughing with each other until it was almost getting dark. That's when they decided that they should go back to their homes and sleep.

All of a sudden, Ben feels his conscience being disturbed and he can sense something. He looks at Chuck and Uri. They nod at Ben like they sense it too. All of them quickly turn around and see The Ferals just a few feet in front of them.

Ben can't believe that all the sense training that Chuck has been giving them, they still can barely sense The Ferals approaching them. The Ferals are a high-power group of cats, and Ben starts tensing up when he sees them. All of them prepare fighting stances.

"Woah, hey now! We're not here to fight! We're here to talk!" Nour, the one with the crown, shows his paws innocently.

Ben frowns. "Yeah, right! I don't trust you!"

"Listen, Ben, isn't it?"

"Don't say my name, you cat bastard!"

"Listen, I know how you feel."

"Excuse me? How can you possibly know how I feel? You're just a bunch of evil cats."

"Listen, you got it all wrong. We're not evil at all. In fact, Uri is the one you shouldn't trust, he killed his own people."

All of their eyes go wide.

"You're lying!"

"No, Ben. It's true." Uri blurts out.

"What?"

Ben looks back at Uri. Uri starts shaking.

"What do you mean it's true?"

Uri stays silent.

"See, even he knows it's true. Let me tell you what truly happened to the Kingdom of Zion: Me and my buddies here were traveling to Zion to make alliances with King Yadin, but we're surprised to see everyone dead and only one kid survived. That kid was none other than that criminal you see before you. I suddenly realized at that moment that Uri was the one who killed all the people in his city, including his parents. And so me and my friends have been chasing this criminal down for over a year now."

Strawberry Shores raises an eyebrow. "Psh, that ain't true at all. Right, Uri?"

"Yes, it is." Uri starts crying uncontrollably. "See! I told you guys you shouldn't help me! Stay away from me!"

Uri starts running away into the forests. Nobody goes after him.

"We've tried to chase Uri down and arrest him for his crimes. There's a big bounty on his head and a bunch of creatures are willing to kill Uri if they have the chance. It's safe if you help us arrest Uri, it's only right. We'll reward you greatly if you do, but if you continue to defend Uri, then that counts as helping a criminal, and according to Universal Law we have to arrest all of you too. We'll give you three days to choose."

The Ferals then take off into the woods, leaving the rest of them with a choice. Honey looks at Ben who is just thinking hard right now.

"Ben, we should look for Uri."

"Why should we waste our time looking for a criminal?"

Honey's eyes shot up. "Seriously, Ben. After all the things you did to protect Uri, you're willing to give up now? You seriously don't believe what The Ferals said, do you?"

"I don't know what to think anymore."

"Ben, don't believe every word you hear. They're just trying to confuse your mind. This is the Devil's doing." Chuck chimes in.

"Maybe it is, maybe it's not. I don't know anymore."

Ben just walks away.

"Ben!..."

Chuck raises his arm at Honey. "Let him go, Honey. This is a lot for him to sink in right now. Let him rest. It's probably best that you all rest too."

Slam raises an eyebrow. "What about you, Chuck? What are you going to do?"

"It's best that me, Strawberry, and Ocean look for Uri by ourselves. All of you go to your homes now."

The Wolf Pack reluctantly agree, and so all of them leave Chuck and the two raptors behind.

Ben's chest feels tight. First Baxter, now Uri—both lied to him today. His mind races, twisting every word, every glance.

339

He blinks, tries to steady his breath, but the weight presses down. He needs to sit still, let the noise quiet down. Tomorrow, maybe tomorrow, things will make more sense.

Chapter 34- Challenge Accepted

Cedric's POV, the busy cowboy

They finally squeeze in their horseback ride. Sarah has been bugging him for hours, as usual. On the trail, two riders come toward them—the Sharp twins, Anna and Edwin, with their unmistakable white hair. Cedric knows them well. Their hair stands out like a spotlight at a rodeo. Some tease them, others admire them, but either way, they draw attention—not just for their looks but for how successful they are.

Edwin scowls, but Cedric isn't surprised. They've never gotten along. Edwin's a Cougar, sure, but Cedric hates him more because their fathers were rivals too—racing horses, trucks, even running on foot. Their dads drilled one rule into them: never trust the other. Cedric hates Edwin not just for the name, but because Edwin cares about winning—

everything's a competition. Rodeos, finishing food, racing—Edwin always boasts about beating Cedric. Every time they meet, Cedric expects a fight.

He hopes Edwin stays quiet. No time for this. His heart pounds, sweat trickles down his face as they draw closer. Trouble feels close—just inches away. But when they pass, Edwin says nothing.

Cedric breathes a sigh of relief, but...

"Hey, Cedric!"

Damn.

"I heard you got a new truck. I heard it's a 2017 Ford F150 just like mine, except it's the Canadian model."

"Yeah, what about it?"

"Tomorrow at 4:00 pm. You and me. Race. Let's see which model is better, the US or Canadian."

"Nah, sorry man. I'm busy."

"Oh, I see. Still a pussy." Edwin laughs.

Anna frowns. "Hey, Edwin! Quit it!"

Edwin frowns back. "Oh, okay. Trying to go on the other side, I see. It ain't my fault that his father was an idiot and died during that car accident."

"Jesus Christ, you never seem to stop, will you?" Anna gives Edwin a malicious frown.

"Fine, then! If you want to race so much, then how about it?" Cedric asks.

Edwin smirks at Cedric. "Oh, finally. He grew a pair of balls."

"Under one condition though."

"What?"

"We need partners."

"Partners?"

"Yes, I know how much bragging you're going to do afterwards that you beat me without any help. You partner with your sister, while I partner with my sister, to make things even."

Edwin growls. "Alright, fine then! Partners it is. You and your little sissy over there are going to lose to us anyway. Let's go, Anna."

As Edwin rides away, Anna gives Cedric a concerned look, then she follows her brother. Cedric doesn't know why she was looking at him that way, but he doesn't think too much about it.

Cedric looks at his sister. "Come on, let's go home."

Sarah frowns. "Hey, why did you bring me into your mess? I don't want to be a part of it."

"Well, too bad, now you are."

Sarah sighs in annoyance. "Why do you always agree to race him?"

"Because he's an annoying ass."

"I don't really care. As long as you take me to Starbucks, then we're even."

"Hell naw. I ain't taking you anywhere."

"Oh, what? Come on! I deserve it after you just forced me into helping you."

"Alright, then. Jesus, I can't wait until you get your license, so I won't have to drive you anywhere."

Sarah frowns at Cedric. Cedric ignores her and continues riding.

Chapter 35- I Wanna Help

At The Coy's Ranch, Ben is feeding colorful hay from Sweetopia to Cedric's cattle as a favor to his friend. According to Chuck, the hay can make one stronger and faster. So hopefully it helps Cedric's cattle in some way.

More than this, he is trying to keep his mind off the encounter with The Ferals and learning about what actually happened to Uri's people. With little luck. He doesn't know what to think, but questions swirl in his mind.

Why would Uri kill his people? Was that even true?

He feels like all they did to protect Uri was for nothing.

Well, at least he might use his special ability to help his friends. And beat The Cougars. Ben hasn't forgotten about that. Well, another feline group he wants to be destroyed. He's starting to hate cats now.

Cedric isn't home when Ben arrives, so he goes straight to the cows, but he notices Sarah sitting on a fence nearby.

"Hey, short stuff. Where's Cedric?" he asks.

Sarah frowns, like she always does when Ben calls her that.

"He's busy running errands."

"Oh, I see. Do you know when he'll be back?"

"No."

Silence besets them as they wait and watch the cattle. Ben throws more of the colorful Sweetopian hay to the cows.

Sarah raises an eyebrow. "What is that?"

"It's called Sweetopian hay."

"Sweetopian hay? Never heard of it? Why is it colorful?"

"Because it's a special kind of hay."

"Where did you get it?"

"Now that's something for me to know and for you to not know."

Sarah frowns again, then winces, reaching down to rub a cast on her leg.

"What happened?" Ben asks.

"I accidentally broke my leg during PE class. God damn it!" Sarah slaps her forehead. "I forgot!"

"Forgot? Forgot what?"

"Cedric and Edwin are having their silly race today, and I'm supposed to be his partner."

"A race?"

"Yeah, we're racing against Edwin and his sister at four tomorrow. Cedric and Edwin are racing their trucks, while I'm racing Anna on horses." Sarah looks at Ben. "Hey, can you replace me?"

"Replace you? I don't know how to ride a horse."

"Oh, come on. I'll teach you."

Suddenly, the roar of an engine joins them. Ben turns to see Cedric's truck pulling up. Cedric waves as he walks up to Ben and Sarah, then stops short when he sees the colorful hay.

"What the hell are you feeding my cows?"

"Sweetopian hay."

"Sweetopian hay?"

"Yeah, Chuck says that it can help an animal to become stronger and faster. I'm testing it on your cattle."

Sarah raises an eyebrow. "Who's Chuck?"

"Now that's also something for me to know and you to not know."

Sarah frowns again.

Cedric sighs. "Ben, stop giving my cattle that... stuff."

"But it will help them."

"I don't care, stop."

· "Ok, fine. By the way, I heard from Sarah that you're planning to race Edwin."

"Oh, did you now?" Cedric frowns at Sarah, and she rolls her eyes at him.

"I wanna help." Ben says.

"No."

"What? But why not?"

"Ben, do you even know how to ride a horse?"

"No, but I could try."

"Nah, Ben, sorry, but I can't let you help me. I know I have been teaching you many times how to ride a horse, but this race is not like the others. I wagered that if I win this race, Edwin will help cover my expenses for the ranch, but if I lose to him, I will have to give some of my best cattle away."

"That's why I want to help you. I want to help you beat Edwin."

Cedric grows silent for a moment, but then he says. "Alright, you can help. I know you're just going to intervene some way or another, but here's the problem. You need to learn quickly how to ride a horse, and I mean actually ride one, because the race starts tomorrow at four."

Ben smirks. "Hey, don't worry. I'll use my special ability to help us win."

"Alright, whatever it takes to win, I guess."

Sarah raises an eyebrow. "Special ability? What's that?"

"Now that's something that I know and—"

"Oh my god! Can you just shut up already and tell me now!?" Sarah glares at Ben. Ben runs away from her while she's trying to kill him.

"Cut it out, you two," Cedric says. "Ben and I have work to do if he's going to learn to actually ride."

"Hey, I can teach Ben how to ride too," Sarah whines.

Cedric shakes his head. "Oh, no. You have to do your homework."

"Pff, alright fine then! You never really spend time with me and mom anyway, so why bother? You're not my brother anymore!"

Sarah runs off to the house. Cedric is half-shocked by Sarah's reaction.

"What the hell was that all about?" Ben asks.

Cedric shrugs. "Ah, nothing. Sarah is just being a twerp. She doesn't know any better. She needs to realize how to take responsibility."

Ben's eyes narrow as he watches Cedric, tension tightening his jaw. Family runs deep—his mom's a Coy, and Cedric's part of that bloodline. The weight of the Coy Ranch presses on him, a quiet determination settling in. He pictures the Sharps' sprawling fields, their success shining like a challenge. Ben clenches his fists. He'll cross that finish line first—for Cedric, for the ranch. If he has to tap into his special ability to do it, he won't hesitate.

***

Ben falls from the horse for probably the dozenth time in the last few hours, his ego is hurting almost as much as his rear end.

Cedric sighs in frustration and says, "I think we should switch to a slower and more experienced horse." After disappearing into the stable, he returns with another equine. "This is Scrappy. I think you should start with him instead and get back to the basics, but you need to remember that Anna is an experienced barrel racer. I don't think you're going to beat her on your own, but with your special ability, the match is pretty uncertain."

Ben growls. "I don't care if that idiot woman is the best horse racer in the world. I can still beat her ass with my ability. Just you wait. I don't even need to know the basics. Just teach me how to stay on when I take this horse zooming."

Just as Ben is about to get on Scrappy, someone screams.

"Hey, help!"

Cedric turns as Sarah runs by, chasing after some flying papers. With a sigh, he says, "Hey, Ben. Wait here. I'm going after her."

He gets on his horse and chases after Sarah, leaving Ben alone with Scrappy. He doesn't want to wait and decides to get on by himself. He tries to make the horse move, but he won't budge.

As he struggles with the new horse, he hears someone trotting in his direction. He thought it might be Cedric, but he turns around as Anna trots up on a horse of her own. *You gotta be kidding me? Just after I mentioned her, really?*

He ignores her, focusing on trying to move Scrappy. He doesn't want to talk to her. She's the girlfriend of his enemy after all.

Despite Ben's effort to ignore her, Anna trots toward him. "Hey, Ben. Where's Cedric?"

"I don't know," Ben mumbles as he tries to make Scrappy move.

"What are you doing?"

"Trying to make this horse move."

Anna smirks. "Man, you should probably get Cedric to help you."

Ben grows more irritated and urges Scrappy on harder, but the beast suddenly lies down. Ben falls off next to the obstinate horse with a leg trapped underneath.

Anna laughs. "Man, you're pretty hilarious."

Ben's heart beats faster and his cheeks get warm as he struggles to free his leg. *That's it! I about had it with this woman.*

"By the way, that big hole that you dug during the field trip was clever. I kept laughing at Jack's face when he was stuck in it."

Ben just grumbles as he pushes against Scrappy's side, hoping to get the horse off his leg.

"Let me help you out, Ben. I think Scrappy is just hungry. Cedric told me he refuses to move when he wants to eat."

"I don't need your help, you slut!"

"Excuse me?"

"Just get out of here, you asshole!"

Anna frowns. "Okay, fine! You know, I thought you weren't as bad as Jack says about you, but I guess he's right!"

Anna gallops away on her horse. Ben shouts in a rage. Scrappy finally got up. Ben clambers to his feet and brushes dirt from his pants.

Anna seemed to want to help him, but after Baxter and Uri, he has no intention of trusting anybody outside of Cedric, Tom, and Honey. Even Slam, he isn't sure about. However, what she said about Scrappy being hungry gives him an idea. He grabs a handful of the Sweetopian hay he left by the fence and feeds it to Scrappy. The horse eats it immediately, then his eyes grow wide and his tail swishes around frantically.

Oh boy. What did I do?

Chapter 36- No!

Cedric's POV, the busy cowboy

Cedric gallops after Sarah and her flyaway homework papers, just one more problem to add to the hundred more that he has. He needs to get back to training Ben. Cedric prays to God Ben doesn't do anything stupid while he is gone. That's another problem he definitely doesn't need.

However, Cedric sees an opportunity to talk to Sarah about her outburst. She's young, but she needs to learn that life isn't full of fun and games. Cedric learned that the hard way after their dad died, but Sarah was only a baby then. He was like her when he was younger, but he had to become the man of the house and work to support his family.

Cedric passes Sarah and grabs the flying papers one by one.

As Cedric glances at them, his sister yells, "No!"

It's too late. Cedric frowns at a family picture of them all, even Dad, but Cedric's and their dad's faces are scratched off. Cedric put two and two together...

She's upset at me, isn't she? He's becoming like his dad more and more. Their dad never spent time with the family, and now Cedric is doing the same thing. He has always been focused on getting money, there's almost never enough. He's always working hours straight on end, never getting enough sleep. It's hurting his grades at school, it's hurting his health, it's hurting his family, and it's hurting Jehovah as well.

He remembers what Chuck taught him about what the Holy Scriptures say at Philippians, chapter one, verse ten. It says to "Make sure of the more important things." He's been focusing too much on work. It's time to stop this.

Cedric looks over at Sarah and smiles. "I've been neglecting you and mom, have I?"

Sarah nods, her eyes cast down at the ground.

"Hey, you don't have to feel guilty. I should be the one who's guilty. How about this? After the race, let's take mom and go to the rodeo this weekend, okay?"

Sarah smiles and nods. "Yeah!"

"Okay, then it's settled. Now let's go back home."

Suddenly, Ben zooms by on Scrappy, the older horse going far faster than he should be capable of. Cedric notices colorful hay floating in front of Scrappy's face, which the horse seems to be desperately trying to catch.

Ben must be using his special ability. That could work. Even if not, Cedric doesn't actually care about the race at all. He's been spending too much time focusing on work and useless distractions like animosity with Edwin when he should be spending time with the more important things, his family. He's just planning to take a break with his family after this race.

When Ben finally stops, he looks at Cedric all smug and confident. Cedric sure hopes Ben doesn't do anything to hurt himself, knowing him. Ben has that same Coy stubbornness to always win like his dad.

Chapter 37- The Race Begins

If Cedric could wish for something right now, it would be not staring at an ugly looking white-haired varmint for minutes. Yet, here he is with Edwin, staring each other down, standing next to their pickup trucks, as the race is about to begin. Edwin's colleagues have the roads blocked, so they won't crash into any random cars passing by. Cedric knows that Edwin has something up his sleeve for this race, he just knows it. That stupid grin of his is proof, but Cedric doesn't care at this point.

Before they get into their pickups, Cedric offers his hand. "May the best man win?"

Edwin slaps Cedric's hand. "What kind of bullshit are you playin'?" Edwin walks toward his truck. "Pff, 'may the best man win,' my ass."

A typical taunt from his enemy. Cedric ignores him, and they both get in their pickups. Cedric is more worried about the second race with Ben against Anna on horseback. He would expect Ben to lose if not for his special ability.

Cedric snaps back to the present trial as one of Edwin's colleagues waves the flag for the race to start.

***

Ben is laying on Scrappy waiting for Cedric to show up so he can "pass the baton" to him. Anna is on her horse next to him. They rarely look at each other, but when they do, they both shoot daggers of hostility to each other. However, the only thing he's focusing on right now is the race.

Suddenly, Ben hears a truck coming. He turns around to see Edwin's truck, and Cedric is a few hundred feet behind. *Oh, great. It looks like I have to win this race for us.* Edwin gets out of his pickup and rushes over to Anna. Anna is about to stretch her hand for Edwin to touch it, but he shouts out, "Hey, get off the horse! I'm going to ride!"

"What? I'm not getting off!"

Edwin ignores Anna and climbs onto the horse even though she's still on it.

"Hey!"

Anna tries to stop him but seems to have no choice but to hold on when Edwin starts riding.

Seconds later, Cedric arrives and touches Ben's hand.

355

Ben immediately creates colorful hay out of thin air and Scrappy eats it, and another handful floats in front of his muzzle. Ben holds on, praying his idea will work...

Toot!

The biggest fart Scrappy could ever make was made in his rectum and the sheer force, along with the hay in front of his eyes, creates the speediest horse demon the world has seen. Leaves are nearly coming out of bushes and trees as they pass by. Not before long, he is catching up to Edwin and Anna.

"Jesus! That's the fastest horse I ever seen!" Anna's eyes go wide.

"Get off! You're adding too much weight!"

"Excuse me! This race is supposed to be with partners!"

Edwin pushes Anna off. She falls and rolls into a small ditch next to the race path.

Ben pulls back on the reins on Scrappy. Scrappy stops to happily nibble on the floating Sweetopian hay.

Anna is hurt. She can't get up. Ben pauses for a second. He doesn't know what to do. Should he help her or continue the race? He really wants to win this race for Cedric, and besides why would he want to help Anna? She is a jerk. He hates her for what she has done.

Ben is about to continue the race until he looks back at Anna again... She's crying...

I can't believe what I'm doing. He climbs down from Scrappy and helps Anna up.

Anna looks stunned for a moment, then pushes Ben away. "Get away from me, asshole!"

Ben almost shouts back at her, then realizes she's right. "I'm sorry that I was mean to you."

Anna lets out a huff, but her expression softens.

Ben smiles. "I know that you were just trying to be friendly back then. I was a jerk, but... I'm sorry."

Ben takes a water canister he has strapped to his back and offers it to Anna. She hesitates, then takes it and drinks. She takes a step and stumbles, but Ben offers his arm to help her catch her balance. He stabilizes her and he leads her over to Scrappy.

"What are you doing?" she asks.

"I'm taking you to the finish line."

That's where Cedric is anyway, and Ben knows he has a med kit in his pickup to help Anna's injury. Anna lets Ben help her onto Scrappy, then he gets on, and they ride together to the finish line.

Everyone looks surprised to see Ben with Anna. When they cross the finish line, Ben gets off Scrappy and helps Anna off.

"You alright?" Ben asks.

Anna nods.

"Hey, Sarah," Ben calls out. "Grab the med kit from Cedric's truck, will you?"

Sarah immediately runs to Cedric's pickup.

Ben walks over to Edwin and pushes him. "You son of a bitch! You could have killed Anna."

Cedric and the others try to break them up. Anna just stands there looking dumbfounded. Ben finally relents and turns to Cedric. "Sorry for not winning the race, man."

Cedric smiles. "It's alright."

"But you're going to lose all of your cattle though."

"Honestly, Edwin can keep the cattle. I'm done ranching for a while. You know how much time and money is spent caring for them? It's a wonder why my dad didn't have time with the family."

"Yeah, but how are you going to make money now?"

"Do you know Justin, our cousin? His dad has a construction company. I'll think about working for him. At least his hours are more flexible than the cattles.' Besides, I want to make more time to improve my ability and serve Jehovah more."

Suddenly, they hear a loud thwack, a whine, and a thump. They turn around to find Edwin on the ground, unconscious, and Anna is standing over him. All of Edwin's colleagues back away from Anna.

Ben smiles. "Jesus, that woman can really punch."

"Tell me about it." Cedric smirks. "I'm surprised she didn't punch you. It looks like you two are getting friendly with each other."

"Don't tell Honey about this." Ben smirks. "Besides, I know you got a crush on Anna, so..."

Cedric blushes. "Okay, let's just go."

As Ben, Cedric, and Sarah walk away, Ben looks over his shoulder and sees Anna smiling at them. Ben smiles back and waves goodbye.

***

Cedric drops off Sarah before taking Ben home. When they get to his house, Ben opens the door and gets out of the truck.

"Hey, Ben..." Cedric begins.

Ben turns back.

"Don't worry so much, alright?"

"Alright."

"Hey, I love you."

Ben smiles. "Yeah."

Ben closes the truck door, and he walks toward his house. Cedric smiles. Life isn't all about winning anymore for Cedric, and it seems Ben picked up on that too by helping Anna. Hopefully he did, but knowing Ben and how stubborn he is, he might not. He just sees right through things and lets his emotions take a slide. Cedric loves that kid though...

Why does he keep hurting himself?

Chapter 38- Finding Out

Tom, Cedric, Honey and Slam stroll through town. They're all quiet, not a word spoken, not even from Slam. A crept silence until all of their phones buzz at the same time. Ben's message pops up: **"Wolf Pack, meet at the Wolf Den tonight. We're searching for Uri."**

Tom blinks. Ben had given up on Uri last time they talked. What changed?

Another text follows: **"Also... I want to make peace with Jack."**

Tom frowns. *That stubborn kid?* Changing his mind was almost unheard of.

He glances at the others. They shrug, except Cedric, who grins.

"I think he's had a change of heart," Cedric says. "Come on, let's get some breakfast at the café, and I'll fill you in."

When they enter the café, they find Baxter sitting alone at a table, eating. The four of them decided to sit with him.

Baxter leans back, looking surprised. "Why are you sitting with me?"

"We forgive you." Tom blurts out.

"What? But I've betrayed you guys. Why?"

"You came clean and fessed up to what you did," Honey says. "That just proves you still want to be part of The Wolf Pack. And besides, you're still wearing that wolf chain, are you? 'No Wolf Works Alone'."

There's a long silence. Baxter holds onto the wolf chain Ben gave him. Baxter smiles. "Thank you."

Tom knows Baxter is a good man at heart. Even though he doesn't seem like it from the outside. He was too judgmental of the kid when he first met him, but when getting to know him better, he can see Baxter from the inside.

He was just like Ben. Hurt from the inside, but now he came clean and confessed. Tom is just praying that Ben will come clean to them too.

***

Shortly after they have eaten, Anna walks up to them. *What's she doing here?* Cedric wonders. His heart skips a beat, and he isn't sure what to say to her. He doesn't know what she's going to say to him either.

It's kind of embarrassing to have someone like Anna that you had a major crush on for years just to lose to her brother in front of her. He's still bothered about losing that race, even though winning isn't important to him anymore. Cedric is just silently biting his nails off as she gets closer and closer.

"Hi." Anna waves shyly.

Cedric smiles. "Howdy."

Anna looks around. "Where's Ben?"

"I don't know. Somewhere."

"I just want to thank him for helping me during the race."

Slam raises an eyebrow. "Race? What race? Was there a race at school that I didn't know about?"

Cedric shakes his head. "Oh, no. That's what I was going to tell you about. Edwin and I had one of our silly races again, but I wanted a relay with partners. Long-story-short, he pushed Anna off her horse, and she got injured, but Ben decided to help her, giving up on the race to make sure she was okay. Unfortunately, that made us lose."

"You guys didn't lose. Honestly, you won. My brother is the real loser, as well as his other lousy friends. That's why I came here." Anna rubs her arm. "I'm wondering if you guys are willing to add one more member to your 'pack'?"

Cedric rubs his head. "I don't know, Anna. What will Jack think when he sees his girlfriend with a bunch of men he despises?"

"Oh, Jack? Don't worry, I dumped his ass. I don't want to be with him any longer. You guys are nice."

Cedric blushes.

"Hey, another girl added to the team! Man, and who says we have no rizz?" Slam smirks.

"Please don't ever speak again," Cedric says, rubbing his forehead in embarrassment.

Tom rubs his chin. "Hmm, well, that explains why Ben changed his mind, but this raises another concern."

"Really? What?" Cedric asks.

"Ben texted us something about 'making peace' with Jack. I thought he was joking, but I have a feeling Ben has something more serious in mind."

"What? That he's going to kill Jack? Come on, that's too far, even for Ben," Cedric says.

Tom scratches his head. "I don't know. Ben has been acting odd lately. We need to find out what he's planning."

"Where do you think he might be?"

Tom looks at Anna. "Hey, Anna. Where does Jack usually go at this time?"

"He usually runs through the woods near Silvertown River Park."

"Well, that's where he might be then," Tom says. "I better call Ben just to see if he answers."

As Tom dials his phone, everyone heads to their cars...

Chapter 39- One Last Brawl

Ben leans on a tree at Silvertown River Park, waiting for Cougar Jack to show up and eager to get things over with. He's ready to show Cougar Jack how much stronger he has become.

All these years since Ben has known Jack, he has wanted to find a way to show him how successful he and his pack are. That wolves are at the top of the food chain, not cougars.

He almost felt successful when he and his friends learned special abilities, but that ultimately failed. Even with this special ability, he doesn't feel valuable at all.

Honestly, he's just tired. He's tired of fighting with Jack. He's going to show Jack what Chuck trained him these past months and that's to show peace.

When he hears someone coming, Ben ducks into a bush. Jack approaches, looking like he's out for a run, and stops for a break, drinking his water.

Ben leaps from the bush to surprise Jack.

"How long have you been waiting for me?" Jack asks, not seeming surprised.

Ben's eyes shoot up, then he frowns. "I have been waiting long enough. I'm tired of this, Jack. I want to make peace."

"Peace? What are you on drugs?"

"No, I just want to make peace. I realize how much we're hurting each other, hurting our friends."

"Hurting our friends?" Jack laughs. "The thing is I don't have any friends anymore. They all left me, including my girlfriend. And it's all your fault, you bastard."

"Excuse me?"

"You know, over the years I've known you, I never understood how a poor kid like you can attract somebody. I also don't get why you were so determined to beat me either. Then I realized something: it's because you and I are the same."

"What? What do you mean?"

"We both know that the rich and successful are the only ones to survive in this cruel world. People only care about who is more successful, and you know it, Ben. Success is the only way to help your friends, it's the only way to make your dad not leave you."

"You shut up about my dad!"

"I'm just like you. My parents are jerks who only care about how successful I am. I know that all the good times I had with my friends are a waste if we are not successful. All the things you did with your mom, Ben, didn't matter at all. You know it to be true. You know the only way to help her now is to be on top of the food chain. So fight me, you bastard! I want to see how weak you truly are!" Jack continues to laugh.

Ben stays silent. He hears all this rambling nonsense from Jack. Ben doesn't disagree with Jack. Hell, the words he's saying used to be true to him, but he can't take the stupidity of this jerk anymore. *I swear, if this guy mentions my mom again, I'm going to kill him.*

"You shut the hell up, man!"

Jack smirks. "Make me shut up. Come on!"

Ben runs toward him. They trade blows for several minutes with no clear winner, both bruised and battered, until Ben falls to the ground. Ben tries to get back up again, but the muscles ache so bad that he can't. *Come on... Get up... Prove this idiot you're not weak.*

Jack smirks. "Jeez, all that punching just to fall on the ground in defeat? Man, no wonder your dad left you."

That's all? All that training I did with Chuck, and I still manage to lose? That's it! I have about— %$%*%^^%^*%^*^

Ben's vision glosses over with a red glow.

Jack stumbles back in surprise as Ben gets up and summons a knife in his hand. The Devil is giving him what he wants, and Ben couldn't care less. The only thing he wants to do is shove this knife up Jack's gut.

"What... How the hell did you do that? Who... Who the hell are you?" Jack stammers in shock.

Ben rushes forward...Stab...

His vision clears. His conscience is back. *What... What have I done?* He stumbles back as regret flows through him.

A chorus of yelling draws Ben's attention, and he looks up at a nearby hill to see all his Pack members, with Anna and Baxter running toward him, rushing over to Jack once they're close enough to see that he's wounded.

Honey tries to heal Jack, vines wrapped around his torso, but soon shakes her head in frustration. "He's too hurt. I can't fix it. Here, help me lift Jack. I'll take him to the hospital."

Cedric and Baxter pick up Jack.

"I can drive." Baxter says.

Honey nods. "Okay."

They take Jack to Honey's car and drive off.

Tom frowns at Ben. "What the hell were you thinking?"

Ben breathes heavily. "I... I don't know."

"Jesus Christ, you might have killed him! You will be lucky if they manage to save him!"

Ben panics. "I'm sorry."

"Pff, there is no way you can make up this one! I'm done with your troublemaking! You need to figure something out because I'm done!"

Tom then storms away, joined by Anna and Slam, to his truck.

Ben wants to say something, but is speechless as they drive away...

What... What have I done?

Chapter 40- ...

Ben throws another bag into his truck. Just a few more, and he can drive away from everything and never come back. After what he's done, nobody will accept him. Nobody will ever respect him. Not to mention, he'll be going to prison for attempted murder if he doesn't run. Prison is honestly not a thing he thinks he deserves. He thinks he deserves to just die. He doesn't know why he even exists if he is just made to harm people, harm his friends...

After packing everything, he was about to turn on The Howler until—

"Ben!"

Honey runs up his driveway with tears in her eyes. "I know what you're doing, Ben. Please don't."

"Forget about me."

"Ben, please don't."

"Why do you love me so much? Look at me: I'm useless."

"Ben, I care about you. Despite anything you're going through, I still love you. Please, don't leave."

"Forget about me!"

Ben turns on The Howler and drives away. In the rearview mirror, Honey is trying to catch up to him, holding her hand out. He just puts more gas in the gas pedal. Farther and farther away from Honey because he doesn't deserve her. He's sorry to make Honey cry, but she deserves better. He knows she can find a person that's far better than him... She doesn't have to suffer any longer.

***

In the middle of the forest, Ben takes out a picture of him and his parents from his pocket. He was such a young naive little twerp back then, and he still is.

He then takes out his phone, the screen showing a picture of him and his Pack members. He's put everybody through so much crap, but they won't have to worry any longer.

If he were a better man, his father wouldn't have left. If he were a better man, then God would love him. Instead, he knows how much of a worthless man he is.

His emotions are ablazing, just like the fire he set before him. He's burning some of his stuff, all the good times with his friends were only memories. Good memories to hide the person he truly is. Now he's burning it all.

He throws the picture of his parents into the fire. He deletes the picture of his friends on his phone. There's only one thing left to do.

Only one thing to get rid of... He takes out a gun from his pocket. His father's pistol he kept inside his closet. What a good way to die. Have the thing that his father loves better than him... kill him...

Suddenly, he hears a shuffling in the bushes, and he turns just in time to see Uri running toward him. He is about to tell him to go away, but Uri hugs him with tears in his eyes before he can say anything.

"I'm sorry that I lied to you. I don't know why I did it, but I know how much of a bad person I am. You don't have to deal with me anymore. I'm going to turn myself in to The Ferals, and I will be punished. I deserve to die for what I did."

Ben is stunned into silence, Uri's words reflecting his own thoughts about going back and turning himself in to the police. But before the thoughts overwhelm him, someone shouts, "Hey, what are you doing here?"

Ben looks over as The Ferals emerge from the tree line.

Nour shrugs. "Well, it doesn't matter. Hand Uri over to us, Earth human. If you do, we'll give you whatever you want."

"No."

"What? What do you mean, 'no'? That child is a criminal! He killed his entire people! Why do you still want to protect him?"

"Because God's heart is greater than mine. I did something bad too, but Jehovah's mercy is great. I have been judging myself too much. God is the real judge. That's one thing you cats wouldn't understand."

Nour and The Ferals just stand there, seemingly stunned by his words. Ben summons a huge pile of cotton candy to engulf The Ferals, sticking them in place. He then rushes Uri to his truck, and they drive off...

***

"Ah, you see. Your plans always fail." Nader frowns at Nour.

Nour just growls as he sees them driving away. Slipping away from his paws like an invasive rodent. He thought his trick of lying to The Wolf Pack would work. Lying to The Wolf Pack and the others that Uri killed his people, but that's not actually the truth.

Sure, they did find Uri back at Zion with all the people dead, but he also saw King Yadin, his dead body was next the unconscious Uri under some debris, but yet Uri is still alive.

His father protected him from the destruction of the Babylonians and those Babylonians didn't realize they left one of King Yadin's sons alive. The king made a good sacrifice toward his son, Uri doesn't know that. He doesn't want to believe it despite how much Nour and The Ferals have been telling him. It was hard, Uri was right in their hands, but yet again, they failed.

"Honestly, Nour. You shouldn't lie anymore. Just tell the truth." Tito says.

"Oh, just be quiet and get out of this pink mess. We're going to the hospital in the human village."

Sebastian raises an eyebrow at him. "What? The hospital? Why the hospital?"

"I secretly threw a poison dart on both Ben and Uri before we got covered. They're probably going to pass out anytime soon and be taken to the hospital. I'm planning to go there, capture Uri, and head out once this is over and done with. We've already captured those Sweetopians that were with them, now we just need Uri."

***

"Hey, thanks for forgiving me."

As they speed through town, Uri smiles at him.

Ben laughs. "It's going to be okay."

Suddenly, Uri sweats profusely. "I feel dizzy."

"Are you alright?'

Uri passes out.

"Hey!"

Ben stops the truck and tries to wake Uri up, but he feels dizzy himself and the world suddenly fades to darkness.

Chapter 41- Forgiveness

Cool air brushes his skin—too cold, too sharp. Ben blinks at the pale ceiling, the blur of spinning fan blades above. Fluorescent lights hum. His limbs feel heavy, like they're made of sand.

Where—?

The stiff sheets, the sterile scent. *A hospital?* His pulse stutters.

Uri.

He shifts, tries to sit up—

Footsteps.

The door creaks open. Ben freezes and sinks back against the pillow, heart thudding. Honey steps in, not in scrubs, just in her favorite black overalls and her black-and-yellow striped t-shirt. No words. She sinks into the chair beside him, hands folded in her lap. A man follows, older, doctor maybe, clipboard in hand. He walks straight to Ben's bedside, expression unreadable.

The man is the same doctor that Ben visits more times than he can count. Dr. Morrison has fixed Ben a lot as a result of being hurt a lot over the years doing stupid things.

"How's it going, Ben?" Dr. Morrison asks.

"Good."

"Are you hurt at all?"

"No."

"Good. Some people found you and a little boy passed out on the side of the road."

"Um..."

Dr. Morrison smiles. "Don't worry, you don't have to explain anything. Honey told me you were running away. She called the police, and they found you. Honey also told me that the little boy is your cousin, is that correct?"

"Yeah."

"He's been living with you, is that right?"

"Yeah."

"Honey says that you were sending your cousin to the Coy's house so you wouldn't have to take care of him any longer. I'm sorry, I can't imagine how bad your home life is, Ben. I have to tell the police that both of you are alright. Do you need anything before I head out?"

"No, thank you."

"Alright."

Dr. Morrison closes the door behind him, leaving a heavy silence in the room. Honey stares at the floor. Ben shifts in the bed, eyes flicking toward her, then away. The silence stretches. His throat tightens.

She hasn't looked at him once.

"How's Jack?"

"Jack is fine. He is recovering."

"Good…" Ben pauses for a moment. "I'm sorry. I'm sorry that I hurt you."

"You didn't hurt me, Ben."

"No, I know I did, and I'm sorry. Please forgive me. I don't feel like fighting anymore…" Ben sheds tears. "Please forgive me."

Tears spill before he can stop them. Honey's shoulders shake, and in the next moment, she crosses the room and wraps her arms around him.

He holds her like he's afraid to let go.

For the first time in forever, winning doesn't matter. He doesn't care about Cougars or powers or being the strongest. All he cares about is the girl in his arms, and the friends who didn't give up on him, even when he gave up on himself.

He presses his forehead against hers. "We're gonna make this right," he whispers. "I promise."

But first—he has to protect Uri. Wherever the Ferals are, Ben knows they're not done. And neither is he.

"Honey?" Ben starts wiping his tears away, and she does the same.

"Yes?"

"We need to get Uri out of here, quickly."

Honey looks at Ben, seeming puzzled. "Why?"

"We were being chased by The Ferals. They are probably searching for us. We must leave with Uri, quickly."

Without hesitation, they both get on their feet. They sneak through the hallways of the hospital so they wouldn't get caught and they go to where Uri is.

Chapter 42- The Big Raid

Tom's POV, the police boy

The Wolf Pack, Anna, and Sarah move fast through town, the hospital in sight but still too far. Tom keeps his head down, jaw clenched. He'd yelled at Ben after the Jack incident— maybe he had a right to, but it doesn't sit right. Not now. Not with Ben found unconscious in his truck, and Uri somehow involved. If the Ferals were after them...

Tom shakes the thought away. He just needs to get there. Fast.

A sharp scream cuts through the street.

Everyone freezes.

Then—BOOM.

The explosion knocks the air from his lungs. A plume of smoke bursts into the sky a block away. People pour from the corner building, panicked, screaming.

"Silvertown Pet Grooming?" Tom mutters, staring. "What the hell—"

Out of the haze, a figure steps forward, dragging rage behind him like smoke. One of the Ferals. Fur streaked with red arrows. Eyes locked on them.

Tom's pulse spikes. So much for just getting to the hospital.

"Hey, look at what you stupid Earth humans did to my hair!"

He points to a red bow in his orangish hair on top of his head. "What do you think I am? A female?"

Another Feral is on someone's car, a white one, talking to one of the groomers employees.

"Sorry, miss, but have you seen a little boy with a blue headscarf anywhere?"

The woman panics and runs away screaming. Other people must notice the talking cats, and the panic spreads.

Baxter rolls his eyes. "Oh, great. They finally decided to show up, huh?"

"What the hell is going on?" Anna asks, looking at the two talking cats horrified. Sarah hides behind Cedric.

"Oh, I forgot. You two don't know, do you?" Cedric says.

Anna raises an eyebrow. "Don't know what? Why are there two talking cats? Am I high?"

Cedric rubs his head. "Well, I don't know about that one, but I'll explain it to you two later." Cedric looks at Tom. "Should we run toward the hospital, or should we stop them?"

Tom shrugs. "I don't know. We're not that far away from the hospital. That means the rest of them are nearby."

Tom's phone rings, and he takes it out to find Ben is calling.

"Ben, where the hell are you?"

"Well, hello to you too."

Tom frowns. "I'm not joking around, Ben! Two Ferals are terrorizing the town right now!"

"Don't worry, we already know. Me, Uri, and Honey just left the hospital. We're driving toward The Wolf Den right now. I have a plan."

Tom rubs his forehead. "Oh, great. What's your plan?"

"We should all meet together at The Wolf Den. We can lead The Ferals out of town. Does that sound good?"

"Yes, I guess I'll see ya later."

"Bye."

Tom turns off his phone and looks at the rest of The Wolf Pack. "Follow me."

Cedric raises an eyebrow. "Was that Ben?"

"Yes. They're out of the hospital. They're going to The Wolf Den to draw The Ferals out of town."

Cedric scratches his head. "What are we going to do? All of our cars are parked too far away."

"Don't worry, I have a plan."

Tom walks up to a random car nearby and breaks the window. He then hot-wires it and turns to the others. "Come on. Jump in."

They all look at him with puzzlement, but they jump in. Tom slams on the gas and pulls up to where the Ferals are still terrorizing the neighborhood.

"Hey, you cats! Remember me?" Tom shouts.

One frowns at Tom. "Hey, you're that Earth human's friend!"

"Yeah, that's right! Come and get me!"

The two cats sprint after them. Tom floors the gas, tires screeching as the stolen SUV lurches forward. He's never hotwired a car before—never broken the law, period—but desperate times call for desperate measures. His friends are probably still in shock watching him pull that stunt. His dad would've lost it.

Tom clenches the wheel. He's always followed the rules, but ever since Ben came into his life, the lines have blurred. He's done things he never thought he would. This one takes the cake.

He'll yell at Ben later. Right now, he's getting them out alive.

Chapter 43- Plan Failed

Nour's POV, the angry feline

Nour stalks through the hospital, looking for Uri. All the humans run away screaming as he approaches. He doesn't want to hurt them; the faster he finds Uri, the sooner he will get out of here and forget about this planet. Nader is with him, meanwhile Sebastian, Tito, Ginger, Antar, and Ebo are off in the middle of Silvertown doing whatever they please.

Nour and Nader finally catch Uri's scent that leads them to a room, but there are a couple of Earth soldiers with golden badges blocking the way. There is also a person with a white robe, whom Nour assumes is a doctor, talking to the two soldiers.

Nour looks up at them. "Excuse me, but you're in my way."

They suddenly jump, and the two soldiers grab their guns. Nour and Nader move before the humans can react. They moved so quickly that they decided to have a little fun.

It must have looked like a bolt of lighting for the policemen and the doctor, but when they had time to react, they saw that their pants had fallen, their belts removed. They look behind them.

Nour and Nader spit out their belts.

"Hmm, it looks like you didn't lose all of your sense of humor." Nour says.

Nader rolls his eyes. "Just get Uri, will you? I'm going to take care of these three."

"Fine, then."

Nour opens the door and enters the room where the nurses were so kind enough to tell them where Uri is kept. Meanwhile, his brother is tying up the two policemen and the doctor. Nour feels the room and it's cold. It's empty? At first, Nour thought he entered the wrong room, but then there's an open window. *Uri? Did he escape?*

He grinds his teeth. Great, Uri could be anywhere around town and to make matters worse that Ben human is probably with him too.

"What happened?" Nader asks.

"They escaped."

"Great, they could be anywhere at this point."

"Hold on."

Nour calls the rest of The Ferals using his phone.

"This is Nour. Uri has escaped from the hospital. He's probably roaming around town. Have you guys seen him?"

"Um, Nour. We got a slight problem." Tito answers.

"What?"

"Well, I know you told us to not get ourselves involved, but me and Sebastian just saw this cool grooming place in town and really wanted to go there. We kind of... destroyed it. Well, it was only Sebastian who destroyed it, but... Sorry."

"Hey, it ain't my fault those human workers ruined my hair! They thought I was a female! Do I look like a female to you?" Sebastian speaks up.

"Well, to be honest, I kind of have a hard time myself." Ginger interjects.

"Shut up!" Sebastian yells.

Nour sighs. "You gotta be kidding me right now. Why didn't you guys listen to me?"

"Um... Nour?" Ebo asks.

"Oh, great! What is it now?"

"Well, I found Uri."

"Really? Where?"

"I just saw him inside a car with the Ben human and his girlfriend. I will give you the coordinates."

"Please do. Thank you."

"Will do, boss. Yay, I'm finally useful for on—"

Nour hangs up. Him and his brother spring into action, getting out of the hospital.

Nour doesn't know what Ben is planning, but he wants to get to them before they try to do anything.

Chapter 44- The Final Confrontation

Ben, Uri, and Honey wait at The Wolf Den for the rest of their friends. Ben's hoping this plan—luring The Ferals here—keeps the town safe. He doesn't want a fight. Not unless talking fails. And if it does, he's ready.

He's sure The Ferals aren't all bad. They've had chances to kill, but haven't. Not even during the Sweetopian village attack—no deaths, just damage. Strange for trained assassins. Maybe, like him, they're trying to protect Uri.

A car approaches. Ben watches as their friends step out.

Then something shifts in his gut. A flicker of tension. His conscience bristles.

They're here.

The Ferals have arrived.

"Hey, watch out!" He yells, but it's too late, as suddenly two bombs come out of nowhere, hurtling toward them. They luckily dive clear of the explosions and get up as The Ferals finally step into the clearing.

Their leader, Nour, stares at The Wolf Pack with malicious eyes. "Okay, I have had enough of this chasing around! Give us Uri, or else we'll have no choice!"

"I know that you're hiding something, Nour." Ben yells back.

"Excuse me?"

"You and your friends are just like us. We both want to protect Uri."

"We're nothing alike! At least you have your lover, and what do I have? She's dead!"

When Ben hears this, he knows the true reason The Ferals are chasing Uri. It's because Nour, just like him, doesn't want those he loves to leave him, and that's why he tries everything he can to make sure his friends don't leave his side... He doesn't want to be alone.

Ben looks at Nour. "I know how you feel, not wanting your friends to leave you, and that's why you keep chasing Uri, is it?" he smiles. "Well, you don't have to chase him any longer, because we'll protect him."

Tito looks at Nour. "Nour, we should stop. It's clear they can take care of Uri better than we can."

"No, I know how many dangerous and powerful creatures there are out there in the universe that would do anything they can to find Uri."

"But he's safe. They will protect him," Ginger says.

"Yeah, a bunch of Earth humans that barely know how to use their abilities? Sorry, but I don't think they can defeat any powerful creature. Let's just stop them, grab Uri, and get out of here."

Nour leaps forward, and The Ferals follow his lead. Ginger encases the Wolf Pack in sand.

Nader then makes bombs appear above each of The Wolf Pack's heads. The bombs explode, and smoke fills the air...

Once the smoke clears, Nour sees... *Nothing? Wait a minute, my conscience—*

"Hey, watch out! They're behind us!"

Nour yells out. The Ferals turn around, they see all The Wolf Pack including Uri standing ready to fight.

"Oh, great. One of them knows how to teleport. I don't know who it is though." Nader says.

Nour growls. "Isn't that fantastic, but I got an idea. If they are anything like us, they work well together. That's why we need to separate them. Let's see how well they can fight by themselves. Plus, that will give us more of a chance to capture Uri."

Nader shrugs. "Alright, sounds like a plan."

The Ferals get in formation to split. Sebastian is the only one smirking excited to fight. They captured those three Sweetopians, so Nour knows they stand a chance. They won't be relying on their Sweetopian teachers. This will be a piece of cake.

Chapter 45- Fighting Begins!

Slam

We're fighting. We're actually going to fight! I don't even know how to feel about it. I'm nervous—Chuck, Strawberry, and Ocean aren't here. And Anna and Cedric's little sister? They don't have any special abilities. They're probably wondering what the heck is going on. Honestly, same. But I know one thing: I have to help my friends.

It's kind of wild. I only met The Wolf Pack on the first day of school, and here I am, months later, running into battle with them. Fighting against—of all things—a deadly cat gang. The Ferals. Ferocious cats. This feels like the kind of thing you'd read in a fantasy book.

Actually... it'd make a great book. Our stories, our chaos, all of it. If our lives were in a novel, this moment right here would be the climax. We've come so far. We've learned a lot. Messed up a lot, too. But that's what makes a story worth telling, right? We can't rewrite anything now. Only the author can do that. But now's not the time to start breaking the fourth wall.

Wait... What was I doing?...

Oh, yeah that's right. I'm fighting. I'm running alongside Baxter. You know, I'm surprised Baxter changed his ways and is willing to help The Wolf Pack too, even though he only knew them as long as I had. I can see what a loyal and good group The Wolf Pack are and now it's time to help them fight these ferocious cats.

I don't know how these cute and cuddly cats can be so deadly.

I mean come on, just look at them! They are not even mean looking, they look like cute furballs that can't even hurt a fly not to mention that their eyes, I mean, as I'm running along with my friends toward them I can see just how cuddly their—

Oh, wait. We're fighting now.

Me and one of The Ferals charge at each other, but I'm not ready to fight. The cat leaps up with a summoned spear, but I use a top hat to disappear before he can strike.

I emerge from my top hat to find red arrows covering the cat's gray fur. They turn into actual arrows and fly toward me.

I summon a top hat and it swallows up some of the arrows, then I make another hat next to the gray cat.

The arrows fly out at the cat, who seems to be able to control them, changing the trajectory of the fletchings to soar back at me. I dodge out of the way, but while distracted, the Feral lunges at me. I nearly avoid a blow from the cat's claws, but an arrow pierces my arm, and I scream in pain.

Blood seeping a little from my trench coat. Once dirtied with food stains is now more dirtied with blood.

"Hey, let me give you some advice kid," the cat says. "Just let me kill you because you're no match for me. You chose the wrong cat to fight. Unlike my friends here, I will kill no matter who you are."

"Hey, why so violent?" I ask. "We can have peace."

"Peace? Man, you're like my brother, Tito. You both are peaceable people. It would've been best if you chose him instead of me. Peace doesn't exist in the universe. Every planet I've been to, there's no peace at all. The only point in life is to survive. That's one thing you and my brother won't understand. The both of you are living a lie."

That reminds me of Baxter. This cat probably cares about his friends, even though he doesn't act like it. I realize that's his weakness and try to think of how to exploit it. I've got it.

I use a top hat to stop more arrows from the Feral. This time, I make another hat appear over a nearby cat who the gray cat keeps looking at—possibly the brother he mentioned.

"Hey, look out!" The gray cat calls out as he runs toward the other, but he's too slow and the arrows are nearing the oblivious target.

I make another top hat above the other Feral and catch the arrows before they strike.

I then make another hat in front of the gray one, gobbling him up. Another suspending above his brother, sending one furball flying into the other. My victory! Oh, yeah! I haven't had this much fun about a victory ever since I—

Baxter

Baxter has been waiting for so long to fight. To get himself bruised or to bruise someone else. He's planning to make peace with these alien cats, but that doesn't mean he can have a little fun. Baxter charges at one of the Ferals, but the cat doesn't seem like he wants to fight. When Baxter takes a swing, the cat dodges and steps back.

"Hey, you white fur ball, fight me!"

The Feral shakes his head. "No, I don't want to fight. I can't fight with people I know are good."

Baxter shows his teeth in anger. Of course he had to choose the weakest out of all The Ferals to fight with. Baxter creates bombs next to the cat, but again his foe simply dodges away, summoning bubbles to catch the bombs and sending them back at Baxter.

Baxter barely dodges his own bombs, then suddenly can't move. He looks down to find bubbles encasing his feet.

The Feral stands still as the bombs explode harmlessly around them.

"Get this crap off me," Baxter yells as he struggles to free himself.

The cat shakes his head. "Man, you remind me of my brother Sebastian."

Baxter is not going to give up that easily, Baxter has an idea.

Baxter's rage grows until his entire body begins to glow red. An explosion erupts from Baxter's body, bursting all the bubbles around him, leaving him standing there with smoke rising from his skin.

The cat summons more bubbles, but suddenly one of Slam's top hats appears above him. The hat disgorges a hail of arrows at the cat, then just as suddenly, another hat appears and catches them.

"What the hell is he doing?" Baxter mumbles.

Just as he says this, another hat appears and a Feral shoots out of it, bowling Baxter's opponent over, and both the cats roll off in a ball of tangled fur. Victory is complete. Baxter wishes it would stay longer.

***

Honey

Honey shifts her weight from foot to foot, her fists clenched at her sides. Her heart thuds in her chest, loud enough she swears the others can hear it. She's not a fighter—not really—but she plants her feet anyway. She's ready to give everything she has.

She repeats her mom's voice in her head: *Keep your stance. Watch the eyes. React, don't flinch.* Then Strawberry Shores' tips echo in too: *Use your conscience wisely. Breathe. Let God's holy spirit guide you.*

Anna and Sarah are behind her. She's got to hold the line.

Then she feels it. Grit. A soft scrape under her boots.

Her eyes flick down. Sand. Creeping like fingers between her toes.

Before she can react, a rush of wind slams into her. A wall of sand, thick and fast, bursts toward her—ginger fur flickers through it, a cat staring at her from a distance.

She gasps as the sand coils around her legs and starts to rise. It clings to her like wet cement, tugging her down inch by inch. She twists, yanks, but it's no use—she's stuck.

Then, just as sudden as it began, the sand stops.

The air stills.

Honey stands frozen, breath shallow, waiting for the next move.

"I'm sorry for how things are," the Feral says. "I'm not going to kill you, but I must stop you. You don't know the dangers involved with protecting Uri."

"Yes, we do, but Jehovah is going to help us."

"Pff, yeah. I used to believe that Jehovah was going to help us too until I realized it's all a farce. There's no peace in the universe."

"Yes, but if you just realize the little things Jehovah did for you and your friends in the past, you'll see that He does care about you."

"I love your optimism. You remind me of Nour's girlfriend, Angel. She was optimistic about the world. If only there were more people like you. That's why you need to stay alive. Unfortunately for me, I'm a worthless cat. My dad thinks I'm worthless after he left me. I'm just like my sand; worthless and nothing good can grow on me."

After hearing this, Honey looks at Ginger with sympathetic eyes. She can't imagine what sort of things he and The Ferals have gone through, but she knows that he's not like sand. Honey tries to think of how to use that to escape from the sand attack.

Ginger renewed the waves of sand, threatening to suffocate Honey, but she can tell the cat's heart isn't in the fight. He said he was like the sand, 'worthless with nothing good growing on it. '

But Honey knows that good things grow even in sand. She creates a cactus, growing from the sand right next to the cat, and strikes him on the rear end with it. The Feral yowls in pain, and with his concentration broken, the onslaught of sand ceases.

Honey walks up to the Feral and says, "You're not worthless. You said that you're like sand that has nothing good growing on it, but there are always good things growing everywhere, including in sand. You just have to look for the good."

The ginger cat smiles but doesn't say anything. Honey knows that there's good in everything, even in this evil cat.

***

Cedric

Winning isn't the top priority for Cedric now, but he feels like they have to win this one because it means their lives. Some of his buddies just charged at The Ferals like a bunch of chimpanzees not giving second thought. He is just going to stay with Anna, his sister, and Uri. Keeping his eyes out... Wait, he senses something.

He winds up his lasso as a Feral charges his way. He hesitates as the cat grows bigger and bigger, becoming a muscled, hairless monster.

The only time Cedric tackled something so large was when he rode a bull. This gives him an idea.

"Hey, Anna. Time me," he calls out.

"Time you? Why?"

"I'm going to ride this cat like a bull. I want to see how long I can stay on."

"What? Are you crazy?"

Cedric smirks. "Yeah."

Anna shakes her head and takes her phone out. "Alrighty, then."

When the monstrous cat charges, he tosses the lasso over its neck, and jumps on the beast for the ride of his life. He isn't able to hold on for long until he's bucked off, but he manages to loop the lasso around the cat's legs.

"What time did I get?"

"Five seconds," Anna calls back.

He's disappointed. He would have liked to make it to eight seconds, but it seems it was long enough. He has his lasso be invisible. He just needs the cat to come a little closer.

"Hey, kitty kitty. You're a wild one, aren't ya?" Cedric makes cute chirping noises.

The cat growls. "اسكت. (Shut up.)"

"Yeah, sorry. I don't understand you."

The giant cat creature takes one big step forward. *Perfect.* Cedric quickly swings his hands up. The giant cat stumbles and falls, then shrinks back down to its regular size as the lasso drains all its energy.

With the weakened Feral tied up by his lasso, Cedric looks around to see if anybody needs help, but they all seem to have things under control.

Sarah and Anna are safe, so Cedric checks on Baxter and Slam. Their opponents seem more intent in fighting each other, so Cedric ties them up while they're distracted.

He checks Honey next, but her cat's already entangled in vines.

"Hey, have any of you guys seen Uri anywhere?" he asks.

All his friends shake their heads.

"He ran away with a dark cloud chasing him," Anna says.

Cedric slaps his forehead. "Oh, great. It looks like Uri decided to fight as well."

"Don't worry, I'm sure we can find him." Honey chimes in.

"I sure hope so."

***

Uri

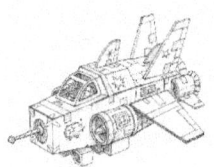

Uri's chest swells with gratitude. They forgave him. They still care. After everything, they stayed.

I'll repay them, he thinks. *I have to. I will.*

He stays back with Cedric, shoulders tense but heart steady—until a creeping thought claws its way in.

They shouldn't be protecting me. I don't deserve it.

A chill brushes the edge of his mind.

I deserve the darkness.

Darkness answers. It seeps in from the edges of his vision, swallowing light, flattening sound. The world vanishes. Cedric. The Wolf Den. Gone.

"Hello?" Uri's voice breaks in the void.

No reply.

He runs.

His footsteps slap against nothingness, swallowed by the silence. His breath comes fast, fogging in front of him—but there's no cold. Just absence. Then—

Whack. A blow from nowhere slams into his ribs.

He stumbles, gasping.

Crack. Another—his shoulder. Then again. Shadows attacking from every side.

He flinches, shifts, *transforms.*

Feathers burst from his arms, his body lightens—he becomes a kestrel and launches upward, wings slicing the air.

Higher. Escape. But even the air feels thick. A shape emerges in front of him—floating. A face, twisted and hollow-eyed, grinning. He veers hard. Tries to climb. Then claws. A paw—massive, unseen—snatches him mid-flight.

Uri struggles against whatever is holding him as the strange face grows closer. He is about to give up when he remembers what Ben said back in the woods. He said he doesn't care about the bad thing Uri did because he sees the good in him, that Jehovah sees the good in others, despite the bad things they've done.

His determination renewed, Uri keeps fighting to free himself and think of a way to defeat the darkness.

As the creepy face inches closer to Uri, he tries to wiggle out of the paws grasping him. He isn't afraid because he knows that The Wolf Pack care about him and are willing to protect him. More importantly, he knows that God will protect him.

Uri's faith is renewed, and he regains his power. Suddenly, Uri's body glows white, driving away the darkness. He breaks through the Feral's grasp and soars at the cat, landing blow after blow until Edo slumps to the ground. Ebo is now seeing tweety birds. Victory is complete.

Suddenly, some of The Wolf Pack come running toward him, and he returns to his human form and scoops up the fallen cat. The others have captured some of the Ferals as well.

"Where did you run off to?" Cedric asks.

"I got surrounded by darkness and tried to fly away. I didn't realize how far I went, but I was able to overcome the darkness with my own light." Uri looks around. "Where are Tom and Ben?"

"They're still fighting. We've lost both of them," Cedric says.

Uri shrugs. "Well, guess I'll join you guys in the search party. We better make sure they're okay."

"Alright."

So Uri joins them in trying to find Ben and Tom. Uri hopes that Ben and Tom manage to defeat Nour and Nader. Uri knows how strong Nour and Nader are. Those two cat brothers are what Uri is most scared of. Uri wants to find them quickly before something goes wrong.

***

Tom

Tom charges at one of the Ferals, the one with robotic legs, the cat doesn't move, not even an inch. He summons multiple swords around the alien, but it still doesn't react. As the blades near their target, the Feral blinks out of existence.

Tom looks around, seeing no sign of his foe, but his conscience senses something coming at him. He summons a shield.

An explosion erupts against the shield, tossing him to the ground, but he's unhurt. He shakes his head to clear the ringing in his ears and looks over the edge of the shield.

The cat is just standing there, gloating. "Those Sweetopians trained you well on how to use your conscience. It's unfortunate I have to fight you, but I have to follow orders from my leader."

"Why are you so devoted to him?"

"Nour isn't just my leader, but he's also my fleshly brother and a good friend. Even though he makes questionable choices, I still want to protect him."

This reminds Tom of how he always follows Ben, even though he's nothing but trouble, because he's his friend and he wants to look out for him.

"I can see that you're a good protector of your friends too. We're going to have a respectable battle."

The Feral pulls out one of Tom's favorite music CDs. Tom doesn't know how this cat has one of his music CDs, he probably stole it somehow. He sees him do something very peculiar.

His robotic eye opens up like a CD player and he puts the CD in his robotic eye. His robotic eye closes and turns into like a CD player as Tom's CD inside turns around and around. The cat opens his mouth and it's making music. Musical sound waves are visible.

The cat springs into action, sending out waves of music. Tom holds up the shield as it's battered by what seems to be sound waves. His ears ring with pain as the shield is buffeted, but he holds his ground. How much longer he can hold, he isn't sure. *Have I failed?* He wonders as the sonic waves push him back.

But he recognizes the rhythm. Maybe he does have a chance. He gets his groove on. He dances to the rhythm of the music as he avoids the sound waves. It's a good thing his friends aren't around to see him. His dancing is a complete embarrassment.

Suddenly, the music's over. Tom stops.

"You dodge well, but I got more tricks up my sleeve."

No pun intended, the cat literally pulls another of Tom's CDs out of his sleeve, but this time it isn't a music CD. It's a CD of Tom's favorite childhood cartoon: Tom The Big Fat Lion. It's a story about a gluttonous lion who is a king trying to protect his pride. No wonder he's a screwed up child now.

The Feral immediately switches the music CD out and replaces it with Tom The Big Fat Lion. The cat's pupil suddenly changes into a camera lens, and the camera lens shoots out a holographic image of Tom, the big fat lion himself, but the king lion doesn't look like his normal self. The lion's eyes turn red, looking at Tom with the intent to kill him.

"How the hell are you doing this? It's impossible!" Tom looks at the cat wide-eyed.

"In the universe, everything's possible. I bet that those Sweetopians taught you that your special abilities are based on your dreams, right? Your dreams can become your reality if you are willing. That's what the outside universe is like that you people of Earth don't have, but even with my dreams coming true, I still feel sad for some reason..." The cat looks at his robotic arm. "I see different people in different worlds across the universe and they don't seem like they are happy even though they have their dreams. I don't know what to do now except protect my friends, but they're sad also."

While he gives Tom this monologue, Tom is barely paying attention because he's busy trying to fight the evil gluttonous king lion trying to eat him.

The Feral shakes his head, getting back to his senses. Tom is using his shield, protecting himself from the king lion. Tom is so busy using his shield that he barely notices the Feral charging at him.

Tom struggles against the force of the lion, holding tight to his shield as he is pushed back, his feet digging into the earth. He peers over as the cybernetic Feral approaches with a blade in each paw, moving in for the kill. He can't do anything. Has he failed?

No, he isn't going to give up yet. No, there's somebody that can help. Tom closes his eyes and prays...

When he opens his eyes, his shield and his entire body are glowing white, and the Feral recoils at the sudden brilliance. The light is so powerful that it disintegrates the holographic lion.

Tom's filled with holy spirit as he summons a flurry of swords. The Feral tries to dodge them, but one cuts through a robotic foreleg, sending it spinning to the ground.

The cat draws back, seeming stunned by the blow, but then he creates a holographic cloud.

He flies around on the cloud, avoiding every sword, but one catches him off guard. He gets cut real badly. He falls...

Tom makes the other swords hover near him, their points near inches from the cat. He just holds his wound. Breathing heavily, defeated.

"Go on," He hisses. "finish it."

Tom dismisses the swords and his shield.

"Why...why are you sparing my life?" He asks.

"Because your friends need you. You may think life is always going to be out of order, but that's why both of us need to stay alive, because our friends need us to keep them in line."

The cat is speechless. A long silence ensues until Tom hears some people running toward him. The rest of his friends, his Pack members. Perfect timing for Tom's sake. It's a good thing to see that his friends also won their fights.

***

Ben

What a crazy roller coaster these past few months have been for Ben and his friends—mostly because of Ben. There are plenty of things he'd do differently if he could rewind, but he can't. He can't control what happens, only how he responds. Now, his focus is clear: help Nour, the leader of The Ferals.

At first, Ben thought Nour was just another ruthless villain. But now he sees it's not that simple. Nour's like him—trying to protect Uri, trying to prove himself. Ben wants to show him that success isn't everything. And Uri? He doesn't have to worry about him anymore. The Wolf Pack has Uri's back.

Ben charges. Nour draws his sword in response. Ben knows he can't win a straight fight, so he needs to catch him off guard.

He summons fluffy clouds of cotton candy above Nour, but the cat's lightning-fast reflexes let him dodge every sticky clump. The blade keeps coming, gleaming in the light.

Ben grabs the hardest, stalest baguette he can imagine and raises it just in time to block Nour's strike.

Slash after slash, Ben deflects every attack. Nour takes a step back, frustration flashing in his eyes. Then, he stretches out an empty paw and hurls a ball of fire toward Ben.

Ben calls forth a giant scoop of ice cream that melts the fireball with a sharp sizzle.

Nour snarls as his sword bursts into flames, charging forward again with the fiery blade blazing.

Ben creates more ice cream balls and shoots them at Nour. The cat dodges all of them and shoots out more fireballs. As he is dodging them, Nour charges forward, but Ben summons a banana peel in front of the Feral, causing him to slip and fall to the ground.

Ben smiles. It seems his plans are working. It looks like all that training he did with Chuck is paying off. It wasn't a waste of time after all.

"How the hell are you doing this? It doesn't make sense. You're just throwing food at me." Nour gets up on his four legs.

His eyes and entire body glow red. Ben panics as he realizes The Devil's Eye is overcoming him. Ben doesn't know what to do, faced with The Devil's Eye. He refuses to give up, no matter how powerful Nour may be now that the Devil has led him astray.

Ben looks around for help, he's alone. He's not truly alone though, because he knows Jehovah's with him. Ben may be scared, but he knows his friends are fighting alongside him, and God is too. He decides the only way to save Nour is to put faith in God…

His body starts glowing white. The Feral leader charges, but Ben stands still and calm. When Nour lands his blow, there is an explosion of light...

Ben opens his eyes. His ear rings but stops. There's a bunch of broken trees lying around him, but that's not the only thing lying. He finds Nour lying at his feet.

"Hey, Ben!"

Ben hears voices. His friends. His Pack is here. They're carrying the rest of The Ferals with them. *That's good, it looks like we won.*

"Ben, are you alright?" Honey yells.

"Yeah."

Ben turns back to Nour. The galactic assassin is crying and holding a picture of another cat, a white one with eyes as green as fresh pine needles. Is that— Wait—

Nour's paw tightens around the knife, his eyes wild. For a split second, it looks like he's about to plunge it into himself.

Ben's heart pounds. Without thinking, he summons a heavy ball of ice cream and hurls it straight at Nour.

The icy mass slams into him, knocking the knife from his grip. Nour stumbles back, stunned and disarmed.

Ben doesn't care about winning. He steps closer, voice steady but soft. Now's the time to help—if Nour's willing to listen

Chapter 46- Help Is On The Way

Nour lies on the ground, tears streaming as The Wolf Pack surrounds him. His friends are tied up, defeated—and it's all his fault. He clutches a picture of Angel, the weight of his mistakes crashing down.

He led them on a wild goose chase chasing Uri, thinking capturing him meant success. He promised to protect Uri but only brought terror instead.

Since Angel died, Nour's been desperate not to lose anyone else, but he's only caused more pain. He feels worthless, undeserving of life.

Slowly, he looks up at Ben—the one who stopped him from ending it all.

"Why are you trying to keep me alive?" Nour asks. "I've been trying to kill you and your friends."

"Yeah, I know." Ben picks up Nour and hugs him. "But I also know that you're a good cat who was just trying to protect Uri."

This surprises Nour. Nour realizes how nice Ben and The Wolf Pack are as they untie Nour's friends. Nour stops crying as Ben sets him down on the ground.

Nour smiles. "You guys proved that you can protect Uri better than we ever will. Um..." Nour rubs his head in embarrassment. "We'll also release your Sweetopian friends that we kidnapped too."

Nour laughs awkwardly as he turns on his teleportation watch. Chuck, Strawberry, Ocean, and a bunch of other Sweetopians appear out of nowhere in front of The Wolf Pack.

Jeez, how many Sweetopians did The Ferals kidnap? What strikes Ben as more of a surprise is the old brown velociraptor that's within the Sweetopian crowd. Jegu.

Ben immediately runs over and hugs Jegu.

"Glad to see you guys alive." Jegu says. "What happened?"

"Sorry that I kidnapped you, my Sweetopian friend." Nour blurts out. He walks, head down, to Ben and Jegu.

Jegu stares at Nour, then nods. "It's okay. I know you're a good feline at heart. Jehovah forgives you."

"I'm sorry for all the mess we've done to you and your planet. We won't be bothering you any longer." Nour looks at Ben and his Pack members. He then turns to his cat buddies. "We should probably head to BS Lion and go back to Misr."

All The Ferals nod at their leader as they walk away until—

"Wait, you guys are leaving already? Oh, come on, stay a little while longer. I want to learn more about you alien cats," Slam blurts out.

Nour laughs awkwardly. "I'm glad that you think we're interesting, but unfortunately, it's been a while since me and my friends have been back home. Our friends back home probably miss us."

Honey smiles. "Oh, I see, but you guys should come back. We'd love to talk more, or we might even go to your home nation and see what it's like."

Nour nods. "Yeah, maybe."

"Wait, I want to come with you guys." Ben blurts out.

Cedric frowns at him. "What are you nuts, Ben?"

Ben shrugs. "What? Come on, you guys. Don't you want to explore the rest of space to see what it's like?"

Tom raises an eyebrow. "Yeah, but Ben. Do you realize that you have an attempted murder charge against you from Cougar Jack's parents? That's why they're trying to keep you in the hospital. The police are probably looking for you. You're not doing any favors by continuing to run away."

Ben chuckles. "Oh, yeah. I forgot about that. How long do they keep you in jail for attempted murder? I hope it's not that long because I want to space travel pretty soon."

Tom yells. "What are you, crazy? You just did something seriously wrong, and the only thing you care about is wanting to have an adventure, seriously?"

"Well, I just killed a lot of my people, so Ben's charge is nothing compared to mine." Uri chimes in.

Nour looks at Uri. "Oh, yeah, about that. What I said was a lie, sorry Uri. You didn't actually kill your people."

Uri raises an eyebrow at Nour. "Yeah, I know you told me a bunch of times when chasing me, but is it actually true? How come was I the only one still alive?"

Nour nods. "Yeah, I didn't know exactly what happened, but when we found you, you were unconscious under some debris with your dead dad. It was those damn Babylonians that killed everyone. I'm sorry we didn't arrive earlier to save your city, Uri. If we had been there earlier, we would have saved King Yadin and the rest of your family, but those Babylonians are too sneaky and powerful. They're spreading their spiritual prostitution everywhere across the universe."

Tom asks. "I'm sorry, 'spiritual prostitution'? What the hell is that?"

Nour looks at Tom. "Oh, I'm sorry. I forgot you Earth humans don't know much about the outside universe. There's this powerful woman, the most powerful woman in the entire universe. They call her 'Babylon The Great,' or 'the mother of the prostitutes' because she's known to seduce many creatures into serving her. Her servants are called The Babylonians. There's so many Babylonians in fact, every nation you come across in the universe has people serving her, and unfortunately there were even some in the nation of Zion and there was nothing we could do to stop them from destroying Uri's city."

"Yeah, you're right, Nour. There's nothing we can do to stop her." Jegu chimes in. "Only Jehovah can stop her. We'll continue to share the good news about Jehovah, so we can save some who are victims of her."

Nour grins. "Yes, thank you, Jegu."

"Ah, you see. This is the reason why I want to join you guys in space traveling. Now I want to learn more about this 'Babylon The Great' woman. Come on, let me join you." Ben blurts out. He walks over to Nour, about to give him a hug again, but then Cedric holds him back.

"Ben, you're crazy. Stay here." Cedric struggles to hold Ben back.

Nour can't help but laugh at the two humans. "I wish I could let you join me, but it's best if you stay on your planet for a while."

Jegu nods. "I agree with Nour. And I think us Sweetopians need to head back home too and rebuild our village."

Nour slaps himself. "Oh, yeah, sorry Jegu. Man, there's so much I have to apologize for, but first, I'm going to help you rebuild your village before heading home myself."

Jegu shakes his head. "Oh, there's no need to help. We can—"

"No, I insist." Nour interrupts.

Jegu smiles and nods. "Alrighty, then. Guess we'll be leaving too. How about you Uri?"

Uri pauses for a moment as he looks at The Wolf Pack. "You know what, I think I found my new family here on Earth. I'm going to stay."

Jegu says. "Very well, then. We'll meet again soon."

Nour nods. "Yes, we will. Sorry, Uri, for chasing you for so long."

Uri laughs awkwardly. "It's okay, you guys have a safe trip back home to Misr."

"Yes, thank you."

Nour stands with The Ferals and the Sweetopians, sharing quiet goodbyes with The Wolf Pack and Uri. The roar of the BS Lion fills the air as they take off.

Through the window, Nour's eyes find Ben—the human who cracked open his stubborn heart, who showed him that friends come before selfish wants.

It's a lesson Nour never grasped until now.

As the city shrinks behind them, he steals himself. Back in Misr, The Ferals will change. They'll face the problems head-on, help those who need it—finally living up to what they were meant to be.

And deep down, Nour feels a quiet thanks to Ben—for the first time, truly grateful.

Chapter 47- Graduation

Ben and The Wolf Pack graduate High School a few months later after a hectic year. Meeting Uri and then having an evil gang of alien cats trying to kill you can make for a crazy time. Ben is glad that his friends didn't give up on him, and he didn't give up either. They trusted in one another— they trusted in Jehovah— and now they made friends with aliens that nobody knows about.

The thing is Ben had to stay in prison for two and half years. The sentence was originally five years, but luckily they were nice to him. They found out that he was a good kid and behaved himself, so they reduced his sentence by half.

He's on good terms with Cougar Jack now, though that's only because Ben thinks Jack is afraid of him after just stabbing him. He doesn't want to fight him any longer.

While Ben sat in prison, Silvertown was still buzzing from the chaos The Ferals brought. No one was hurt, but buildings wore the scars of the fight.

Ben chuckled when he heard the story about Dr. Morrison and two cops caught pantless—Nour and Nader had swiped their belts during the chaos.

Social media exploded with photos and videos, sparking curiosity worldwide. News crews and tourists poured in, hoping to catch a glimpse of these so-called cat aliens terrorizing the town.

The police stayed on edge. Tom's dad kept pushing him to go to the police academy, and Tom had been buried in training ever since Ben's arrest. Once he graduates from that academy, he'd finally get real police duties.

Most hoped the whole mess would fade into a weird memory, a fluke soon forgotten. Luckily, nobody thought of Uri as an alien or connected Ben and his friends to the madness.

The Sweetopians and The Ferals had gone, promising to return once Silvertown calmed down.

After a long time of imprisonment, Ben is finally a free man. Now that he's a free citizen, he's been planning to do something that he wanted to do for a long time ever since he met Uri.

He stands on a hill with Honey and Uri, waiting for the rest of their friends to show up. The three of them plan to go on a space adventure together, to a planet Uri said that he always wanted to visit. Ben thought it would make for a good date, third wheel or no.

Cedric's truck rumbles up with the rest of the Wolf Pack, including Anna and Sarah, riding on the bed. When Cedric stops his truck, they all get out and walk over.

Cedric smiles. "Hello there."

"Hey..."

An awkward silence fills the air. Ben isn't sure how to say goodbye to his friends.

Ben laughs awkwardly. "Hopefully we'll meet again soon."

Tom nods. "Yes. Just make sure you don't cause trouble on another planet."

Ben smirks. "I'll try not to. How did the police academy go?"

Tom sighs. "It went well, which is bad because now my dad is wanting me to do so much crap for him."

Cedric laughs. "Yeah, but I'm glad you're going to be back, though."

Tom shrugs. "Well, don't say that, because now you're making me want to go with them to space."

"Hey, how long will this space adventure take, anyway?" Slam asks.

Honey shrugs. "I don't know. Uri says maybe two months, right, Uri?"

"Well, that's just an estimate. It might take longer depending how smooth the trip goes, but you'll love it."

Honey smiles. "Well, no matter how long it takes, we're going to make sure we're back."

Tom raises an eyebrow. "Where exactly are you guys going? I forgot."

Uri replies. "We're going to The New World. I can't believe out of all the planets I went to, I never been on The New World before, and it's close to The Old World where I used to live."

"The Old World and The New World? I remember you telling us, Uri, those two planets are where the two most powerful rulers of the universe are. The king of The North and the king of The South." Slam says.

Uri nods. "Yeah, that's correct. The king of The North lives on The Old World and the king of The South lives on The New World. In fact, that's where I want us to travel to."

"To where? To the king of The South?" Cedric asks.

"Yeah, I always wanted to know what The South looked like," Uri points at Cedric's cowboy hat. "I heard the people there wear hats similar like that. They even talk like you guys. I'm curious what you guys might think of it. All of you should come with us."

Cedric awkwardly chuckles. "We would like to, Uri, but some of us have important things to attend and families to feed, sorry."

Honey smiles. "Well, whatever the case, we'll make sure to come back soon."

Ben smirks. "Yeah, because 'No Wolf Works Alone.' "

Ben raises his wolf chain. All of them howl like wolves, except for Honey, she just shakes her head.

"Jeez, I swear. This stuff is getting old now. We need a new motto." Honey blurts out.

Ben frowns. "Hey, don't disrespect the old motto."

"Whatever. Are we going yet?"

Ben pulls them into a tight hug, the moment heavy and real. Around him, his friends wave, their faces glowing in the fading light.

The Imaginator hums to life and lifts smoothly off the ground. It climbs toward the sunset, streaks of orange and pink painting the sky like a promise.

Ben's heart pounds—nervous, hopeful. Whatever waits out there in the vastness of space, he isn't alone. With the light guiding him and Jehovah by his side, he feels ready to face whatever comes next.

The End

How To Be An Alpha Series

How To Be An Alpha

What's up, homies!

Today, me and my buddies are going to teach you how to become alpha males in an alpha world, bros. I see a lot of weak ass males in the world who think they are no good.

Well, don't worry, because your buddy Ben is here to teach you how to become alpha males in an instant.

No charge to you because I hate charging people....

Well, maybe if you pay me a little, then that would be great because rent is running high and I need to pay for the expenses, but nevermind that.

Let's just get to the lesson here, shall we? My name is Ben, by the way, and these are my friends...

Ben: Hey, come on you guys! Introduce yourselves.

Tom: Seriously Ben, do we have to do this?

Ben: Hey, just stick to the script, okay?

Cedric: Ben, why am I shirtless?

Ben: Because the women love you, Cedric.

Cedric: What do you mean, what women?

Ben: The women that are reading this right now.

Cedric: Ben, I'm pretty sure no woman is ever going to want to read this piece of junk.

Ben: Oh, come on. Don't say that. There's going to be tons of women chasing after us as I get this story out.

Tom: Your ambitions and goals are beyond my understanding, Ben.

Ben: Whatever, just stick to the script.

Hello, my fellow males of the earth and everyone outside the Earth! There might be someone who's reading this in outer space, and if you are, then why? Why are you reading this? Anyway, back to introducing my friends here. It looks like my friends, Tom and Cedric, have already introduced themselves, so I guess I have to introduce my other two friends. My new pack members! Ladies and gentlemen, meet Slam and Baxter!

Baxter: Hi

Slam: Hey, this is kind of interesting! I've never expect to see so many people reading this. Man, Ben, I think we're going to get tons of women after this story comes out.

Ben: You really think so?

Slam: Sure!

Tom: Slam, I wish I had your optimism

Slam: Hey, you just have to look at the brightest side of life, my friend.

Ben: Okay, can we stick to the script here because we're getting distracted?

Slam: Okay, sorry. Continue.

Anyway, these are all of my homies. We call ourselves "The Wolf Pack!"

Speaking of wolves, they are a great example of how to be alphas. That's what me and my homies are here to teach you, the ways of the wolves. So hold your buttcheeks because I'm going to show you the first step to becoming alpha males. The first step is to know who your enemies are. Every wolf knows who their buddies are and who their enemies are just by smelling them.

Now, I'm not saying that you should smell those around you, but it all starts by knowing your buddies very well so you can distinguish who is actually your friend and who is not.

We all got our enemies. Those types of people who you just want to pound their face to the ground and tell them: "Got you now, bastard! Who's the weak one now!?"

Man, enemies are just a pay in the ass to deal with in this life. I wish there weren't any enemies. We could all just get along, but no! They just have to be a bunch of assholes to ruin your life!

Tom: Um, Ben? Are you okay?

Ben: Yeah, I'm fine. Just continue sticking to the script.

Everybody has enemies in their lives. You could be the nicest person in the world, and you will still have some people who try to bring you down. Well, don't worry, because The Wolf Pack is going to teach you how you can defeat your enemies and get a second hand over them. Come along and I'll show you.

Cedric: Ben, where are we going?

Ben: Just follow me and I'll show you

Tom: Ok? This place looks strangely familiar.

421

Ben: It should be because this is Cougar Jack's neighborhood.

Tom: Cougar Jack's? Ben, don't tell me you're planning to destroy Jack's house?

Ben: Wow, good job. I don't have to explain anything to you. You already know. This is a great example of how good our relationship is.

Tom: Ben, I swear to God if you try to destroy Jack's house, then I'm leaving.

Ben: Hey, where are you going?

Tom: I'm not going to get involved in this.

Ben: Tom, get back here.

Tom: No.

Ben: But I had so many plans to use you in this story that are going to be funny.

Tom: Hell no.

Ben: Alright, fine then.

Anyway, now that one of my homies left. I guess I have to change some things that I had planned to do, but nothing's going to change for those of you who are reading.

You'll still be entertained, I promise you. And you'll soon learn to be alphas.

Okay, so now that you know who your enemies are, what I want you who are reading this to know is that in order to survive in this world and become alphas, you need to find out where your enemies live and where they hang out. For example: my enemy lives in a big house right next to the shores of Silvertown Lake.

Now that you know where your enemy lives, the next step is to figure out how you can infiltrate their base without them noticing.

Cedric: Okay, I'm not doing this either.

Ben: Oh, come on. Not you too.

Cedric: Ben, we're literally doing something that's illegal. We're literally breaking into somebody's house and destroying it.

Ben: Well, if you put it that way, then yeah. It does sound illegal, but if you add Cougar Jack to the equation, then it's quite alright.

Cedric: I can't believe this. I'm outta here.

Ben: Hey, you can't leave as well.

Cedric: Sure can.

Ben: Uhhhh, let me guess, you two want to leave too?

Baxter: As long as I get paid a good sum of money, then no.

Slam: Hey, are you sure you want to do this, Ben?

Ben: You know what, I'm tired. Let's just go home already. This was just a waste of time for us and the reader.

Slam: Well, we can't let the reader be disappointed. What should we do now?

Ben: I don't know. It's a crappy story idea, anyway. The author didn't put too much thought into it.

Baxter: Well, how does this story end? I got a lot of better things to do than just hanging out with you idiots.

Ben: Well, do you just want to end it here?

Baxter: Please do.

Ben: Alrighty then....

How To Be An Alpha 2 (Getting Cute Girls)

Oh, yeah!

I'm excited for today, boys! Why?

Because we're going to teach you how to get cute girls! I know all you beta males who are reading this right now think they can't get any women out there, but The Wolf Pack is here to tell you that yes you can!

Tom: Nope, sorry. There's no hope.

Shut up, Tom.

Anyway, me and the boys are going to video ourselves trying to talk to girls we haven't met before out in public and see if we can get their numbers. If we can do it, then so can you! So are you guys ready because right now it's summer break for us and everyone is out and enjoying the sun, so there's going to be plenty of women out. Right, boys?

Cedric: I sure hope so.

Slam: Oh yeah, we can do this! Man, we're going to get tons of girls' numbers today.

Tom: We'll see.

Baxter: Psh, man, you guys aren't going to get any girls' numbers at all. Girls these days love a bad boy like me. They don't like nice guys.

Cedric: Oh, really? Is that so?

Baxter: Yeah, just wait and see, my man. All of the women are going to be chasing after me.

Well, it looks like the boys are ready. Hopefully, we'll get at least one girl's number for each of us, but we'll see. Fortunately for me, I already got a girlfriend, so I won't be participating in this for the sake of my girlfriend not kicking my ass. For those who are reading right now, I'm going to video every encounter my boys have with a girl and see if they can get their numbers.

Tom: Oh, boy. You know, I really don't want to do this, Ben.

Ben: Oh, come on, Tom. Don't be shy. I know you can do it.

Tom: Oh, yeah, easy for you to say because you already got a woman.

Cedric: Yeah, you lucky bastard

Ben: Heh, heh...Nevermind me...let's just get started, shall we?

Tom: Ben, I'm going to—

Okay! Let's just get started! My boys here are going to travel to different areas around town to see if they can find any women at all. And if they do, then for those who are reading; get ready because it will be show time.

***

Alright, my boy Baxter is driving around in his sweet muscle car in town looking for some hot chicks. All of my other homies are driving around in other places right now. I really want to show you homies that are reading this right now that I really appreciate you guys taking the time to even take a glance at this stupid thing I'm doing with my friends, but I just want to show you readers the typical life of an average alpha male.

Isn't that right, Baxter?

Baxter: Hey, get that stupid camera off my face, man!

Ben: Olp, sorry...Wait a minute. Baxter, look, there's a cute girl over there.

Baxter: Over where?

Ben: There! She's sitting in front of the Safeway.

Baxter: Wait, does that girl go to our school?

Ben: Oh, yeah. I think you're right. I don't know her name, though.

Baxter: Oh, I know her. Almost too well, actually. Hannah, she's a wild one. Watch and learn, Ben, because I'm going to show you how to tame a wild beast.

Ben: Um...Okay?

Baxter: Oh, yeah! Just wait here in the car. I don't want you to ruin the scene with your...presence.

Alrighty then...well... as my boy Baxter gets out of the car and runs towards this Hannah chick, I'll be filming with my camera to show you bros who are reading this what Baxter can do. Hopefully, Baxter gets her number. He's the most confident person I've ever met...

Well, Baxter is approaching Hannah right now, but she seems to be looking at him like: "What the heck is going on? Why are you here?"...

Oh, it looks like Baxter is putting his shades on and he's putting his hand on the table. Hannah looks like she just wants to get out of there. I secretly put a mic on Baxter. Let's see what he's saying to her:

Baxter: Hey, girl. What are you doing this weekend?

Hannah: What do you want, Baxter?

Baxter: Oh, hey. A girl who likes to be forward. I like that.

Hannah: Excuse me?

Baxter: So, do you want to come to my place and have sex or what?

Hannah: Pff, like anyone would sleep with you?

Baxter: That's not what you said to Frank last night.

Oh, boy.... Well... it seems like Hannah didn't like what Baxter said, because she just smacked him in the head. Hannah is rushing away from Baxter right now to her car, and she just drove off.... Well, okay then... I wonder what Baxter said? I guess we'll find out because he's running towards us right now.

Baxter: Man, what an asshole!

Ben: So... How did it go?

Baxter: Man, women these days are a bunch of jerks!

Ben: So it didn't go well then?

Baxter: No, it did not! That girl was a jerk!

Ben: I thought you said girls love jerks?

Baxter: Yeah, they do.

Ben: Then, how come she left you?

Baxter: Oh, just shut up!

***

Cedric: Ben, why am I shirtless again?

Ben: Because women are just going to love you. I don't know why you don't show your abs, bro, because ladies love that.

Cedric: Man, this is ridiculous. I'm putting my shirt back on.

Ben: Alright, fine then.

Alright, my fellow male readers. My friend Cedric here is going to show you how you can get the ladies with music. Cedric, grab the guitar.

Cedric: Man, this is going to be so embarrassing, but you know what? Screw it.

Ben: Oh, come on. Don't be like that.

Cedric: Whatever, let's just walk over to those two girls already.

Oh, yeah! Get ready, male readers, because there's two more girls at Safeway and they're hot and ready for a sexy man in their life and that sexy man is Cedric.

Cedric: Okay, please stop talking.

Ben: Okay, fine.

As you can see here, my buddy Cedric is approaching the two women. It looks like he has his guitar ready. Let's see what he says.

Cedric: Um…hello…

It looks like the women have finally noticed him. What will my buddy Cedric do next?

Cedric: Um…do you guys like music?

Girl: Yeah, sure.

Oh, and it looks like one woman is talking and she's smiling. That's a good sign. My buddy is doing well so far. It looks like my buddy Cedric is getting ready to strum his guitar. He's playing a little tune.

Oh, yeah, baby. There you go.

Good job Cedric....

Wait...Hold on.... He stopped?

Cedric, what are you doing?

No, oh come on!

Why are you running towards me?

Cedric: Ben, I can't do this, man.

Ben: What? Sure you can.

Cedric: Nah, I can't. Let's just go already.

Ben: Man, I can't believe you.

Alright, well it looks like my buddy Cedric is too much of a coward to play his guitar in front of two delicate ladies, but lucky for you male readers, my other buddy Tom is next and I'm sure he's going to do great. His dad is a sheriff, so that's an instant level up to his "rizz-o-meter".

Tom: Ben, I don't think me being the sheriff's son is going to give me more "rizz."

Ben: Oh, sure it will. Come, try it on that one girl that's sitting alone on the bench.

Tom: Alright, fine.

Alright, well my buddy Tom is going to show you male readers how sheriff's sons pick up chicks. You readers will get a close look at my buddy Tom's rizz. He'll do great, you'll see...

Alright, well, it looks like he's walking slowly up to her. She hasn't noticed him yet. Tom is sitting on the bench now next to her, but she still hasn't noticed him yet because she's on her phone. Come on, Tom, tap her shoulder. There you go! Now she is looking at him.

Tom: Uh… sorry to disturb you, miss, but are you waiting for the bus?

Girl: What does it look like?

Tom: Oh, right. Sorry, stupid question…

Well, it looks like my buddy Tom started a conversation, but they've stopped talking all of a sudden. Come on, Tom, say something.

Tom: Um…I don't know if you know me or not, but I'm Tom, by the way. What's yours?

Girl: Tasha.

Tom: Tasha? That's a nice name, a nice name indeed…So, one thing that you can know about me is that I'm actually the sheriff's son.

Tasha: The sheriff's son?

Tom: Yeah, I mean, I'm not trying to brag or anything, but my dad is a good sheriff. Almost too good actually…But he's a wonderful dad. I mean, he's so dignified, but what do you expect, you know…. It's like he's always trying to force me to become something I know I'm not. He always expects too much from me, like okay, nobody's perfect dad. Why do you expect me to be perfect when you're not perfect yourself? I mean, come on!...

Tasha: Um… I need to go now. The bus is here.

Tom: Oh, yeah, sure. By the way, can I get your number?

Tasha: Um, no.

Tom: Well, that's fair. You have a good one.

Tasha: You too?

And it looks like my buddy Tom has finally come back after talking to the girl at the bus stop. I wonder what they said? It looked like a friendly conversation, but I don't know. Olp, he's getting close to us.

Tom: Ben, turn off the camera.

Ben: How did it go? Did you get her number?

Tom: Nah.

Ben: What? But it looked like you guys had a pleasant conversation.

Tom: Yeah, 'a pleasant conversation.' It's more like hell.

Ben: Alrighty then?

Well, it looks like not even the sheriff's son can get the ladies, but lucky for you male readers, there's one of my friends left. Slam, you're up next...Slam?...

Ben: Hey, did you guys know where Slam went?

Cedric: I have no idea?

Slam: Oh, boy! You guys wouldn't believe it! It's amazing!

Ben: Jesus Christ! You scared me!

Slam: Oh, sorry. I just had a good conversation with a lady who I thought was cute.

Cedric: Wait? Really? That's good for you. At least one of us was successful.

Slam: Yeah, the lady was nice. I just felt sorry for her because she was carrying all those groceries by herself with one hand. Man, I just felt bad for her walking across the road on her cane.

Tom: Her cane?

Slam: Yeah, isn't that sad? People have no respect when they see old ladies walking across the street. I've seen so many people walk past this cute old lady carrying groceries that it just made me sick, so I just had to help her.

Tom: Slam, we were talking about young ladies. Have you asked any young ladies out?

Slam: Oh, okay...Yeah, I have, but they turned me down.

Tom: Great, fantastic. Apparently, all of us suck at talking to girls.

Slam: Hey, don't look down on yourself. Look at it this way; at least we know that the girls we talked to are not right for us.

Tom: Is that supposed to be encouraging?

Slam: Yes, it is. I mean, there's plenty of fish in the sea, and as fishermen, we must exercise our patience to find the right one for us.

Baxter: Psh, you're too optimistic. What's wrong with you?

Slam: You know what, I ask the same question every time I wake up. Hahaha!

Baxter: Okay, you know what, I'm leaving. This has been a shitty day.

Tom: For once, I agree with Baxter.

Cedric: Yeah, let's just go home already.

Alright, well, it looks like my friends here are done for today.

Sorry for those who are reading this junk story. Until next time, my readers, continue moving forward in this stupid world where we can't even find at least one decent woman who is nice enough and wants to have an actual relationship. But there's no woman like that in this world, so for those who are reading, just give up.

As long as you have your boys with you, that's all that matters. "Bros before hoes.," is what we say..........

One Year Ago

Hey, why are you still here?

I thought I turned the camera off. Stop reading and do something with your life.

I'm walking towards my house, alright. That's all I'm doing, then I'm just going to sit on my recliner and watch TV because it has been a disappointing day today ok, so stop reading...

Man, come on! Why are you—

Honey: Hey, Ben! How's it going?

Ben: Uh, what?

Oh, great.

Honey is here.

It looks like she got out of her house to say hello to me. Oh, great. I don't feel like talking right now, but I guess I will talk to her. She is the only girl I actually like. In fact, I actually have a crush on her—Don't tell anybody—But I'm not right for her. She's out of my league.

Honey: Hey, Ben. I want to talk to you for a second.

Ben: Yeah, sure.

Honey: Hey...uh...

She's pausing? That's kind of odd? Honey is the type of person that never pauses, so she must be about to tell me something important.

Honey: Ben...I can't hide this feeling for you any longer...I like you, Ben, more than a friend. I hope you feel the same way. I don't care if you don't. It's just that I've been holding this feeling for you for a long time now and need to get it off my chest...I'm sorry I—

Ben: I love you too.

Honey: Really? Um...Well...Do you want to watch a movie together or something? I mean, not right now, but sometime later in the future?

Ben: Sure, I'll be glad to.

Honey: Ok, good. Well...I guess I'll see you later.

Ben: Sure.

Honey starts walking away quickly. Oh, great. I didn't know what to say to her. I hope I said the right words, but who knows? Man, I couldn't get the words out, but she does love me! More than a friend, but more like a...

Man, I can't believe it! This is incredible! And here I thought my day today was in the dumpster, but no...Man, I don't know what to do right now...Well, probably getting off the street would be the first step I should do.

So that's what I did. I rushed towards my house. I immediately opened the door and went inside just to hear the TV on in the living room. It sounds like my dad is watching TV right now, but no worries. I don't feel like talking to him anyway, and I'm pretty sure he doesn't feel like talking to me because he usually doesn't. But wow! I can't believe it!

I hurry through the kitchen and not through the living room, because my dad's there. I get to the stairs leading up to my bedroom.

Once I enter my bedroom, I quickly shut the door and let a joyful shout as I jump around. I'm making sure to be quiet enough, so my dad won't hear me, but inside I feel like jumping across the whole entire house, but I just start laying on my bed thinking about what just happened to me...Man, oh, man!

Forget what I told you, readers, that there isn't any hope of finding a delicate woman in this world because there is! If they're like Honey, that is.

But boy, am I glad to meet a girl like Honey!

I just hope I don't disappoint her like I do with the rest of my life.

Fingers cross...

How To Be An Alpha 3 (Being A Real Cowboy)

Howdy there, partners!

Today we'll be teaching you city folks how to become real cowboys. Cowboys are the most alpha-thing there is in this goddamn country. Right Cedric?

Cedric: Ben, stop speaking in that accent. That's the most terrible country accent I have ever heard in my entire life.

Well, it seems like my cowboy friend doesn't think well of my voice, so I guess I'll— *Cough* Cough*

Well, boys and girls... whoever is reading this right now. Today me and my boys are going to a rodeo, and this is perfect timing to teach you readers about what we do here in the USA. We live in the beautiful state of Montana, some of you might know, and most people when they come to Montana think everyone who lives here is just a bunch of rednecks with no lives.

Well, I'm here to tell you readers that you need to stop assuming things because Montana's filled with diverse people. We're just like the rest of America. It ain't different at all, but if you insist on continuing to be an idiot, well I guess I have to show what a real cowboy looks like and lucky for you, I got a friend who's a cowboy and he's right here. Say hello, Cedric.

Cedric: Um...Hi.

As you can see, he just looks exactly like a normal American white boy looks like, expect he's wearing a cap, jeans, and cowboy boots and actual knowledge of how to take care of animals unlike what most of you idiots who travel to Yellowstone do. You people like to irritate the buffalo just because you want to get close to it and take a picture. Seriously, what the hell is wrong with you people!?

Anyway, enough of me rambling a bunch of nonsense. Cedric, you do the talking now.

Cedric: Um...Ben, what do I talk about?

Ben: Just talk about anything. What's it like to be a real cowboy?

Cedric: Well, I don't know. Well, the first thing I will show you, I guess, is the fact that we are busy people. I mean, right now I need to take care of the cows, but my friend here decided he wanted to film me for no reason and show you whoever is reading this about my life... Seriously, Ben, why am I doing this? I have a lot of things to do today.

Ben: It's okay, just pretend I'm not here.

Cedric: Alrighty, then.

Okay, well, it looks like my cowboy buddy is walking towards the corral where he keeps his horses.

Tell me, Cedric, all of your horses' names?

Cedric: Well, see that white horse that's sticking his head out of that shelter canopy over there? His name is Frosty.

Ben: Frosty? Like Frosty the Snowman?

Cedric: Exactly. He's my bucking horse I'm taking to the rodeo. Hey, Ben, go over to that trailer and open the door for me, will you please?

Ben: I can't right now. I'm carrying this camera.

Cedric: For Christ's sake, put the camera down and help me!

Ben: Alright, fine....

...Sorry, for those who are reading right now. I was busy trying to help Cedric here put his stupid horse into the trailer. It only took a hundred hours, but we finally managed to put the horse inside. Man, Cedric you need to hire some more help around here.

Cedric: Yeah, yeah. I know. Hey, Josh, thanks for helping.

Josh: No problem.

Oh, by the way. For those who are reading, our cousin Josh is here with us too. He's also a cowboy. Say hello, Josh.

Josh: Um...hello.

Cedric: Man, Ben, stop putting the camera in front of our faces!

Ben: Oh, come on. You guys are going to be famous. Plus, there might be some cute cowgirls reading this.

Cedric: Yeah, I seriously doubt it. Anyways, are we going to the rodeo or you're just going to continue wasting our time filming us?

Ben: Wait, I need an epic shot of you guys with your shirts off.

Cedric: Oh, for Christ's sake! Just get in the truck already!

Ben: Fine.

Well, me and my two cowboy buddies are going to the rodeo right now. I'm wondering if you guys are going to win it all today.

Josh: Er...Probably not.

Ben: What? Why do you say that?

Cedric: Well, Ben, do you also know who's competing at the rodeo as well?

Ben: No, who?

Cedric: None other than Cougar Jack and Edwin Sharp.

Ben: You can't be serious right now?

Cedric: Yep.

Ben: Well, the both of you better win then.

Cedric: Sorry, that's just going to be impossible because those two have beaten us every single time. We haven't won one time against them.

Ben: Well, that's going to change.

Cedric: Really? Why is that?

Ben: Because I have a plan?

Cedric: Oh, great. Ben, don't even try.

Ben: Oh, that's why you shouldn't have said anything.

Well, readers, it looks like you guys are going to see what a real western showdown looks like soon.

Cedric: Oh, great. What are you planning, Ben?

Ben: Just wait and see, my friend.

***

We finally made it to the rodeo, readers. While Cedric and Josh are busy preparing for the rodeo, I'm just walking around looking for my other friends. They said they are going to be here, but I don't see them...

Jeez, and my friends say that I'm so hard to find in a crowd. I should say the same thing about them... Oh, wait, I see them. Hold on, let me hurry up to them and tell them about my awesome plan...

Ben: Hey gang!

Tom: Oh, great. Here comes trouble.

Slam: Hey, Ben! How's it going?

Ben: Good.

Slam: Ah, that's good to hear. Man, I'm excited for the rodeo, are you Baxter?

Baxter: Nah, "rodeoing" and "cowboying" is not my thing.

Slam: Yeah, this is not my thing either, but I'm just excited to see what Cedric and Josh can do. I hope they win, Ben.

Ben: Yeah, I hope so. Speaking of, I got a plan.

Tom: Oh, boy. Not now. I want to take a break.

Ben: Oh, come on. This will help our buddies win.

Tom: Help them win? Yeah, the only help you can give, Ben, is giving heart attacks.

Ben: Hey.

Tom: I'm sorry, Ben, but I can't help you. My parents are here, and I don't want to get in trouble with my parents if they find out.

Ben: Hey, you can't be serious?

Tom: Yeah, see ya.

Ben: Wow, alright. Well, I guess it's just the 3 of us then.

Slam: Okay, what is your plan, Ben?

Ben: Well, I was just planning to have us look for The Cougars.

Baxter: The Cougars? Wait, The Cougars are here? Isn't that just great?

Ben: Yeah, and apparently Jackass and Edwin are competing with Cedric and Josh.

Baxter: So what is your plan?

Ben: Well, first off, take this camera because we're going to look for Jack and his "friends." Wherever they are?

Slam: Hey, I think I know where they might be.

Ben: Really? Where?

Slam: Here, I'll show you.

Alright, well, sorry for those who are reading because Slam is taking us through the crowds of people here at the rodeo. So I do apologize for not commentating as well as I should be because there's a lot of people here and it will just be weird talking to a camera...

Alright, well it looks like Slam is taking us to the secret behind-the-scenes area of where the contestants are. I don't think we should be here, and I don't know how we managed to get here without anyone kicking us out, but hey we're here anyway, so let's just make the most of it and find where Jackass and Edwin are.

Slam: Yeah, I think I know. Just follow me.

Ben: Alright.

Slam: Oh, wait. I see them.

Ben: Yeah, I see them too. Good.

Slam: What do you want to do to them?

Ben: Well, it seems like we can't go to them because if we do, then security will probably kick us out.

Baxter: Now what?

Ben: Wait, I think Jackass is walking towards our direction.

Slam: What should we do to him?

Baxter: Heh, heh. Don't worry, I know. Just wait here.

Okay, well, it looks like Baxter has a plan, so we'll just wait here to see what Baxter does. It looks like Baxter is walking up to him. Jackass doesn't see him yet. Baxter just tapped Jack on the shoulder and Jack turned around.

Baxter: Hey, Jackass...

***

Oh, Baxter, what have you done!? To be honest with you it was pretty funny, but Baxter could have warned us ahead of time. I'm sorry to you readers, but we're running away from an angry Jackass who just got smacked in the head with a stink bomb that Baxter unexpectedly chucked at him, but the thing is Jackass isn't the only one who's chasing after us.

Look, see.

Some other people are chasing after us because Baxter's stink bomb worked too well. Now we are running for our lives right now. For those who are reading this, wish us luck.

Anyways, I don't know what to do in this situation.

Hey guys, what should we do?

Baxter: Run! That's all we can do!

Ben: Where though?

Baxter: Quick, follow me! Let's go to my car!

So, we're going into Baxter's car now. Let's get out of here already!

Baxter: I'm trying to, man!

We've finally escaped, that's good, but we're going to miss seeing Cedric and Josh competing at the rodeo. Oh, well. What can you do?

Baxter: Man, I didn't want to go to this stupid rodeo in the first place!

Slam: Man, I sure hope Cedric and Josh win.

Ben: Yeah, me too. Guess they'll let us know tomorrow.

Well, for those who are reading this. Sorry, again, for the unexpected situation that we put ourselves in. I hope you were entertained reading this. If not, then apologies for wasting your time. Hopefully in the next adventure we'll finally successfully show you readers how to truly be alphas…

Hopefully.

How To Be An Alpha 4 (Hunting)

Alright, readers!

It's hunting season! And when it's hunting season, that means us alphas must scavenge around looking for some food. The Wolf Pack needs to find food quickly this hunting season and we're going to teach you readers how to hunt so you'll develop your skills as an alpha and get more rizz... Maybe.

Cedric: Yeah, right? Hunting is not going to get us more rizz, Ben.

Ben: Oh, come on. It sure will. You'll see.

Anyway, my readers, before I even teach you how to hunt, it is probably safe for me to teach you how to use a gun properly. We're going deer hunting right now and we have our hunting rifles here, but you readers need to realize how to use a rifle safely. Otherwise, you might end up shooting your friend.

Now, I don't know where you readers live, but if you live in the United States, then chances are there's going to be different rules for each state on gun laws. Here in Montana, there are no laws, so we can just do whatever we want.

Right, Cedric?

Cedric: Ok, that's not true at all. There are rules here.

Yeah, and if you can legally possess a firearm, then you can shoot whoever you want too, right Cedric?

Cedric: What are you trying to do here? Start a controversy?

No, no, no. Alright, when it's all been said and done, safety is the number one priority here and you really need to know how to handle a gun properly or any weapon that you use to hunt. Anyway, enough talking. I will show you readers a live demonstration on how to shoot a deer. Cedric put this suit on.

Cedric: Wait, what? Ben, what are you planning to do?

Ben: Just be quiet and put the suit on.

Cedric: What is this?

Ben: It's a deer costume.

Cedric: Oh, no. I know what you're planning to do. I'm not going to do it, Ben.

Ben; Why not?

Cedric: What do you mean "Why not"!? What are you trying to do!? Kill me!?

Ben: Hey, calm your nerves. I'm not going to shoot you with an actual gun. I'm just going to use this airsoft gun on you. Here, put this vest on to protect you.

Cedric: Oh, wow! A vest! That's sure going to change my mind on doing this.

Ben: Hey, listen. I promise to pay you if you do it, Cedric.

Cedric: I can't believe I'm doing this. Fine.

Well, as my buddy here is busy putting on his vest and deer costume. I'm going to show you how to shoot properly. First off, make sure you don't have your gun pointing at you at all times and your finger is off the trigger...

Cedric: Jesus Christ, Ben. Where did you get this costume at?

Ben: I got it at Walmart during Christmas.

Cedric: Yeah, I can tell. It has Christmas decorations on it, and it smells like Christmas too. Did you even wash this, Ben?

Alright, sorry as my friend interrupts me here. Now that you have a good grip on your gun, make sure you continue to have a good grip as you're taking aim. Cedric, are you done yet?

Cedric: Yes.

Ben: Alright, cool.

Cedric: Hey, don't point the gun at me! What are you doing!?

Ben: I thought you were ready? Anyways, just stand still and act like a deer.

Cedric: Jesus, I can't believe I'm doing this...

Alright, as you can see, my buddy is very terrible at acting like a deer.

Ben: Hey Cedric, get on all fours at least.

Cedric: Man, I'm just glad nobody is around watching this.

Alright, as you readers can see... Well, you can't see anything right now, but just imagine Cedric in a deer costume and he's on all fours acting like a deer.

Cedric: Please don't imagine that.

Anyway, now what you need to do is take a good aim at your deer. Aim for the rib cage because that's the bread and butter. Alright Cedric, just stand still. Now make sure you still have a good grip on your gun because it's time to shoot your target.

Cedric: Ben, wait!

Bang...

...Alright, you readers, now that you have shot your target, it's time to run away from them as they try to kill you.

Ben: Hey Cedric! I'm sorry, man!

Cedric: Shut up! I'm going to kill you!

Well, boys, there's a lesson to learn today: Never do a live demonstration of shooting an animal. And never let your friend be that animal because you'll end up shooting them in the ass like I did...

Well, I hope you readers learn a valuable lesson here today. If not, then oh well. It's your choice. Just pray that you can run faster than your friend.

How To Be An Alpha 5 (Boxing Match)

Hello ladies and gentlemen!

Welcome to the Alpha Boxing Club! Where we take the best alphas of the world and make them fight each other to see who the best alpha is. Right now, you readers are going to be in for a treat because today's boxing contenders are two high school teenagers. These two have been fighting with each other ever since they knew each other and today they want to take their fight to the next level and have it seen for the whole public to enjoy.

It's going to be like Rocky, folks, except scratch the romantic bit.

Well, let's show you folks the two contenders already. This man is the best, most toughest, most bestest in all of America, in the whole world actually.

It's none other than... COUGAR JACK!!!!!!!!!

As we try to get Jack ready, let me tell you folks, unfortunately, he's not single. I know, I know. You ladies are very sad right now, but don't worry because you can get his autograph at the end of the boxing match after he beats his opponent. It's going to be an easy and quick match anyways of who Cougar Jack is fighting.

Speaking of his opponent, here comes Benjamin Uno!

Alright, well, let's forget about Benjamin as we can see Cougar Jack has finally made it on the stage.

Hey, Cougar Jack, tell me some wise words before your match up.

Cougar Jack: Oh, yeah! I'm going to knock this pip squeak on the ground!

Alright, it looks like Cougar Jack is all hyped up. Let's see if his opponent is ready. Let's go over to Ben real quick....

Hey, Ben. What the hell is wrong with you, man?

I'm mean, come on!

Do you realize who you are fighting up against?

Man, you must be very brave or very stupid, but I'm choosing the latter.

Ben: Excuse me?

Alright, that's enough talking for you, Ben. I know how you like to talk too much, but the readers here want to see some action and the action is coming to you folks, don't worry. Alright, Cougar Jack! Ben! Are you two ready?

Cougar Jack: Oh, yeah. Don't worry, Ben. I'll make sure to make this quick and painless.

Ben: Shut up.

Woah. Hey, now. There's some pushing going on, but the fight is not starting yet. Wait until the whistle blows, boys... Alright, blow the whistle already!

Rrrrr

Alright, the fighting begins!

And immediately Ben takes the first jabs, but Cougar Jack, being so elusive, dodges it without a blink of an eye. Ben keeps on jabbing, but it looks like Cougar Jack is just trying to see if he can waste Ben's energy.

Oh, wait!

Hold on!

Oh, Cougar Jack takes multiple jabs at Ben and one of them was successful as Ben stumbles backward!

Now, it looks like Ben is pulling away after that first hit. It seems like that first jab from Jack really hurt him.

Oh, crap!

Jack takes another jab, but Ben dodges it with ease. But oh no! Jack gives a right hook, and it hits Ben.

Ben is stumbling now!

Oh, no!

This might be the end for Ben! It seems like my prediction of this being an easy and quick fight is correct, as Ben continues to stumble backwards, trying to dodge Jack's jabs. If Jack lays another hit, folks, this will be the end.

Oh, boy! Jack finally lays another hit, and it's over! Jack wins!

WOOOOOOOOOOOOOOAAAAAAAAAAAAAAAHHHHHHHHHH!!!!!! !!!!!!!!!!!!

Alright, way to go Jack! I mean, we were expecting this to happen, but it was still a good fight. It clearly showed that you really trained well, Jack.

Jack: Hey, I just practiced and practiced. That's all that matters, folks. If you guys give it your all, then you can be successful too. It was a good fight, Ben, but unfortunately you lost. Better luck next time.

Ben: Shut up!

Jack: Woah, hey now. We got a sore loser at our hands. But that's okay, Ben. Honestly, for you Ben, I think trying is probably not good for you.

Ben: I want a rematch!

Woah, okay now.

There are no rematches. This is just a one-time thing. If we do this every time, we'll get in trouble with the principal.

Speaking of... I'm sorry, readers, but we'll have to end this story short because I think I see a group of people coming our way and it's probably some teachers, so we'll see you later. But before we leave, always remember readers, don't be a lousy wolf who relies on his lousy friends. Be a tough cougar instead and just be yourself. Nobody can tell you what to do.

Cougar Jack: Hey, Larry! Put that camera down and run!

Larry: Alright, alright.

Well, it looks like it's time to go! Bye!

Larry: Haha, man. This was great. Bye bye, Ben. You can have your stupid camera back...

...Why ...Why is my life like this?...Why...Why am I even born?....Why do I even exist?...

I can't take it anymore!...

Just kill me now!...

Uh, What?...

Who's here?...

Tom: Ben, get up buddy.

I can't see who it is because the bright sun is blinding my eyes. It also doesn't help that I'm crying like a dumbass, but it sounds like Tom.

Tom: Ben, come on.

I see a figure blocking the sun and I begin wiping my tears away. I can see a little clearly now. Yeah, it is Tom... Oh, great, he's not the only one here.

Honey: Ben, are you alright?

Great, all of my friends are here, including Honey. I don't want them to see me in the state I'm in right now. It's hard enough for you readers to see what state I'm in, but now my friends know... Well, I can't do anything now. I just grab Tom's hand and get up.

Honey: Ben, we need to take you to the hospital.

Ben: Hospital?

Honey: Yeah, your face is messed up. You're bleeding.

Ben: Nah, I'm fine.

Cedric: Ben, you stubborn fool. We're taking you to the hospital, anyways.

Ben: Fine.

Well, readers... Sorry if you don't know what's going on right now.

The stupid Cougars just took my camera for no reason and decided to film me fighting Jack.

Those jerks!... Well, I can't do anything about it now.

It's a good thing my friends came at the right time... I don't deserve them.

Uri's Scrolls of Information

On a journey through time and space, Uri has seen tons of different planets. To keep track of where he's been, Uri keeps a catalog of scrolls with him to record the places he's discovered. One of those places he discovered recently is planet Sweetopia. Here's what Uri has drawn and written in his scrolls about Sweetopia:

Here's a slightly accurate image of planet Sweetopia. Usually, you won't see the islands on the planet if you're looking from space because the atmosphere of the planet is always covered with cotton candy-colored clouds. The clouds make the islands look bigger or smaller than they are on the surface, or it can even change it's shape and make it look like there's tons of islands all at once. These are usually hallucinations that the inhabitants of planet Sweetopia use to confuse newcomers and make them go away.

The Sweetopians have become experts on controlling the weather of the planet and protecting it. The only problem is that it's very hard to draw an accurate diagram of the planet and where the islands are. The islands don't stay in one place, and if you don't have a UPS (Universal Positoning System) in handy, then it will be nearly impossible to land your spaceship. If not careful, you'll end up sinking in the Sweetopian seas and get eaten by the Sweetopian Sea monsters.

What's also kind of hard to show on the maps is the black areas some of the islands have. The black areas were created by these dark creatures that are simply called "The Creatures of Darkness". They bring out the bad in everything around them and ruin the colorful planet. Thet's why the inhabitants try to find and kill off these dark creatures before the whole colorful planet turns into a dark gloomy wasteland.

Discovered Islands:

This image shows all the islands discovered so far on planet Sweetopia. The Sweetopians are only able to keep track of the three because, as written before, the islands move and change a lot on the planet. Plus, the sea creatures keep them at bay as well. The three main islands that the Sweetopians can inhabit are: Banana Island, Grape Cluster, and Rainbow Apple. Rainbow Apple is the most populated out of the three. Banana Island is the largest island by mass and second most populated. Meanwhile, the Grape Cluster is just the small outcast that nobody wants to go to unless you want wine.

Rainbow Apple:

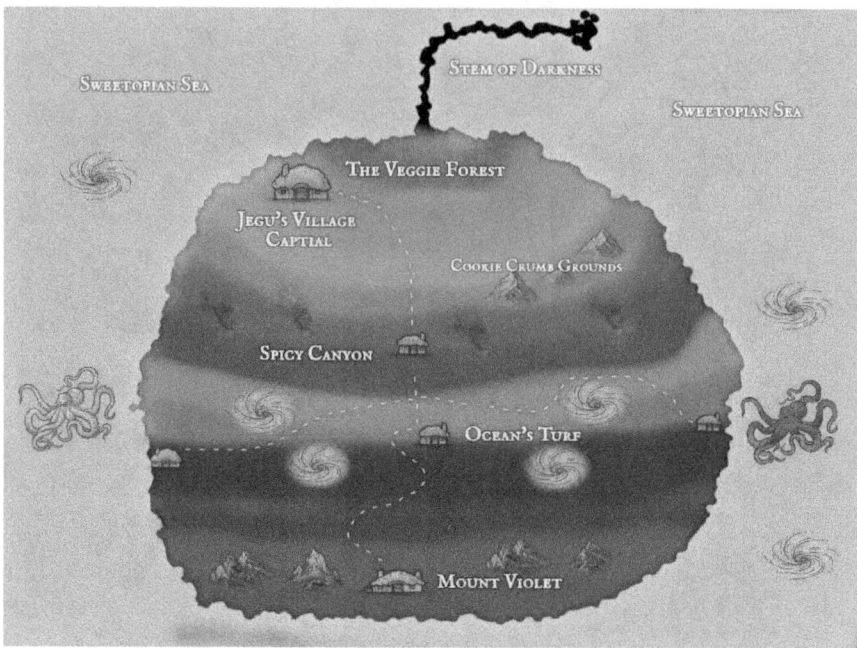

This image shows Rainbow Apple in its entirety. Rainbow Apple is the first island the Sweetopians found. It was founded by Jegu "The Great Candymaker", who helped his raptor kind escape a terrible war. When they discovered the island, it was just a big black rotten apple controlled by the Creatures of Darkness. With Jehovah's help, Jegu and his allies were able to defeat the Creatures of Darkness and make Rainbow Apple a colorful island that everybody can enjoy. Now, Jegu oversees the entire planet to check on and protect his people. The Sweetopians spend most of their day trying to find any more islands and kill more dark creatures off. If a newcomer arrives on their planet, they will welcome them as long as they're not crooks.

The Wolf Pack Members

Name: Benjamin Uno
Role in the Pack: Alpha Leader
Age: 18
Special ability: Ben doesn't know what he wants to do in his life. The only thing he wants to do is be with his friends and protect them no matter what it takes. That's why his abilities and powers started off random, like his ability to summon random food, because he didn't know what he wanted to do in his life until he realized the truth. Then his food making ability started to make more sense to him and he wanted to learn more skills.

Name: Tom Dunkley
Role in the Pack: Second in command/ Enforcer
Age: 18
Special ability: He's very dignified and wants to protect his friends. That's why his superpowers are like that of a soldier; he's able to create shields to protect himself and his friends, and he's also able to make swords and shoot them at people for defense.

Name: Cedric Coy
Role in the Pack: Hunter/ Worker
Age: 18
Special ability: He's a rancher and a cowboy, so all his superpowers relate to cowboy things like his lasso ability that makes him be able to use a lasso to wrap around his enemies and his enemies can't escape or do anything. He can even make his lasso invisible, so his opponents won't see it coming, but he must be very accurate with his throwing as most of his opponents move a lot, that's the only downside of his lasso ability.

Name: Honey Barnes
Role in the Pack: Alpha Female
Age: 18
Special ability: She loves helping people, that's why she is training to be a nurse at the hospital. That's also why her superpowers are that of healing. Because of her love of plants, she uses her ability to grow plants that can heal her allies when they are injured. She can also defend herself using her plants as well.

Name: Baxter Rodriguez
Role in the Pack: Weapons Expert
Age: 18
Special ability: He is very skilled at fighting and has a violent temper. That's why his superpower is to make bombs instantly out of nowhere. His abilities always involve explosives because he is sort of a pyromaniac and plus his explosive abilities really represent his angry mood.

Name: Slam Dickson Dolly
Role in the Pack: Omega (Peacemaker)
Age: 18
Special ability: Slam is very good-natured and curious about the world. He loves many different things. One of his favorite things he likes is magic tricks. That's why his superpower is that of a magician because he wants to travel instantly to destinations he wants to go using his top hat. Slam loves traveling and meeting new people, that's why he is a very good communicator as well.

Name: Sarah Coy (Cedric's sister)
Role in the Pack: The Misbehaving Pup
Age: 10
Special ability: To be annoying.

Name: Uri
Role in the Pack: The New Pup
Age: 10
Special ability: Uri is a playful and high-spirited kid. He represents King Solomon when he was a young boy yearning for the truth. Uri has good knowledge of the Holy Scriptures because he was taught by his father King Yadin (who represents King David). King Yadin had taught Uri a few things about taking care of animals and being a good shepherd. That's why his special abilities revolve around animals. He's got his dad's staff that he uses to shapeshift into different species. The staff used to be for sheep herding, but just like Moses' staff from the Bible, God's holy spirit is upon it.

The Sweetopians

Name: Jegu "The Great Candymaker"
Role in Sweetopia: The Overseer
Age: 60
Special ability: He can use his bushy black chocolate mustache as a weapon to wrap around his enemies, so they won't move. He is a candymaker, so his special abilities have to do with everything related to candy. He has different kinds of candy instruments that he uses as weapons like his candy sword.

Name: Chuck "The Chocolate Monster"
Role in Sweetopia: The Assistant
Age: 23
Special ability: His special abilities are related to everything chocolate, that's the reason why he is called "The Chocolate Monster" because he is a very skilled warrior who can use chocolate as a defensive weapon against foes. He can make the chocolate form into shapes of weapons, like spears, and he can use them to fight. He can also make a chocolate version of himself to trick the enemy into thinking that he is there, but in reality that's just his chocolate clone.

Name: Strawberry Shores
Role in Sweetopia: The Strawberry Gardener
Age: 20
Special ability: Similar to Chuck's ability, except everything revolves around strawberries. She can turn herself into a strawberry to hide or even turn someone else into a strawberry to play a trick.

Thanks for Reading!